The shining splendor of our Zebra Lovegram logo on the cover of this book reflects the glittering excellence of the story inside. Look for the Zebra Lovegram whenever you buy a historical romance. It's a trademark that guarantees the very best in quality and reading entertainment.

A MAN'S KISS

Intending to bestow a swift peck on his forehead, she marched over to him and brushed her lips against the tousled hair covering his brow. Strong golden-brown arms reached up and seized her, pulling her down on top of a hard, muscular body. "That was no kiss, woman! *This* is a kiss."

Jordan gripped her waist with one arm, while with his free hand, he somehow managed to tilt up her chin. In the next moment, the hot pressure of his lips found her open mouth. She struggled to right herself, but he did not give her the chance. His hand slid to the back of her head and held it in place. Then he began to kiss her—*really* kiss her—to ravish her lips and mouth.

She flailed against him, fought to regain her balance and pull away, but she could not. Her hair came undone, entangling itself in her own thrashing limbs. The blood rushed to her head and her body throbbed with unfamiliar sensations, yearning for some unknown, but wondrously exciting conclusion . . .

HISTORICAL ROMANCES BY EMMA MERRITT

RESTLESS FLAMES (2203, $3.95)

Having lost her husband six months before, determined Brenna Allen couldn't afford to lose her freight company, too. Outfitted as wagon captain with revolver, knife and whip, the single-minded beauty relentlessly drove her caravan, desperate to reach Santa Fe. Then she crossed paths with insolent Logan MacDougald. The taciturn Texas Ranger was as primitive as the surrounding Comanche Territory, and he didn't hesitate to let the tantalizing trail boss know what he wanted from her. Yet despite her outrage with his brazen ways, jet-haired Brenna couldn't suppress the scorching passions surging through her . . . and suddenly she never wanted this trip to end!

COMANCHE BRIDE (2549, $3.95)

When stunning Dr. Zoe Randolph headed to Mexico to halt a cholera epidemic, she didn't think twice about traversing Comanche territory . . . until a band of bloodthirsty savages attacked her caravan. The gorgeous physician was furious that her mission had been interrupted, but nothing compared to the rage she felt on meeting the barbaric warrior who made her his slave. Determined to return to civilization, the ivory-skinned blonde decided to make a woman's ultimate sacrifice to gain her freedom—and never admit that deep down inside she burned to be loved by the handsome brute!

SWEET, WILD LOVE (2834, $4.50)

It was hard enough for Eleanor Hunt to get men to take her seriously in sophisticated Chicago—it was going to be impossible in Blissful, Kansas! These cowboys couldn't believe she was a real attorney, here to try a cattle rustling case. They just looked her up and down and grinned. Especially that Bradley Smith. The man worked for her father and he still had the audacity to stare at her with those lust-filled green eyes. Every time she turned around, he was trying to trap her in his strong embrace.

Available wherever paperbacks are sold, or order direct from the Publisher. Send cover price plus 50¢ per copy for mailing and handling to Zebra Books, Dept. 3037, 475 Park Avenue South, New York, N.Y. 10016. Residents of New York, New Jersey and Pennsylvania must include sales tax. DO NOT SEND CASH.

KATHARINE KINCAID

ZEBRA BOOKS
KENSINGTON PUBLISHING CORP.

ZEBRA BOOKS

are published by

Kensington Publishing Corp.
475 Park Avenue South
New York, NY 10016

First printing: June, 1990

Printed in the United States of America

For My Son, Paul
Who Loves Truth, Justice, and Adventure
Hold Fast To Your Dreams and Ideals

Prologue

Boston, 1899

When Spencer Kathleen O'Rourke heard the frantic clang of the front doorbell, she had no doubt whatever that her life was about to undergo a drastic change. The Irish called it "second sight," but Spencer, being of a determinedly practical nature, viewed such premonitions as mere instinct and paid them as little heed as a fly buzzing about her head.

She left off dusting the jars and bottles that made up her pharmacopoeia, and with quick, efficient strides walked to the small, square mirror hanging beside the cherished medical diploma stating she had graduated with honors five years previously from Johns Hopkins University School of Medicine. Every crinkly, carrot-red hair was still in place where she had stuffed it earlier that morning beneath the white, gauze cap that resembled a nurse's cap more than a doctor's but at least restrained her unruly mane and made her look more dignified and professional.

She just wished there was something she could do about the freckles liberally dusting her nose and cheekbones, and the blue-green, thickly lashed eyes that leaped out of her face. Sparing a moment to examine herself critically, she ruthlessly searched for whatever it was that made people doubt her abilities as a doctor. She was dressed in funereal black, which helped subdue her too-vivid coloring, and over the austerely cut, ankle-length skirt and puffed-sleeve blouse, she wore an immaculate, starched white apron that modestly concealed her ample bosom.

Except for her lush bosom, she was painfully thin and spinsterish-looking, given to sharp angles rather than curves. On her last birthday, at age twenty-seven, she had abandoned all hope of ever marrying. Not only was it impossible to find a man who appreciated a woman brazen enough to become a doctor like her father, but she had finally realized she was simply unattractive to men. The current standard of beauty called for women to be pale, languorous, and deferential—also flat-chested as pancakes. She was anything but and determinedly proud of the fact. What did she care if men were put off by her, so long as they valued her medical skills? Medicine was her whole life, making up for everything she had ever lacked as a woman.

Unfortunately, ever since her father's death four months before, few patients had jerked on the bell-rope beside the front door. Despite her excellent record of saving patients, the residents of this poor Irish neighborhood still did not trust a woman to cure their ills or set their broken bones. Adding insult to injury, they went to midwives to deliver their babies. As long as her father had been there to drunkenly peer at them, shake his head, and cluck his tongue, no one had seemed to mind that *she* had usually provided the diagnosis and treatment. Now that he was gone, his love for "a wee nip" having been his undoing, people had begun taking their business elsewhere. This was the first time in a week anyone had rung the bell.

Another angry clang made Spencer jump. Angry with herself for shamelessly procrastinating, she smoothed down her already unwrinkled apron and assumed her most professional, unsmiling attitude. If only her eyes and hair were not so bright and garish, or her chest so demonstrative of her gender! Spreading the palms of her hands against her breasts, she attempted to flatten them, but the effort did little good.

Her father had always said that her eyes, hair, and bosom were her finest assets, but they were also the reasons why men refused to take her professional accomplishments seriously. It was bitterly ironic that at the very same time, potential suitors scorned these attributes as being too far removed from the ideal of feminine beauty. What did men *want,* anyway? Muttering in frustration, Spencer resolved that on the morrow, she would tighten the gauze breast binder she had taken to wearing and would also purchase a small tin of face powder to tone down her freckles. A deep sigh escaped her; ready or not, she must answer the clanging bell before whoever was there lost patience and went away.

Hurrying to the front door, she flung it wide open, admitting a gust of fierce March wind. A desperate-looking man in worn, tattered clothing stood on the doorstep, hunched over in the biting blast. "The doc . . ." he gasped. "I gotta see the doc . . ."

"Come in . . ." Spencer stepped back to grant him passage. "You've come for yourself? If so, go right into the examination room."

The question proved unnecessary. As the man stumbled into the entrance hall, Spencer could see he was gripping a deeply gashed right hand. Blood dripped onto the scuffed but meticulously clean and polished floorboards she had spent half the morning scouring on her hands and knees.

"You're bleeding. Come quickly. I'll fetch a basin." Whirling on her heel, she marched ahead of him down the hallway and turned into the small room with narrow table and several wooden chairs that served as an examination room.

"Sit here on the table's edge . . ." She grabbed a basin and thrust it under his dripping hand. "That's a nasty cut. What were you doing?"

"A bit of woodwork for a neighbor two doors over. The chisel slipped and bit into me palm." The man spoke with a deep brogue reminiscent of Spencer's father—the same brogue she had worked so hard to eradicate from her own speech during her medical school days. Her brogue had been one more thing to set her apart from the other medical students, ninety-nine percent of whom were young men from well-to-do families.

"A few stitches should set you right," she assured the man who was trembling and looking anxious. At the mention of stitches, he paled even more than he was already.

"Can't ye just bind it good so it closes by itself?"

"Stitches are quicker. And they'll help keep out infection. Really, there's nothing to it. You've naught to fear."

"Where's the doc, then?" The man eyed her preparations with dark suspicion. "If I got to be stitched, I want the doc t' do it."

Spencer paused in gathering the necessary items. "*I* am the doctor," she quietly informed him. "Unless you're looking for the elder Dr. O'Rourke. He passed on to his eternal reward four months ago."

"The sign out front says Dr. *Spencer* O'Rourke. Is that *you?*"

"Yes. Me name is the same as me father's—a bit unusual, I admit, but me da always wanted a son, and I was the only one t' come along. Me ma died givin' birth t' me."

She deliberately lapsed into the same thick brogue he was using, but the man did not seem in the least comforted. Snorting belligerently, he jumped off the table's edge. "I'll not have a wee lass pokin' me with a sharp needle."

"For the love of Saint Brigid, sir, take a good look at me!" Spencer exploded. "I'm hardly what one would call a wee lass. I've been stitchin' gashes and mendin' broken bones for many a year now. It's a rare sad thing that a hale, hearty man such as yerself should fear a few stitches. Summon yer courage, sir, and let's get on with it."

The brogue was effortless now; when she was angry or upset, she couldn't stop it. Fuming, she picked up a tray containing suturing materials, disinfectant for flushing the wound, and bandages, but the man backed away, edging toward the door. He had a pugnacious nose, gaunt cheekbones, and dirt under his fingernails. His clothing was worn and filthy, and he smelled faintly of whiskey, an odor Spencer found distressingly familiar. Probably the silly bloke had cut himself because his hands were unsteady from drinking. Far too many men in this neighborhood did as her father had done: drowned their sorrows and disappointments in cheap Irish whiskey instead of facing their troubles fair and square.

"I'd never a come here had I known ye was a woman," he said. "I dinna hold with women gettin' above themselves."

"And where have ye been for the past thirty years, sir? Johns Hopkins University did not think me above meself when they handed me a diploma five years ago. I admit there were few females in a class of nearly forty, but the New York Medical College for Women was founded in 1870 and has been turning out practitioners ever since—every one of them, women. Before that, in 1864, Dr. Mary Edwards Walker was commissioned Assistant Surgeon in the U.S. Army, where she served with admirable distinction."

Spencer rattled off the names and accomplishments of her heroines, whose achievements were as familiar to her as her own family history. The man simply stood, glowering at her and bleeding carelessly down the front of his trousers and onto her clean floor.

"So ye see, sir, whatever prejudices ye may wrongly harbor, women have made significant contributions to the medical profession. I meself am *more* than capable of doing a good job on that poor hand of yers."

Still scowling, the man snatched a length of bandage off Spencer's tray and wrapped it around his wound. "Naught ye say can convince me, lass. I'll not have a *woman* doin' a *man's* job. I'll just take meself over a few streets t' Doc O'Brien's. If there's any stitchin' t' be done, *he* can do it."

"That's ridiculous, and ye know it! Ye're losin' so much blood ye'll probably faint dead away before ye can even reach the O'Brien residence . . . And if I were ye, I wouldna want Seamus O'Brien touchin' me with his dirty hands. He doesna believe in asepsis—rejects all the latest theories. Besides, now that ye've bled all over me hallway and examination room, the least ye can do is let me *fix* the problem."

Shrugging contemptuously, the man looked down at the blood-smeared floor. "Now, *there's* a proper job for a lass—moppin' up blood. But the tricky things—like stitchin' and cuttin'—are best reserved for gentlemen. Ye've a great nerve postin' a sign with a man's name on it, hoodwinkin' folks into thinkin' they're gonna be treated by a *real* doctor."

"I *am* a real doctor! I've treated hundreds of patients! I can give ye references. Why, I was first in me class!"

"Ye're wearin' a skirt, lass. That's all the convincin' *I* need t' seek another practitioner. I don't know where this world is gettin' to with women takin' work away from honest men with fam'lies t' support. Doc O'Brien's got an ailin' wife and four half-growed children dependin' on him."

"I have to eat, too, sir!"

"Then git yerself a husband. And if ye've still a hankerin' for cuttin' and sewin', take up dress-makin'. I've no quarrel with a woman *assistin'* a man, mind ye, but what ye're doin' ain't right, an' I'd rather take me chances with *no* treatment than let a female stitch me up."

"Then get out and be damned to ye, sir!"

Spencer shakily pointed to the door. She almost hoped the man's hand *would* become infected and have to be amputated before he was through. Seamus O'Brien's stubborn, primitive practices had resulted in several such tragedies; why did everyone choose *him* over her?

"I'm a-goin', lass." He strode past her and yanked open the front door, revealing a small boy just about to dart away without ringing the bell.

Spencer started forward to intercept the child, then realized he was not another patient—only the delivery boy leaving the latest edition of the evening newspaper on her doorstep. As the man exited, she snatched the paper and clutched it to her bosom; newspapers were too precious to trust to the capricious March winds. Also, it was the last paper she could afford to have delivered to her doorstep—or indeed, afford to purchase. Her savings were rapidly dwindling, and the rent man was clamoring for his due; in another week, she'd be forced to find cheaper accommodations in a neighborhood even less enlightened than this one.

Retreating back inside the house, she proceeded toward the kitchen at the back of the house to make a cup of tea. Solaced by half a pot of scalding orange pekoe, but still fuming and determined to change her circumstances, she opened the newspaper to the section advertising employment opportunities. It was time to set aside pride and abandon her dream of maintaining her father's private practice and ministering to the needs of her old neighborhood. The neighborhood obviously did not want her. What she would have to do was find work in a hospital—not a happy decision but necessary, assuming such a thing was even possible, and she could stand to work in one. All of the prestigious positions in Boston hospitals were occupied by men, and even if they weren't, hospital work was horribly depressing.

Despite recent efforts to improve them, hospitals were still dreaded places where people went to die, when there was no longer any hope of recovery. Spencer hated the mere idea of hospitals; her father had always gone to people's homes and performed surgery on the kitchen table. That was what she had always wanted. Now, it seemed she had no choice. If a hospital position proved impossible, the only other means of support open to her was nursing, where women *were* accepted but for paltry pay, long hours, and the sacrifice of all she had struggled so hard to obtain.

Her heart rebelled at the mere thought of admitting defeat. Between sips of the now-cooling tea, she ran her finger down the page, pausing at each possibility. An advertisement in bold black type caught her eye. "WANTED: medical practitioner for rubber plantation in Amazon jungle. Must possess moral integrity, resiliency, ability to adapt to primitive living conditions, and sense of humour. Transportation provided.

Respond to Jordan King, 13 Avenida Marshal Deodoro, Manaus, Brazil."

Her finger lingered on the ad as if controlled by some supernatural force. She had read of the great rubber boom currently underway in the jungles of Brazil. People of all nations were pouring into the steamy tropics in search of "black gold." They had built a fabulous city hundreds of miles upriver from the Atlantic Ocean. Manaus reportedly possessed all kinds of amenities—except, perhaps, doctors to treat the ills of mankind so far from civilization. Would anyone care if a *woman* were that doctor?

Spencer scanned the advertisement a second time; it made no mention that the practitioner must be male. Her earlier sense of premonition returned with stunning force, causing her to rattle the paper in sudden, surging certainty. Maybe *this* was what she had sensed lay in wait for her when she first heard the clanging of the doorbell this afternoon. Here was a chance to cast off her failed dreams and ambitions and seek adventure in a new, exciting land. It might *still* be possible to live a life of dedication and service, using the skills she had worked so long and hard to acquire.

Dashing to a cupboard, she seized writing materials, returned to the table, sat down, dipped pen in ink, and began writing: "Dear Mr. King. In response to your advertisement in a Boston newspaper for a physician, I am pleased to inform you of my interest in accepting employment at your rubber plantation in Manaus . . ."

The boldness of her intentions made her pause a moment and stare down at what she had written. Most people would say she was being highly impetuous, if not downright foolhardy, but she had never been one to adhere to or be bound by other people's expectations and restrictions. Tomorrow, she would mail her letter, then book passage immediately for Brazil. If Jordan King refused to hire her, another rubber baron probably would. In the tropics, there had to be a great shortage of doctors, male *or* female.

Yes, she decided, it was time to rely on her "second sight." This was the right thing to do. She was fated to travel to exotic lands and discover whatever destiny held in store for her. She had just enough money left to embark on the long journey, whereas if she waited for Jordan King's reply, her entire savings would be depleted. She finished the letter and signed it with a flourish, making no mention of her sex which had nothing to do with her qualifications, anyway. "Spencer K. O'Rourke, M.D.," she wrote, then added as a postscript, "I especially liked your requirement of a sense of humour. It is a quality which I also demand in an employer."

There, she thought, *now I have shown him that I, too, have expectations and will make demands.*

Without another moment's consideration of the enormity of her decision and its possible consequences, she began making a list of what she ought to take with her to the jungles of Brazil. At the top of the list, she wrote "quinine." Malaria was, she remembered reading, quite prevalent in the tropics.

Chapter One

"Francisco Dos Santos! Where are you? Answer me!" Jordan cocked his head and listened for a response, but the only sound was his own rapid breathing and the incessant whine of the insects rising in clouds around his feet.

He chopped his way through a tangle of liana vines thick as his wrist and stumbled into a small clearing. In the center of the clearing was a soaring, silver-barked rubber tree. From an oblique incision in the side of the tree, milky latex flowed freely into a tin cup clamped to the trunk. At the base of the trunk lay an overturned, galvanized, two gallon bucket spilling precious latex onto the spongy ground.

"Damn my aunt Milly's corset!" Jordan swore, using his favorite childhood profanity. Damning his aunt's corset had seemed terribly bold and daring when he was a boy, but now, in the hushed depths of the Amazon jungle known as the "Green Hell," his words rang hollow and childish, shaming him into silence.

An awful certainty swept him: Something terrible had happened to Francisco, the Brazilian tapper whose job it was to collect the latex from the rubber trees on this particular *estrada* or section of the vast tract of land along the Amazon River belonging to Jordan. Jordan had hired the gaunt, gap-toothed, checker-shirted man in Cearã five months before, transported him first to Belém and then up the Amazon to Manaus, and then farther up the Amazon to Paraĩso, the remote outpost near the mouth of the Putomayo River, where he was attempting to make his fortune from the collection and sale of rubber.

At Paraĩso, Jordan had taught Francisco how to tap the trees and collect the latex from the hundred and sixty-seven rubber trees scattered throughout his assigned *estrada,* and then how to convert the latex into crude rubber over a smudge fire of oily nuts from the *urucuri* palm tree. Jordan himself had hefted the long, broad-bladed wooden paddle, dipped it into a calabash of smoking, coagulating latex, and demonstrated how to form the latex into a solid black ball of cured rubber, which might eventually weigh a hundred pounds or more. For each ball of rubber, Jordan had promised to pay Francisco the almost unheard-of sum of one British shilling per pound. The going rate was five pence per pound, and some only paid a penny, but Jordan prided himself on offering decent wages and supplying adequate food and clothing to his employees rather than hiring gunmen to keep them hard at work, or even, God forbid, forcing hapless Indians into slavery to collect his rubber.

Righting the overturned bucket, Jordan peered into the dense gray-green jungle hemming him in on every side. No stray shaft of sunlight penetrated the thick forest growth; overhead was a solid ceiling of greenery. Trees and vines competed for every precious drop of golden light, while below, in semidarkness, men competed for the "black gold" of the forest—the sap of the rare hevea trees outnumbered by lesser varieties at least eighty to one.

"Francisco!" Jordan shouted in a ringing tone.

The tapper would never have gone off and left a whole morning's work oozing out of a bucket onto the forest floor. Belatedly, Jordan wished he had brought along the .44 Winchester lying in the bottom of his *batelão,* the cedar log canoe pulled up on the riverbank. He chided himself for carelessness; after four years battling mighty, conscienceless rubber barons to protect his comparatively modest holding, he should know better. A man could go for days, even weeks, without a single incident, but he must never forget that violence was a way of life here. If he wanted to survive and triumph, he had better recognize and come to grips with that grim fact.

"Francisco! Don't be afraid. It's me, Senhor Rei."

Jordan used the name by which the Brazilians called him. "Senhor Rei" was now as familiar to him as King, his name in English. But while he prided himself on his mastery of Portuguese, he still could not pronounce the way the Indians fractured the name in Tupi, the *lĩngua geral,* or universal language, of the Amazon tribes. Despite his best efforts to learn it, Tupi remained incomprehensible.

"Francisco Dos Santos, if you're still alive, get your butt out here where I can see you!" he shouted in frustration.

A quick shuffling sound emanated from the giant, twisted roots undulating across the forest floor. Jordan paused again, listening, but it was only some small forest creature scurrying away. Then, in the distance, he heard the howler monkeys screaming alarm and outrage. Abruptly, he shifted direction and began running toward the racket.

"Senhor Rei! Senhor Rei!" a voice called excitedly, babbling in Portuguese. "Come quickly! I have found Francisco!"

"Keep talking, Raymundo!" Jordan directed, making a beeline for the voice of his overseer who had accompanied him upriver to Francisco's *estrada* to check on the tapper, bring new supplies, and see how the man was doing collecting his rubber quota.

Jordan had to employ his machete with great vigor before he broke through the jungle and saw his friend and the missing Francisco. On his knees, Raymundo was bending over a prostrate body—a body already stiffened, mutilated, and grotesque. The sudden, sickening stench of decay was overpowering, and Jordan's stomach turned over with nausea.

"God Almighty!" he breathed, joining Raymundo. "He's been dead some time, hasn't he?"

"Sĩm, senhor," Raymundo confirmed, pointed to a thin shaft—like a long needle—protruding from the man's neck. "Poison dart. It killed him quick. He probably never knew what happened."

"No identification on the dart, I see." Swallowing hard, Jordan gripped the awful thing, extracted it with a quick jerk, and threw it aside.

Raymundo shook his head dolefully. "Could be any tribe, Senhor Rei. The Huitotos roam the area, but they are a gentle people. I do not think it was them. More likely it was that band of Marubas we heard was passing through the territory. They will shoot their blowguns at anything."

"Or maybe it was someone who *wanted* us to think it was Indians, when, in reality, it was white men," Jordan darkly hypothesized. "Curare can be applied to the tip of a dart by white hands as well as by brown ones."

Raymundo lifted his head and stared at Jordan, reminding him of an anxious, sad-eyed bloodhound. His eyes were a chocolate-brown, his skin *cafẽ con leite* or coffee with milk, and his hair dark as night. But he considered himself a white man, far removed from the aborigines who ran naked through the forest and could neither read nor write. Haltingly, Raymundo could do both; he was also a good shot with a Winchester, a great cook—at least of *arroz e feijão,* the Brazilian staple of rice and black beans—an excellent tracker, and from what the whores in Manaus claimed, a wonderful lover who could keep at it all night long. Slender, wiry, and graceful, he was good-looking by Brazilian standards; his single, gleaming silver front tooth lent his smile a rakish, charming air. But he was not smiling, now.

"Sĩm," he gravely agreed. "It could be . . . who you are thinking of."

His thin shoulders slumped, and a trace of fear flashed across his face. He lowered his eyes—afraid to even speak the man's name aloud.

"Don Julio César Arana . . ." Jordan said loudly, rolling the hated name off his tongue as if it, too, were tipped with curare. "This is the third rubber tapper we've lost in as many months to mysterious accidents or 'stray darts,' Raymundo. I no longer believe we're just having a run of bad luck. Today has confirmed my worst suspicions. Someone—most likely Loayza, Arana's trusty guard dog—is systematically killing off my tappers. When word of this death leaks out, the rest of my workers may bolt and run, leaving me with no way to collect my rubber before the next rainy season shuts us down entirely for six months."

"Why do the others have to find out about Francisco?" Raymundo eyed the vultures hunched in the trees above the body. "We'll bury him before the *urubus* get any more of him, collect his rubber as we planned, and return to Manaus without saying a word to anyone. For now, we can pretend he is still out here, working his *estrada,* and later, we can claim he ran away. No one will really miss him."

Jordan stood and paced up and down beside the body, his thoughts exploding. Collecting them required great effort. Finally, he stopped and smacked a fist into his palm. "Damn it all, Raymundo, I can't just ignore a man's death! He's probably got relatives back in Cearã. His death must be reported—just as I reported the others to the authorities in Manaus. Besides, this one we *know* was deliberate; we found the body before the *urubus* finished tearing it apart. This man didn't die because of the usual reasons—snakebite or fever or an attack by a jaguar. He was murdered, plain and simple."

"Sĩm, Senhor Rei. What you say is true, but how does that change things? No one in Manaus will care that another *seringueiro* has died; *seringueiros* die every day. And you have no proof that Miguel Loayza ordered Indians to do this or did it himself. Especially, you have no proof that Arana ordered Loayza to try and scare away all your workers."

"I may not have proof, Raymundo, but I'll tell you one thing: If Arana thinks he can drive me off this land and claim it for himself, he's badly mistaken. It's all I've got left from my father's holdings—the only thing he didn't gamble away before he died. Of course, at the time, he didn't recognize the land's value. Had he known that the whole world would one day go crazy for rubber, he would have sold it or gotten rid of it the same way he got it, on a turn of the cards. Fortunately, he thought it was useless, an impassable, fever-ridden jungle fit only for Indians and anacondas. *Un*fortunately, he then gambled away my inheritance, leaving me with nothing but a Green Hell and my own two hands to support my sisters . . . Thank God, my mother didn't live to see the downfall of the proud King family."

Overwhelmed with bitterness at his father's foolishness and betrayal, Jordan stalked the little clearing like a caged jaguar. Over the years, one would think that his grief and anger might have abated, but occasionally, it resurfaced to drive him half mad with frustration. Alexander King had owned four hundred acres of the finest blue grass grazing land outside Lexington, Kentucky. His Standard-bred trotters were known all over the world for their speed and endurance. His stallions were the most prepotent, booked for years ahead by eager broodmare owners; his box stalls held national and international sulky champions, and his only son had cherished every new foal, every frolicking weanling . . . seeing them as his future, his birthright, his destiny . . .

Alexander King's chance encounter with the hooves of a prized stallion had brought Jordan's world of luxury and dreams tumbling around his ears. Everything had had to be sold at auction to satisfy his father's gambling debts—debts incurred when grief-stricken over the death of Jordan's frail mother, Jordan's father had turned away from his son and daughters and lost himself in the false excitement of cards, whiskey, and glittering women. While his father still lived, Jordan had taken over the job of raising his three young sisters. Following the old man's death, Jordan had been forced to sell cherished family mementoes and his own favorite horse, High Stepping Boy, to keep a roof over all their heads.

Then the rubber boom had erupted, and the opportunity to recoup the family fortunes and once again breed and race fine horses had been too good to bypass. After installing his tearful sisters in an East Coast boarding school, Jordan had set off for the Amazon, knowing nothing whatever about rubber but determined to learn. Four years of backbreaking labor, enlivened by numerous brushes with death as he struggled against disease and predators, both human and animal, had yielded a fulfillingly swollen bank account, but still, it was not enough. Not only did he need a staggering amount of capital to buy back Castle Acres, but he also needed money to purchase the best quality broodmares and studs—all the while providing for the needs of his sisters until such time as they grew up and married.

Only one of his sisters, Victoria, was old enough to marry; she now taught at the boarding school and had taken lodgings near it so the younger girls, Eleanor and Grace, would have a place to go during holidays. Despite Victoria's protests that she was capable of supporting herself, Jordan regularly sent her a generous allowance and also paid all of the younger girls' expenses. Unlike his charming, devil-may-care father, Jordan took his responsibilities very seriously; if the rubber boom held out long enough, he intended to settle a large sum of money on each of the girls, which could then be invested to protect them from ever again being "thrown out on the street" because of a man's profligacy.

All of this family history hammered in Jordan's brain as he paced the clearing, pondering how best to put an end to Don Julio César Arana's subtle campaign to force him off the Amazon. Certainly, Amazonas was more than big enough to sustain them both, but Arana was in the process of a militant takeover of the Putumayo which flowed into the Amazon near Paraîso. Except for four stubborn Colombian squatters, Arana already owned all of the land abutting the smaller river. Now, it seemed he would not rest until he had destroyed not only the Colombians but Jordan, as well.

Complicating matters, the Putumayo itself was disputed territory, claimed by both Colombia and Peru. As a Peruvian, Arana had the backing of his country's government to seize the territory for Peru. Since Jordan's land was all in Brazil, he had considered himself safe from the two warring factions. Now, realizing this assumption was mistaken, he must decide on a course of action.

"All right, Raymundo, let's bury what's left of Francisco, then head straight downriver to Manaus. We won't even stop at Paraîso."

"What will you do, senhor?" Raymundo inquired anxiously.

"Don't worry, my friend, I'm not going to shoot Don Julio on the street—but I *am* going to have a heart-to-heart talk with him, maybe even embarrass him publicly. It's time he understands I'm not leaving or selling out to him no matter *what* he does. And if these little accidents continue to happen, I may start planning a few accidents of my own."

"What do you mean, senhor? What kind of accidents?" Raymundo's chocolate-brown eyes were as big as dinner plates. "No one challenges Arana and lives to boast of it."

"No Brazilian, Colombian, Peruvian, or Indian, you mean. I'm an *Americano,* Raymundo, have you forgotten? And I've got good connections with the British. Arana wouldn't *dare* take on the governments of the two countries who buy all his rubber. He especially wouldn't take them on at the very moment when he's trying to gain additional financial backing to expand his operations here on the Amazon. . . . The man may rule like a king in the jungle, but he's still a nobody in the marketplace of the world at large."

"Are you certain of that, Senhor Rei? It is said his *jeito* reaches everywhere."

Jeito. Jordan considered the Brazilian word, for which no English translation truly sufficed. It meant influence, pull, the right connections. In Brazil, if you had no *jeito,* you were nothing. You had no protection against stronger men, no chance of advancing your fortunes, no one to turn to when things got rough. As one of the richest, if not *the* richest man on the Amazon, Don Julio César Arana certainly had plenty of *jeito*—but Jordan had his American citizenry and his willingness to do whatever was necessary to protect his hard-won assets.

"My jeito is every bit as good as *his,* Raymundo. Where did I toss that dart? I think I'll take it with me when I have my little talk with Arana."

Raymundo searched around the body for a moment, then proffered the slender lethal weapon. "Here it is, senhor."

Jordan gingerly took it, tore off the tail end of his shirt, wrapped the dart inside it, then stuck the whole in his front pocket. "This will be my present to Don Julio—and also, a warning. Who knows?

The next time he visits El Encanto on the Putumayo, a stray dart might find its way into *his* neck. Ever shoot a blowgun, Raymundo?"

"*Não,* senhor."

"Neither have I. It's a skill I might have to develop, if I can find an Indian to teach me. However, blowguns aren't really my style. I'd much rather pummel Arana's arrogant, Castilian features into a bloody pulp."

"*Sĩm,* senhor. I will go and fetch two shovels from the *batelão.*" Raymundo was not really listening now. He had shifted his attention to the unpleasant task of burying the stinking remains of Francisco Dos Santos.

"While we're in Manaus," Jordan said to Raymundo's retreating back, "remind me to check and see if I've gotten any responses to those advertisements I placed in American newspapers for a doctor. If I'm going to battle Arana, I'd sure like to have a doctor at Paraĩso. I should probably amend the qualifications I listed to include a facility with Winchesters. If anyone's stupid enough to actually accept an offer of employment out here, he had better be a good shot with a rifle. Life may get very dangerous in the next year or so, Raymundo. Of course, it's always dangerous on the Amazon, but I've a feeling it's going to get worse."

"*Sĩm,* senhor." Raymundo's reply was all but inaudible.

Realizing he was talking to himself, Jordan fell silent. What he actually hoped to gain from his advertisement was not just someone to treat the illnesses and injuries of his workers—and his own malaria, when he had a bout of it—but also the company of another white man, an educated person with whom he could hold a decent conversation built upon shared cultural experiences and backgrounds. He was hungry for companionship and the chance to speak English during his long sojourns at Paraīso. Many in Manaus spoke it, but he could not afford to spend much time there. He kept his tappers working through encouragement and close supervision—*not* by hiring gunmen as Arana did.

Sadly, he concluded he might need to hire his own guards and "protectors" if these mysterious attacks continued. Could he bluff and bully Arana into leaving him alone? He had heard rumors of Arana's cruelty and violence—or rather, Loayza's, on Arana's behalf. The rumors might be true, or they might merely be jealous grumblings. Personally, Jordan did not care what the Peruvian did on his own land but he would *not* allow the man to threaten him or *his* workers. Probably Arana was so accustomed to having his victims flee in terror that he thought he could get away with anything, even murder.

If so, Jordan would let him know he was no coward who would soon take flight. He would fight for what was his—fight as hard and ruthlessly as his opponent. It was up to Arana. If Arana wanted war, he would have it. But maybe, just maybe, like the bully he was, once he knew Jordan would fight back, he would leave him alone.

Poor Francisco Dos Santos. Jordan resolved that while in Manaus, he would find out if the man had a family back in Cearã. If he did, Jordan would send them not only Francisco's wages but a handsome bonus. Not that a bonus could make up for the loss of a man's life, but it might help ease the poverty of the rubber tapper's family. Jordan already knew that Francisco's family, if he had one, must be poor; only a poor man ever consented to go up the Amazon as a *seringueiro*.

Only a poor and desperate one, Jordan thought, a man like himself who had no choice.

Chapter Two

Caught in a crush of people on Eduardo Ribeiro Avenue, Spencer paused to furiously fan herself with the straw bonnet she had bought to protect herself from the fierce tropical sun. After so long a time aboard ship, the city of Manaus, one thousand miles upriver from the Atlantic Ocean, was overwhelming; she ought to have taken Captain Clairmont's advice and hired a carriage to convey her from the steamship to the Grand Hotel Internacional, where he had insisted she must lodge until she could locate Jordan King.

Wanting to save money, Spencer had opted to walk, protesting that she was most anxious to view the fabulous city up close, on foot, instead of from the confines of a carriage lurching through the wide but crowded streets. Over her protests, Captain Clairmont had then engaged porters to transport her various trunks and crates to the hotel. As she could scarcely haul everything herself, she had thanked him profusely and bade him good-bye. The elderly steamship captain had been wonderful to her on the long journey from Boston, regaling her with tales of life in Amazonas, lending her books about Brazil, and even helping her to learn Portuguese, which she had been studying day and night.

Now she was about to faint from the combination of heat, excitement, and the heady, conflicting odors of roasting coffee, sulphuric-smelling rubber, spoiling fruit, sugarcane rum, cinnamon, sassafras, ginger, and raw sewage. Her system still had not adjusted to the suffocating humidity; the farther they had traveled up the Amazon, the more humid it had become. It was like breathing the vapor from a steam kettle, or inhaling through a layer of wet cheesecloth. Would she ever adjust to this tropical climate?

At least she had the relief of being on land again, in the midst of civilization, without the jungle pressing on either side. The river journey had been fascinating but also an intimidating foretaste of what life in Amazonas would be like. Clouds of mosquitoes and sandflies had often engulfed the ship, and the loglike bodies of enormous alligators had frequently parted the yellowish-brown waters, rolling away from the ship as if completely unimpressed by it. Brilliantly colored jungle birds and monkeys screamed from the shores. After Belém de Pará and one or two smaller towns, only rudimentary villages of thatched-roof huts on stilts broke the monotony of endless stretches of dark, menacing jungle.

Spencer had had plenty of time to doubt the wisdom of this entire undertaking—especially with Captain Clairmont taking such a dim view of her intentions. Repeatedly, the kindly ship's captain had warned that she ought never to debark in Manaus; for all its culture, wealth, and sophistication, the city was the "devil's own playground." Entire streets were given over to sumptuous brothels catering to every known depravity of mankind, featuring women from all over the world. Bars and cafes claimed every corner.

Prices were ten times higher for the basics of living than they were anywhere else, reflecting what seemed to be the city's credo for spending lavish amounts of money—"as though fifty pounds were two shillings," as Captain Clairmont had put it. People indulged themselves outrageously, he said. A man might tip twelve shillings to have a parcel carried three blocks or fling a golden sovereign to a boatman for a five-minute journey. Often, to impress a beautiful woman—of whom there were more legendary beauties here than in any major city in Europe—a man would light his cigars with bills of enormous denomination or tip a comely cafe waitress ten pounds wrapped around a rough-cut diamond.

As if all that wasn't bad enough, high-stepping prized carriage horses were sometimes fed Cordon Rouge champagne to slake their thirsts, the captain claimed, while legless beggars went hungry in the marketplace. Shamelessly gawking, Spencer saw no champagne-guzzling horses or legless beggars, but what she did see took her breath away. Manaus was indeed a modern city, with bottle-green, electric streetcars and streets paved in cobbles. Clipped trees—figs, crotons, jacarandas, and sweet-smelling eucalyptus—lined the avenues, overshadowing electric lamps, fine public buildings, dress shops, and milliners featuring the latest Paris fashions, fancy restaurants, and elite gentlemen's shops.

From the corner of Municipal Street and Edwardo Ribeiro, she could glimpse the magnificent opera house cresting the hill a hundred feet above sea level near San Sebastian Square. It was even more breathtaking than Captain Clairmont had described it: Its blue and gold tiled dome glittered beneath the noonday sun like a beckoning courtesan. Spencer wondered if she would ever get to see inside it, where Venetian crystal chandeliers, Carrara marble, and tall vases of Sevres porcelain were said to dazzle the eye.

The homes by the opera house were no less impressive. Two-story mansions bulked the square, flanked by high stone walls faced with colored tiles from Portugal in jewellike colors—azure, rust-red, apple-green, primrose. The houses all had flat tile roofs, crowned with classical statues and heavy, ornate vases. European styles abounded: everything from Swiss chalets through English Tudor, with a few Turkish minarets thrown in for good measure.

Spencer daubed the perspiration from her upper lip with a plain, unbordered handkerchief and gazed longingly at the beautiful men and women passing in their shiny carriages. Nearly everyone was dressed in cool, spotless white, as if they had just stepped out of ice-water baths. The men wore white linen suits, white suede shoes, Chile hats, and Irish linen shirts. They carried ornate walking canes topped with gold or silver. Women in pale gowns as airy as feathers twirled peekaboo lace parasols to protect their flawless complexions. Their wrists, fingers, and bosoms glittered with diamonds, making Spencer feel old, dowdy, and most of all, *hot* in her somber black traveling gown, unrelieved by even a starched white apron.

She had spent all her savings and the proceeds from the sale of the house furnishings on drugs and medicines rather than on clothes for herself, and she was paying the price for her practicality in this stifling heat. How she longed to find the hotel and obtain something cool and refreshing to relieve her great thirst!

"Excuse me," she said, plucking at the sleeve of a passing gentleman.

"Oui, mademoiselle?"

Smiling, he stopped and turned. Upon getting a good look at her, he frowned, seeming surprised and slightly annoyed by her audacity. But Spencer was growing desperate. His use of French surprised her, and she debated whether or not to attempt her faltering Portuguese. At her hesitancy, his face registered deepening irritation, and his eyes scornfully swept her dark, heavy, unfashionable clothing. Spencer could have sworn they lingered on the patches of dampness beneath her armpits and below her bosom. Feeling ugly as a toad, she blurted in English: "Excuse me, I was wondering if you could tell me where to find the Grand Hotel Internacional."

"Of course, mademoiselle," he responded in perfect English. He gave directions, then coolly tipped his hat and hurried on his way.

Spencer followed his directions, but when she saw the gleaming, huge building across the street from her, she wondered if he had been mistaken. Somehow, she had conceived the idea that the hotel would not be this large or luxurious; she had warned Captain Clairmont that her funds were severely limited, as surely he must have known when they reached the warmer climes, and she had been unable to change to lighter clothing like everyone else aboard the ship.

Recollecting that conversation, Spencer now remembered how he had brushed aside her concerns and assured her that she *must* stay in the Grand Hotel Internacional while in Manaus. Nowhere else would be safe for an unescorted woman. Again, she stopped a passerby.

"Is that the Grand Hotel Internacional?" she inquired of a tall, silver-haired gentleman wielding a solid silver walking stick.

He responded in Portuguese, so rapidly she could not make out all he was saying—only that yes, the building across the street was indeed the hotel. Then he added in thickly accented English: "Grand Hotel Internacional, thee finest een all Chreestendom."

She smiled her thanks, though inwardly she was quaking. What would it cost to rent a room for a night "in the finest hotel in all Christendom?" Well, it could not hurt to find out. At least, she could go to the dining room first, and no matter what it cost, order something to drink. Her throat was so parched she could hardly swallow. If she did not sit down soon in a cool place out of the sun, she was sure she would faint, for the first time in her life.

Crossing the street, she took note that each and every window on the first floor of the hotel was topped with a graceful, arching fanlight, and each window on the second floor was really not a window at all but a set of sparkling glass doors opening onto tiny balconies. Scrollwork adorned the highest level of the building, which gleamed almost blindingly in the sunlight.

As she entered the building, her feet skimmed marble floors, then sank into thick carpeting. The interior was high-ceilinged, but dim, cool, and hushed, except for the tinkle of crystal and murmur of cultured voices. Spencer quickly found her way to the dining room and was ushered to a small, damask-covered table by a white-jacketed gentleman who haughtily gazed down his nose at her. He pulled out her chair reluctantly, but she was too eager for refreshment to care much about his condescending attitude.

Brilliant, tropical-looking blossoms in a cut-crystal decanter graced the center of her table, and after ordering a *limonada,* which she hoped was lemonade, Spencer leaned back in her gilt-and-velvet chair and admired first the flowers and then her surroundings. A wave of embarrassment suffused her as she realized that she was the only lone female in the ornate, gilt-and-velvet dining room. Her dowdy, sweat-stained traveling gown made her stand out like a weed in a bouquet of roses. Fortunately, no one was noticing her, so intent were they on being charming, handsome, and beautiful as they conversed with each other in a half dozen different languages.

Intensely fascinated, even awed, Spencer studied the occupants of the luxurious room. One woman had egret feathers in her hair; her fingers were so heavy with diamonds it was a wonder she could lift them, let alone gesture theatrically to the handsome, mustachioed man across from her. The two were conversing in German. Another couple was speaking French, as were three women seated nearby, sipping champagne from crystal stemware.

Spencer's attention caught on a man seated at a table with four other men. He was very striking and important-looking. Impeccable white linen emphasized his black eyes, swarthy complexion, and impressive physique. He had a closely trimmed black beard and mustache, and black hair parted in the center. A cigar jutted from his massive, strong jaw, and he held his leonine head high, as if he agreed with Spencer's opinion that he was somehow better than other men. His white, well-manicured hands gestured gracefully. Now and then, his nostrils flared as he made some point to the other men, who all treated him with humble deference.

He must be Spanish, Spencer thought, probably a nobleman and rich as Midas. The largest diamond she had ever seen winked from a ring on his pinkie. He also wore a diamond tiepin. The waiter brought her lemonade, and as she gulped the tangy, iced liquid, a sense of relaxation flowed through her. If she could not afford to spend the night in the hotel, at least she could enjoy the surroundings before she had to face the hot streets again. What would it be like to be the wife, daughter—or merely an acquaintance—of the swarthy Spanish nobleman? To live in the luxury to which he was undoubtedly accustomed? Such a fairy-tale existence was beyond Spencer's powers of imagination, but she relished the effort.

She sipped more slowly at her lemonade, anxious to make it last because she probably could not afford another. The ice alone must cost a fortune. The waiter served luncheon to the five gentlemen, including the Spaniard, and Spencer grew conscious of her own sharp hunger as she viewed the succulent meat and vegetables ladled onto gold-rimmed plates and the mounds of fluffy white rice and black beans to which the men helped themselves.

Suddenly there was a loud, angry shout. "Arana, you bastard! I was told I might find you here."

The Spaniard looked up from his heaped plate in surprise. Spencer's own gaze leaped from the Spaniard to a tall, disheveled blond man stalking into the dining room and glaring at the Spaniard as if he were his worst enemy. "Don't look so surprised, Arana. Surely you know who I am."

The blond man's challenging voice carried into every corner. Silverware clattered as people turned to watch him advance upon the Spaniard's table. Noting the intruder's attire, Spencer was amazed. He was dressed as if he had just come in from the jungle. He wore tall, black, mud-encrusted boots, soiled, buff-colored trousers that fit as tightly as a second skin, and a torn, dirty shirt open to the waist. The beginnings of a golden beard stubbled his jaw. His wet-looking, naked chest sported the same gold curly hair, as did the darkly tanned forearms poking out of his rolled-up shirtsleeves. He was filthy, his shirt drenched with sweat, his eyes a murky green—so dark they were almost black—or maybe it was his obvious fury that made them so menacing.

In this lavish, genteel setting, the glowering blond man exuded raw, primitive violence and an almost palpable masculinity, as potent as the Spaniard's but without the dark man's cool elegance. Simultaneously revolted and attracted, Spencer shivered. She had never seen a man so angry. As he approached the seated Spaniard, he reminded her of a jaguar stalking its prey. She had spied one on the shores of the Amazon, just before it pounced on a tiny, hapless deer drinking at the water's edge.

The Spaniard acted unconcerned. Slowly, he wiped his mouth with his snowy white napkin, then folded it and set it down beside his plate. He said something in Spanish to his companions, then silently pushed back his chair. "You flatter yourself, sir," he announced in precise, accented English. "I have not the least idea who you are."

"Then allow me to refresh your memory." With coiled calm, the blond man reached in his front shirt pocket and removed a long, skinny object that resembled a huge needle. With a flourish, he speared the slab of beef swimming in gravy on the Spaniard's plate. "Recognize that, Arana?"

Stuck upright in the meat, the needlelike object quivered obscenely. Spencer wondered what it was; could it possibly be one of those darts the Indians reportedly shot from blowguns?

With great dignity, the Spaniard fingered the shaft but did not remove the needle. "That is, I believe, a dart. And if it's tipped with poison, you have spoiled my meat."

"Who better than you should know if it's tipped with poison, Arana? Go on, finish your lunch. I'll just take it back, and you can continue your meal as if nothing happened."

The Spaniard's eyes bulged, his first show of annoyance. "You must be mad! I don't know what you're trying to prove with this disruption, but I warn you I won't tolerate it. Only a fool would touch that food now, and I, sir, am not a fool."

"Thanks for the information, but that was not the question. The question is: Are you a murderer?" The blond man—obviously an American, he spoke English with a slightly southern drawl—casually leaned against the corner of the table, drawing looks of outrage and confusion from the other occupants and causing the Spaniard's lips to tighten.

"How do you know the dart is contaminated?" the American continued conversationally. "Unless you know where I got it. I plucked it from the neck of one of my *seringueiros,* near the Putumayo. The man was dead, the dart still intact, so I said to myself, why not return it to its rightful owner? I still have plenty of other rubber tappers, and the dart might be needed to eliminate one of them. I've been told curare lasts a long time; I'm sure there's enough poison left to kill another man."

"I haven't the slightest idea what you're talking about. However, if you are accusing me of murder, I must remind you of the penalty for slander and false accusation. If you just tell me who you are, my solicitor will contact you within the hour, and the

Brazilian authorities will also be informed of your accusations."

The American straightened, an exaggerated look of innocence on his dark, dirty face. "Damn my aunt Milly's corset! Did I accuse *you* of murder? I believe I simply *inquired* if you were one. I do think it quite telling that you refuse to eat your meat now. Not *all* darts sold in Manaus as souvenirs to tourists and sightseers are tipped with poison. I'll ask you again: how did you know this one was?"

Trembling, the Spaniard rose to his feet. His height was impressive, but he was not as tall as the blond American. His face flushed a deep, wine color, and his eyes flashed dangerously, as if keeping his temper was the most difficult thing he had ever done. "Get out of this dining room! Get out of this hotel! You take your life in your hands by coming here, ridiculing me in front of my friends, suggesting that I had anything to do with the death of some obscure little rubber tapper."

"Are you threatening me?" the American inquired silkily. "If you are, I should imagine the Brazilian authorities would be interested to know that, too."

"I threaten nobody," the Spaniard denied. "You are a stranger to me; why would I even *bother* to threaten you?"

"I admit we've never met, Arana, but I'd hardly say we're strangers. My land adjoins yours near the Putumayo. I already know a great deal about you, and I expect you know a heap about me. Your overseer, Miguel Loayza, has several times attempted to buy me out on your behalf. Now I think he's trying to *scare* me off my land. It won't work, Arana. Neither you nor your ravenous, guard dogs will ever succeed in driving me off the Amazon. That's why I'm here—to return this dart, *if* it belongs to you, and to warn you to leave me alone."

"I am sorry if you're having difficulties," Arana said stiffly. "But I assure you I have nothing to do with them. I have not been up the Putumayo for many months. Business here in Manaus has occupied all my time. Should you doubt it, these gentlemen can attest to that fact."

"Are you saying you're unaware of Loayza's offers?"

"My emissaries are seeking to acquire more land on many fronts. If Senhor Loayza has indeed approached you, I shall inform him at once to desist in future—if you will but give me your name."

"What a cool character you are, Arana, denying you even know who I am! You're the perfect gentleman, aren't you? At least, in public. But I wonder if anyone here in this room really knows what goes on up the Putumayo. Do *you* even know, Arana?"

The Spaniard locked glances with the tall, lean American. Though Spencer was certain his feelings ran much deeper, his face never revealed anything but polite irritation and wounded dignity. "Of course, I know, senhor. And so does everyone else. My business practices are above reproach. The Arana name commands great respect. Can you say the same for *your* name—whatever it is?"

"If you really don't know my name, I'll tell you, Arana. I want you to remember it, because the next time I come looking for you, I won't be nearly as polite as this time . . . I'm Jordan King, son of Alexander King, formerly of Lexington, Kentucky, in the United States. I'm an *American,* Arana, not some damn *caipira* you can push around. If you push me, I'm gonna push back . . . Is that understood?"

"Sĩm, senhor, I understand completely. Your pride

has been injured because you have been unable to protect your workers from the *Indios* who still roam the jungles and have no respect for the laws of civilized men. However, that is no reason why *we* should lack civility. Come . . . why don't you join me for a brandy? I, too, have problems with the *Indios,* and we can discuss our mutual difficulties like gentlemen."

Incredibly, considering the insults and accusations the American had leveled at him, the Spaniard extended his hand for a handshake. For a moment, the American looked nonplussed. He glanced down at the extended hand as if it were a weapon aimed at his midsection. When he lifted his eyes, they were a brilliant hard green.

"No thank you, Arana. I had sooner share a brandy with a bushmaster. At least then I'd know for certain the nature of the serpent I was facing. If my instincts about you are wrong, I apologize. If they're not, then beware: You and I will meet again, and as I said, next time I won't be so polite."

The Spaniard dropped his hand, his black eyes glittering. "Have it your way then, Senhor King. Now, if you will excuse me . . . I must get back to my guests."

He reseated himself at the table, picked up his wine-glass, and unconcernedly sipped it. Then he beckoned to the others still staring in wonder and consternation. "Come, come! Do not let this unpleasant incident spoil your appetites. I shall order another plate at once. Colonel Luis, you were going to tell me about the new carriage you recently purchased. How can we all get rich on rubber if you persist in buying carriages instead of automobiles . . . ?" His voice trailed off in the welter of awkward laughter from the men at the table. Every man seated there pointedly ignored the blond American who had been so cunningly dismissed.

The American's face reddened slightly, and his fists clenched. Spencer could not decide whether to feel sorry for him or pleased at his comeuppance. As he turned and stalked from the room with only a shade less hostility than he had shown upon entering, she suddenly realized who he was. He had said his name was Jordan King!

She had been so enthralled by the drama of the moment and the contrasts between the two men she had scarcely registered all that was said. Now, the very man she had come all this way to see was leaving the dining room and probably also the hotel. Jumping up from the table, she nearly upset her lemonade, but there was no time to worry about spoiling the fine damask or paying her bill.

"Mr. King!" she cried breathlessly. "Mr. King, wait!"

All eyes swiveled in her direction. Paying no heed to anyone, she dashed after the tall, departing American.

Chapter Three

Jordan King was nearly out on the street before Spencer caught up with him. When she did, she almost wished she had not. He paused in the lobby and glared at her with such green-eyed ferocity she wondered if he even saw her. Obviously his thoughts were still on the Spaniard he had challenged in the dining room.

"Mr. King? Mr. Jordan King?" She had to tilt back her head to look up at him. Tall as she was, he was taller still and whipcord lean, his body nicely proportioned but stripped of all unnecessary flesh.

"What do you want?" he rudely demanded. His eyes skewered her, as if she were some loathsome creature that had just crawled out from beneath a rock.

"Mr. King, my name is Spencer O'Rourke. Do you recall receiving a letter from me?"

His blond brows plunged downward in puzzlement. "No, I can't say I do. But then, this is the first time in months I've been to town. I was just going home to sort through my mail. Why would *you* be writing me, anyway?"

Spencer moistened her lips. Despite the lemonade, her mouth felt full of cotton. "Isn't there somewhere private we can go to talk?"

He snorted impatiently. "I haven't got all day, miss. Say what you have to say now and be done with it."

His curtness offended her, rousing her Irish temper. She had nothing about which to be furtive or embarrassed; *he* was the one who had just made a spectacle of himself in the dining room. "Mr. King . . . I'm actually *Doctor* O'Rourke. I wrote to you in reponse to your advertisement in a Boston newspaper for a physician. It's possible that I arrived here before or at the same time as my letter. In any case, the letter is now superfluous. I've come to Manaus for the express purpose of accepting your offer of employment."

Jordan King stared at her in disbelief, then threw back his head and barked with laughter. "Damn my aunt Milly's corset! Paraíso needs a doctor bad, but not *that* bad. You think I'd hire a *woman* to work for me up the Amazon?"

"Surely you would not reject my application before I've had a chance to state my case, Mr. King. I'll ask you again; why don't we go somewhere quiet and discuss this matter?"

"It would be a waste of time, Miss O'Rourke—excuse me, *Doctor.* I wouldn't consider hiring a woman. Had I gotten your letter, I would have written and *told* you that."

"But you know nothing about me, Mr. King! How can you make up your mind so quickly? I'm just what you're looking for. So sure am I of my qualifications that I've spent every last penny I possess to get here."

"You mean you're broke—flat broke, without a *cruzeiro* to your name?" Studying her in amazement, he folded his arms across his near-naked chest and rocked back on his heels.

Recalling that *cruzeiros* were the Brazilian form of money, though most financial transactions in Manaus involved the British pound, Spencer nodded. "I've barely a penny, shilling, or *cruzeiro* to my name. But I *do* have my medical skills to offer, and you are the man to whom I wish to offer them."

"Just your *medical* skills?" he inquired archly, cocking one eyebrow.

Spencer flushed to the roots of her carrot-red hair. "Of *course,* just my medical skills. What other skills could you possibly mean?"

As he pondered the question, his eyes roamed her face and figure. Then he chuckled and shook his head. "Forget I ever mentioned it, *Doctor.* If you *have* any other skills, I'm sure the price would be way too high for them . . . Since *I* won't hire you—and I assure you I won't—what do you intend to do?"

"I intend to talk you into it—to change your mind."

"I've already told you: that won't work. So what, now?"

"Why, I . . . I dinna know what I'll do," Spencer confessed, too shocked and disappointed to even dissemble. "I only arrived here a few hours ago. As soon as I finished my lemonade, I intended to go looking for you. Then, when I overheard your argument in the dining room and realized who you were . . ." she trailed off uncertainly, at a momentary loss as to what to do or say next.

Jordan King sighed. "Look . . . it's getting a bit late in the day for traipsing back down to the riverfront. Besides, you look exhausted. It's the humidity—takes a long time to adjust to it. In any case, I doubt you'd be able to find a berth on a steamship out of here today; you'd just be stuck in an unsavory part of town with no accommodations for the night. Why don't you check into the hotel, and go to the riverfront first thing in the morning?"

"I canna . . . *can't* afford this hotel, Mr. King. And I'm *not* leaving Manaus. Perhaps you can recommend cheaper accommodations where I'll be comfortable until I can find employment with someone else."

"It costs four pounds to spend the night here, a healthy sum, I admit. But isn't it worth the price to keep your virtue intact and maybe even your life?"

"Four pounds!" Spencer burst out. "That's highway robbery!"

"No, that's simply life on the Amazon . . . Tell you what. Instruct the guy at the front desk to put it on *my* account. It's the least I can do to compensate you for the trouble you've gone to. I'll pay for one night only. After that, you're on your own."

"Never mind, Mr. King! If ye won't give me a chance to prove me competency, ye can take your charity and . . . and stuff it where the sun doesna shine! I'm quite capable of looking after meself."

"My, my . . . What an unladylike thing to say, little Miss Irish! I assume you're unmarried. No man in his right mind would allow his wife to come to the Amazon and work for a man she's never met. For all you know, I could be a rapist or a murderer, escaping punishment in my own country. Doesn't that *bother* you just a tiny bit?"

"Now that I think about it, it does, Mr. King. From what I've seen of ye so far, ye very likely are a dangerous man. I'd be far better advised to seek employment from the gentleman ye insulted in the dining room—Mr. Arana. I doubt he would force a lady to stand about, debating her future, in a public lobby."

Jordan King's face lost its faintly amused, condescending expression. Before her very eyes, his sun-darkened, chiseled features hardened to their previous state of barely leashed violence. "One thing I'd advise you while you're here in Manaus, Doc. Steer clear of Don Julio César Arana. If one can believe all the rumors—and I can—that cool, cultured Peruvian in his impeccable white linen is a murderer. Up the Putumayo, at El Encanto, he beats his Indian workers—sometimes to death—forces their wives and daughters to serve the lusts of his hired gunmen, and makes their children wait on his table. I believe he killed one of my rubber tappers, or ordered his death, which amounts to the same thing. You can go work for him if you want to, but if you do, there's no telling what might happen . . . Having warned you, I've done all I can. So if you'll excuse me, I'll be on my way now."

"But, Mr. King! Wait, please wait . . ."

As the tall American began walking away from her, Spencer darted after him, plucking at his sleeve. Once again, he turned to her—this time, with a growl of exasperation. "Haven't you any pride, Doctor? Women should never beg."

"I'm not begging! I merely wanted to say . . . should ye change yer mind later tonight, ye may contact me here, where I have decided t' stay, after all. Tomorrow, when I find new lodgings, I will leave a message at the front desk as to where ye can reach me."

"There's no need for that. I won't be contacting you either tonight or tomorrow. I doubt we'll meet again. Not that meeting you hasn't been diverting, but I rarely come to town. I only came this time to warn Arana to leave me alone and to inform the authorities of my employee's death. Now that I've done that, I'll be leaving as soon as possible."

"Where is your rubber plantation?"

"Eight days upriver—when my launch is working properly. When it isn't, the journey takes longer." He glanced impatiently toward the doorway. "Good afternoon, Doctor—and good-bye."

"Good-bye, Mr. King," Spencer answered coolly, masking her burning ire in regal hauteur.

The infuriating Mr. King did not know it, because he did not know *her,* but she had no intention of allowing him to escape so easily. This was only the first round in her battle to gain employment. She had not come all this way to be dismissed upon first meeting. Jordan King needed a doctor at his plantation, and she needed a job. Tomorrow, she would confront him again at the address he had listed in his advertisement. Once he saw how persistent she was, he would undoubtedly reconsider. The same stubborn perseverance that had made her a doctor against overwhelming odds would eventually make him hire her.

More determined than ever, Spencer turned back toward the dining room, where going in, she met Don Julio César Arana coming out. The elegant Spaniard—no, Peruvian—nodded and stepped aside for her. As Spencer swept past him, she got a good look at the supposed monster. This attractive, sophisticated gentleman could not be a murderer; Jordan King must be mistaken, just as he was mistaken if he thought she would meekly accept his refusal and bow out of his obviously troubled life.

After a bath, a decent dinner, and two reviving shots of French brandy, one of the few luxuries he allowed himself, Jordan finally felt well enough to tackle the stack of mail awaiting him in the wicker basket where his houseservant, Chico, deposited it every day. The basket was filled to overflowing, and Jordan eyed it with great distaste. All day he had been plagued by a grinding headache and a sense of impending weakness. He still felt slightly ill, but as yet, had no fever—a good sign. Maybe his malaria was not flaring up again, after all. His illness could be blamed on his encounter with Arana; the man was enough to justify a headache in anybody.

Seated at the big desk in the front room of his modest, whitewashed, red-tiled house, he began sorting through the stained, travel-worn letters. Usually, he found several from his sisters, which he would set aside to enjoy at leisure, but mostly, he found bills, some overdue, which would have to be paid immediately. In the current stack were two letters from Victoria and one from Eleanor. In vain, he searched for something from Grace, the youngest, a talkative, engaging little minx who regarded letter-writing as a great chore, though she loved to receive letters.

An engraved invitation from a business associate caught his eye, and, tearing it open, Jordan discovered that the sixteenth-birthday party for the daughter of the man with whom he made shipping arrangements to transport his rubber from Manaus to Belém, had taken place three weeks previously. Sighing, he shook his head. When he had first arrived in Manaus with no wife in tow, the Brazilians had launched a vigorous campaign to marry him off to one of their nubile young daughters, but the girls had all reminded Jordan too much of his sisters. Most of his acquaintances had since given up on him, so he doubted his presence had been missed at this party. Nevertheless, it would have been nice to mingle with civilized people, eat and drink abundantly, and forget about the hardships of jungle life, if only for a little while.

It often seemed as if the jungle was swallowing him alive, and he would never be a normal person, engaged in normal living. Before he got rich enough to go home, his sisters would all be married and strangers to him, and he himself would be an old man—too old to marry and found a family dynasty of his own.

Tossing bills in one heap, announcements and advertisements in another, and personal letters in yet a third, he came across a letter postmarked Boston and written in a decidedly feminine but unfamiliar hand. He ripped it open and scanned the contents of the single sheet of thin paper. The signature at the bottom read Spencer K. O'Rourke, M.D.

Why, she had never even identified herself as a female! Jordan thought in astonishment. Had he received the letter before meeting her, he undoubtedly would have written back, enclosed passage money, and hired her on the spot. Hers was the only response to advertisements he had placed in both Boston and New York newspapers, the two U.S. ports where steamship passages were readily available for journeying to Brazil and elsewhere in South America.

She certainly had a great deal of nerve, he groused. But then, it must have taken great nerve to become a physician in the first place. Female medical practitioners were strange oddities; Jordan himself had never before met a woman doctor and would on no account entrust his health to one, though Victoria might. His sister possessed many radical, upstart ideas, the most controversial being that she actually believed women were equal to men and should be allowed to vote, a point of view with which Spencer K. O'Rourke would undoubtedly agree.

Crumpling the letter in one hand, Jordan shuddered. He tolerated Victoria's views because he loved her; she was his sister. But he would think long and hard before entering into any sort of relationship with a self-proclaimed suffragette. The skinny, red-haired woman with the brilliant, blue-green eyes and freckled face had "suffragette" written all over her, and a second S-letter word every bit as frightening: *spinster.* Her mode of dress, forthright manner, and lack of any feminine artifice which might have made her more attractive had probably all contributed to her inability to attract a husband. Unable to find one in the United States, she had more than likely assumed that the jungle was full of ripe pickings—men so starved for companionship they would consider marrying anybody.

"You've come a long way only to be disappointed, Doctor O'Rourke," he said aloud, then clamped his jaws shut, chagrined to be holding a conversation only with himself. He had picked up the habit of speaking his thoughts aloud in the remote reaches of Paraïso, where he sometimes feared he might go mad if he couldn't talk to *someone.* Damn! Why couldn't the outspoken Miss O'Rourke be a man—one with an appreciation of good Irish whiskey? She had a man's name and ambitions; all she lacked was a man's body.

Leaning back in his chair, Jordan pictured Spencer O'Rourke as he had seen her that afternoon; the only feminine thing about her had been her bosom. He would not have minded getting his hands on a pair of beauties such as she possessed. But as for the rest of her . . . well, he wasn't quite that desperate, at least, not yet.

Thinking of bosoms, Jordan was reminded that it had been a long time since he'd had his hands on any woman's breasts—"beauties" or otherwise. And tomorrow he wanted to leave again for Paraíso. He shoved aside the piles of mail and decided that if he rose early, he could still dispose of the most urgent matters and take the rest of the mail with him to read on the journey. Chico did an excellent job of handling his city business and almost always followed his instructions to the letter; the little Brazilian houseservant could especially be counted upon to pay the bills, because half of them came from his own relatives who somehow managed to supply nearly everything Jordan needed.

Perhaps an hour or two with one of Manaus's famed whores would cure his headache, and also keep him from fantasizing about fondling such a plain Jane as Spencer O'Rourke. How could he even consider tumbling that dried-up old maid? Jordan supposed that his association with his sisters—knowing the agonies they had gone through wondering if they were pretty—made him more sympathetic than most men toward plain women. If he could not court them, he could at least pity them. Fortunately, none of his sisters were as unattractive and therefore doomed to spinsterhood as Doctor O'Rourke.

Rising to his feet, Jordan pondered which nationality of woman he wanted this night. A place down on Itamaraca Street boasted girls from as far away as Moscow, Tangier, Cairo, and Budapest. According to ads in the newspaper, an evening with a thirteen-year-old Polish virgin, imported direct from Warsaw, would cost as little as seventy pounds. Of course, if a man wanted "real quality," an hour with one of the reigning queens such as "Trinidad" with her bolero hats and little black poodle, Zizi, he would have to pay a small fortune, and a whole night could cost an inheritance. Rumor had it that Trinidad had once charged the price of a glittering diamond necklace worth fifteen hundred pounds.

Jordan finally decided on Aria Ramos, a Brazilian, whose poignant violin solos were the highlight of every carnival. Aria was a dark, vivacious beauty who always welcomed him with open arms and a joyous outpouring of the latest news, gossip, and scandals. First he would enjoy her luscious body, then he would engage her in sprightly, frivolous conversation, and if he had to choose which he most anticipated, it would probably be the conversation. Making love to a beautiful woman was certainly pleasurable, but when a man spent as much time alone in the jungle as he did, *talking* to one was every bit as delightful, if not more so.

Yes, why couldn't Spencer O'Rourke be an Irishman full of bonhomie and blarney? That's what he needed: a congenial companion who could speak English and serve as a heartening reminder that somewhere in the world human beings still met, discoursed, and conducted their business in a friendly environment. He had been too long in that dim, silent, dangerous world of the jungle . . .

Jordan carefully counted out the cash he thought he would need, went out, and spent several idyllic hours locked in the passionate embrace of Aria Ramos, who knew many things to do with her mouth, the least of which was talking . . . But afterward, as he staggered home through the darkened streets, his headache returned with renewed ferocity, and his vision blurred more than the moderate amount of liquor he had consumed would have warranted. In the morning, instead of rising early, he slept late; awakening to find himself sweat-drenched and shivering. His flesh felt hot to his own touch, and he was so weak he could not stand upright.

"Chico . . . Chico . . ." he called in a raspy voice. "Go fetch a doctor. I'm ill, again . . . probably another attack of that damn malaria that keeps plaguing me. If a doctor won't come, at least get me some quinine. I don't care what it costs."

"Sĩm, senhor, I will go at once," answered Chico, rushing into Jordan's bedroom in the black, flapping slippers he always wore with a white shirt and trousers. "But what shall I tell the lady downstairs in your office? She has been waiting to speak with you for more than three hours already."

"Lady? Damn it, Chico, *what* lady? . . . Oh God, my head. I think it's coming off my shoulders."

"Ugly lady with red hair like a jungle bird's feathers, a black dress, and brown dots all over her face. She says she is not going away until she sees you."

Doctor Spencer K. O'Rourke. Who else could it be?

"Tell her . . . tell her . . ." Jordan panted from the effort of trying to think clearly and translate his thoughts into Portuguese for Chico, whose English was far from perfect. "Tell her to get her ass up here and bring her little black bag, if she's got one."

"Sĩm, senhor."

Closing his eyes, Jordan collapsed on the bed in a wave of dizziness. He thought about getting up and putting on his pants, at least, for it was his custom to sleep in the nude, but decided what the hell; she was a doctor, wasn't she? If she wanted to peer under the sheets, she should not be surprised by what she might see. A moment later, there were footsteps on the stair, and then a rustling sound, like a woman's skirts.

A cool hand touched Jordan's brow. "Mr. King, you're quite ill. You have a very high fever."

"I *know* that," Jordan gritted through clenched teeth. "What I want you to do is fix whatever's wrong with me. Why else would I invite you into my bedroom?"

"Just lie still and rest, Mr. King. Don't upset yourself with further conversation. I only have one question, and you can answer yes or no. Do you suffer from malaria?"

"Yes, damn it!"

"That's all I need to know. Go back to sleep, Mr. King. I'll take care of everything."

Jordan had one last thought before an all-too-familiar blackness closed in on him: *I hope she knows what the hell she's doing.*

Chapter Four

By nightfall, Jordan King was delirious, in the throes of the first, full-blown attack of malaria Spencer had ever witnessed. She was afraid to leave him in the care of his distracted houseservant, who kept babbling incoherently in a mixture of Portuguese and English and dashing in and out of the room with basins of water and pots of black, sweet coffee or noxious-smelling tea neither she nor her patient were in any condition to drink.

It was time to take matters into her own hands. Searching Jordan's desk in the downstairs front room, Spencer found pen and paper and wrote a note in English, which she hoped someone at the front desk of the Grand Hotel Internacional would understand. In it, she requested that her two trunks, several crates of medicines, and other baggage be sent as soon as possible to Jordan's address. She then pressed the folded note into the hands of the short, slender houseservant with the black, flapping slippers.

The man's age was impossible to guess; he had wrinkled, nut-brown features, dark hair and eyes, and moved with quick, jerky motions—rather like a monkey, Spencer thought. "Grand Hotel Internacional . . ." she said slowly, trying to pronounce it the way Brazilians did. "Take my note to the hotel and give it to the desk clerk."

The man stared unblinkingly, looking from her to the note and back again.

"I'm going to stay here to look after Mr. King, so I need my things," she explained. She tried saying it in Portuguese, but the words came out all wrong. By his puzzled expression, she knew he did not understand. "Hotel!" she finally shouted at him. *"Va para hotel!"*

A flicker of recognition lit his brown eyes. "Hotel?" he repeated wonderingly.

She nodded. "Grand Hotel Internacional."

"Hotel Grand Internacional?" He mixed up the words, and the accent was different, but they were finally communicating.

"Sĩm, senhor," she assured him in the only Portuguese word she found easy—the one for "yes."

He astounded her by breaking into a grin and asking in halting English: "What . . . is . . . you . . . name?"

"I'm Dr. Spencer O'Rourke."

"Doutor?" He frowned, either not understanding the word or else not believing her.

"Yes, I'm a doctor . . . Now, what is your name?"

"Chico Paulo Roberto Antonio Morais," he said proudly. "But . . . you . . . call Chico."

"Well, now that we've settled that, Chico, do you understand what I want you to do?"

He nodded. "Hotel Grand Internacional."

"Yes. Go to the hotel. My room is number 11. I have a few things there, and the rest they are keeping in storage. Tell them I want everything brought here at once—either tonight or first thing tomorrow."

"Sĩm, Doutor."

For the first time, Spencer smiled at the man. He had called her by her professional title and seemed to understand what she wanted. "I am going to work for your employer and make him well again. In order to do that, I must be near him. Is there a spare room upstairs which I might occupy?" When he frowned again in puzzlement, she dismissed him with a wave of her hand. "Oh, never mind . . . I'll explore the upstairs for myself. Go quickly now to the hotel. I want everything brought here before Mr. King wakes up . . . and realizes what I'm doing," she added under her breath.

The little Brazilian released a torrent of Portuguese which she took to be assurances that all would be done as she asked. When he finally left the house, she went back upstairs to check on Jordan King. Finding him in fitful slumber, she took advantage of being alone by picking out which of the two other unoccupied, upstairs bedrooms she wanted for her own.

That decided, she explored the house from top to bottom. With Chico gone, there was no one else in it but her and Jordan. How odd! If Jordan King was a rich rubber baron, why did he live so modestly? Compared to the luxurious residences scattered around Manaus, his house was remarkably plain and simple. Of the five rooms on the second floor, one was Jordan King's bedroom, two were empty except for simple, palm-fiber hammocks strung up in lieu of beds, a third was used for storage, and the fifth was a tiny, tiled room with chipped accoutrements for bathing and other intimate necessities.

The rooms downstairs were no less utilitarian. Besides Jordan's office, there was a large front parlor almost bare of furniture, a small dining room, and several other rooms opening onto what was obviously the heart of the house—a central, ill-kept courtyard, where brilliantly colored flowers bloomed in tangled profusion. Plain wicker furniture, white-washed walls, and a lack of carpeting, drapes, or decorative items proclaimed this a very masculine, temporary abode. No effort had been made to give the house character or clues to its main inhabitant; indeed, it looked scarcely lived in, except for a small, cluttered room in the back of the house at the very end of the courtyard, where Chico apparently stayed.

Spencer decided that one of the empty downstairs rooms would do well for storing her belongings. She wrinkled her nose at the dust and grime in the kitchen, and resolved to have Chico spend the next day cleaning it. Jordan King would need plenty of hot broth and light, nourishing foods when he was able to eat again, and if Chico was unable to provide decent meals, *she* might have to cook them or find someone who could. She expected the current siege of her prospective employer's malaria to run its course in no more than a week. After that, he would need several weeks of rest and good food to regain his strength. Obviously, he had not been taking care of his health or eating properly; his agitated emotional state may also have had something to do with provoking this most recent attack.

Returning to the bedside of the man she was determined first to cure and then to accompany to his rubber plantation, she checked his vital signs and was relieved that he had not worsened. Malaria claimed over three hundred lives annually in Manaus; she could not remember where she had read this, but the figure stuck in her mind. Well, what did people expect? Alongside the luxurious homes, shops, municipal gardens, and parks in the city, there were heaps of garbage and offal, topless cisterns and rainwater barrels, stagnant puddles in the streets, and the stinking huts of the poor . . . all combining to produce an abundance of mosquitoes, flies, and other insects.

Realizing it was the hour to lower mosquito nets, Spencer let down the one bunched and fastened to a frame suspended over Jordan King's bed. As she was tucking it under the mattress of his big four-poster, he stirred. Pushing down the light sheet covering him to the waist, he kicked it aside, where it toppled from the bed onto the floor. Spencer already knew he was naked; she had discovered his nudity in the course of her first examination, when his glassy green eyes had stared challengingly up at her: "I hope I'm not embarrassing you, Doc," he had said through chattering teeth. "I presume you've seen naked men before."

"Hundreds," she had stiffly assured him, though in fact, most of the male patients she had dealt with in the past had had far more modesty than Jordan King.

Now, more than the first time, the sight of his flaccid white genitals in their nest of blond hair startled her, reminding her of the awkwardness of her situation. Here she was, a stranger in a strange country, alone in this man's house and embarked upon a course of insinuating herself into his life when he was too helpless and ill to stop her. What in the name of St. Brigid did she think she was doing?

Powerless to look away, she stared at Jordan King's nude body. It was actually quite a beautiful body, with wide shoulders, a narrow waist, and slim hips. From the waist up, his skin was tanned a rich, golden honey color; below, he was dead-white, the curly blond hair pale as moonbeams. His legs and thighs were lean and muscular, his belly flat, his navel deeply indented. Even lying down, he appeared strong and undeniably masculine. He was certainly exceedingly well endowed, she thought, and could not help speculating on just how large he would be when sexually aroused.

For shame. Such wanton thoughts were totally out of character and a blight on her professionalism. Cheeks flaming, Spencer averted her eyes, picked up the sheet, lifted the mosquito netting, and covered him again. The heat, humidity, and his current state of helplessness made the idea of clothing him seem ridiculous, but from now on, whenever she examined him, she would make certain Chico was present—and Chico could also perform the more intimate nursing chores. She vowed to confine her activities to the management and treatment of the dreaded disease assaulting his attractive body and rendering him as weak as a kitten.

Regular doses of quinine should soon set him right—and then she would insist upon a proper convalescence, with plenty of rest and good food. "Never fear, Mr. King," she whispered softly. "You are going to get well—and then you are going to hire me. I'm going to build a new life here on the Amazon."

Jordan King mumbled something and tossed his head from side to side. He was sweating profusely. Spencer softly clucked her tongue. No wonder he needed a doctor at his rubber plantation. To be ill like this in the middle of the jungle would be a terrible test of fortitude and human endurance. The number of deaths occurring *outside* the city must far exceed the number occurring within. It was a good thing she had brought plenty of quinine; she had a feeling she was going to need it.

* * *

So weak he could hardly lift his head, Jordan opened one eye and stared up at the mosquito netting bunched above his head. The room was hot and flooded with bright sunshine, indicating late morning or early afternoon. He wondered where Chico was and why it was so noisy; he could hear babies crying and women chattering. At first, he thought they were out on the street, where something exciting must be occurring. But as he lay there listening, he realized that the noise seemed to be coming from below—*inside his own house.*

The effort of raising his head off the pillow nearly killed him. Where in hell was Chico? And why hadn't he brought quinine to get this damn malaria back under control? By a sheer act of will, Jordan managed to sit up, then had to rest a moment until the room stopped spinning. Good Lord, he was dying, and his worthless Brazilian houseservant was nowhere around. Hadn't he sent Chico to fetch a doctor?

Jordan frowned, trying to remember. As usual after one of his attacks of fever and chills, his thoughts were muddled, and he had lost all sense of time. He might have been lying in bed for only an hour, or it might have been two days.

"Chico!" he croaked, his voice barely a whisper.

On a stand beside his bed was a tray with a pitcher and a glass of water. Reaching for the glass, he drained it and immediately felt better, except for the awful taste still lingering on his tongue. Brushing his hand across his mouth, he felt a thick stubble—several days growth of beard! How long had he been lying there unattended?

Furious, ready to fire the faithless Chico, he

swung his legs over the side of the bed and lurched to his feet. He had to cling to the bedpost to remain upright, but gradually his dizziness lessened, and he was able to snatch up the sheet, wrap it around his waist, and he set off in search of his houseservant. As he left the room and approached the stairwell, a baby's high-pitched wail floated up the steps amidst a babble of female voices.

Oblivious to his employer's suffering, Chico must be having a party! Jordan thought. With each stumbling step, Jordan's fury grew—fueled by the noise drifting up the stairwell. From the top step, he could see down into the front hallway but not into the parlor or his office. Jordan again shouted Chico's name, but no one answered or came to his aid. With all the chatter and commotion downstairs, he could shout all day, and no one would hear him.

Lurching back into his bedroom, Jordan went to the stand by his bedside and opened the top drawer. He fumbled inside and removed the Smith & Wesson six-shooter he kept loaded and close at hand, in case thieves broke into the house. Grasping the pistol in one hand and the sheet in the other, he stumbled back to the stairwell. "Chico!" he shouted one last time. "Damn it, someone down there answer me!"

When no one did, he raised the pistol and fired a single shot into the ceiling. Chunks of plaster and chips of red tile rained down on his head, but he was past caring. He'd get someone's attention or die trying. In the wake of the shot came dead silence, then people began spilling out of the parlor into the hallway.

Jordan had a fleeting impression of women and children with soiled clothing and dirty faces, wide-eyed babies, Chico—the damn rascal!—and a tall, black-garbed woman with fiery red hair and snapping, blue-green eyes. Staring up at him, she recovered her aplomb much faster than he did.

"Put that gun down at once, Mr. King, before ye kill someone! What are ye doing out of bed?" She handed a sniveling baby back to its mother and rushed toward the bottom of the stairs.

"Stay right where you are!" he rasped, waving the pistol at her. "Who *are* all these people? What are they doing in my house?"

Shards of memory pierced the blackness throbbing behind his eyelids; he had a dim recollection of this red-haired woman—Spencer O'Rourke—and Chico bending over him, spooning liquids into his mouth, bathing his hot face, neck, and arms with cool water, combing his hair, bringing him basins. Someone had helped him relieve himself into one of them . . . Had *she* been taking care of him, touching him intimately, all this time? The thought made him flush with combined anger and speculation; who in hell did she think she was?

The object of his irritation paused at the foot of the stairs. "These people are Chico's friends and relatives who need medical care for themselves and their children. One baby has a very bad case of dysentery, another a rash, and one of the women has female troubles . . . I was just doing what I could for them."

"In *my* house?" Jordan roared, recovering his voice all at once. "You were curing potty rash while I was dying of fever upstairs?"

"Ye're not dying, Mr. King. If ye were, ye couldna be standing there waving that gun at everyone. And the only reason I invited them to come here is because I wanted to repay them for all they've done for ye."

"*Done* for me? Damn my aunt Milly's corset!

What have they done for *me*—except wake me with their loud chatter and crying babies . . ."

He trailed off as her eyes flashed indignantly and her shoulders straightened. "That one . . ." she pointed to the woman holding the nearest pot-bellied, stick-legged baby, "brought a chicken so Chico and I could make broth for you. And Dona Clotilda over there brought eggs. Dona Maria brought rice and beans. Ye owe these fine women yer humble gratitude, Mr. King, for they've been feedin' yer entire household durin' yer unfortunate illness."

"*What* household?" Jordan shouted. "There's only me and Chico. If we need food, he has only to go to the market and *buy* some."

"He had no *money,* Mr. King. Ye were going t' give him some t' pay bills and run the household, but ye became ill quite suddenly, and *I* certainly dinna have enough money to pay for everything. Why, the prices in Manaus are simply outrageous—twenty-five shillings for a scrawny chicken and sixpence for a single hen's egg. I dinna know how anyone survives here, much less prospers. Fortunately, Chico's family came to our aid, and, in return, I decided to hold an open clinic and treat their illnesses while I'm here, looking after ye."

"Who gave *you* permission to look after me?" A wave of dizziness crashed over Jordan. Struggling to keep his balance, he almost dropped his pistol *and* his sheet.

Spencer dashed up the stairs. "Chico! Come quickly! Mr. King is about to collapse."

"*Sĩm,* Doutor!" The cowering Chico, who had been hiding behind a fat woman in a red skirt, detached himself from the crowd and raced toward the stairs.

Letting go of both pistol and sheet, Jordan

clutched at the wrought-iron newel post at the head of the stairs. Whatever energy had gotten him this far had suddenly deserted him; Spencer reached him just as his legs gave out, and he would have toppled headfirst down the stairs if she had not caught him around the waist. For a woman, she was surprisingly strong. She managed to keep him on his feet long enough for Chico to get there and support his other side. While she rewrapped the sheet around his exposed lower half, Jordan caught a glimpse of upturned faces and staring eyes; every woman and child in the house was watching with unbridled fascination.

As the two partners in crime helped him back to bed, Jordan groaned, pathetically glad to escape the onlookers and lie down again, though his anger had not dissipated one bit.

"Chico . . . more quinine," Spencer O'Rourke directed. "Downstairs . . ."

She pointed toward the door. Jordan's houseservant was only too glad to do her bidding. Darting Jordan a worried glance, Chico flap-flapped out of the room.

"Wait a minute . . ." Jordan grabbed Spencer O'Rourke's arm just as she, too, turned away from him. "Wait just a damn minute . . . I've got a few more questions to ask, and you better be able to answer them."

Spencer's blue-green eyes scanned his hand where he clutched her arm. As she raised her eyes to his, the strength and determination in her vivid face astounded him. "I shall be happy to explain, Mr. King," she said precisely. "You have been ill and delirious with malaria for nearly a week."

"A week!"

"And I thought it best to move into your house so

I could care for you."

"Move into my house! Hell's bells, you've got me sounding like a damn parrot!"

Spencer O'Rourke's lips twitched, but she refrained from cracking a smile. "Chico has been here, too, so it has all been perfectly proper, Mr. King. Lucia, Chico's sister, comes during the day to cook. Yesterday you slept all day, and your temperature was almost normal. So today seemed a good day to repay the kindness of Chico's relatives. When I first extended the invitation, the women seemed a bit hesitant to bring their babies to me—I suppose because I'm a woman—but once Chico told them what a good doctor I am, they decided to take a chance."

"How would Chico know what a good doctor you are?" Jordan inquired sarcastically. "I've had many attacks such as this one; Chico himself usually gets me through them—or else my overseer at Paraîso administers the quinine and bathes my fevered brow."

Spencer O'Rourke drew up the sheet to cover more of his chest, then tucked the ends firmly beneath the mattress. "This time, your attack was quite severe, Mr. King. Chico feared you might die. I like to think I had something to do with the fact that you are still alive, and if you want to stay alive, you had better heed my warnings: *rest,* Mr. King. You need plenty of bedrest and nourishing food. Your body is utterly depleted. Under normal circumstances, I would say you have a strong constitution, but these attacks have severely weakened it—perhaps because you don't give yourself enough time to recover from them afterward."

Jordan did not want to tell her how weakened he felt at the moment, especially upon hearing he had been sick for nearly a week. A whole week of his life had passed, and he had only the haziest recollection of anything occurring during that time. It was a sobering, frightening revelation; had he collapsed like this in the jungle, he would not have lasted a single day.

"I . . . I suppose I should thank you . . ." he said reluctantly, still not liking the way she had moved into his house and taken over, without his knowledge or permission.

Looking down at him, Spencer O'Rourke half smiled. Her lips thinned at the corners, and her eyes twinkled. Suddenly, she seemed almost pretty. She did have good bones, he noticed, and her eyes were actually quite stunning.

"Ye should," she liltingly advised. "But somehow, I think ye won't. I know me presence here comes as a great shock t' ye, Mr. King. I apologize for being so forward, but it would have been foolish to send for another doctor when I was right here . . . Please rest, now, and we can talk again, later."

"Oh, we'll talk again, Dr. O'Rourke. I wouldn't want you to think I've reconsidered and decided to hire you, after all. I will, of course, pay you for the services you've rendered so far."

Spencer O'Rourke's smile faded, and the light went out in her eyes. Once again, she was a plain, intimidating spinster, with a ramrod up her spine. "We shall leave unpleasant discussions for another day, Mr. King—until ye're feeling better. In the meantime, I'll finish with the women downstairs, then instruct Lucia t' bring ye something t' eat."

Jordan closed his eyes, utterly exhausted. So she had hoped he would hire her; she had thought to take advantage of the situation by making herself indispensable. Well, he could see right through her little plan, and he was not going to approve it. Spencer O'Rourke had not the slightest idea of the dangers lurking at Paraîso. She may have succeeded in getting one foot in the door, but as soon as he was fully recovered, he would send her packing without a single qualm of conscience.

After he had rested a few moments, he would also find his trousers. Spencer O'Rourke might be a doctor, but she was also a woman and he a man. There was no sense tempting fate. Were he the one administering to a member of the opposite sex, he doubted he could maintain such a cool detachment in the presence of his patient's nakedness. The fact that she could do so irked him; he knew from experience that most women found him highly desirable and would show some reaction to seeing him in bed without a stitch of clothing.

He briefly speculated on what Spencer O'Rourke would do if he suddenly reached up and cupped her abundant bosom in both hands. Had any man ever touched her so intimately? Jordan doubted it. Dr. Spencer O'Rourke did not invite intimacies. It would be interesting to test her aloofness and see if he could dismantle it; she was indeed a challenge. He sighed to himself. At the moment, he was in no condition to even think about seducing a woman, nice bosom or not. Besides, there were plenty of buxom—and far more beautiful—women in Manaus. Very few presented the complications of Dr. Spencer O'Rourke. He thought of Aria Ramos: Now, there was the perfect woman. He fell asleep dreaming about the charms of the beautiful, dark-eyed prostitute, but when he awoke again, it was the red-haired, straitlaced doctor who occupied all his thoughts.

Chapter Five

"Here's your pay, Dr. O'Rourke. You'll find I was quite generous. I've also included a letter of recommendation I hope will result in employment wherever you now choose to look for it."

Jordan King handed over a long parchment envelope and gave Spencer a small, tight smile. "I am truly grateful for all you've done; I feel better than I have in years. Unfortunately, I still believe that the life to which I'm returning is totally unsuitable for a woman."

Without even looking at it, Spencer took the envelope and shoved it into the pocket of her long black skirt. "You're leaving for Paraíso this afternoon?"

Jordan shook his head. Dressed in a clean white shirt with rolled-up sleeves, tan trousers, and black boots, he stood behind the big desk in his front office. On the desk were several untidy piles of correspondence.

"No, not this afternoon, but first thing tomorrow morning. Chico has sent word to my overseer, Raymundo, to ready the launch, and purchase supplies. I must also finish sorting this mail. Chico will see to it that your things are sent wherever you wish, which I sincerely hope will be to a steamer bound for Boston."

Tears pricked Spencer's eyelashes, but she was too proud—and too angry—to cry in front of Jordan King. No sooner was the man out of his sickbed when he was dismissing her. Despite saving his life, she meant no more to him than Dona Isabella, another of Chico's relatives who had been bringing fresh vegetables every day. Was this why she had kept the lonely vigil at his bedside all those hot, humid nights—so she could be banished without ever having a chance to finally state her case?

"But you aren't well enough to return to the jungle, Mr. King," she disputed miserably, struggling to keep her anger—and her telltale brogue—from surfacing. "You are far too weak."

It was true, she thought. To one who did not know him well, he presented a picture of glowing, golden good health. His blond hair, rakishly dipping over his brows, gleamed with silvery highlights. His lean, handsome face was smooth-shaven and ruddy-cheeked, his intensely green eyes lucid and shining. Only another doctor would notice the small signs of recent illness: the hint of pallor beneath the deep tan, the tiny webs of lines at the corners of his mouth and around each eye, the slightly weary inclination of his tousled head . . .

"I don't feel weak," he said. "But you can give me a couple of bottles of quinine to take along, and if I do have another episode of fever, I'll just dose myself . . . Come to think of it, I'll buy all the quinine you've got. I used to keep enough on hand at Paraïso to treat my workers in case they needed it, but it's been too costly lately. For what used to be a shilling bottle, druggists are now demanding two pounds, ten shillings. How much do you want for yours?"

Spencer did some hasty mental arithmetic and realized she had more than enough quinine to pay for her passage home, even if Jordan King never paid her anything for taking care of him; in the next room, she had nearly a crate of the drug!

"I'm not inclined to sell the quinine I have, Mr. King. If I secure a position at another rubber plantation, I'll need all I brought."

"Oh, surely you could spare a few bottles, Doc . . . Tell you what. I'll buy all your medications. Just tell me what each one is for, and I'll keep them until my workers need them. I'll make you a good deal on the whole batch, enough to pay your passage home. You've got to face facts. If I won't hire you, you can bet nobody else will, either—and for the same reason. They won't want a female doctor. Another reason is that unlike me, they don't give a damn about their workers. When one dies, they don't even bother saying a prayer over him."

Fury clogged Spencer's throat. For a moment, she could not speak. How dare he offer to purchase her precious medicines in the same breath he was refusing to hire her to administer them? The mere idea of allowing some arrogant layman to diagnose ailments and treat patients made the hairs rise on the back of her neck. He must take her for a complete fool, spouting that nonsense about other plantation owners. He was probably the one who didn't give a damn about his poor workers; he only wanted the medicines for himself.

In a voice shaking from the effort of maintaining control, she said: "If you won't hire me, Mr. King, why don't you just allow me to accompany you and set up a clinic for your workers on my own? I could charge them modest fees for treatment. If no one cares about them, and they have nowhere else to go,

I'm sure they would come to me. Much as you yourself hate women, you never noticed my sex when you were severely ill; it no longer mattered."

"Oh, I wouldn't say I never noticed," Jordan King drawled.

His green-eyed glance swept over her, lingering longer than it should on her bosom. Spencer sucked in her breath. Few men of her acquaintance were as bold-eyed as Jordan King. A sharp glance or cutting comment was usually all it took to make them mind their manners. She scowled her hardest at him and desperately tried to summon some rapier remark. None occurred. Feeling tongue-tied as a timid schoolgirl, she was only able to stutter helplessly.

"If . . . if I set up a . . . a clinic of sorts, you could just forget I was there. I wouldn't expect anything from you. In n-no way would you be responsible for me."

Jordan King's gaze returned to her face. "You mean I wouldn't have to feed you? What would you do—hunt your own food? Would you also kill the jaguars that prowl Paraïso at night and the 'gators that threaten to tip our *batelãos* on the river?"

"I shall do whatever *you* do to deal with these problems, Mr. King. I doubt you yourself encountered them before you arrived here. If you can learn to survive in the jungle, so can I. And whatever help you do give me, I'll repay in . . . in quinine."

His brows lifted consideringly. "In exchange for a bowl of stew from the common pot, you'd dose and cure me when I got sick?"

"Of course. Other than that, I would look after my business, and you could look after yours. The only other thing I require is separate living quarters. My own hut . . . which I'm sure I could persuade your workers at Paraïso to build for me. It could also serve as my clinic, where the workers could come seeking treatment."

"Your own hut . . ."

"My hut and my food shouldn't be too difficult to provide, Mr. King. If that doesn't seem fair to you, I could pay for my food out of the modest fees I shall charge your workers."

"Oh, food isn't what I'm worried about. Most of my workers would probably pay you in food instead of money, anyway. What bothers me is that you'd still expect me to come running whenever you scream at the sight of a snake."

"No, I wouldn't! Do *you* scream when you see a snake?"

Jordan King's gaze was unwavering. "Only when I see a really big one."

"Then I shall try to scream no more than you would."

Breaking into a chuckle, Jordan King pulled out his chair and sat down. But when he raised his head and looked at her, his face and eyes were again deadly serious. "This is an entertaining but futile conversation we're having, Doc. You can't go with me. I don't want to feel responsible for you. I've had three men die recently, and while I'm quite certain Arana's behind their deaths, I have no proof. At Paraĩso, the only certainty right now is the danger . . ."

"The danger is precisely why you need a doctor at Paraĩso. I might be able to save lives that otherwise would be lost." In her eagerness to get through to him, Spencer leaned over the desk. "You see, Mr. King, I'm not like other women you might have known. I don't run from danger, I stand and face it. I *fight*. What do you think malaria or any other disease is? They are enemies. I have been trained to vanquish them; I have the weapons to fight back. Just give me a chance . . ."

Spencer suddenly realized she was almost nose-to-nose with Jordan King. He was staring at her with narrowed eyes and an incredulous expression. Embarrassed by her impassioned outburst, she straightened and stepped back.

"You are a fool if you don't take me with you, Mr. King," she finished quietly. "I left Boston because of the prejudice I encountered there, in my own neighborhood, where I had foolishly hoped to spend my life curing the ills of my fellow Irish. When I was sick at heart over my failure to win their confidence, your advertisement offered me exactly what I wanted and needed—a new life in a place where my skills would be valued, not scorned. If you, too, are so prejudiced you cannot see past my gender, then I won't plead with you anymore. I'll keep my skills—*and* my quinine—until I can find someone who will appreciate them."

Jordan King leaned back in his chair, still studying her with his intensely green eyes. "That was quite a speech, Doc," he said softly. "Something to think about."

"I don't want you to think about it, I want you to decide—here and now. If you are uncertain whether or not I'll manage, why not grant me a trial period? How long a time do you usually spend at Paraïso, without returning to Manaus?"

"I'm usually gone two to three months, depending on how my supplies and ammunition hold out. Then I come back to Manaus, check my mail, and load up again. That's during the dry season. During the rainy season, since rubber can't be collected anyway, I spend more time here in the city. I suppose I could give you a chance—see if the workers would even permit you to treat their illnesses."

"You do owe me that, Mr. King."

"No, I don't—I've already paid you. As far as I'm concerned, we're now equal. If you do go with me, I'll treat you the same as I would a man. I'll expect you to defend yourself, look after your own needs, and pull your own load, so to speak. You'll have to take your turn bailing out the *batelão,* when necessary, and cooking common meals. As I said, I don't think food will be a problem. As for separate quarters, there is a spare hut you can use, once minor repairs are made to it."

Spencer struggled to conceal her elation. "That would be most satisfactory, Mr. King. If either of us are displeased with the arrangement, then on your next journey to Manaus, you can simply bring me back with you."

"Exactly what I intend, Doc. I really don't expect you to last long. However, may I make a few suggestions that will at least better your chances of success?"

"Of course . . ."

"Take some of that money I just gave you and get down to the marketplace this afternoon. There are a few things you'll need—your own hammock, mosquito netting, some white lightweight clothing, for example. You'll expire from the heat and humidity on the river in those heavy dark clothes you always wear. I presume you have sturdy foot gear."

"My traveling shoes have served me adequately thus far." Lifting the hem of her skirt, Spencer nodded at the low-heeled, high-button shoes she wore.

Jordan King did not even rise and look at her shoes over the desktop. Instead, he snorted contemptuously. "Buy *boots,* Doc—the best you can find. Alligator leather is good; buy more than one pair. And get a bonnet with a wide brim and a gauze scarf you can tie over your face to keep out the gnats. Buy an oilskin to stay dry in a downpour. And a pistol and plenty of ammunition. A six-shooter is best, and a rifle would not be amiss. I have an old machete you can use, but it's best to bring your own. Everybody takes a machete with them into the jungle . . ."

Jordan King mentioned several other useful items, and as soon as he dismissed her, Spencer hurried to write them down before she forgot something. She wondered if she would have enough money, considering the city's exorbitant prices. Before leaving for the marketplace, she tore open the envelope Jordan had given her—and gasped at its contents. The money inside surpassed what she would have made in a year back home in Boston; Jordan King might not live as richly as his peers, but he was definitely not stingy. She decided to purchase some tins of sardines and fruit preserves, just in case she did occasionally have to furnish her own meals. With the funds that remained, she would then open a bank account. Her heart thudded almost painfully with a combination of joy and excitement: *She had won a place for herself; she was on the road to a new life!* And, she congratulated herself, she hadn't lapsed into her hated brogue even once during the entire conversation.

Jordan had named his launch *Evangeline,* after his mother. Evangeline King had always been a gentle soul, trustworthy and kind; the only time she had ever let him down was when she died. His old, battered, typical-of-the-Amazon steam-powered launch was much the same way. It would chug along unceasingly for weeks on end, and then, without warning, suddenly cough and expire. He kept a ready supply of rusty spare parts in the engine house for those unexpected moments and always muttered a little prayer for a safe journey to Paraïso and back whenever he left Manaus.

On the occasion of his departure this time, a sunny, hot morning, he felt more anxious than usual. He knew from Raymundo's big grin and the steady chug-chug-chug of the engine that everything was going well. Still, his stomach was knotted, and his palms clammy. Ever since he had agreed to allow Doctor Spencer O'Rourke to accompany him upriver, he had been mentally kicking himself. Why had he changed his mind and given permission, when any fool would have called it sheer stupidity to take a woman into the jungle?

The damned nuisance of a difficult female sat unconcernedly amidship atop a crate of her own medicines and gazed enraptured at the passing scenery as they departed Manaus. Jordan noted she had taken his advice and switched from somber black to pristine white, effecting a remarkable change. A high ruffled collar cupped her face, softening her jutting chin and calling attention to the rosy color of her cheeks. With her bright hair and vivid turquoise eyes, she compelled attention, rather like an orchid or bromeliad blooming unexpectedly in the darkened gloom of the jungle.

Unfortunately, the demure white blouse and long skirt skimming the tops of absurdly large brown boots only served to emphasize her frail femininity. Black garments had at least-made her appear hardened and strong, but white revealed her for what she was—a skinny, weak female. Excepting her bosom, her body was slender as a blowgun; if she turned up her freckled nose at their sometimes unappetizing fare, she would fade away to nothing.

He could not fathom why he had done it. Possibly it was because of the look in her eyes when she spoke of the prejudice she had encountered back home. That look had reminded him of his sister, Victoria; their father had once told Victoria she could not ride a particularly wild horse she favored, and Victoria had been deeply hurt—not so much because she was not allowed to ride but because of the reason. "You're a girl," Jordan's father had said, as if that explained everything. But it hadn't, at least not to Victoria, who rode every bit as well as Jordan, if not better. That single thoughtless remark had fueled Victoria's determination to obtain many rights denied women. Jordan would never forget his sister's seething indignation—the same indignation flashing in Spencer O'Rourke's blue-green eyes. And somehow, because of "that look," he had allowed himself to be persuaded to do something he never should have done.

Angry with himself for giving in, he picked up his Winchester, and leaving Raymundo to navigate the river and steer the launch, took a position in the starboard bow, from which vantage point he hoped to spy some creature to serve up for dinner.

Though loaded down to a point where the water was a bare four inches below the paint-blistered gunwales, the launch was not packed with much in the way of ready foods. Once away from the hubbub of Manaus, game was plentiful along the river, and Jordan preferred to hunt or fish for the main course rather than consume the precious supplies that might stave off hunger farther upriver or at Paraĩso where the smokey fires for curing rubber had a tendency to drive away many forest creatures.

In silence, he scanned the densely green riverbank for any sign of movement. Other than a white heron taking flight in a flurry of silvery wings, there was none. The river was wide at this point and a golden-brown color; it was also deceptively calm and quiet. Jordan knew that both the river and the jungle teemed with life, but probably he would not spot game until late afternoon.

Still, watching for game was better than making polite conversation with the red-haired woman intently studying the scenery and ignoring him. He wondered if she ever allowed her shoulders to slump or wore her hair down. When she wasn't wearing the silly white cap that covered the mass of her fiery tresses, she kept her hair tightly bound into a kind of double knot at the back of her head. Today, he remembered, she wore no cap, and the sun glinting off the thick coils struck bronze and amber sparks.

Irritated to be spending so much time thinking about her, he raised his rifle and idly shot at what was either a log or an alligator lying on the riverbank. Woodchips flew, and Raymundo shouted congratulations on his good aim, but Spencer O'Rourke never said a word. Prim as a saint, she sat—her blue-green eyes fastened on the bank. Discomfitted, Jordan strode to the stern, putting the engine house between him and his annoying passenger; evidently, she intended to "mind her own business," come hell or high water.

Late in the afternoon, Jordan took over the running of the launch, while Raymundo did a bit of fishing. The slender, brown-skinned Brazilian caught a good-sized catfish and quickly skinned and gutted it in a small, open space on the crowded deck, amidst the crates and barrels they were taking to Paraïso. Leaving the bloody mess where it lay, the overseer then busied himself with cooking dinner on the makeshift stove Jordan had fashioned out of half a metal drum.

Spencer offered to help, amusing Jordan by her efforts to speak Portuguese with Raymundo. Since her arrival in Manaus, she had made good progress with the language but still spoke it hesitantly and with a stilted accent. Raymundo seemed not to know what to make of her and would not permit her to touch the slabs of white meat or the dented pot in which he was boiling rice. He did, however, indicate with a nod of his head and some exasperated muttering that she could dispose of the fish guts he had left lying on the deck. Affronted, she had haughtily retreated to her spot on the medicine crate. When the boat's single-screw propeller began making an odd sound, as though it had struck something or become ensnarled, Jordan reluctantly dragged his eyes away from her thin, ramrod-straight figure.

He shut off the engine and let the boat drift while he bent over the side of the stern and tried to see what had happened. Snags were commonplace on the river, and the only way to avoid them was to watch the water carefully for the slight ripples that indicated some hidden obstruction. During the rainy season, the river rose, sweeping all manner of debris downstream and depositing it in surprising places. Then, as the water level descended, watching for snags became a tedious but necessary occupation. While he had been distracted by his female passenger, the *Evangeline* must have gotten hung up on one.

He heard a slight splash near the bow—either a flying fish or a 'gator rolling away from the launch—and called to Raymundo in Portuguese. "Do you see anything?"

"Não, senhor," Raymundo answered coming quickly to stand beside him. "But I will go down and check while you keep watch with the rifle."

Jordan nodded and fetched his Winchester in case the splash he had heard turned out to be a 'gator, after all. Jumping into the Amazon was not something a man did lightly; the river was home to all sorts of dangerous creatures: snakes, fresh water sharks, spiny catfish weighing in at three hundred pounds . . .

Raymundo shucked his shirt and shoes, but with an embarrassed glance toward the bow and the doctor, retained his trousers, merely rolling them up to the level of his thighs. As he swung one thin leg over the side, Jordan stopped him. "You're sure you have no cuts or open wounds?"

Raymundo flashed his silver tooth. "I would never offer to jump in the river if I was bleeding, Senhor Rei. The piranhas would make short work of me."

"Well, just in case, take the end of this rope." Jordan handed him a mooring line. "If you get in trouble, I can pull you aboard in a few seconds."

"Thank you, senhor." With another flash of his silver tooth, Raymundo went over the side.

He landed with a splash and easily treaded water while he oriented himself. Jordan watched as he then ducked below the surface of the water to check on the propeller. A minute later, he resurfaced and shook the droplets out of his eyes. "It is nothing, senhor—only the vines from a submerged tree that have twisted themselves around the blade. I can free us with no trouble."

"Do you need a knife or machete?" Jordan inquired.

"Não, senhor. With my bare hands, I think I can do it."

"Better tie that rope around your waist first."

"Don't worry, senhor. It will only take a moment, then I will quickly climb back into the boat."

"Can I help?" A female voice asked.

Jordan looked up see to Spencer O'Rourke standing not two feet away and peering interestedly over the side. "Not at the moment, Doc. Everything's under control. If you really want to do something, keep our dinner from burning. I despise burnt rice."

"Oh, I've already stirred the rice and removed it from the stove, covered the fillets to keep the flies off them, and cleaned up the disgusting mess Raymundo entrusted to me. I'm not sure, but I thought he said to . . ."

A horrible scream erupted from the water. The unearthly sound sliced through Jordan's bones and muscles, exposing every nerve ending to scalding horror. "Senhor! Piranhas! They are eating me alive!"

Raymundo was flailing his arms and legs, trying to beat them away, but Jordan could see the water moving with hundreds—thousands?—of silvery bodies, darting to and fro, tearing at the overseer's flesh.

"The rope! Raymundo, have you got the rope?"

"Mamãe de Jesus!" Raymundo screamed, past rational answer.

Jordan leaned far out over the stern and grabbed one of the man's flailing arms by the wrist. "Help me drag him inside the boat!" he shouted to Spencer, who had thrown herself half overboard trying to grab Raymundo's other arm.

Together, they managed to lift the screaming, hysterical overseer into the launch, but when Jordan saw the lower part of Raymundo's body, he nearly dropped him in sick dismay. The remnants of Raymundo's trousers hung in shreds; so also did the flesh on his legs. From the knees down, muscles, tendons, and sinew had been slashed and torn into ribbons.

Gently, they lowered the writhing man to the deck. As they did so, Raymundo's eyes rolled back in his head, and he ceased uttering any sound whatsoever. Jordan expelled a harsh sigh. "Good God, I think they've killed him."

"No . . . he's fainted, but he's still alive. If we work quickly, we might be able to save him. You'll have to help me."

"I . . . I don't know if I can." Jordan gagged on the bile surging up from his stomach. Dashing to the rail, he was sick into the river, where the water was churned pink and frothy from the blood frenzy of the piranhas.

"Get hold of yourself, Mr. King," he heard Spencer O'Rourke say in a perfectly calm voice. "I'll have to operate right away, and I need your assistance."

Operate. She said it as casually as if announcing dinner. Ashamed of his weakness in the face of her strength, Jordan wiped his mouth, straightened, and turned. "All right . . . what do you want me to do?"

Chapter Six

This was why she was here, Spencer told herself—to save people's lives, to snatch them from the jaws of death. Nevertheless, as she made hurried preparations to perform surgery in the middle of the Amazon, miles from a hospital or even a clean kitchen table, she could not keep her mouth from going dry or her stomach from churning.

While Jordan King shoved two crates together to make an elevated, flat surface, she thrust her surgical instruments into the smoldering embers of the little drum stove to purify them and enable her to cauterize some of the ragged lacerations. Jordan hefted his overseer onto the makeshift table, and she quickly began tying off exposed blood vessels, at the same time giving directions on administering chloroform to produce a state of deep anesthesia.

"Will this stuff work?" Jordan inquired, for once doing as he was told. "If I were in his place, I think I'd rather have a few good snorts of *cachaça.*"

"I'm unfamiliar with the anesthetic properties of *cachaça,* Mr. King. However, the chloroform should do quite nicely. I'll have to remove whatever I can't save and repair the rest as best I can. The important thing is to maintain proper asepsis until we can get him to a hospital."

"There *are* no hospitals where we're going, Doc. In all likelihood, this operation will only postpone the inevitable. Out here, men die from mere cuts, and before they do, they go mad from the flies swarming all over them."

"If we turn about immediately, Mr. King, we should be back in Manaus by morning, if not before. As soon as I no longer need your help, you can turn the boat around, and until we get there, we'll keep him under a mosquito net."

Jordan King raised his eyes to hers. "I'm afraid we can't go back to Manaus just now. We've already lost more time than we should have. The workers will be out of supplies, and some might be ill or injured every bit as badly as Raymundo. He'll understand the necessity of pressing on toward Paraïso. If he survives the journey, I'll drop off the supplies, pick up anyone else who needs hospitalization, and head back downriver."

"Well, I won't argue with you at the moment, Mr. King. But neither will I permit this man to die for lack of proper nursing facilities."

"Can't *you* take care of him, Doc? If I'm not mistaken, that's why you insisted upon coming with me, so you could look after my workers, isn't it?"

"With injuries such as these, this man shouldn't be moved, much less subjected to a rigorous journey and primitive living conditions. There is a limit to what I can do for him, Mr. King, regardless of how hard I try. Look at his left leg. I believe it's damaged beyond repair. If he survives at all, he'll never walk again."

"Then I guess we'll have to pray for a miracle, won't we, Dr. O'Rourke?"

To that, Spencer had no reply. When a man's life

dangled by a mere thread, it was hardly the time for a verbal sparring match. Giving her attention to the difficult task before her, Spencer all but forgot about Jordan King. She did not think of him again until the surgery was nearly completed, and all that remained was to stitch up the smallest of the wounds where the fish had torn away Raymundo's flesh.

Suddenly, Jordan's hand reached across Raymundo and dabbed at her brow with a pad of gauze. Startled, she jerked her head away. "What are ye doin'?"

"You're perspiring, Doc—and no wonder. I've never seen anyone give such wholehearted concentration to their labors. You have my deepest admiration."

"I wish I had your money," she retorted. "You ought not to waste gauze pads like that; I can't afford it."

"Sorry. Next time, I'll use a piece of dirty, old burlap—or maybe I'll just let you drip on your patient's wounds."

Realizing how churlish she sounded, Spencer softened her responses. "Forgive me, Mr. King. You mustn't mind my outspokenness. I believe in saying what I think. While I'm at it, I must compliment you. You assisted me like a true professional. I forgot you were there."

"That's hardly a compliment, Doc. I like to think women find me *un*forgettable."

He was starting to rattle her again. Spencer bent to her work but could not resist a parting shot. "Maybe they do, Mr. King, but in what capacity I canna imagine."

An hour later, Raymundo was resting more or less comfortably in a hammock stretched across the deck beneath the overhang of the engine room. Having emerged from the anesthesia long enough to mutter his thanks, he had then sunk into a deep sleep. It was early evening. While cleaning up the mess from the surgery, Spencer discovered she was starving. Jordan was reheating the rice and cooking the fish, and her nose twitched in anticipation of the simple meal.

Hefting a basin full of bloody refuse from the surgery, she made ready to toss the contents over the side of the boat—and then it came to her. Earlier, she had done the same thing with the fish guts. She had scooped them into a bucket and tossed them overboard, following Raymundo's instructions. At least, that's what she *thought* he had told her to do. Shortly thereafter, Raymundo had jumped into the river to free the boat propeller and been attacked by the piranhas.

Jordan King's voice broke into her stunned preoccupation. "What's wrong, Doc? You look like you're going to swoon."

"I . . . I . . . Mr. King, those blood-thirsty little fish that attacked Raymundo . . . Where did they come from?"

"The piranhas? Damned if I know. They don't usually attack without provocation. If there was a meat-processing plant in the vicinity dumping its refuse into the river, I could understand it. Such places draw them from miles in every direction. But out here on the open river, it's rare for them to go after a swimmer—unless he has an open sore or wound. I asked Raymundo before he went overboard, and he said he didn't have any so I don't know what set them off."

The deck seemed to tilt beneath Spencer's feet. She clutched the basin to keep from dropping it. The piranha attack was *her* fault. By tossing the bloody fish guts overboard, she had drawn the vicious little creatures straight to Raymundo.

"Dr. O'Rourke, what is it?" Jordan King grabbed the basin from her hands, set it on the deck, and made a grab for her. "Hey! You'd better sit down before you fall down."

He led her to a barrel, but instead of sitting, she leaned against it and tried to still her inner quaking. Raymundo had lost several toes and the use of one leg because of her ignorance and stupidity; he might even lose his life. "Stupid . . . stupid . . ." she muttered in an agony of self-accusation.

"Who's stupid?" Jordan King demanded. "What are you talking about?"

"I'm stupid!" she screamed at him. "I threw the fish guts overboard just before Raymundo went into the water to free the boat."

Jordan King's green eyes seared to the bone. "That is stupid," he mercilessly agreed. "Whatever possessed you to do it? We do dump our garbage over the side but not usually until we're leaving an area. Raymundo sure as hell wouldn't have jumped in the river knowing you had just tossed bloody fish guts into it. Why didn't you say something?"

"I dinna realize the danger! We dinna have piranhas in Boston, ye know. If anyone should have thought of it, it was ye or Raymundo himself . . . Oh, what are we arguin' about? It *is* me fault. Because of me, he'll never walk again." A sob broke from her throat. Spencer could scarcely breathe for the guilt she felt.

"Damn my aunt Milly's corset!" Jordan exploded. "I *knew* something like this would happen if I let you come along! It's exactly what I feared would . . ." His tirade trailed off in midsentence, but in her head, it went on and on. Nothing he could say was worse than her own condemnation of herself. Undoubtedly, she had misunderstood Raymundo's Portuguese. Even if she hadn't, why had she been so quick to act without thinking?

Sighing deeply, Jordan King suddenly gripped her shoulders. "Wait a minute, Doc. He's still *alive* because of you. What you did this afternoon—why, it was incredible. You took charge, stitched and cut flesh, mopped up blood, and saved a man's life as easily as most women would mix a cake. You never so much as blinked or wrinkled your nose at the stench or the heat . . ."

"Dinna patronize me, Mr. King! I know when I've behaved irresponsibly. Before I threw anything overboard, I should have asked if it was the right thing to do. At the very least, I should have stopped Raymundo from going into the water. I *do* know about alligators, after all. I should have realized something like this would result."

"Yes, damn it all, you should have. But it's too late now to be sorry. Nothing in the world is less productive than self-recrimination, so you might as well forget it. Anyway, I'm hungry. Let's eat, and you can feel bad about it *after* dinner."

His magnanimous dismissal of her guilt amazed Spencer—and also made her feel pathetically grateful. What he said made sense. No matter how harshly she blamed herself, she could not change what had happened. The best she could do now was make certain Raymundo lived. They ate dinner in silence. Jordan offered her a glass of wine to go with her fish, but needing a clear head to stay awake and watch her patient, Spencer refused it.

Night fell swiftly. There was no lingering twilight. Jordan lit lanterns and slowed the launch to a snail's pace but kept going upriver. Spencer wondered how he could see where they were headed. The lantern on the bow cast little light into the murky waters; it was eerie to be gliding into black nothingness. He stayed away from the nearest shoreline, but the jungle noises echoed across the waters. The drone of insects was unnerving, the mysterious groans, shrieks, and howls spine-tingling.

Occasionally, unseen wings sliced the air overhead. Spencer surmised that bats were swooping low over the launch. She put on her straw hat with the veil that Jordan had suggested she buy. Now and then, a mosquito whined near her ear. She longed to sling her own hammock near Raymundo's and crawl under her new net—but she dared not chance falling asleep. After an hour or so of chugging upriver in the darkness, she decided to ask Jordan the uppermost question in her mind.

"Aren't we going to stop for the night?"

"Not if I can help it. Don't worry . . . this stretch of river is deep and wide. As long as I keep the *Evangeline* in the middle, we should negotiate it with no trouble."

"Mr. King . . . I really think we should return to Manaus instead of pressing on to Paraïso. Raymundo's worst days lie ahead. The risk of infection is so great . . ."

"I've been thinking about that, Doc." Jordan glanced toward her but continued to steer a steady course. "Maybe we'll meet another launch or steamboat headed downriver with a load of rubber. It's not unusual; if we do, we'll simply ask them to take Raymundo with them. Once he gets to Manaus, Chico will see he gets the help he needs."

"But what if we don't meet another boat?"

"Then we'll do as I said—keep going and come back when we can."

"I canna accept that, Mr. King!"

"You have no choice, Dr. O'Rourke. I'm going as fast as I can; that's why we're traveling at night. By tomorrow night, our fuel will be running low and we'll have to tie up to the riverbank and collect more wood. By then, we'll also be in a section of the river where night travel would be especially dangerous. Why don't you get some sleep? I'll wake you if Raymundo needs you. If he doesn't, I'll wake you in an hour or two anyway, so you can check him."

"When will you sleep?"

"Tomorrow night, when we tie up to the bank. Go ahead, Doc. You look ready to drop. Don't concern yourself with me; I'm used to this."

It was too dark to find her hammock without using a lantern, but whenever Spencer got close to one, she was inundated by huge insects dive-bombing the light. A moth as big as her outstretched hand brushed the brim of her hat, and she shivered in revulsion; moths and bats were not her favorite creatures. Neither did she like the idea of resting while Jordan King worked, but fatigue was creeping over her so she finally lay down on top of the same crates where they had performed surgery on Raymundo.

The next thing she knew, someone was shaking her, and a shaft of sunlight was stabbing her eyes. She sat up with a sharp cry. "Mr. King! Why dinna ye wake me? Is Raymundo all right?"

"Relax, Doc. Your patient is fine. He did awaken a time or two during the night, but I gave him more of that sedative you left out, and he went right back to sleep."

"Ye shouldna have done that! How did ye know how much t' give him?"

Jordan King held up one hand to forestall further questions. "Why don't you examine him first and argue later? There's a launch headed our way. As long as it isn't one of Don Julio César Arana's, I intend to stop it and transfer Raymundo aboard."

Spencer looked past Jordan King's darkly tanned, gold-stubbled face and saw a boat coming toward them through the mist that still clung to the river. "Wait!" she cried. "Ye canna put him on that boat before I've changed his dressings and cleansed his wounds."

"Why do you think I woke you? Hurry, Doc. There's no time to lose."

Spencer moved as fast as she could, but even so, things happened far too quickly. Jordan hailed the boat, ascertained that it belonged to a *seringueiro* known to both him and Raymundo, and speedily made arrangements for Raymundo to return to Manaus with the man. Spencer barely had time to dose her patient with more sedatives before Jordan was demanding that Raymundo be moved right in his hammock from one boat to the other. Raymundo himself barely seemed to register what was happening, but as soon as the overseer was safely transferred, Jordan bent over him and spoke in a low, reassuring tone.

"Rest easy, old friend. You're going to be fine. Don Allejo will take you back to Manaus, and I know a good doctor there who will fit you out with crutches and teach you to walk again. Don't worry about losing your job; you've got a job for as long as you want it."

"Obrigado, senhor." The little Brazilian gave Jordan a fleeting, silver-toothed smile. Then Jordan leaped from the deck of the rubber-laden launch back into the *Evangeline.*

"Happy now, Doctor O'Rourke? If you aren't, say so now, because this is probably your last chance to return to civilization. My friend wouldn't mind taking you back to Manaus. When you weren't looking, he asked me if you were my woman. That's the only explanation he could think of for why I'd be crazy enough to take you with me to Paraïso."

"I hope ye told him the truth!" Spencer could feel her cheeks reddening. "As for my returning to Manaus, more than ever, I am convinced of my usefulness at Paraïso . . . Did ye give my instructions for taking care of Raymundo to Don Allejo?"

"Of course . . . Look at all the *bolachas* of rubber he's towing, will you? After he sells them in Manaus, he'll be a rich man."

Annoyed at Jordan King's lightning-quick changes of subject, Spencer followed his gaze to the rear of the launch which was loaded down with huge, blackened balls of rubber. More balls of rubber bobbed at the end of their tethers behind the launch.

"Do ye really know a good doctor in Manaus who can help Raymundo? His one leg is all but ruined," she stated in a biting tone. "Me Portuguese canna be trusted, but that's what I understood ye t' say."

"I gave instructions to Don Allejo on where to find him. Doctor Jorge is a favorite of wealthy rubber barons. I imagine he'll charge a fortune to treat a poor Brazilian, but between him and Chico, Raymundo will be well taken care of . . . Damn, but I'd sure like to bring a load of rubber like *that* into Manaus the next time I come!"

"I hope Raymundo gets there safely," Spencer grumbled, envious of Jordan's high regard for the other doctor.

"Oh, he will. *Até mais tarde, meo amigo!*" he shouted to the departing launch. Saluting Spencer, he quickly went back to work getting the launch underway, again.

* * *

Spencer pushed around the distasteful object lying in a puddle of gravy on her dinner plate and contemplated pouring it on top of Jordan King's blond head. They were sitting on the riverbank on two overturned half barrels in an area Jordan had cleared with his machete just before he collected fuel for the launch then shot and killed the little brown monkey they were having for dinner.

She was sure he had deliberately fished out one of the two front paws to put on her plate—a paw that even in its boiled state bore a startling resemblance to a human child's hand. Jordan had eaten his own paw with great relish, cracking the tiny bones and removing the meat with no more disgust than he would have shown toward a chicken wing. Spencer was revolted.

"I'm really not hungry, Mr. King. I think I'll pass."

"Then I guess I'll have to eat your share. The only thing better than monkey stew is roasted monkey. Raymundo always spits them and roasts them over an open fire. Once you get over the shock of how human they look, you'll find them every bit as tasty as beef. Yes, we have exotic fare at Paraïso, Doc. Tapir, deer, quail, partridge, snakes—whatever the hunters catch . . ."

Spencer saw an opportunity to change the subject and did so. "The hunters?"

"The hangers-on at Paraïso. When I get up in the morning, I never know who will be there. They creep into camp like a morning mist and melt away again just as easily. All of them are hoping for work. That's the trouble. You can't depend on them, unless of course, you beat and enslave them like Arana does."

"But how can he beat and enslave them? Don't they fight back?"

"Oh, they're no match for Arana's toughs. These men are *caipiras*—illiterate peasants. Some speak Portuguese or Spanish, but others only speak one of the Indian dialects. They often are half-Indian. Why, I've had Colombians, Peruvians, Brazilians, and even a Frenchman suddenly show up at Paraïso. I give them short-term jobs—hunting, building, fixing things—whatever I need done."

"You don't put them to work collecting rubber?"

"Most of them, no. They're too fond of *cachaça* to be trusted for weeks alone in the jungle, working an *estrada*. However, if I run across a man who's reasonably healthy and can stay sober, I'll hire him. I'll assign him one to two hundred trees, give him everything he needs to live alone in the jungle for a month, and see if he can withstand the loneliness and still produce those big rubber *bolachas* you saw in that launch this morning. If he can't, he's finished. Most times, the *caipiras* can't; they haven't got the physical stamina or discipline to be working on their own, without an overseer wielding a whip."

Spencer set down her untouched dinner. "Then where do you get your workers—the ones who collect the rubber?"

"I go south to Cearã, Sergipe, or Bahia and hire men from off the *sertão*. That's where Raymundo came from. It's dry cattle country there, except for along the coast. The people are poor but seem to be hardier. If you pay decent wages and treat the workers well, they last a lot longer. Arana should try it—but he's too damn greedy. Besides, it's easier just to enslave men, and the easiest of all are the Indians."

"Then why doesna someone *do* something?" Spencer demanded, outraged. "It's utterly beyond me how such cruelty can exist without causing a hue and cry that will ultimately put a stop to it."

Brandishing his cleaned plate, Jordan King shrugged. "If you stay here long enough, Dr. O'Rourke, you'll find out why. This isn't Boston. In the jungle, there's no law and order: The strong simply destroy the weak. It's the law of nature applied to men—and women. I hope you're strong, Doc. In many ways, you seem to be, but in others . . ."

He glanced down at her uneaten food. Stung by the unspoken criticism, she snatched up the plate, balanced it on her knees, and resolutely began eating. Jordan King was infuriating, but he was also right; if she wanted to build a new life for herself, she had better adjust, starting with the food.

A sardonic smile curved Jordan King's mouth as he watched her struggling to swallow a morsel of monkey meat, which did, in fact, taste a little like beef. "Now, isn't that good, Doc? It's actually quite tasty, isn't it?"

For fear of gagging, Spencer did not answer. She merely nodded and speared another morsel of meat. Jordan's grin became a hearty laugh. "Damn my aunt Milly's corset, Doc! I must say you've got guts. When I myself first got here, I turned green just thinking about eating monkey meat. It was weeks before I dared try any, and the first time I did, I got sick."

Spencer desperately feared she was going to disgrace herself. Her stomach heaved alarmingly. Just in time, Jordan got to his feet and clapped her on the shoulder. "Excuse me, but I think I had better get everything neat and tidy before it's too dark to see. I don't like to use lanterns any more than necessary in the middle of the jungle—attracts too many insects. Sleep when it's dark, get up when it's light. That's what the Indians do, and I've found it a good practice."

As soon as he turned his back, Spencer bolted into the underbrush and lost what little she had eaten. Afterward, she hurriedly disposed of the left-over stew and cleaned up the mess from their dinner. By the time she got back to the launch, the light was waning.

"I've taken the liberty of stringing up your hammock, Doc. You couldn't have been too comfortable on top of those crates last night." Jordan King was stripping off his shirt, his wide shoulders and narrow torso starkly outlined against the darkening riverbank.

"Thank you, Mr. King, that was very thoughtful of . . ." She stopped in midsentence when she saw where he had placed the two hammocks. His and hers were right next to each other under the overhang of the engine house where Raymundo's hammock had hung; indeed, they were practically on top of each other.

"Of course, if it rains, we'll both have to share the engine house in *very* close quarters."

His tone mocked her. Not for the first time, Spencer comprehended the delicacy of her situation; she was alone with a man she barely knew in circumstances most people would consider compromising. Before, when he was ill, she had been able to ignore the possibilities for inappropriate conduct. Now that he was better—and looking exceedingly virile as he casually stripped in front of her—she could ignore them no longer.

"Why are ye takin' off your shirt, Mr. King?"

"Why, I thought you knew. I always sleep in the raw. Saves on clothes and makes me feel cooler. Why don't *you* give it a try? You'll be lying under a net, after all, and I promise not to peek."

She wasn't sure he was teasing; even if he was, his comments were entirely too suggestive. In no uncertain terms, she must let him know that she would brook no assault on her virtue. Just because they would be spending lots of time alone together did not mean he could expect a gradual erosion of her morals. Marching to her hammock, she quickly untied the knots, grabbed her mosquito net, and slung the hammock over her shoulder.

"Going somewhere, Doc?"

"Back to the clearing where we ate. I'm sure I can find two trees t' support my hammock. I wouldna want t' intrude on yer privacy, Mr. King, nor do I wish ye t' intrude on mine."

"That's not a very good idea."

"Do ye mean t' say ye've never slept ashore on yer journeys, Mr. King?"

"No, I've done it many times. I only meant to say you'd be safer here on the launch."

"Safe, Mr. King? Safe perhaps from jaguars and snakes, but the worst danger on this launch has nothing to do with jungle beasts."

Jordan King cocked a blond eyebrow. "Surely you don't fear me, Doc. Why, I'm an absolute lamb around women."

"A lamb who insists on shearing his own fleece in a lady's presence," Spencer said primly.

"Now, now . . . I wasn't going to remove *everything*."

"I dinna care if ye do remove everything! I'll not be here t' see it."

His mouth twitched, and his eyes twinkled. Spencer knew he was laughing at her; she could read his amusement in his slanting green eyes. "You ought to at least take a pistol. You did purchase one, didn't you, as I advised before we left?"

"Of course, I'll take me pistol—and my oilcloth." Spencer quickly fetched them. "I'll see ye in the morning, Mr. King. And dinna worry, no matter what happens, I shan't need yer assistance."

"I doubt I could get there fast enough to give it. Jaguars and snakes work fast. One scream is all I'll hear; then it will all be over."

"I know when someone's trying to frighten me, Mr. King. Good night. And if ye do come runnin' at the sound of a scream, be sure and don your trousers first. Insect bites on the privates can be quite serious."

She was gratified to see his grin disappear. "Insect bites on the . . . ?" he repeated disbelievingly.

"Yes, a severe bite in the wrong place could cause ye t' swell up like a hot air balloon—and I dinna think I could do a thing about it."

That should give him pause, she thought triumphantly. Carefully, she negotiated the narrow plank spanning the space between the launch and the riverbank, then ran lightly across the spongy ground. Better to face the dangers of the jungle than the temptations of the flesh. The image of his torso outlined against the approaching darkness flashed through her mind. Oh, yes, much better . . . But was she running from his desires—or her own?

Chapter Seven

Jordan lay in his hammock in the humid darkness and imagined his sister Victoria scolding him. "Jordan, you should be ashamed of yourself, teasing Dr. O'Rourke so unmercifully. See what you've made her do—go running off into the jungle where she'll probably get killed and eaten by a jaguar."

No, she won't, Jordan told his sister, whose disapproving voice always sounded amazingly like the voice of his own conscience. Dr. Spencer K. O'Rourke is tougher than you are. Pity the poor jaguar who attacks her! She'll probably un-man him with a single look—same as she does men. Why, she actually tried to eat that monkey paw, the first one she's ever seen!

He grinned to himself and poked at the mosquito netting, where a score of determined insects were trying to bite him through the barrier. He was very warm and wished he could take off his trousers, as the good doctor had feared he was going to do, but if she did need his help, he could hardly dash to her rescue without any clothes on. The mosquitoes would have a feast, and Spencer would give him another of "those looks"—the kind that could shrivel a lemon.

Jordan sighed and rubbed his bare chest. Tired as he was, he could not sleep for worrying about the proud, straight-laced redhead. Her rigid insistence on observing proprieties might well get her into serious trouble. What did she think he would do—creep into her hammock at night and rape her? She should be so lucky, he thought contemptuously. Doctor O'Rourke really had nothing to worry about on that score. Though not as plain and unattractive as he had first thought, she was definitely more intimidating. While he could not help but admire her, having seen her in action, he also felt uncomfortable around her. In her brusque competency, she was more than a match for him, and where women were concerned, that was a new experience, one he did not think he liked.

Closing his eyes, he strained to sift the familiar, jungle sounds. Everything sounded normal, though what seemed normal to him might not be so to Spencer. She was probably terrified and cowering under her mosquito net—but far too stubborn to return to the launch. Well, if she didn't get any sleep tonight, it was all her own fault. On the other hand, she might be sleeping like a baby, while he was doing all the worrying.

Gradually, the fatigue he had been fighting all day once again crept over him, and he succumbed to the urge to sleep. How long he drifted in a sea of cotton he had no idea, but suddenly a shrill scream sent him bolting from the hammock. He stood stock-still on the deck and listened intently. The scream came again, an unearthly, piercing wail, as though someone was in terrible pain.

His reflexes sent him stumbling for boots, gun, and lantern, without which a man could die in the jungle night. Then he was dashing down the plank spanning the stretch of water between the launch and the shore.

"Oh! Oh! Oh!" the scream continued, raising hairs on the back of his neck.

"Spencer! Hold on—I'm coming!" Jordan bellowed, crashing through the underbrush in his haste to get to her.

He found her in the clearing, jumping up and down in her bare feet and clawing at herself. "Oh, they're all over me! They're biting and stinging!"

Holding up the lantern, he discovered the source of her terror and pain: inch-long red ants with huge, busy pincers.

Quickly, Jordan set down the lantern and began brushing them off her body. Fortunately, she was still clothed, but when he had brushed off all he could see, she was still hopping up and down and clawing at her bosom. "Oh, dear God! Oh, no! No!"

Her rising panic called for desperate measures. Seizing her white, ruffled blouse at the neckline, he tore it open straight down the middle. Ants scurried across her bosom, which was tightly wrapped in some kind of bandage.

"What the hell?" Jordan muttered questioningly. Despite a thorough knowledge of women's undergarments, he had never before encountered this sort of apparel. As he brushed off all the ants he could see, he wondered if the wide bandage covered an injury or wound.

When a fleeing ant disappeared into the hollow between Spencer's breasts, Jordan realized he would have to tear off the bandage, too, in order to repel all the determined invaders. Using both hands, he ripped at the gauze binder. It was much stronger than it looked. Finally, he succeeded in releasing one end of it but was then defeated by its length. Apparently she had wrapped the bandage several times around the upper half of her body, for what purpose he could not imagine, but was growing more and more curious to learn.

Hurriedly, while she screamed and sobbed, he removed her blouse, then tugged on the length of gauze, turning her round and round, until it came undone. Her white, rose-tipped breasts—the fullest, most beautiful, perfectly formed breasts Jordan had ever seen—spilled into the lantern light. Jordan expected Spencer to protest his stunned appraisal of her pulchritude, but she was too far gone with hysteria to even notice she was now naked from the waist up.

"For the love of Saint Brigid, help me! Get them off! Get them off!"

Her loose hair flew around her shoulders like a curtain of flame as she clawed at the vicious creatures stinging her tender flesh in an orgy of hungry abandonment. Jordan grabbed one in the act of pinching her with its huge pincers; the ant's body came away, but its pincers remained fastened in place. Large red welts dotted the magnificent breasts where other ants had already feasted. Finally, he succeeded in knocking them all to the ground.

"What about under your skirt?" Jordan inquired, by no means ready to stop at her bosom.

"No, I dinna think . . . Oh, yes! Yes, there are some under there!"

Spencer's skirt and undergarments came off more easily than her blouse and the strange, gauze bandage. She was narrow-hipped but possessed sweetly rounded thighs and calves, Jordan noticed, as slapping at her bare legs, Spencer made little sobbing sounds. "Oh, they're so beastly! So huge! I've never seen ants as big as these! Their bites sting like . . . like fire!"

"That's what they are—fire ants." Jordan shook out Spencer's long skirt. Any minute now, she would notice her nudity, and all her concern would shift toward that.

"Oh! Oh! Ye awful things! Get away from me! Get away!"

Now, the ants were running back and forth over her bare feet. Screaming, she continued jumping up and down. Jordan saw no hope for completing the rescue but to pick her up bodily and carry her back to the launch. Scooping her off her feet, he swung her into his arms, then had to stamp his own feet to deter the ants from running up his boots.

He felt one sting his knee, and it did feel like fire. Making a mad dash for the launch, he escaped the swarming creatures, and as soon as he reached the safety of the deck, set Spencer on her feet and pulled in the plank linking the launch to the shore.

"That should do it. They can't get to us now."

When there was no response from the woman behind him, Jordan turned to look at her. In the dark shadows of the deck, Spencer stood sobbing quietly with her hands over her face. A cloud of fiery-red hair effectively concealed her body; she seemed not yet to have realized she was naked as the day she was born. Feeling a surge of pity, understanding completely how unnerving the last few minutes had been for her, he pulled her into his arms. She sobbed unrestrainedly on his shoulder, then choked and hiccupped, trying to regain control.

"There . . . there . . ." he crooned. "The bite of a fire ant is devilishly painful, and if you get enough of them, you *can* die. But I don't think you got that many, and what you did get will soon quit stinging."

"It's not the pain. It's . . . it's . . . the feel of them running all over me. It's a *terrible* sensation. A person could go mad from it."

"There . . . there. You're safe now." Stories he had heard popped into Jordan's head, but he refrained from mentioning them. It was said that a favorite punishment Arana's overseers inflicted upon recalcitrant Indians was to tie a wrong-doer spread-eagled to a Palo Santo tree, the favorite haunt of fire ants, then howl with laughter as the man went mad under the attack of the insects.

"I dinna know where they came from," Spencer blurted. "One moment, I was lying quietly in me hammock, and the next, I felt them crawlin' all over me. I'm probably not bitten all that bad—but if ye hadna come when ye did, I . . . I dinna know what I'd have done."

"You probably tied your hammock to a Palo Santo tree where they had a nest. I should have thought to warn you about that. However, you mustn't dwell on the incident," Jordan counseled, worried by her shivering and the paleness of her lips. "Such frightening things happen all the time out here. After a while, you learn to live with danger and even to relish it. Compared to the boredom of most people's lives, it's not a bad life . . . and after all, I did warn you."

She stiffened in his arms. "Yes, ye did. I'm sorry I broke our bargain. I hadna meant to scream. Ye should not have come runnin'. Next time, just ignore me."

"I'll do no such thing," Jordan chided. "I don't really expect you to be totally self-sufficient. Besides, if something bad happens to me, I hope you come running when *I* scream."

She lifted tear-drenched lashes to gaze into his

eyes. "Thank ye, Mr. King, for helping me when I really needed it. I hope I can do the same for ye someday."

Her uncharacteristic humility touched him as her haughtiness never had. In the semidarkness, her blue-green eyes were liquid and shimmering, her mouth soft and moist, with a vulnerability he had never before noticed. He felt an odd, twisting sensation in his gut, followed almost immediately by an overwhelming urge to kiss her. He bent his head, but before his lips touched hers, she jerked away.

"I . . . I really must get dressed and find some salve to sooth these stings," she murmured distractedly.

"Yes, of course . . ." He suddenly remembered the odd bandage she had been wearing. "Are you sure you're all right? You haven't any injuries other than the stings, have you? That gauze you had wrapped around you . . ."

She dropped her gaze and flushed a deep, embarrassed red. "No . . . none. Excuse me, Mr. King. I'll fetch some clothes and dress in the engine house." Arms folded primly across her bosom, she stepped back from him into the darkest shadows on deck.

"I'll go back and get your things if you'd like, though I think it would be best to wait until morning. By then, all the ants should be gone."

"Mornin' will be soon enough, thank ye." She had put a crate and two barrels between them now. "Would ye mind, please, turnin' your back?"

He turned around, piqued that he hadn't kissed her while he had the chance. "Glad to oblige, Doc, though I see little need for such modesty. You've seen me naked, and now I've seen you. That makes us even . . . Of course, I don't know how you felt about seeing me, but seeing you was a real pleasure.

You're a stunning woman, Dr. O'Rourke, and why you'd wrap yourself up in a gauze bandage is more than I can figure out. Most women would give their eye teeth to be as well endowed as you are."

Profound silence greeted his observation. So he was right. She *was* embarrassed by her God-given bounty—to the extent that she sought to hide it. The discovery gave him an insight into her character. Why, she had stifled her femininity! What a challenge it would be to see if he could unearth the passion so carefully buried beneath the layers of gauze and efficiency!

"You know I'm going to kiss you eventually, don't you, Doc?" he goaded, intrigued to see how far he could push her. "It's only a matter of time. I expect it will happen before we get to Paraïso. So tell me; how many times have you been kissed? Now, I don't mean a chaste, little peck on the cheek—I mean a real soul-shaking, gut-clenching, spine-tingling kiss? One that makes your toes curl. The kind that makes you want to tear off all your clothes and rub bare flesh against bare flesh."

Except for the jungle noises on shore, the silence deepened.

"I bet I could teach you things about kissing that you've never imagined, Doc," Jordan continued. One small part of him insisted he was a cad for going on like this, but another part assured him he was doing her a favor by taking her mind off the horror of the ants. "You could look at it as sort of a medical experiment. How much can I accelerate your pulse and increase your rate of breathing? How long can you hold your breath while your lips are pressed against mine?"

Behind him came a faint rustle. He turned around. Spencer stood there, calmly regarding him, as if all he had been saying was so much monkey chatter. She had dressed in a plain white outfit almost identical to the one she had been wearing. What had she done—bought several of the exact same garments? If so, she had buried her femininity absurdly deep, and the challenge of unearthing it was doubly fascinating.

"I'll sleep on a crate in the engine house tonight, Mr. King. Tomorrow, when you retrieve my hammock, I'll figure out a way to hang it in there, where I can close the door on you if I feel the need to do so."

"Whatever you say, Doc. You'll find two convenient hooks inside expressly for the purpose of holding a hammock when it rains. Unfortunately, you don't get a good breeze in the engine house; it's unbearably hot and stuffy."

"I'm sure I can survive the stuffiness, Mr. King." She gave him one of her quelling looks. "Once I get my pistol back, I will of course keep it close at hand, in case you misplace your manners."

"Back in control again, I see, aren't we? What a pity! I liked you better naked and sobbing on my shoulder."

"I *hated* myself naked and sobbing on your shoulder. Good night, Mr. King."

With a haughty lift of her chin, she walked away. Jordan had to stop himself from going after her and kissing her until that foolish pride melted and was gone forever. "Good night, Doctor O'Rourke," he said softly.

When Spencer awoke the next morning, she saw her hammock, pistol, and torn clothes lying on top of the crate beside a basin and pitcher of water for washing, a small bar of soap, and her hairbrush and hairpins, all neatly laid out as if she were a guest in a hotel or someone's private home. A delicious smell was wafting through the partially open door of the engine house; Jordan was obviously cooking breakfast. Just as obviously, he had been spying on her while she slept.

Quickly and quietly, she rose, performed some hurried ablutions, and yanked the brush through her long hair. Then she carefully pinned it in place in her usual severe style. At last, except for the wild fluttering in her lower abdomen, she felt ready to face him again.

Stepping out on deck, she addressed his backside—attractively muscular, like the rest of him—which was all she could see as he bent over the cook stove. "Good morning, Mr. King."

Immediately, he straightened and turned, bestowing a glowing, white-toothed smile that lit his tanned face from within. "Good morning, Doc! You're looking fresh and lovely, a regular jungle orchid. Did you sleep well?"

His outrageous flattery reminded her of the danger of permitting him to become too familiar. Last night, she blushingly recalled, he had almost kissed her, and she had almost allowed it. The fact that he had seen her naked—and undone her breast binder and speculated about its purpose—was bad enough, but the fact that she had almost succumbed to him was shocking in the extreme. For a few short moments, she had experienced a curious, melting sensation, unlike anything she had previously known. Why, she had actually *wanted* him to put his hands on her . . .

"I believe I would sleep better if I had a lock on the engine house door, Mr. King."

"Sorry, I'm fresh out of locks . . . How about a taste of piranha?"

"Piranha! You mean . . . you've actually caught and prepared the same little fish that attacked Raymundo? And you expect me to *eat* them?"

With a hurt look on his handsome face, he gestured to the sizzling fish laid out on the grill of the drum stove. "Piranha make *wonderful* eating. I doubt these are the same ones who attacked Raymundo, but if they are, then they've met a just fate. Raymundo would be delighted to know we're having piranha for breakfast."

Spencer doubtfully perched on the edge of her medicine crate. "They do smell delicious," she ventured, having quite forgotten the matter of the lock—or at least, having pushed it to the back of her mind.

"Here, try one . . . I'll bone it for you first." He picked one up with an iron spatula, slapped it on a tin plate, and boned it almost faster than she could swallow her apprehension.

Timidly, she took the plate, accepted the fork he handed her, and tried a bite. The fish was sweet and flaky, done to perfection and melting on her tongue. "Why, it's delicious!"

She smiled up at him and was rewarded with another charming grin. "Eat all you want. I've already had mine. Now that I've got more fuel, I want to start the engine and get underway."

Spencer devoured every morsel of the succulent fish, then sat quietly, enjoying the sweet, fresh air as the launch chugged up the river. It was a beautiful morning, not yet hot, and golden bars of sunlight lay across the broad expanse of brown water. She and Jordan did not speak again until almost noon, when it had grown quite humid, and the insects were buzzing loudly on shore.

"Look there!" he suddenly pointed, drawing her attention with a wave of his hand. "On the riverbank."

She peered into the dense green tangle and saw a streak of orange, black, and white.

"Jaguar," Jordan said in a tone of deep respect. "One of the jungle's most magnificent predators. Not as dangerous as a bushmaster, perhaps, or one of the big anacondas, but an animal you want to avoid, if you can."

Spencer's attention caught on a flash of blue—a huge, turquoise-winged butterfly skimming across the river. Jordan laughed at her delight in it.

"Oh, I see those all the time. Usually they fly in flocks. However, this is the first time I've ever seen one and thought of a woman's eyes."

The compliment elicited a ripple of pleasure down Spencer's body. Embarrassed, she chided herself for being so gullible as to believe anything Jordan King said; the man was *not* to be taken seriously. In the great, tall trees, unseen monkeys chattered and screamed. Jordan angled the launch close to shore, and a tiny, delicate deer leaped away. "Damn my aunt Milly's corset! There's dinner, and I wasn't ready."

Spencer was glad he had had no time to grab his rifle; the deer was too pretty to kill. Eventually he spotted a small tapir and brought it down with a single shot. He dropped anchor, rowed to shore in the tiny dinghy, hacked off the choicest meat, and left the rest behind. Late in the afternoon, it clouded over, and the scent of rain came to them from the darkened sky. Jordan found a sheltered bend in the river and tied up to a half-submerged tree whose limbs were poking up like the outstretched hand of a drowning victim.

"We better eat early tonight and retire to the engine house. We're in for a storm . . . and don't argue, Doc. It's gonna rain buckets, and I don't intend to sleep on deck."

Worried about spending the night together in such close quarters, Spencer set about arranging the engine house to allow for privacy. There wasn't much to be had. The steam-powered engine took up the entire rear of the shelter, and stacks of wood and other items took up the rest. No matter what she did, she could not find space enough to hang two hammocks without putting them side by side, closer than Jordan had hung them the day before beneath the overhang.

Dinner was a hurried affair, eaten standing up in a rising wind. Spencer hardly had time to register the taste of tapir, much less decide if she liked it or not. Afterward, Jordan bustled about the crowded deck, checking to make certain all barrels and crates were secured. He then lit a lantern, brought it inside the engine house, and shut the door. Not ten seconds later, a crack of thunder shook the entire boat. The rain began, hammering on the roof like a crazed drummer.

Spencer sat primly on a small crate near her hammock; did Jordan King play cards or chess? Did he have a deck of cards aboard? What on earth would they talk about all evening? She hoped the deluge would pass quickly and she could persuade him to leave the engine house and sleep outside. The rain drummed steadily for a quarter of an hour, the boat rocked and the wind blew, then the storm seemed to settle down into a quiet, monotonous downpour that promised to last all night.

Jordan grinned at her from the depths of his hammock. "Let me know when you want to douse the light, Doc."

"I . . . I believe I'll read a bit, first, Mr. King. I brought a Bible along, and I've always found reading it to be a good prelude to a sound night's rest." She picked up the fat leather-bound book lying in her lap and opened it.

"Puts you to sleep, does it?" He gave her a rakish, discomfitting grin. "Well, I've got my own methods for settling the weary mind."

He rummaged in the dark shadows beneath his hammock and produced a bottle of amber-colored liquid. "Care for a snort of French brandy? It's just the thing for a night like this."

"I don't imbibe spirits, Mr. King. I thought I made that clear the other day when I refused the wine you offered."

"You didn't, exactly. That was the night you had to keep a close watch on Raymundo; I thought that's why you were refusing the wine."

It *had* been the reason she had refused it. But she also rejected spirits on almost every other occasion. Having seen what drink had done to her father, she had no desire to blunt her own faculties. "It's not wise for a doctor to drink at all, Mr. King. One never knows when one must perform surgery or make a decision involving someone's life."

Undeterred, Jordan uncorked the bottle and took a generous swig straight from its mouth. Afterward, he recorked it and winked at her. "Ah, wonderful stuff . . . warms you to the bone . . . Look. Why don't we abandon this stuffy formality and call each other by our first names? Dr. O'Rourke is such a mouthful."

"I don't think we should, Mr. King. We must strive to keep our relationship on a strictly professional basis. Besides, most of the time, you don't call me *Doctor* O'Rourke. You call me Doc, which I detest."

Jordan King barked with laughter. "Sorry about that, Doc. If I'd known it offended you, I'd have started calling you Spencer right off. However, I was afraid you'd think I was thinking about you as a woman—that I was even thinking of seducing you."

Remembering their conversation of the night before, with all the talk about kissing, Spencer flushed. Jordan King apparently enjoyed teasing people. Every other word he spoke held an underlying spark of pungent humor, as if he might be silently laughing at her, though he had not, she suddenly remembered, been laughing during Raymundo's surgery.

"Does it please you to try to embarrass me, Mr. King? Is that how you amuse yourself—at the expense of other people's feelings?"

For a moment, he seemed taken aback. Then he grinned and nodded. "Yes, it does please me—for some perverse reason I don't quite understand, I particularly enjoy teasing you. That's why I want to kiss you, so I can figure out what it is about you that so pricks my fancy. Maybe I'm half in love with you; I'm not usually so rude and boorish. A single kiss could explain a lot—to both of us."

"It wouldn't explain anything to me. I feel nothing whatever for you . . . That is to say, nothing personal. As one who has learned to survive in the jungle, I respect you, but in a perfectly ordinary manner, of course, as I would respect any man who has achieved your skills."

"How can you be so sure, Doc? Doesn't the chemistry between a man and woman intrigue you? Wouldn't you like to know if you do feel something more for me?"

"Not really," Spencer denied, unable to look him in the eye while she said it.

"What harm could one kiss do, Doc? If we kissed and got it over with, then we would both feel relieved of a great deal of pressure and could continue our relationship on the business level you so much desire . . . that is, if the kiss indeed does nothing to us."

"I don't *want* to kiss you, Mr. King."

"Not yet, perhaps, Dr. O'Rourke. But you might change your mind once we begin."

Irritated at herself for once again allowing such an inane conversation to get started, Spencer set down her Bible and rose from the crate. Obviously, the only way to beat this man at his own game was to meet his challenge and demonstrate that nothing he did had the power to really rattle her.

"All right, Mr. King, I'll kiss you. Then I'll turn out the light and go to bed, and so will you, and it will *not* be in the same hammock. In exchange for this great favor, you will cease mocking me and never again initiate these distastefully intimate conversations. I will insist upon respect and professionalism between us . . . Agreed?"

Jordan King regarded her solemnly, though his mouth had a suspicious twitch. "Agreed, Doc."

Intending only to bestow a swift peck on his forehead, she marched over to him, bent down, and brushed her lips against the tousled hair covering his brow. "There! It's done . . . and I felt absolutely noth—"

Strong, golden-brown arms reached up and seized her, pulling her down on top of a hard, muscular body. "That was no kiss, woman! *This* is a kiss."

Losing her balance, she all but fell into the hammock. Jordan gripped her waist with one arm, while with his free hand, he somehow managed to tilt up her chin. In the next moment, the hot pressure of his lips found her open mouth. She struggled to right herself, but he did not give her the chance. His hand slid to the back of her head and held it in place.

Then he began to kiss her—*really* kiss her—to ravish her lips and mouth. She gasped for breath, inhaling the sweet fumes of French brandy, as potent as if she herself had drunk it. She flailed against him, fought to regain her balance and pull away but could not. Her hair came undone, entangling itself in her own thrashing limbs. She felt his hand on her breast, kneading her fullness. The blood rushed to her head, to her nipples, to her loins. Her body throbbed with deep, pulsing sensations, rushing toward some unknown but wondrously exciting conclusion. Streaks of light—lightning?—flashed before her eyes.

Suddenly, Jordan King stopped kissing her. She jerked back, her feet finally finding the floor. They stared into each other's eyes; his were a brilliant green, so green it hurt to look at them.

"My God!" he breathed, releasing a deep sigh. "Dr. O'Rourke, do you think it's physically possible for two people to make love in a hammock?"

Chapter Eight

Jordan had not meant for things to actually go this far, and he was not a bit surprised when Spencer O'Rourke leaped backward, like a scalded cat. Her turquoise eyes blazed with a blue-green fire, her cheeks sprouted roses, and her face and body radiated crackling disapproval. In that moment, even with a scowl on her face, she was truly a beautiful woman.

"I think we'd have to be contortionists to manage it, Mr. King. Ye may be one, but I'm not, and if I were, I could hardly be expected t' fall into a hammock with ye on so brief an acquaintance."

"Why, Doc, I wouldn't call our acquaintance brief. We've been through a lot together. At any rate, we aren't strangers. I've bedded women I knew far less intimately than I know you."

"Ye scarcely know me a-tall!"

"I know what you look like without any clothes and in the morning before you've had a chance to brush your hair."

"That's not *knowing* me!"

"You're absolutely right. That's a mere skimming of the surface. What I want to do is get to know the *real* you—the woman within. To put it bluntly,

I want to get inside you, mind and body."

"Mr. King!"

The blue-green eyes darkened to a steely gray. Before Jordan guessed her intent and could take steps to protect himself, Spencer seized the side of the hammock, exerted all her strength—grunting with the effort—and neatly flipped it over. One minute he was comfortably ensconced in the hemp hammock, enjoying their verbal battle, and the next he was plunging face downward onto the hard floor of the engine house. Startled but unhurt, he got to his knees, then was stunned to feel the firm pressure of a booted foot square in the seat of his pants. Spencer gave a mighty shove and sent him sprawling a second time.

Rolling over, he tried to grab her by the ankle, but she was already yanking open the door and running out on deck into the rain. "Spencer! Get back in here!" he shouted. "For God's sake, it's a deluge out there. Besides, I didn't mean it; I was just teasing you."

But he had meant it, he realized. He did want to make love to her—wanted it with a burning desire that stunned him with its dark ferocity. No wonder Spencer had bolted into the wet night. Until now, he had been toying with her, merely playing with the possibility of seducing her. But that kiss! It had unleashed a torrent of feeling that overshadowed even his wounded dignity. He wanted to strip off all her clothes, explore those magnificent breasts, and make Doctor Spencer K. O'Rourke whimper with helpless pleasure.

"Spencer! Dr. O'Rourke!" he shouted again, standing in the open doorway where the rain lashed his face and plastered his shirtfront against his chest. "Hey, look . . . I'm sorry. I didn't mean to scare you. You can come back inside now, and I'll promise not to even talk to you, if that's what you want. Word of honor. I'll be a perfect gentleman."

"Ye don't know the meaning of the word, 'gentleman!' " came the angry, lilting reply. "Ye've been leading up to this from the day we first met!"

"No, I haven't—not consciously, anyway. But if I had been plotting to get you into bed with me, what's so wrong about that? I should think a woman would be flattered to know a man wants her."

"Ye'd want any woman ye couldn't have. Seduction is only a game with ye. Ye enjoy the chase."

"Of course I do. All men do, and women enjoy it, too, though they won't always admit it. At least, most of them enjoy it—not you, though. I can see that. You're too prim and proper to ever let yourself take pleasure in being chased . . . Why don't you come inside, and we'll continue this discussion where it's warm and dry?"

"I dinna want t' come inside with ye! Ye can't be trusted! I'd rather drown out here in the rain!"

Spencer's brogue was thickening along with her anger—an interesting phenomenon, Jordan thought. Whenever she lost her temper or forgot herself, she sounded more like an Irish spitfire and less like a stiff, starched spinster. Maybe the key to unlocking the real woman inside the caricature was to keep her in a state of perpetual anger.

"All right, Doc. Suit yourself. Do you mind if I close the door though? I dislike being wet and cold."

"Ye can close the door on yer bloody foot, for all I care, an' I hope ye do, lad! Just don't ask for me help if ye break any bones. For the love of St. Brigid, I'd just have t' refuse it!"

Jordan burst out laughing, which only seemed to inflame Spencer's ire even more. She let loose with what sounded like a string of colorful Gaelic curses, and as he softly closed the door on them, an object struck the wood, glanced off it, and shattered; she had actually thrown something at him!

It occurred to him she might be crazy. What sort of woman went around throwing things at a man for simply trying to kiss her? For that matter, what sort of woman swathed herself in gauze bandages? Or came to Brazil all alone to work on the lonely, dangerous Amazon? Or operated on a man's legs as if she did it every day on top of a crate in the middle of a river?

If Spencer O'Rourke wasn't crazy, she was certainly damn close to it. He was lucky he hadn't bedded her, or he might come down with the exact same illness and start doing similar, peculiar, astonishing things. Congratulating himself on having the good sense to shut the door on her, he returned to his hammock, righted it, and climbed inside. However, he was unable to relax, knowing she was out in the rain, while he was safe and dry. Instead of lessening, the downpour increased, drumming harder than ever on the roof, as only a rainshower on the Amazon River could do.

He tossed and turned fitfully, trying this position and that, unable to find any comfort. Finally, with a long-drawn-out sigh of defeat, he got up, rummaged around for a piece of filthy, old canvas, and finding it, flung open the door. "All right, Doc, you win! You can have the engine house, and *I'll* sleep on deck."

At first, he thought she had not heard him or else was too stubborn to come in out of the rain.

But a moment later, she suddenly appeared in the lanternlight spilling through the open doorway. She looked like a skinned rabbit—all wet and bedraggled, hair and clothes molded to her head and body, thin, pale, and shivering.

"God Almighty! You'll catch your death of cold! Get in here, you stubborn fool!"

Through blue lips and chattering teeth, she responded grimly. "Only if *you* get out."

"I said I was coming out, and I am." Stepping on deck was like stepping under a waterfall. Quickly, Jordan flung the canvas around his shoulders to shield himself from the cold cascade of water, but it managed to find its way beneath the canvas and into every crevice of his body anyhow. "Happy now? You won't be satisfied unless I get pneumonia, will you?" he barked at her.

"No, I won't be satisfied until ye treat me with the respect I deserve!"

"Deserve!" he bellowed. "What about the respect *I* deserve, as captain of this launch?"

"When ye *earn* it, I'll *give* it!" she retorted. "Now, if ye'll excuse me, I'm going to bed."

She marched into the engine house, whirled about, and shut the door in his face—leaving him alone in the driving rain to figure out how he was going to spend the long, lonely, cold night.

The next morning, taking her cue from Jordan, Spencer acted as if nothing whatever had occurred between them the previous evening. She came out of the engine house to find the sun rising, breakfast cooking, and a hollow-eyed Jordan calmly setting two places atop the crate that had come to serve as their dining table.

"Good morning," he said cheerily. "Sleep well? I certainly did. There's something mighty cozy about listening to the rain drum on the roof at night, then awakening in the morning to find everything washed clean and sweet-smelling."

What roof? she wondered, casting a wary glance around the deck. Try as she might, she could not discover where Jordan might have slept, all snug and cozy, listening to the rain. Other than his haggard eyes and the note of fatigue in his voice, his demeanor revealed nothing. He was newly shaven, his clothing dry, and his usually tousled blond hair neatly combed. Sometime during the night, the rain had stopped, obviously allowing him the chance to recover from the discomforts he must have experienced. She had not been certain when that was—only that her guilt had at last eased to the point where she herself was able to snatch a few hours of badly needed sleep. All night long, she had worried about Jordan being out in the rain. Despite the canvas in which he had wrapped himself, he might catch a chill, or suffer another attack of malaria, or, indeed, contract pneumonia.

But if he was not going to acknowledge the tensions of the past evening, she certainly would not allude to them. "It does look like we're going to have a lovely day," she politely conceded.

"And I can't think of a thing I'd rather do right now than share breakfast with a beautiful woman," Jordan said, flashing his rakish grin.

So that's what he's up to, Spencer thought. *Since force didn't work, now he thinks he'll charm me into his hammock.*

She returned his smile with a chilly one of her own. "Then ye havna much imagination, have ye, Mr. King?"

Grinning more broadly, as if her brogue amused him, he nodded toward a barrel. "Sit down, Doc. Breakfast is almost ready. I hope you like your eggs boiled in the shell."

"Eggs? Where did you get fresh eggs?"

"These are turtle eggs—a bit different from what you're used to, but I think you'll find them tasty just the same. I've fixed a whole mess of them—found them exposed on shore this morning. The rain must have washed away the sand the mother turtle used to cover them. Luckily, I got to them before the jungle critters. Turtle eggs are a great delicacy for both man and beast."

As usual, Spencer found herself warming to his irresistible magnetism; when he wanted, he could be so interesting and informative. She could almost forget the danger simmering beneath the surface of his smooth manners. Last night, when he had kissed her, that danger had exploded, all but knocking her off her feet. Never had she suspected that a kiss could be so potent—rather like the kick of a mule. She had once treated a man who'd been kicked by a mule. "Never saw it comin'," the man had said. "Caught me by surprise, it did—an' afterward the mule just stood there, like it surprised him, too."

Jordan King had appeared every bit as surprised as she had been. But whereas her instincts had advised her to flee, his had urged him to press the matter. They had experienced two entirely different reactions; perhaps that was why the woman bore the most responsibility for keeping things from getting out of hand. She was the only one with a level head on her shoulders. Of course, she was also the one who might get pregnant if the man had his way with her.

Anticipating another unique but delicious breakfast, Spencer sat down and accepted the plate of boiled turtle eggs Jordan gave her. The eggs resembled golf balls, but the shells, she discovered, were rubbery rather than hard. Jordan ate with great relish, but Spencer could not help conjuring a tantalizing image of fluffy scrambled eggs and thick toast slathered with orange marmalade, a *real* breakfast!

After breakfast they got underway again, and the day passed uneventfully, except that every time Spencer looked Jordan's way, her glance collided with his. He would flash his mocking smile, and his eyes would slowly, rudely roam over her, bringing a hot flush to her cheeks and making her insides turn somersaults. It was as if he were undressing her, one garment at a time, and enjoying every moment of it. He did not bother to hide the fact of his base desires; if anything, he flaunted them. His eyes and his smile telegraphed scorching messages impossible to ignore or misinterpret. Spencer would quickly look away, before she, too, became obsessed with the idea of Jordan King making passionate love to her.

After dinner that night, while Jordan was busy doing something on shore, she secured the little fortress of the engine house against whatever assault he might choose to make upon it. Closing the door, she jammed two heavy crates against it, and with a weary sigh, partially undressed and sank into her hammock. No sooner had she done so when a knock sounded on the door.

"Spencer? Are you in there?"

Jumping out of the hammock, she glared at the closed door. The engine house was stifling hot and smoky. For some reason, the kerosene lantern was giving off fumes and an unpleasant, acrid odor. It would be heaven to open the door and allow fresh air to circulate—but the reason she could not open it was standing outside, very likely grinning his mocking grin and hoping to feast his hot-eyed gaze upon her.

"Of course I'm in here," she carefully enunciated. "I'm not coming out, nor are you coming in. Go away, Mr. King. I've retired for the night."

"But I need your help. I . . . I've suffered an injury."

"What sort of injury?" she demanded suspiciously, not for a single minute trusting the scoundrel.

"While I was on shore . . . It was . . . um . . . getting dark, and a . . . a vampire bat suddenly swooped down and bit me."

"Bit you where?"

"Um . . . on the thumb. The little bastard got me right on the thumb."

"I dinna believe it! I've never heard of such a thing."

"You've never heard of vampire bats? They're common in these parts. Why, if you take horses or cattle to your plantation, the bats will kill them in a matter of weeks. Every night, they suck the blood right out of the poor beasts, and in the morning, you find bites all over them."

"Why don't ye get under your mosquito net, Mr. King? I'm sure ye'll be safe from them, there."

"But what about my poor thumb?"

"I'll see to it in the morning."

"I could be dead by morning."

"I'm not opening this door, Mr. King! Not for any reason! Do ye understand that?"

"I don't know what you're so afraid of, Doc. I've

never in my life raped a woman. I sure don't intend to start now."

"For the love of St. Brigid! Will ye just go away and leave me alone?"

For a moment, there was silence on the other side of the door. Spencer thought she had finally gotten through to him, but then his voice came again, low and wheedling. "Couldn't you just take a look at my thumb?"

"No!" she screamed. "No, no, no!"

Aghast at the wildness of her response, she jumped back from the door. What was happening to her? Why was she allowing this man to make her behave in a wild, undisciplined manner, utterly at odds with the careful control she had worked for years to obtain?

A deep, masculine chuckle resounded outside the door. "Oh, all right, Doc . . . I'll leave you alone, if you're sure that's what you want. It was only a little bite, anyhow—nothing serious. If I lose a thumb over it, I can always grow another. What's a thumb compared to the possibility that if you open this door, you might lose your virtue? Better my thumb should fall off than you should fall from grace."

She gritted her teeth while he chattered on, enjoying himself immensely. In a little while, he went away. She extinguished the lantern and lay down in the hot, humid darkness, her body trembling, her heart pounding. Unwittingly, she pictured herself in Jordan King's arms, kissing him with wild abandon, even kissing his thumb, which she knew was unblemished but needed her kissing just the same, as badly as she needed his.

* * *

Three or four days passed. Spencer found it difficult to keep track of time when all her thoughts centered on Jordan King's incredible virility as he went about his daily activities of running the boat, hunting their food, chopping firewood, and diving into a sheltered spot on the river for a quick, cooling swim. As he climbed back into the launch after one such late afternoon, impromptu bath, she stared at the water sheeting off his splendid, half-naked body, raised her eyes to his, and realized she had never in her life been so attracted to a man. Nor had any man ever laid such exciting siege to her staunch defenses.

He grinned lazily, his green eyes sliding over her with warm calculation. "Wouldn't you like a quick swim? There are no piranhas or alligators about today. No eels or sharks, either."

"How can you be so sure?"

"The birds. I've been watching the shore birds skimming the water and bathing, having themselves a good time. They don't do that if predators are lurking beneath the surface, just waiting to catch them."

"Sounds risky to me," she snorted. "Putting your faith in the whims of a few birds."

He grabbed a rough piece of toweling and began to wipe himself dry. "You don't like risks, do you, Doc? Oh, I don't mean all risks. Certainly, you took a very great risk just by coming to the Amazon. What you guard against is personal risk, the possibility of losing control by having someone really get close to you. You're afraid of what might happen if you start to care for someone."

"I dinna think that's an accurate assessment of me personality at all, Mr. King!"

"Isn't it?" His eyes probed deeply, reaching for

her very soul. "Then why do I scare you half to death? Why does the thought of intimacy—a kiss or a caress—send you scurrying to find a safe hiding place, where a man can never get to you?"

"Why do *you* find it so necessary—so challenging—to try and get to me, Mr. King? Why is it so impossible for a man and woman to be alone together without leaping into each other's arms?"

He shrugged and grinned. "Nature, I guess. That and the fact that you're a fine-looking woman, despite all your efforts to make yourself look like some old schoolteacher no man would ever want."

"I'm *not* fine-looking," Spencer said bitterly, glancing away from his too-knowing gaze. "I'm tall, thin—except for my bust—and too vivid and gaudy. I even have freckles. Men like pale, delicate women who would never dare *dream* of saying what they think—or even *thinking* for themselves."

Jordan shouted his laughter. "Well, you've got a point there, Doc! You are rather unusual. However, I find you quite intriguing." Falling silent, he cupped her chin in his hand, turned her face toward him, and gazed deeply into her eyes. "Indeed, I find you . . ."

Something whined past Spencer's ear and thudded into the roof of the engine house. A split second later, there was a loud crack! Both she and Jordan jumped. Several other cracks followed, accompanied by pings and mini-explosions. Jordan flung one arm around her and dragged her down on the deck beside him. "Get down! Somebody's firing at us!"

"Who?" Spencer demanded, cringing as the wood splintered on a nearby crate.

"How the hell should *I* know? We're only a half day's journey from Paraíso. It's got to be someone who doesn't want us to reach there alive—probably Loayza and a few of his buddies."

"Blessed saints in heaven!" Spencer gasped.

"Stay here while I get the engine started. You'll have to help me untie the launch and get underway. Don't worry; all we have to do is outrun them."

"I'm not worried. Just tell me what to do."

"For the moment, keep out of sight. As soon as I get the engine fired up, I'll be back."

Without another word, Jordan began to crawl toward the engine house on his belly. Rifle fire marked his progress. Whoever was on shore had obviously guessed his intent, because the engine house was soon peppered with shot holes. The entire launch rocked from the force of being hit repeatedly. Showers of wood splinters erupted each time a crate was hit. Loud pings resounded whenever metal was struck. Spencer spotted the kerosene can sitting in plain view atop a crate. If it got hit, and the can started leaking, a fire could easily break out.

Inching forward on her elbows, she maneuvered her way toward it. Cautiously, she stretched one arm and discovered she could not reach it without rising to at least her knees. Taking a deep breath, she scrambled to her feet, grabbed the can, and ducked back down again. A shot creased her head, the heat of it singing her hair. Then a heavy weight fell across her.

"What do you think you're doing?" Jordan growled in her ear, his tone furious. "I thought I told you to stay put."

As she lay sprawled under Jordan's heavy body, the can dug into her rib cage. "The k-kerosene can. I dinna want them t' hit it and start a fire."

"Damn the kerosene can! They almost hit *you!*"

"I'm f-fine, except for bein' ground into bone meal!"

He rolled off to one side. "Damn my aunt Milly's corset! There must be two dozen of 'em out there. The bullet holes alone will sink us."

"Did ye get the engine started? I dinna feel any vibrations."

"The *Evangeline*'s being temperamental. I came back out here to retrieve a little part I was working on this morning. I think it will do the trick, but for God's sake, don't do anything so stupid as raising your head again. You've got a new part in your hair; it could just as easily have been a hole in your forehead."

Spencer gingerly touched her head. "Funny . . . it doesna hurt."

The menacing staccato of rifle fire drowned out the conversation. Jordan scrabbled about on deck and finally located what he was looking for—a small, squarish-looking metal object, whose purpose Spencer could only imagine. Holding a finger to his lips in a last warning gesture, he shimmied toward the engine house on his stomach. Several moments later, Spencer heard the engine belch and sputter, then roar to life. Back Jordan came—this time, with his Winchester in hand.

"Here . . ." he said, handing it to her. "Cover me while I untie the launch."

"I . . . I doubt I can hit anything," Spencer whispered. "I've never fired one of these."

"Hell's bells! You don't have to aim it, just point it at the shore and squeeze the trigger."

Spencer shoved the rifle back at him. "No, ye cover *me* while *I* untie the launch."

Before he could argue, she jumped up and began running toward the bow, where a long mooring line held the launch fast to a tree trunk tilted at an impossible angle over the water.

"Spencer!" he shouted.

In the midst of the pop-pop-pop of the gunfire from shore, she heard the satisfyingly loud and comforting boom of his rifle going off behind her. In seconds, she had the launch freed. As the current quickly carried the boat toward the center of the river, she dashed into the shelter of the engine house, with Jordan hard on her heels.

"Keep feeding wood to that fire!" he barked, grabbing another box of cartridges and exiting as fast as he had entered.

She had little time to wonder how he was going to steer the vessel outside, where he would make an easy target. Most of the stacked wood was too large to fit into the little oven that produced the heat that in turn made the steam and powered the launch. She had to crack the large pieces of kindling over her knee, then stuff them into the oven as best she could. Twice she burned her hands on the hot oven door, and every time she opened it, the blast of fiery heat nearly singed her eyebrows. Her clothes clung to her like sticky, wet rags, and her hair curled itself into tight, springy little coils. In the oven itself, an inferno blazed, and the engine was soon chugging along faster and more efficiently than it ever had before.

In no time at all, Jordan was standing in the doorway, grinning the biggest, widest grin ever to grace his handsome, rugged face. "We've done it!" he exclaimed. "We're past them now. Quit using up all my wood, Doc, and come give me a big victory hug."

Chapter Nine

"I . . . I'm so hot—so dirty," Spencer demurred.

"You've never looked better," Jordan contradicted. He walked toward her, his green eyes glinting in the dimness of the engine house. "I especially love the streak of soot on your cheek and all those curls falling down in your eyes."

"I . . . I probably smell bad, too!"

"It's honest sweat—nothing to be ashamed of."

He stalked her into a corner, his wide shoulders seeming to fill the entire engine house. The sight and scent of him flooded her senses. Her stomach muscles clenched and knotted—quivering with expectation. He was so wholly male: all ridged, rippling muscles, tousled, golden-blond hair, and tight-fitting trousers over lean, narrow hips. In a moment, he would take her in his arms and crush her to that massive chest . . .

"Oh, Jordan, I canna do this!" she wailed in an agony, longing mixed with dread. "I'm . . . I'm just not ready!" Only inches away from her, he traced one finger down her cheek and along her lower lip. "Will you wait until you're a wrinkled, dried-up old prune to find out what it's like to be a woman? What a pity that would be—what a waste!"

"A waste for *ye* maybe. Not for me. *I* dinna need this; I was getting along fine without it until ye came along."

"You were getting along miserably, masquerading as a man, trying to bury your femininity under a cold, efficient exterior . . ."

"I wasna!"

"You were, too. Admit it, Spencer. You don't know how to act like a woman. You don't even know how to kiss."

"Ye mean I dinna know how t' take orders!"

"That, too. You almost *never* do what you're told. Here, I'll prove it to you. Put your arms around me, Dr. O'Rourke."

She crowded against the wall. "No . . . No, I canna."

"Yes, you can. Go on, try it."

Feeling sicker by the minute, Spencer stared down at her boots, a great conflict warring within her. On the one hand, she *did* want to meekly succumb to his demands, but on the other, she most emphatically did *not*. It was if he was asking her to surrender some part of her essential self—a part no one had ever seen, no one had ever known about. Even *she* hadn't really known about it. Why did he have to press so hard? Why did he have to make her feel so inept . . . lacking—threatened and uncertain?

"Hold me, Spencer," he urged huskily. "Let me feel your heart beating against mine. Let me touch and love you. You're a beautiful woman. Don't be afraid."

"I'm *not* afraid!"

"You're terrified."

"Stop contradictin' me!"

"Stop fighting me."

"But I dinna *want* this!"

He drew back and gazed at her with heavy-lidded eyes. "You're lying to yourself, Spencer. You want it as much as I want it."

Sudden tears trembled on her lashes, blurring her vision. "I . . . I dinna know *what* I want. I only know I'm not ready for *this*. I may *never* be ready. I'm not even sure ye're the man I'd want to do it with, even if I *did* want it."

Jordan sighed and shook his head. "Spencer . . . Spencer . . . what a difficult, stubborn child you are. All right, relax. Stop sniveling and dry your tears. I'm a patient man. I can wait a little longer—at least, I think I can. Why don't you go wash your face and comb your hair? Maybe if I see you looking like an old maid again, I can forget the Spencer with the tender mouth and luscious figure. I can start appreciating your many accomplishments instead of wasting all my time thinking about wrapping my hands around your sweet little bottom."

He was chuckling as he stepped back and let her go. *Chuckling!* It was all a big joke to him, an amusing game, while to her . . . to *her,* it was the most devastating, confusing, unnerving experience of her entire life! And considering what life had already brought her, that was saying a lot. Brushing past him, she fled from the engine house.

Paraīso, Jordan's rubber plantation near the mouth of the Putumayo River, consisted of several rude buildings which were more primitive than Spencer had expected. Her first view of it as the

Evangeline chugged around a bend in the river was disappointing. Most of the buildings were nothing more than large grass huts on stilts with conical, thatched roofs. There was a wooden dock, also raised on stilts, and a large cleared area. Around the whole, the jungle pressed with menacing determination to take back what must have been wrested from it with back-breaking labor.

"There's my house." Jordan pointed to a roomy-looking, square structure set back from the other buildings. It stood on stilts and boasted the only metal roof Spencer could see gleaming in the late-morning sunlight.

"It's got four rooms," Jordan continued. "Plenty of space for both of us . . . Here, toss this mooring line around one of those posts when we get close enough."

"You said I could have my own hut," Spencer reminded him. "I am not staying in your house."

"You can have your own hut. But I also told you it needed minor repairs first . . . Are you going to take this mooring line or not?"

Spencer took the line and directed her attention to tossing the loop over the big post jutting out of the water. As Jordan expertly maneuvered the launch alongside the dock, she tossed and missed. Fortunately, a thin, brown-skinned man in a tattered white shirt and torn-off-at-the-knee pants was running toward them down the dock. He leaned down, grabbed the line, and quickly secured the launch.

"*Bom dia,* Senhor Rei!" The man flashed a big grin marred by several broken yellow teeth. "Where is Raymundo?" he continued in rapid-fire Portuguese. "I do not see him."

"He isn't with us, Luiz," Jordan answered. "I'll explain why in a moment. First, I want you to tell me who's here. That's not one of our *batelãos,* is it?" He nodded toward a long, low, canoelike vessel tied up to the other side of the dock.

"Não, senhor. It belongs to Senhor Serrano from La Reserva. He arrived yesterday to see you. I told him you were very late returning from Manaus. He seemed worried and decided to wait."

"Yes, well . . . he had good reason to worry. Get a few boys to help you unload, Luiz. I presume there's Indians about, looking for work. I'll tell you everything later. Where's Serrano?"

"Up at your house, senhor. He is not very well. Last night, he drank too much *cachaça,* and I have not seen him yet today."

"I'll check on him," Jordan said, utterly ignoring Spencer and the matter of the hut he had promised her.

"Wait a minute!" Spencer clambered from the launch to the dock. "What about my hut? You could at least point it out to me."

Jordan turned to her, annoyance darkening his features. Gone was the teasing, playful rake who had tempted her so badly over the course of the journey; in his place stood a preoccupied stranger with far more on his mind than seduction. "Sorry, but I have better things to do right now than worry about your accommodations, Dr. O'Rourke. As I warned you before, you won't find the Grand Hotel Internacional in Paraíso. Luiz, show the lady that hut where I slept the first year I lived here. After I see what Serrano wants, I expect a complete accounting of all that's been going on in my absence. Since Raymundo didn't return with us, I'll have to rely on you to be my overseer. Do you think you can handle it?"

"Sĩm, senhor! Of course! I have done a very good job of looking after Paraĩso while you and Raymundo were in Manaus." Luiz bestowed a look of unabashed worship on Jordan and then darted a curious glance at Spencer. "Senhorinha, you will come this way, *por favor,* and I will show you the hut Senhor Rei mentioned."

Spencer was too steamed at Jordan's suddenly hostile, dismissive attitude to take pleasure in the fact that she had understood every word of the exchange between Jordan and Luiz, even though it had taken place in rapid Portugese. "I'm sure the hut will prove most comfortable, regardless of what state it is in," she said loud enough for Jordan to hear as he walked away. Under her breath, she added, "Anything is better than sharing living space with an ill-tempered viper."

However, when Spencer saw the hut, she had reason to wish she had not been so insistent upon staying there. The structure had only half a roof, wild pigs had recently been rooting in it, and it was currently infested with huge cockroaches, spiders, and a host of sand fleas. Luiz gestured to it apologetically. "This was a good hut when Senhor Rei lived here. I myself helped to build it."

"It's not very good now." Spencer wrinkled her nose at the strong odor of pig. "But I'd be happy to pay you to help me clean it and put on a new roof."

Luiz flashed his broken-toothed grin. "Of course, senhorinha. In a month or so, it should be good as new."

"A month or so! No, Luiz, you do not understand. It must be fixed immediately—now, today."

Luiz frowned, his dark brown eyes suddenly wary and stubborn. "Then I cannot do it, senhorinha. Now that Senhor Rei has returned, and I am the new overseer, I will be much too busy."

"Then could you please find someone else to help me—maybe one of the Indians who are going to help you unload the *Evangeline?*"

"I do not know, senhorinha. I will try, but we will all be very busy, today, and for many days to come."

"I see." Spencer sighed, resigning herself to having to fix the hut alone, since it was obvious no one was going to leap to her aid.

"Will that be all, senhorinha? I must go now. Senhor Rei is waiting."

"Yes, you may go, Luiz. No, wait a minute. Did you know that I'm a doctor? This hut will not only be my house; it will also be my clinic. If there is anyone in camp who needs medical attention, please tell them they may come see me at any time."

Luiz stared at her, clearly dumbfounded and disbelieving. Finally he asked tentatively, "You are perhaps a *macumbeiro* in your own country?"

Spencer had not heard this word before. Thinking it must be another term for physician, she nodded. "I have brought many medicines. To the Indians, they will probably seem magical. Tell everyone I have special remedies to cure fever and dysentery, clear up rashes, and treat snakebite and insect stings. They will not be sorry if they come to me for help."

"I will tell them, senhorinha," Luiz assured her. His tone sounded far more respectful than it had at first. Apparently, a *macumbeiro,* whatever that was, commanded respect.

Spencer spent the entire afternoon cleaning the hut, disinfecting it as best she could, and arranging her belongings so that as much as possible was under the protection of the half-roof. She had no idea how to go about repairing the missing section; Jordan would simply have to order it done, and she'd have to keep calling his attention to the problem until the task was completed.

Late in the afternoon, as she was growing hungry, Luiz again appeared at the hut. "Senhorinha, Senhor Rei says to tell you he will be taking dinner soon with Senhor Serrano. He hopes you will join them both."

"Tell him I will be delighted," Spencer responded, matching his polite formality.

She hurriedly fetched a basin of fresh rainwater from a nearby wooden cistern, washed her hands and face, brushed her hair, and changed into a clean white skirt and ruffled blouse. She wanted Jordan to see her cool, immaculate, and in control—complaining about nothing, especially not about the primitive living conditions which scared her more than a little. When she was ready, she made her way to Jordan's large, roomy house, climbed the wooden ladder leading to the upper level, and politely clapped her hands outside the door, as Brazilians did when they wished to announce their presence.

"Spencer? Come around the other side." Jordan called. "We're on the front veranda—at least until the winged invaders force us to take cover."

Spencer walked around the house to a wide, spacious veranda overlooking all of Paraïso. She drew in her breath appreciatively; up here, a cool breeze was blowing, holding insects at bay, and the view was most pleasant. Through a fringe of palm and banana trees surrounding the house, she could see the river glinting golden in the waning sunlight and people moving in and about the buildings.

For a moment, her attention caught on the distant figures. She had been too busy all afternoon to pay much heed to the other inhabitants of Paraïso; neither had they sought her company. Now she was curious to learn which of the people she saw below were Indians and which Brazilians.

"Doctor O'Rourke?" Jordan dryly inquired. "If I can pry your attention away from the scenery, I'd like you to meet a friend of mine, David Serrano. He's one of the few Colombians still battling to keep his land on the Putumayo."

Spencer quickly looked back at Jordan. Dressed in an open-chested cream linen shirt, tan trousers, and customary, tall black boots, he appeared every inch the handsome, self-assured rubber baron. His green-eyed gaze collided with hers and momentarily flickered with the old fire. Then he coolly turned and gestured to a man seated at a small bamboo table, upon which rested an open bottle of brandy and two glasses. Spencer acknowledged the man with a smile and a nod. He was a short, coffee-colored gentleman in his mid-fifties, who appeared cordial and energetic. Rising, he held out a calloused hand and gave Spencer a warm grin.

"I am enchanted, Doutor O'Rourke. Please forgive my poor English. My Portuguese is also difficult to understand, but my English is worse. Since you don't speak Spanish, we will have to make do as best we can."

"I understand you perfectly, senhor, and I'm delighted to meet you. La Reserva is the name of your plantation? You must tell me all about it."

"With pleasure, *Doutor.*"

They all sat down. No sooner had they done so when a young girl in a simple calico frock padded out of the house in her bare feet and calmly began to serve a simple dinner of rice and beans. The girl was quite young, probably only in her early teens, and rather pretty with her large brown eyes, sweet round face, and very black hair. Her facial features were broad and somewhat flattened, leaving Spencer in little doubt she was Indian.

"And who is *this?*" she inquired, unable to keep a note of accusation out of her voice.

Jordan's mouth twitched in amusement at her tone. "I call her Mimi, though that's not her Indian name, of course. She's the daughter of one of the Huitoto Indians who now and then shows up looking for work. Since we had company tonight and you made yourself scarce all day, I put her to work preparing a passable meal."

Bristling at the implication that she had somehow been rude not to offer to cook dinner, Spencer glared at Jordan. "I'm sorry, but the hut needed all me attention. I worked all day on it. Unfortunately, I canna repair the roof by myself. I was hoping that tomorrow . . ."

"Se Deus querer." Jordan dismissed the complaint with a wave of his hand. "In case you don't know the meaning of that phrase, I'll tell you. It means 'if God wills,' a most popular and useful phrase among Brazilians, is it not, David?"

The Colombian grinned. "Ah, yes. If God but wills, we can do anything. And if He doesn't, we poor mortals are never to blame."

"It's not God I will blame if me roof is not fixed tomorrow," Spencer said darkly, then deciding she really was being rude, she turned to David Serrano. "Please tell me about La Reserva. I really am interested. Indeed, I wish to learn everything I can about life here in Amazonas."

"Alas, Doutor. La Reserva is not in Amazonas. My plantation lies outside the area belonging to Brazil. It is in territory belonging to Colombia but currently being claimed by Peru."

"It is on the Putumayo, then?"

"Yes, Doutor. It is not far from El Encanto, Don Arana's plantation, and that is the source of all my troubles."

Before the Colombian could say more, Jordan passed the bowl of steaming black beans to Spencer. "Have some beans, Doctor. And let poor David eat before you start grilling him about La Reserva."

Spencer served herself and passed the bowl to Serrano. The Indian girl, Mimi, brought her a brimming glassful of a sweet, sticky juice to drink with her meal, but the men continued swigging brandy. They ate for several moments in silent concentration, and Spencer noticed that David Serrano seemed somehow sad and distracted, as if his mind was elsewhere while he ate. Dark circles ringed his black eyes, and deep lines were etched on either side of his mouth.

When she had finished eating, she set down her fork. "And how many people do you employ at La Reserva, Senhor Serrano?"

"Forty-five families work for me there," the Colombian said. "Of course, they are scattered; each family has its own *estrada* to work. Some have left me and gone back to the jungle until things calm down at my plantation."

"You've had troubles, recently?"

"Sĩm, Doutor." David Serrano bowed his head and looked away, but not before Spencer saw the glint of tears in his eyes.

"David's wife and young son have been kidnapped and are being held prisoners at El Encanto," Jordan said bluntly.

"Oh, no, how awful!" Spencer burst out.

"Yes, it is—the bastards," Jordan growled under his breath.

Before Spencer could ask who had done such a terrible thing, Mimi served *cafẽzinhos,* the tiny cups of hot, sweet black coffee much beloved by nearly everyone in Brazil. While the men sipped the steaming concoction, she pursued the matter.

"But, how did it happen—and why?"

"I owed a debt to Don Julio César Arana, for supplies I bought at his trading post," Serrano said tiredly. "Arana assured me I did not have to pay for them until my next rubber harvest was sold. I should never have believed him. Now I see he only wanted an excuse to attack La Reserva."

"Arana himself attacked your plantation?"

"Not himself, no—but his overseer, Miguel Loazya. Loayza swept down on me with a gang of armed men, stole rubber valued at one thousand British pounds, and then . . ." His voice broke as he struggled to get out the words. ". . . and then he and his men raped my wife before my very eyes, laughed and jeered at me, and took both her and my son back with them to El Encanto."

"Blessed St. Brigid! Was there no way to fight them off?"

"None, senhorina. They overpowered me completely. There was no one there except myself, my family, and a handful of *seringueiros.* The rest of my workers were all on their *estradas,* gathering the rubber. Even had they been there, they would not have been much good. I employ mostly Indians, and they are terrified of anyone from El Encanto. The tales of cruelty to the Indians there are known everywhere along the Putumayo and even beyond."

In the midst of her shock, Spencer was conscious of Jordan's eyes upon her, gauging her reaction. She bit down hard on her lower lip, gathered her thoughts, then continued calmly. "Have you notified the authorities? Surely they will come and help you rescue your wife and son, then punish this Loayza and also Don Arana, if he is indeed responsible."

Serrana gave a bitter laugh. "What authorities? There is no authority on the Putumayo except for the Winchester .44. And who would help me rescue my wife anyway? She is Indian, my son is half Indian, and even if you are new to the area, you must have heard the old saying: *'Son animales, senõr; no son gentes.'* In Spanish, that means, 'They are animals, sir, not people.' "

"Why, I canna believe everyone feels that way! I certainly don't, and I know Jordan doesna, either."

"I've already offered to go with him to help rescue his wife and son," Jordan said quietly. "But David has refused. I can well understand why; we probably wouldn't get out of there, alive."

"Then you intend to just leave them at the mercy of those awful men?" Spencer demanded incredulously.

Tears streamed down Serrano's cheeks. Helplessly he shrugged. "What else can I do, senhorina? Our workers are not fighters. They are not trained to use firearms. And El Encanto is very well guarded. On my way here to tell Jordano what happened, I saw Don Arana's launch, the *Liberal,* patroling the river. Aboard were more than fifty Peruvian soldiers, fresh from Iquitos. I'll wager they are here on the excuse of 'protecting' Arana's holdings but actually came to wage war on us Colombians. One way or another, Peru hopes to gain complete control of the Putumayo rubber lands—even if they have to destroy us to get them."

"I think you are right, my friend." Jordan poured another shot of brandy for the weeping Colombian. "The appearance of Peruvian soldiers can only mean war between Peru and Colombia—war that will probably spread as far as my place. In fact, it already has. It was probably those very soldiers who opened fire on us before we got here. In the jungle, it's hard to distinguish property lines."

To Spencer, it seemed as if both men were losing sight of the main issue: a woman who had been raped and kidnapped, along with her child.

"I canna believe something cannot be done to rescue yer wife and son," she blurted.

"It may be that something can be done," Serrano conceded. "But I am not the one to do it."

"Who, then?" Spencer probed.

"When last I went to Manaus, I found mail awaiting me from relatives in Colombia. They said an emissary from my government had been appointed to come here and assess our problems, in hopes that the growing land dispute can be settled peaceably. His name is Don Jesus Orjuela. He is a man with powerful connections and a respected reputation as a conciliator. At this very moment, he may be en route to the area. When he comes, I shall tell him what has happened. If anyone can obtain my family's freedom, it is Don Orjuela. I just hope he gets here before Arana's men return to my plantation to finish what they started."

"This is incredible!" Spencer rose to her feet, unable to believe what she was hearing. Here was proof of Don Julio César Arana's wickedness—eye-witness proof. Yet, neither Serrano nor Jordan seemed capable of putting a stop to it, or even trying to put a stop to it. Instead, they sat drinking brandy, bemoaning the injustice of it all but unwilling to really do anything.

All her life, Spencer had been an activist, wading into waters over her head, as her father had always put it, battling forces much bigger and stronger than she was. To learn of an injustice was to seek to right it, just as she had sought to right the injustice of discrimination against women in the medical profession. The more people had tried to discourage her, the more determined she had been to gain the status of doctor and practice medicine, come what may.

If Jordan and Serrano lacked sufficient physical force to stop Arana, then they must look for some other means of doing so—not merely wait for some obscure government official to arrive on the scene.

"Why doesna someone document Arana's cruelties and expose him t' the world at large?" she demanded of Jordan. When he didn't immediately answer, she hurled another question. "T' whom will the rubber stolen from Senhor Serrano be sold?"

"To the regular buyers," Jordan muttered. "He'll sell it to mostly American and British manufacturers of automobile tires and other rubber products."

"Wouldna these people cease doing business with him if they knew how he obtained his rubber?"

A frown furrowed Jordan's brow. "I'm not sure they'd care how he obtained his rubber."

"But you canna be sure they wouldn't care, either, can you?" Spencer saw by his expression he had never thought of the problem in this light. Other ideas began popping in her head: Did Arana have financial underwriters—investors in his business? And if he did, who were they? How would they feel about Arana's thug, Loayza, stealing rubber, raping women, and mistreating workers?

As if he could read her thoughts, Jordan shook his head. "Spencer, you could collect a whole boatload of information about Arana, and it still wouldn't do any good. Nobody would believe you. Worse yet, if they did, they'd just ignore it and go on with business as usual."

"Only cowards 'go on with business as usual,' and all men are not cowards."

Though Spencer did not mean it quite that way, it sounded as if she were accusing Jordan and Serrano of being cowards. She could have clarified her statement, but by then, she didn't care how she sounded. She was angry about Serrano's wife and son, angry that nobody was doing anything about it. What good were a man's tears if he wasn't ready to risk his life to save his own wife and child? Maybe David Serrano was a coward, after all. She looked at the Colombian's tear-streaked face and softly repeated, "No, Senhor Serrano, all men are not cowards."

He dropped his chin and looked away, unable to meet her gaze. Having nothing more to say to either man, Spencer spun on her heel and left the veranda.

Chapter Ten

"Good-bye, my friend . . . be careful," Jordan admonished as he held out his hand to David Serrano for a farewell handshake. The two were standing on the dock in the light of a murky dawn, and David Serrano's face was downcast, his eyes haunted, as he prepared to climb down into his *batelão*. Obviously he had not slept well, Jordan thought.

"Good-bye, Jordano," the Colombian said, clasping Jordan's hand. "Thank you for your good advice, but be sure to heed it yourself. Paraĩso is as vulnerable as La Reserva, and I do not think Arana will stop with us poor Colombians. Your land is every bit as valuable as mine—perhaps more so. It is also convenient."

"Don't worry. I'll keep my Winchester close at hand. Just remember what I told you: Don't take any foolish risks. If you change your mind about going after your wife, let me know, and I'll go with you. Don't let Dr. O'Rourke's attitudes influence what you do or don't do. She doesn't understand the situation. Women always underestimate danger and oversimplify complex matters."

"I am not a fool, Jordano. You and I are no

match for a man as powerful and influential as Arana. Were we to fight him without using guns, as Dr. O'Rourke suggests, we could not win. It would only be our word against his, assuming we lived long enough to tell our story. Besides . . . we must keep our priorities in order, must we not? I came here to get rich on rubber. That is the most important thing. Much as I love my wife and son, I cannot protect them from the sad destiny imposed by their birthright. My wife was doomed before ever I met her, and our children are also doomed. In our lifetime, we will see the Huitotos disappear from the face of the earth. I mourn this sad fact, but I cannot change it. I am only one man; I cannot fight the inevitable."

"You're probably right, my friend—at least, about the rubber. As soon as I get enough money to make a new start in the United States, I'm getting out of here. Arana can have Paraïso, if he still wants it. In a few years, the opportunities here will no longer exist. As soon as the British rubber trees in Asia start producing, we'll be finished. Big as he is, Arana himself won't be able to withstand the competition."

Serrano frowned. "How much longer do you think we have?"

"My guess is only a few more years—a decade, at most. The British have done everything possible to cloak their activities in secrecy, but everyone knows about the seventy thousand high-grade rubber seeds Henry Alexander Wickham managed to smuggle out of Brazil. Of course, with all the mistakes he made, most of the seed has gone to waste. But enough survived for British botanists to finally figure out how best to cultivate them. By now, the young trees should be maturing on plantations in Maláya and Ceylon. Soon, they'll be ready to produce. Trust the British to persevere. Brazil, Peru, and Colombia don't stand a chance against the determination of the English. Given all the secrecy, I've been following the situation as closely as I can."

Serrano's frown grew deeper. "I imagine Don Arana follows it, as well. He, too, must know that time is running out. Why else is he so cruel—so relentless? If we do not make our fortunes before the bottom falls out of the Amazon rubber market, we will all fail. I myself have spent half my life in this 'green hell' and thus far have little to show for it."

"In some ways, we've wasted our lives pursuing this dream," Jordan somberly agreed. "You at least have known the joy of a wife and child, though you may have lost them both—but I've never experienced either. Sometimes, I feel I'm only half a man."

The Colombian suddenly grinned, his normally ebullient personality resurfacing. "Is that why you brought the red-haired doctor to Paraĩso? I know you said it was because Paraĩso has need of her services. But as soon as I saw her, I wondered. Latin women have never appealed to you, but here is an *Americana,* a woman of your own country, one who seems to match you in fire and spirit."

"I assure you marriage never crossed my mind when I agreed to let Dr. O'Rourke come to Paraĩso," Jordan denied. His friend's observation amazed him, but he also recognized the possible truth of it. "Ever since I made the decision, I've been regretting it. Now that the danger from Arana has increased, I'm even more worried—and angry. She had no right to say the things she said to you last night. Her ignorance is appalling, and her manners worse. After you leave, I intend to have a word with her. Believe me, this is the last time she'll insult one of my guests."

"Calm yourself, my friend. She is a woman, and women have enormous, tender hearts but limited intellects. They are incapable of seeing the broader picture, as we men must do. You and I know that I must go back to La Reserva and fight to hold what is mine, but Doctor O'Rourke sees only that my wife and son are in the hands of a vicious man and must be rescued. Who knows? Perhaps she is right. The world may not agree that the life of an Indian woman and a half-breed child are worth more than a fortune in rubber, but it may be true. It is certainly true that no matter what I say or am compelled to do, I will always mourn the loss of them. I won't be able to live with myself if they are never rescued. Always, I will awaken in the night, calling their names . . ." His voice trailed off. Once again, he blinked back tears.

"Let us hope Don Jesus Orjuela will be able to secure their release," Jordan soothed. "In the meantime, until he arrives here, we must both keep a sharp lookout. Incidences of violence or 'unexplainable accidents' may well increase."

"We have both lost good men, Jordano. But do not worry about me; I am developing eyes in the back of my head. And if I ever catch Miguel Loayza alone in the forest, he is a dead man."

"I'll kill him for you, David. I swear to you that if I ever get the chance, I'll kill him on your behalf."

The two men shook hands, then David Serrano climbed down into his *batelão,* slipped the mooring line, and shoved away from the dock. As Jordan watched him paddle away, he waved. Serrano waved back—a single, solitary gesture, almost like a salute. Sadness and anxiety swept Jordan; he might never see his Colombian friend again. Serrano had been helpless to prevent the capture of his family; if Arana or Loayza returned to kill him, how could his friend defend himself?

Spencer was standing on a rickety ladder trying to maneuver a piece of makeshift thatching into place on the roof when Jordan suddenly shouted her name, followed closely by a question. "What in hell do you think you're doing up there?"

Glancing over her shoulder, she gave him a chilly stare and resolved to keep her temper—and her brogue—in check. "What does it look like? I'm repairing this roof. If it rains before I get it finished, all my things will be soaked."

"Damn my aunt Milly's corset! Does nothing at all deter you from your plotted course?"

"Not if I can help it. Would you mind handing me another piece of thatch? I'm almost finished with this one."

She heard a rustling sound, then Jordan was standing at the foot of the ladder, handing up a mass of woven palm fronds. "You call this thatch? It's the worst workmanship I've ever seen; it'll never keep out the rain."

"It's better than nothing and will at least provide some shelter until I can improve my skills."

Jordan rattled the thatching. "You wove this?"

"Of course. Your new overseer, Luiz, has been

far too busy to help me, and no one else has offered. I admit it's clumsily done, but I'll soon get the knack of it. All I had to go by was the thatching already on the roof."

"Amazing," Jordan clipped. "Simply amazing. It seems you are as handy with your hands as you are quick with your tongue. You've spent less than twenty-four hours at Paraîso, and already you can thatch a roof and give sound advice on how to handle all our problems."

His sarcasm gave Spencer pause. After placing the second piece of thatching in the spot where she intended to tie it down, she hiked up her skirt and descended the ladder. When she reached the ground, she confronted Jordan with hands on hips. "I presume you are referring to Senhor Serrano's problems—namely, the capture of his wife and son."

"I'm certainly not referring to the big cockroaches in your hut, though I must admit that particular problem is bigger than I thought." Jordan stamped his foot to remove one from his boot.

Spencer lifted her own boot and brought it down hard on the offensive creature. The resulting crunch was loud in the sudden silence. "I'm not afraid of cockroaches. Did you think I would be?" she asked challengingly.

In fact, she had spent the night jumping at every scurrying sound and had hardly slept a wink for fear of ants invading her hammock as they had that night in the jungle. But she was not about to admit her fears to Jordan King.

"Arana is a far more dangerous adversary than a mere cockroach," Jordan growled. "The way you insulted David Serrano—and me—last night was inexcusable. Neither of us are cowards, simply because we recognize the power of that man."

"I disagree." Spencer forgot all about her resolution to curb her temper. "What is inexcusable is that both of ye are allowing him t' get away with his crimes!"

Jordan regarded her through half-slit eyes, his mouth twisted into a furious snarl. "Would you prefer to see us both dead? That's what would happen if we were so foolish as to try bearding the lion in his den."

"I would prefer to see the man I first saw in Manaus—the one who stood up to Arana and belittled him in front of his cultured friends. Did ye mean what ye said that day—the threats ye made? Or were you only posturin', flexin' your muscles but never really meanin' t' thrash the bully?"

"Damn it, woman! You do know how to slip the knife between the ribs and twist it, don't you?" Jordan's face flushed a dark red color.

"It comes with bein' a doctor," Spencer retorted. "I am well acquainted with the more tender portions of the anatomy—*and* the psyche."

"Just what in hell do you propose that I do about Arana?"

"Expose him!" Spencer all but shouted. "Everyone with whom he does business—everyone who buys his rubber—must be told what sort of man he is. All his wickedness and ugliness must see the light of day. If there's a cancer or infection eating away a person's insides, a surgeon must excise it. In the darkness; evil can only grow and fester, but once exposed t' sunlight . . ."

"And how in God's name am I supposed to do that?" Jordan roared.

"Well, ye're an intelligent man, Mr. King, and ye claim t' know this country far better than I. I'm sure if ye put yer mind to it, ye could think of something."

"Meo Deus! You're an impossible woman!" More angry than she had ever seen him, Jordan raked his fingers through his hair. Then he stalked around the hut, muttering to himself. Finally, he returned to stand accusingly in front of her. "All right, Doctor, I'll think of something! But if anyone gets hurt because of it, the blame will lie on your shoulders. Is that clearly understood?"

Spencer had a sudden mental image of Jordan lying wounded and bleeding on the jungle floor; what if he did something reckless because of her goading? What if he got himself or someone else killed?

"I'm not asking ye t' storm into El Encanto and start shootin' people . . ." she backtracked. "I'm merely suggestin' that we . . . we collect evidence of Arana and Loayza's wrong doing and present it t' the proper parties—people who have the power to stop him."

"And you think such evidence will be easy to come by."

"Why should it be so difficult? Senhor Serrano himself will make a good witness."

"If he lives long enough."

"Why shouldna he? He turned down your offer t' help rescue his wife. It seems t' me he's quite determined to guard his own life."

"And is that some sort of crime?"

"Of course not. But if a man truly loves a woman, he'll go to any lengths t' rescue her. And for his own child—why, he'll walk through the gates of hell."

Jordan stood and stared at her as if she were spouting some sort of nonsense. Then he sighed. "Arguing with you is like whistling in a windstorm. It's impossible to match your gusty logic. You just blow everything away with a few well-chosen words."

Spencer knew he did not mean it as a compliment, but she believed what she was saying and would not back down one inch. "Would ye allow another man t' rape and kidnap yer wife, t' enslave your son? Would ye walk away and let him have them, while there was still breath in yer body t' fight?"

After a short pause, Jordan said softly, "No . . . I suppose I wouldn't. But I don't condemn another man for feeling differently."

"I do," Spencer said. "Last night, I dinna mean t' insult him—or ye. But then I thought about it all night long and realized that people like Arana and Loayza exist because they're allowed to get away with what they do. There must be a way t' stop them."

Jordan looked suddenly weary. "I'll think about it, Spencer. That's all I can promise. I'll think about it."

As Spencer watched him walk away, she thought she ought to have felt victorious, but she did not. She was meddling in affairs about which she knew little or nothing, and more violence could likely be the result. Having succeeded in fanning the fires of Jordan's rage—the rage she had first witnessed at the hotel in Manaus—she might come to regret it. Could she keep him to a course of rational, carefully considered risks? Or would he suddenly explode and do something foolish, sacrificing lives in the process? Even stopping Arana wasn't worth that.

Dear Saint Brigid, she thought, trembling. *What have I done? What in heaven's name have I done?*

As Jordan went about the business of Paraïso—assigning workers to this or that job, planning a schedule of visits to the various *estradas,* and training Luiz to take over the duties formerly performed by Raymundo—his mind replayed his argument with Spencer and shuffled possibilities for dealing with Arana. It angered him that she had gone right to the heart of the matter, saying things he himself had been feeling but had not had the courage to put into words. *Arana must be stopped.* Somehow, someway, the man had to be stopped. It was long past time.

It was also true what she had said about David Serrano. Jordan could not imagine abandoning his wife and child, if he had one, to the mercies of Miguel Loayza. His pride alone would force him to try and rescue them—and if he loved them as much as a man should love his family, he would not be able to eat or sleep until they were safe again. Not even his greed for rubber would keep him from seeking retribution.

Yet he could not completely condemn Serrano, as Spencer did. Serrano's wife was, after all, an Indian, whom most whites regarded as less than human. While Jordan felt sympathy for the plight of the Huitotos and treated his own workers with fairness and kindness, he had no idea how to fight prejudice that ran so deep, and had never thought of trying to fight it. Serrano himself was prejudiced. The Colombian had loved and married an Indian, but his head still warred with his heart. When and if Serrano ever returned to his own country to live, he would not take along his Indian wife and half-breed son. Other *seringueiros* in his situation never did. Some had two families—one in the jungle and another in whatever town they had originally come from. Such arrangements were commonplace and no longer even raised eyebrows.

So what was he going to do about Arana? Jordan asked himself. Thus far, with the exception of Serrano's most recent experience, everything Jordan had heard about Don Julio César Arana was mere rumor. Nothing could be proven. No one of Jordan's acquaintance had personally witnessed Miguel Loayza torturing Indians, nor could he himself be absolutely certain that Loayza had killed Francisco with the poison dart. How was he to go about obtaining indisputable evidence?

Only one idea occurred to him: going to El Encanto and discovering with his own eyes what conditions there were really like. Later, assuming he survived the experience, he could figure out what to do with the information he obtained. Brazilian authorities would not be interested in anything happening outside of Brazil's boundaries, and Peruvian authorities would be understandably reluctant to arrest a leading citizen engaged in establishing Peru's claims to some very rich territory. Only the Colombian government might be outraged, but as yet, Colombia had done nothing to protect its own citizens, let alone fight for the rights of savages.

That left only Arana's investors and the foreign companies who bought his rubber. Spencer's idea was not a bad one, Jordan realized, but he had no illusions that what she was suggesting would be easy. First he would have to find out exactly who was involved. Then he would have to figure out the best way to approach them. Whether or not his "evidence" would be believed was another matter; Arana would claim he was lying. But no matter how the whole thing turned out, at least Jordan would know he had tried, and he could face Spencer O'Rourke without flinching and feeling guilty.

Why did he care so much for Spencer's opinion of him anyway? Jordan wondered disgustedly. He was not in love with the woman—or was he? No, she was simply the only white woman for hundreds of miles in any direction. He had come to admire and respect her, albeit grudgingly, and also to enjoy her prickly, challenging company. More than anything, he wanted to take her to bed. Something about her compelled him to think of lovemaking whenever he looked at her. Maybe it was her obvious innocence—or her stubborn resistance to his charms. Whatever it was, he found himself wanting to kiss her senseless and storm all her defenses, one by one. She was a conquest he could not resist.

Action was the only way to deal with the whole problem, he decided. This very day, he would load a *batelão* with supplies and ammunition, and coach Luiz on what to do in his absence. Then, first thing in the morning, he would embark on the long journey up the Putumayo to El Encanto. By launch, if he dared take the *Evangeline,* the trip would take two days in good weather. By *batelão,* he was looking at three or four days of weary paddling, during which he would have to elude the

Liberal, Arana's big launch, and stay out of sight of his men. With luck, he ought to be back at Paraïso in eight to ten days. Once he got to El Encanto, he would allow himself only a full day to spy on the doings of the rubber depot. More than that would be subjecting himself to too great a risk of discovery.

Not looking forward to the trip, Jordan sighed. There was so much to be done right here; all of his *estradas* needed checking, and the rubber being made at them had to be collected and brought down to the river for transportation the next time he returned to Manaus. Maybe Luiz could take a man or two and begin doing that while he was gone.

He sighed again. If he was indeed in love with Spencer O'Rourke, he did not much care for the condition. She was the only reason he was even thinking of spying on El Encanto. And the worst thing about it was that he dare not tell her where he was going and why. If he did, she'd demand to accompany him—and that, Jordan realized, was the last thing he needed on such a dangerous, foolhardy mission.

Chapter Eleven

After another uncomfortable night in her half-patched hut, wherein the folly of thinking she could complete repairs by herself was made clear to her during a brief, predawn shower, Spencer went looking for Jordan. He would simply have to assign some workers to help her finish the roof. The section she had already fixed leaked excessively; a cascade of cold water pouring down into her face had awakened her that morning.

"Luiz!" she called, spying the overseer crossing the misty area between two buildings. "Have you seen Senhor Rei yet this morning?"

"Sĩm, senhorinha. He is down on the dock. If you hurry, you can catch him before he leaves."

"Leaves? Where is he going?"

"He said I was not to tell you, senhorinha. However, he did not say I couldn't tell you he was leaving."

"But—how long will he be gone?"

"More than one week, less than two weeks. One can never say with certainty on the river."

"A whole week?" Spencer was outraged. Jordan had never told her he was going anywhere, and the fact that he did not want her to know his destination made her immediately suspicious and fearful. Her stomach muscles knotted, and her palms grew moist. Breaking into a run, she caught up to him just as he was climbing into the *batelão* tied up next to the *Evangeline.*

"I demand t' know where ye're goin'!" she cried, eyeing the supplies he had packed and the extra cases of cartridges for his Winchester.

"Uh, oh . . ." Jordan said. "I had hoped to be gone by the time you caught wind of this trip."

"It has something t' do with Arana, doesna it?" she guessed by his guilty expression. "Ye're goin' t' do somethin' foolish and ill-considered."

Jordan's face darkened, and his eyes turned the murky green color that signaled anger. "Make up your mind what you want, Spencer. One minute you're calling me a coward, and the next you're accusing me of being a fool. Yes, this trip has something to do with Arana, but exactly what is none of your business."

"It most certainly is my business! I . . . I goaded ye into this, and I'm not sure I should have. Please . . . tell me where ye're going."

"To El Encanto. But all I'm going to do is take a look around the place—secretly, of course. Once and for all, I'm going to find out if the stories I've heard are true or not. Won't you feel ashamed if I discover that all of Arana's workers are happy and well fed? I know I will."

"They won't be," Spencer said with certainty. "Dinna forget Senhor Serrano's wife and son; they certainly aren't willing workers. Ye're not goin' alone, are ye?"

"I am," Jordan calmly responded. "Alone there's

less chance of my getting caught. Besides, I can't spare anyone from Paraïso. Luiz is the only one who can handle firearms proficiently, and I need him too much here."

"Then I shall accompany ye. Wait right here until I fetch a few things."

"You are not coming with me!"

"Oh, yes I am. If I have to, I'll take me own *batelão* and follow ye; I'll take that one right over there." She pointed to one of the canoes drawn up on shore. "But it really would be better if we shared the same one; that way I can help with the paddlin'. I also suspect ye might find need of my medical services."

"Forget it, Spencer. No way in hell will I permit you to come."

"No way in heaven can ye stop me. What if ye come down with an attack of malaria? What if Loayza shoots ye? Not only might ye need a doctor, but ye'll also need a competent witness. How can it be so dangerous if all we're goin' to do is *spy?*"

"Oh, God," Jordan moaned, rolling his eyes heavenward. "Why, me? Why have you saddled me with this stubborn, meddlesome female?"

"Jordan, be reasonable. I promise to be a help, not a hindrance. Spying on El Encanto is a wonderful idea. That way we can find out for certain just how bad things are. Then we can record our observations and have an attorney witness them the next time we're in Manaus. We'll get David Serrano to make out a deposition also. And when we've collected enough, we'll take them to . . . to the newspapers! I bet if we tell the newspapers what's going on . . ."

"No more! Go get your things. I will give you exactly five minutes to collect what you need. Bring quinine. And writing materials. Your job will be to keep us both healthy and record what we see. Everything else is up to me. You will not do the actual spying. If I have to, I'll tie you to a tree in the jungle. You'll stay where I tell you and wait until I come back."

"If ye insist, Jordan," Spencer demurred, thinking she could fight that battle later, after this one was safely won.

"I do insist. I mean it. You'll hide in the jungle while I do the actual spying. And there won't be any foolishness about where we sleep, either. You'll sling your hammock where I tell you to . . ."

For the first time, Spencer realized exactly what she was volunteering for—another week or two alone with Jordan in the jungle. But just as the journey to Paraïso had been worth the obvious risks, so also was this journey. This one trip might be all it would take to gain enough evidence to stop Arana's cruelties. If they were able to verify every shocking detail—and to supply the information where it would do the most good—they might eventually see justice done. As Americans, she reasoned, their opinions were bound to count more than a Colombian's who owed a debt to Arana.

"I trust ye t' behave like a perfect gentleman," she said stiffly. "Do ye swear to that?"

"If you trust me, why do I have to swear to it?" The old jauntiness flashed in his jungle-green eyes, then his gaze bored into hers. "No, Spencer, I'll take no oaths I can't be sure of keeping. If you insist on coming, you come at your own peril."

Half-hypnotized, she could feel the very air quiver with the peculiar electricity that seemed to characterize their relationship. "I'll get my things," she murmured, trying to keep her voice from betraying her mingled anxiety and excitement. "And wherever I sleep, I'll keep me pistol close by."

His mouth quirked upward in a mocking grin. "Do that, Doc. Never know when you might need it."

Their first night away from Paraîso, it rained in torrents that nearly swamped the *batelão*. Huddled beneath the small thatched roof that leaked almost as badly as the roof of her hut, Spencer was untroubled by Jordan's proximity—at least, in a sexual sense. All he did was growl and complain, calling their mission a "fool's errand," and himself the biggest fool of all for once again allowing her to talk him into something of which he deeply disapproved.

Finally, she could take his grumbling no longer. "Oh, be quiet!" she hissed. "I'm as wet as ye are, and if I can stand it, ye can stand it."

"It's not the rain that's bothering me," he clarified. "It's you. If I were alone, I could tie up near shore, get drunk on *cachaça,* and sleep through this whole miserable night."

"That would be sheer lunacy! Anything could happen while ye were sleeping. Loayza could come and take ye prisoner, or a boa could drop out of the trees into the *batelão*."

"Who the hell cares? Right now, I'd welcome the

diversion."

"If ye feel that awful, go ahead and have a drink of *cachaça*. Maybe it will improve your mood."

"I didn't bring any. Plumb forgot it, more's the pity."

"Then why are ye blamin' me for yer discomfort? Even if I weren't here, ye couldna get drunk."

A low chuckle came to her in the inky, damp darkness. Somehow, his hand found her knee. "I guess I was hoping you'd take pity on me and grant me some other distraction from my misery."

She slapped his hand away. "Well, I won't, so ye can forget the whole idea."

"All right, if you won't make love to me, won't you at least talk to me? Words aren't nearly as effective as kisses, but tonight, I'm desperate."

"What do ye want to talk about?"

"You. What kind of little girl were you? What made you want to be a doctor when you grew up?"

So Spencer told him her life history—all about the mother she never knew, and the way she grew up hanging on her father's coattails, fascinated by the way he could make people feel better and fix their broken bones. In the darkness with only the sound of the rain pelting the thatch, it was easy to unburden herself, and she related things she had never told another living soul. It was almost as if she were talking to herself instead of to Jordan.

"I'm not really certain when me da's drinkin' began t' get out of hand. Before I went to medical school, he was only drinkin' socially, but by the time I returned, he had begun t' drink with real compulsion. Fortunately I was able t' step in and take over the practice, so that no one was ever harmed by a wrong diagnosis or me da's hands shakin' when he performed surgery. That's what made it so bitter after he died; for five years, I had been doing all the work and making the important decisions. But as soon as he was gone, people quit coming."

"Was your father a congenial man?" Jordan's voice startled her. He had been so quiet during her long recital she had begun to think he had fallen asleep.

"Yes, he was most congenial, always smilin' and friendly, always seemin' t' be deeply concerned, even when he was too drunk t' know what was wrong with a patient."

"Well, then, that's why people stopped coming to you after he died. They came in the first place because they liked and trusted your father. After his death, they quit coming because they had never really warmed up to you."

"But I'm so much more competent than me da was near the end of his life! And I'm certainly far more competent than me main rival—Seamus O'Brien."

"Ah, but you aren't congenial. If anything, you're as stiff and rigid as a stick. Instead of reassuring people, you intimidate them. You hardly ever smile. Sometimes, I wonder if you're human like the rest of us."

"Of course I'm human!"

"But not subject to the normal, human temptations—the desire for intimacy, sex, good food and wine . . . all the small comforts and niceties of life."

"But that's not true! I'm not like that a-tall!"

"Aren't you? When was the last time you really savored something, Spencer—the feel of silk gliding across your naked flesh, for example, or the taste of something cold and wet on your tongue? When was the last time you allowed yourself to enjoy life?"

"I enjoy life every day," she protested, though it occurred to her that she had never felt silk on her bare flesh, and the last cold, wet thing she had appreciated was the lemonade at the Grand Hotel Internacional. Even then, she had felt guilty about it.

"Maybe you do," Jordan sighed. "In your own peculiar way. But I think you're missing out on an awful lot. In your determination to be completely self-sufficient and prove yourself equal in every way to men, you've denied yourself simple, basic satisfactions."

"I presume we're talkin' about sex again. It always comes back to that, doesna it? Just because I refuse t' join ye in yer hammock, ye think there's something wrong with me."

"You wouldn't join any man in his hammock—not just me. You're afraid of your own sexuality."

"If I ever find the right man, I'll join him without a second thought."

"And what kind of man would that be? Who could ever measure up to your high standards?"

"What woman could ever measure up to yers? I dinna mean as a lover, but as a wife. Why aren't ye married? Ye are, I suspect, even older than I am—a confirmed bachelor, which is a nicer term than spinster but means the same, in any case."

"Just never found the right woman, I suppose.

And I have been locked away in the jungle for the past several years. However, the difference between you and me is that at least I'm still looking. You, on the other hand, gave up hope long ago."

"I'm thinkin' I've had enough of this conversation," Spencer snapped. "It's time we got some sleep."

"You see? Every time I get too close to you, you retreat."

"I'm tired, Jordan. Will ye please stop badgerin' me?"

"I'm not badgering you. I'm sitting here as innocently as a choirboy, staying on my own side of the *batelão,* and not laying so much as a finger on you."

"Ye are anything but innocent! And just in case ye've forgotten, I have me pistol right here in me pocket."

"You don't need a pistol, Spencer. Your tongue is weapon enough. All right . . . I'll leave you alone, if that's what you really want. At least now, after you've told me how you grew up, I understand you better."

"What do ye mean?" Spencer demanded, instantly wary and regretting that she had talked so much.

"The reason you don't know how to act like a woman is because you never knew a woman's influence. You only had your father, and apparently he neglected you."

"He dinna neglect me! At least, not when I was younger."

"Well, someone neglected you, Spencer. You don't know a thing about love, poor girl."

"And I suppose ye do!"

"Oh, I admit I have my limitations, but I'm trying hard to overcome them."

"Good luck!" Spencer spat.

After that, silence fell. Huddled against a piece of wet canvas, Spencer closed her eyes and tried to sleep. This was only their first night, but already the journey was proving long and arduous. She should have known Jordan would use it to continue his campaign to seduce her; she *had* known it. What she had not known was how vulnerable she was on every front. Tonight he had learned more about her than she had ever permitted any man to learn—and he had managed to do it without revealing anything about himself. That worried and frightened her; it had not been a fair exchange.

Tomorrow, she must be more on her guard. Jordan King must not be allowed to learn all her secrets while his own remained safely locked away. That he had secrets, she did not doubt. What did she really know about him anyway? His past was a complete mystery. For all she knew, he might have a wife and children back in the United States. Her mind recoiled from the image of a beautiful woman with iron-clad claims on him, but still, the possibility existed, bringing an icy chill to her heart. *Please God, don't let him be married,* she prayed without thinking—then was shocked to real ize she cared so much.

In the morning, they turned up the Putumayo and discovered that the smaller river was alive with anacondas. Spencer was leaning over the bow of the *batelão,* watching for submerged tree branches and roots, when a huge, triangular head and several feet of undulating body appeared beside the boat.

"Oh, my goodness! What a huge snake!" she shrieked.

Instantly, Jordan was beside her, rifle in hand. "I bet it's forty feet long," he speculated, taking careful aim at a spot roughly ten feet behind the big head.

"What are ye doin'?" Spencer shoved aside the barrel of the Winchester. "Why must ye kill it?"

"Because it's a monster, that's why. It could tip us over if it wanted to, or wrap itself around the *batelão* and crush it to pieces and us with it."

"Oh, no, there's another one!" She pointed to a second triangular head. Then they saw a third and a fourth.

"Good God, start paddling! We're in a nest of them!"

Jumping to obey the order, Spencer hurriedly made her way to the back of the vessel, which was now lurching and rocking, due to the big serpents. All around them were undulating coils, most of which were twelve inches or more in diameter. While she grabbed the paddle and began paddling, Jordan stood in the bow, sighting down the barrel of his Winchester. She wondered what would happen if he opened fire. Would the shots enrage the snakes, provoking them into attack?

She remembered hearing that anacondas could be quite aggressive, especially when injured. Surely Jordan knew that. Fortunately, the ugly reptiles seemed to be playing about the canoe. They rolled over and over beneath it, jostling it furiously, but otherwise not harming it.

"Won't ye sit down now?" Spencer called to Jordan, fearing he would be tipped overboard from the violent rocking.

"I can't tell which snake is which," he complained. "And if I shoot one, the rest might turn on us."

"Dinna shoot," Spencer pleaded. "Instead, why don't ye sit down and help me paddle? It's the only way we can get free of 'em."

Finally Jordan did as she asked. For several minutes, they paddled hard and fast, skimming over the tops of the snakes and bumping into them in a frantic effort to escape the huge coils. At last they eluded them, but continued to paddle as fast as they could. For the rest of the day, they kept a close watch on the muddy, greenish-brown waters of the Putumayo, spotting many more snakes, and other water creatures, as well.

Late in the afternoon, just as Spencer was starting to relax, she saw another large creature trailing in their wake.

"Jordan! What's that thing?"

He hurried to the stern, rifle at the ready, then laughed when he saw where she was pointing. "Oh, that's nothing to fear. It's only a *bufeo*."

"But it looks so . . . so human."

The huge creature had a large, jowly face that reminded Spencer of an old man with whiskers. But as it cavorted behind the *batelão*, she saw that it had prominent breasts and front flippers like a seal.

"What on earth *is* a *bufeo?*" she questioned.

"It's a member of the manatee species. It follows boats the way porpoises will and is said to be good eating, but I've never fancied killing something that looks so much like someone's benevolent old grandma. Though generally docile, it's anything but helpless. They've been known to attack and kill crocodiles and 'gators."

Despite the stifling heat, Spencer shivered. River travel in a *batelão* was certainly far different than on a launch, where the wildlife could be viewed from a safe distance. Here, on this smaller river in this smaller boat, the wildlife was everpresent and close enough to touch. Huge wasp nests hung low over the water, and there were also the cunning, clay-domed domiciles of a bird called the *hornero,* which Jordan pointed out to her.

"Now there's an interesting and sadistic little creature," he said. "Another bird called a *tavachi,* a member of the cuckoo family, likes to usurp the nest of the *hornero* whenever possible. But the *hornero* knows how to gain its revenge. Upon returning to its nest and finding it occupied by an intruder, it simply walls in the entranceway with clay, sealing the invader inside, where presumably it suffocates."

"I suppose nature has its reasons for everything," Spencer observed calmly, though she again felt a cold chill.

"I suppose it does," Jordan agreed. "But after living in Amazonas, I've come to believe that Mother Nature has very few maternal qualities. She's quite a bloodthirsty tyrant in this part of the world, or else we only notice it more here."

Late in the afternoon, a cloud of tiny, stinging

insects, almost too small to see, enveloped the *batelão,* and Spencer and Jordan were unable to paddle out of them. The minuscule creatures might have been a variety of mosquito or perhaps fly, but whatever they were, they soon made life miserable. It was impossible to breathe without inhaling them. They invaded the hair, eyes, nose, and mouth. Spencer and Jordan struggled into concealing clothing, but the pests managed to penetrate even that, driving both their victims into a frenzy of slapping, cursing, and muttering.

With darkness, the tiny insects disappeared, but the relief was short-lived as the larger mosquitoes went to work. Spencer hung netting over the little, roofed shelter and miserably huddled inside, slapping at the creatures who managed to join her. Jordan crawled in beside her, but they were too miserable even to eat. The only advantage to the situation was that seduction was clearly out of the question. Nor did conditions improve the following day. The no-see-ums were back with a vengeance, until both Spencer and Jordan were praying for more rain to clear the sultry air.

By nightfall, their prayers were answered and then some. A full day and night of heavy rain soaked everything in the *batelão* and convinced Spencer that her own skin might sprout a layer of greenish mildew. The miserable weather slowed them down considerably, but also kept Loayza off the river. They saw no signs of the *Liberal* or anyone else, and two days later were able to tie up in a sheltered spot quite close to El Encanto.

"This is where we part company," Jordan said to her on the steamy morning after their arrival. It was cloudy but not raining, an ideal day for conducting clandestine investigations.

"I'll just come with you part way." Trying to remain calm, Spencer tied down the veil of her bonnet to keep out the no-see-ums, should they return.

"No, you won't You'll stay here out of sight, near the *batelão.*"

"How can I verify what you see if I don't come with you? How can I record it?"

"Spencer, we've already discussed this. You can't come with me to El Encanto itself. It's much too dangerous."

"All right. Go ahead. I'll wait here like a good little girl."

He narrowed his green eyes and studied her suspiciously. "You plan to follow me, don't you?"

Giving up the struggle to subdue her brogue, she shrugged. "I am me own boss, Jordan. Whatever I do is none of yer business."

"Damn my aunt Milly's corset! Why am I so stupid? I should have known you wouldn't keep to our agreement."

"What agreement? Ye mean the one *ye* agreed to and tried to force upon me? Or do ye the mean the one I made to meself, wherein I promised t' help protect ye and t' witness everything with me own two eyes?"

"Christ Almighty! When you lapse into that brogue of yours, I know I'm licked! Can you be trusted to at least stay behind me and keep out of sight?"

"Of course. I'm not a complete fool. Ye'll see. I take most orders very well, especially the ones in which I can see the logic."

"Oh, then I've nothing to worry about, have I?" he asked with great sarcasm.

"Not a thing," Spencer breezily retorted.

But Jordan did look worried as he turned away and began hacking their way through the jungle. And as Spencer followed, she, too, felt a sharp prickle of fear; what lay in wait for them at El Encanto?

Chapter Twelve

Don Julio César Arana's rubber depot on the Putumayo was far larger than Paraîso. It had a huge wharf, at which a half dozen armed launches lay at anchor, all of them as big as the *Evangeline,* though the *Liberal,* Arana's biggest launch, was nowhere in evidence. The largest building in the compound was an ugly, two-story affair with a galvanized iron roof and an open-air veranda running all the way around it. The building was situated high on a shelf of land overlooking the riverbank, which had been claimed for garden plots. Beyond were clustered the laborer's huts, washhouses, bathhouses, and storehouses.

Spencer and Jordan studied it from the safety of the jungle. At first glance and at a distance, everything looked normal and fairly well kept. In one corner of the compound, a noisy game of soccer was in progress. Stripped to the waist, the male players were all dashing about, kicking a ball and shouting encouragement to their teammates. However, in another corner of the compound, guards armed with Winchester carbines were overseeing a long line of workers, most of whom appeared to be small, slender Indians. Lugging huge, heavy-looking oblongs of rubber, the Indians were filing out of the jungle and carrying their burdens down to the waterfront.

Creeping closer and taking cover in a patch of young banana plants, Spencer and Jordan were appalled by the condition of the Indians; they were so emaciated they resembled famine victims. Many could barely walk, much less carry the *bolachas* of rubber. Women labored alongside the men, and children stumbled after, each carrying a load that was far too big for them. What little clothing they wore hung in tatters, and all were barefoot and filthy, their hair hanging lankly in vacant eyes.

"I see scars on most of them," Spencer hissed under her breath. "They've been beaten into submission."

"Now, now. The scars don't prove that the beatings took place here," Jordan cautioned.

Just then, one Indian in the line stumbled and fell, dropping his *bolacha*. When he was unable to get up again, a tall, burly black man descended upon him, shouting and brandishing a whip five feet long and thick as a man's thumb.

"That overseer must be Barbadian," Jordan muttered. "I'd heard Arana sent some up here. I can't quite make out what he's saying, but obviously he's threatening that poor fellow."

The Indian whimpered and groveled on the ground. His skeletal body cringed in anticipation of the lash falling upon huge, raised weals, not yet healed from his last beating. The Barbadian drew back the whip and struck the Indian a terrible blow, laying open the meager flesh on the Indian's shoulders. Spencer stiffened in sympathy, at the same time biting down on her lower lip to keep from crying out.

When the Indian still did not get up, the Barbadian gestured to two others. They quickly dropped their *bolachas* and came to the aid of the fallen man. He was dragged off to a stout post standing in the center of the compound and forced to stand and embrace it, while his hands and legs were bound to metal rings on the other side so he could not fall down.

"The flogging post . . ." Jordan said. "Isn't it amazing they call this place El Encanto, meaning Enchantment?"

"That man will die if they whip him," Spencer whispered, in an agony of dread. "He's half dead now, as it is."

They watched awhile longer, but apparently the beating was to be delayed, for the Barbadian only lashed the remaining workers, hurrying them along the worn path to the river. At midday, the carabineers divided the Indians into groups of four, and each group was given a single cup of farina from a copper caldron and a tin of sardines. No water was distributed, but the Indians divided the scant rations among themselves with every evidence of desperate appreciation. As they ate, they made smacking sounds with their lips and behaved as if they were being feasted instead of starved. Spencer's eyes filled with tears when a woman refused her tiny portion and gave it to a big-bellied, stick-legged child in her group. The child was unmistakably suffering from internal parasites, which were devouring everything that went into his body, and even the body tissues themselves.

"I've seen enough here," Jordan growled. "After those soccer players go inside to eat, let's sneak around to the other side."

Spencer only nodded, not trusting herself to speak. The smell of delicious, cooked food wafted on the sultry air, and the soccer players—soldiers, she could see now, as they picked up discarded, identical green shirts—began heading for the main building, where lunch was obviously being served. She wondered how the soldiers could eat, knowing that the Indians had been given so little for what in Brazil was considered the main meal of the day.

Except for the Indians, the compound was not well guarded, and Spencer and Jordan found it surprisingly easy to slip through the fringe of forest surrounding the settlement. But they had not gone far when a terrible odor assaulted their nostrils.

"Lord, what an awful stink!" Jordan exclaimed. "Wonder what the hell it is."

Wrinkling her nose, Spencer was terribly afraid she knew. In lesser doses, she had smelled similar odors during her medical schools days, some of which had been spent ministering to the dying in a hospital. This was the sickening stench of putrefaction—of death, disease, and pus-oozing infections. Before long, they came to a small clearing carved out of the encroaching jungle, and all about the clearing were prostrate bodies—men, women, and children, groaning in the last stages of fatal illness.

Some of the Indians were already dead. Flies buzzed about their open eyes, mouths, and nostrils. The rest lay on the bare ground, cushioned only by their own excrement. Gagging, Jordan sought to drag Spencer back and prevent her from getting a closer look.

"Wait," Spencer gasped, placing one hand over her mouth and nostrils. "I might still be able to help some of them. It doesna' look as if anyone's guarding them."

"The hell they aren't. Keep your voice down. Here comes somebody now."

Crouching at the forest edge, Jordan pulled her down beside him. Two soldiers with handkerchiefs tied over their faces and carbines in their hands tromped into the clearing. Going from one body to the other, they carelessly examined them, giving a nudge now and then with a boot. When one came to a stiffened body, he motioned to the other, pointed down, and said something. Spencer presumed they were making plans to separate the bodies of the dead from those of the living, though what difference it would make eluded her. In these conditions—with no food, water, beds, or medicines—the living would soon be dead anyway.

As the soldiers shouldered their rifles and bent to lift the body, Jordan tugged at her hand. "Come on . . . my stomach can't take any more of this. At this point, these poor wretches are beyond whatever help you might do for them."

Before complying, Spencer cast one long look around the jungle clearing. Jordan was right; this had to be the place where the dying were brought when they could no longer work, and no amount of abuse could force them. Everyone there was too helpless to get up. Some were completely naked and unaware of it, and those whose eyes were opened had a glazed look in them—as if death were not far off. It was a sight she knew she would never forget.

Grasping his hand, she allowed him to lead her away from the awful place. Neither of them spoke as they struggled through thickly clustered, hanging vines and climbed over twisted tree roots. It was hard going, for Jordan dared not employ his machete this close to the compound. Peering through the greenery, Spencer saw a large, sturdy, palm-slatted hut situated quite close to the jungle's edge.

As a heavy wooden door at the back of the structure began to open, Spencer caught Jordan's arm and warned him to silence. She nodded in the direction of the hut. Hardly daring to breathe for fear of discovery, they watched and waited.

A green-clad soldier held open the door while a young girl bearing a basin exited the building. Spencer stifled a gasp of surprise. The girl was very young, possibly not even in her teens, and obviously Indian. But the way she was dressed belied her tender years. She wore a red silk gown trimmed with black feathers—a gown so low cut as to reveal her childish, budding breasts. A deep slit extending upward from the hem of the garment exposed a slender thigh.

The girl dumped the liquid contents of the basin on the ground, then returned to the hut, where the guard waylaid her with a hand around her thin waist. Roughly seizing her, he bent her backward and pressed his mouth down upon hers. The girl shrieked and struggled but was no match for the soldier's strength. Dragging her inside, the soldier slammed the door. A moment later, a heavy bolt slid into place.

"Stay here," Jordan muttered. "I'm going closer."

"No!" Spencer protested, but he shoved the Winchester into her hand.

"Cover me . . . I'm going to look in the window and make sure I'm right about the purpose of that building."

With shaking hands, Spencer accepted the rifle and dutifully aimed it at the hut, though what she would do if she had to fire it she had no idea. As Jordan should have recalled from the last time he'd wanted her to cover him, the Winchester was far beyond her modest capabilities with firearms. Jordan sneaked around to the side of the hut where Spencer remembered seeing a high window as they had approached. Minutes passed with agonizing slowness; there was no sound except for muffled screams inside the hut and the whine of insects in the jungle. Finally Jordan returned, zigzagging through the underbrush.

"It's just as I thought—only worse," he said, taking back the rifle.

"What did ye see?"

"Girls—pretty little Indian girls all dressed up in tawdry, Paris-style gowns like you see in the worst whorehouses in Manaus. There must have been fifteen of them locked up in that hut. While the soldier raped the girl who came outside, several other men looked on, laughing. I heard one of them call the place the 'convent' and joke about teaching 'the nuns' their lessons. I bet there wasn't one of those girls over thirteen years old, and they all just sat there on woven mats, watching everything with big, frightened eyes."

"Dear God! Canna we do anything t' help them?"

Slowly, his face drawn and haggard, Jordan shook his head. "Not now. Not yet. Come on . . . let's keep moving. There's still more of this hellhole to see."

They moved on, working their way around the compound, getting close whenever they could, watching everything, engraving details onto their shocked, disbelieving minds. They passed the bath-houses, where the overseers and soldiers apparently bathed, and the neat, orderly, long buildings where apparently they slept. They passed large store-houses, crammed with supplies and rubber, and a square pen, where barking hounds in cages almost gave away their presence.

Spencer thought they had already seen the worst El Encanto had to offer, when they came to an-other large, square pen, with another set of cages, and some odd-looking wooden devices. "What do ye suppose those are?" she whispered to Jordan.

Cocking an eyebrow, he studied them a moment. "I can't be sure, but I think they're stocks—you know, like were used in the old days in our coun-try, to punish wrongdoers."

"Yes, they do look like that . . ." Spencer con-ceded, eyeing the holes where hands and feet could be confined, and the larger one in the middle which could hold a person's head.

She tried to imagine what it would feel like to stand bent over as one would have to, and realized that the unnatural position would soon cause great agony. So absorbed was she in studying the stocks that she did not at first notice the cages—or what was in them. Since the area seemed deserted, she and Jordan ventured closer, but as soon as they dared step out of the jungle, a low moan made them jump back.

"What was that? I dinna see anyone." Spencer futilely tried to locate the source of the sound.

"The cages . . . Look in the cages," Jordan directed. Spencer did so and could not believe her eyes. The cages were the same size as those confining the dogs at the previous location. Only these cages held human beings, made to crouch, with no space to stretch out an arm or leg, stand up, lie down, or even sit down. Sunk in misery, men and women leaned their heads against the wooden bars and stared blankly into space. The doors of the cages were held fast by stout lengths of leather tightly tied outside, where the inhabitants could not reach them.

In front of several cages were bowls of farina and tin cups of water, in full view of the caged Indians but impossible for them to touch.

"How can they do this?" Spencer cried, heedless that her voice was loud enough for any nearby guard to hear.

"Hush!" Jordan growled, pulling her back out of sight.

"Jordan, it's awful—so awful . . . !" she began, but he clamped his hand over her mouth and held it there until she came to her senses and subsided into silence.

She could not, however, keep hot tears from spilling down her cheeks—tears of outrage and frustration, tears of bitter anger. The Indians were being treated like animals, *worse* than animals. At least the dogs had been fed and watered. How could any human being treat other human beings so cruelly? And how could Arana not know what had been happening?

"Easy, take it easy . . ." Jordan soothed. "If you want, I'll take you back to the *batelão* and finish up here by myself."

Spencer wiped her eyes with the palms of her hands. "No, I want t' see it all—every bit of it. It canna get any worse than this."

"All right, but from here on, we'll have to be really careful. We're almost to the area where the Indians were bringing the rubber out of the jungle. There will be lots of guards there."

"I'll not make another sound," Spencer promised, squaring her shoulders. But as they left the caged Indians, she could not help looking back at them; surely, before they left El Encanto, she and Jordan could sneak back and free the poor prisoners.

Less than ten minutes later, they were spying on the long line of Indians staggering beneath the heavy loads of rubber. How far the Indians had had to carry the bales of rubber Spencer could not guess, but she knew that rubber trees and *estradas* were widely scattered, and these Indians had a quota to meet. Their destination was a large storage building, in front of which stood a weighing scale. Each Indian hefted his huge *bolacha* onto the scale and then stood waiting fearfully to see if he had brought enough.

As the needle of the balance quivered, hovering on the amount, some of the Indians cried out joyously and leaped into the air, capering with pleasure. Others prostrated themselves on the ground, like animals awaiting a blow. Their punishment was quickly forthcoming. Those who failed to achieve the correct amount were either beaten on the spot or dragged off by the soldiers.

Lying on her stomach beside Jordan and peering through the screen of vines, Spencer whispered, "I canna see the scale clearly. How much are they required t' bring in?"

"According to the scale, a hundred pounds," Jordan answered. "If they've got it, they've met their quota. If they haven't . . ." His voice trailed off, leaving the fate of those who failed unspoken.

Hating what she saw—especially hating the man who stood behind the scale, nodding when it showed the correct amount and angrily jerking his head when it did not—she studied the scene. The man behind the scale was a different sort from the soldiers and armed overseers who disciplined the Indians. He wore an immaculate white suit, had polished black shoes, and was slender, with refined features, wavy black hair, and a luxurious, carefully trimmed mustache. Obviously he was in charge. His word was law. He scarcely paid any attention to the Indians, noticing neither their elation when they met their quotas nor their despair when they did not. His attention remained riveted upon the needle of the scale.

"Who is that man?" she inquired of Jordan.

He did not ask who she meant. "It's Loayza—Miguel Loayza. When you see him, it's hard to believe what a monster he is, isn't it? He seems so young—so much of a gentleman. Arana's taught him well. Only when you get up close can you see his character in his eyes. He's got the black glittery eyes of a lizard. He'd kill his own mother without a second thought."

"He's the one who tried to buy Paraîso from ye?"

"He brought the offers. And I'm sure he's the one responsible for the deaths of my *seringueiros* . . . Come on. If we're going to talk, we'd better get out of here first."

Spencer crept after Jordan as he retreated from their hiding place. When they were far enough away, he turned to her. "Well, Spencer, have you had enough? I'd say we've got what we came for—and then some. Staying longer will only increase the risk of our being discovered."

"Jordan . . ." Spencer hesitated, then plunged ahead. "I want t' go back t' those cages where the Indians were bein' kept. Before we go, I want t' free them."

Jordan's brows dipped downward in a frown. "Free them to do what, Spencer? We can't take them with us in the *batelão*. There isn't room."

"Free them t' go back to the jungle where they came from. I bet if we set them free, they could elude the soldiers. The Indians at Paraîso come and go all the time, don't they? They know how t' survive in the jungle."

"But the Indians in the cages are probably too weak to survive."

"At least it would be a chance for them. If they stay in the cages, they'll only die. Those are probably the Indians who couldna be beaten into submission, so now, they're tryin' t' starve them into it. I canna leave here without trying t' help them, Jordan."

Jordan's green eyes reflected the tall fern concealing them. "You'd risk our lives to try and save theirs?"

"We could do it and be gone before the soldiers discover that the Indians are missin'."

"And I suppose if I say I won't do it, you'll threaten to do it without me."

Spencer thought it better to say nothing, rather than to argue. She needed Jordan's help, and she wanted him to give it willingly, because he himself wanted to rescue the Indians. Otherwise he'd be risking his life because of her, a responsibility she did not want.

He sighed. "You win again, Spencer. We'll try and do it. But we'll do it my way, understand?"

She nodded. "Thank ye, Jordan. I know ye'll not regret this decision."

"Hell," he said gloomily. "I'm already regretting it, along with all the rest of my stupid decisions since the day I met you."

Chapter Thirteen

They waited until early evening to try to free the caged Indians. Spencer hoped that nightfall would provide a chance for the captives to lose themselves in the jungle. She doubted that any white men would be foolish enough to brave the jungle after dark, and for once, Jordan agreed with her.

"Another good reason for waiting is that by then everybody will be getting drunk," he said. "That's what men do at night in a place like El Encanto. They drink and dally with whores, if they have them."

Spencer was reminded of the young girls in the "convent," and she wished she could free them, too. But she knew the girls were too well guarded, and the prospect of losing them might make the men brave enough to dare the jungle, even at night. Their only hope for success in freeing any of the Indians was the element of surprise and the general carelessness of the guards. The soldiers would not mind the escape of a handful of half-dead Indians nearly as much as they would if the pretty little Indian girls got away.

In a small clearing Jordan hacked out of the jungle a short distance from the cages, Spencer laid out her medicines and the modest quantity of food and fresh water she had managed to assemble. As she did so, she reviewed Jordan's plan. He was going to open the cages and herd the Indians toward the clearing, where she herself would be waiting to deal with the most pressing medical problems. The Indians would be offered food, and Jordan would then try and warn them against remaining in the immediate area or trying to free other members of their families.

After the Indians had safely slipped away into the jungle, she and Jordan would return to the river and their *batelão,* hidden in the shallows downstream from El Encanto. Jordan wanted the soldiers to think the Indians had freed themselves; he was counting upon the guards not discovering until morning that their prisoners were gone.

"Everything ready here?" he asked Spencer in a low voice, sneaking up on her unexpectedly.

Minutes before, he had left to scout the vicinity, and she was surprised to see him back so soon. With a nod of her head, she indicated the bananas and mangoes she had set out beside the quinine and other medicines she had brought along in case she or Jordan were injured or became ill. "As ready as we can ever be given such short notice. I just wish I could have made some broth or something more nourishing; fruit won't give them much strength."

"Don't worry about what they'll eat once they get away. They'll hole up for a day or two, make snares, and be catching their own food in no time. Just remember what I told you. If you hear rifles firing, run and don't look back. As soon as I can,

I'll meet you at the *batelão*. If I'm not there by morning, don't wait. Start paddling for home."

"Whatever happens, I won't leave here without you." Spencer eyed Jordan calmly, drinking in the sight of his tall, muscular figure. The thought that something might go wrong and she would never again see him alive cut to the bone, but pride prevented her from letting him see how anxious she felt.

He eyed her back, just as calmly. "Don't risk your neck for me, Spencer. If they catch me, by myself I might be able to escape. But if they catch you, God alone knows what they'll do. These men are animals. They haven't a shred of decency. Because of what we've witnessed here, they'll have to kill us both—but they won't kill you quickly. They'll make sport of you, first—worse than they do with the little Indian girls."

Spencer lifted her chin. "I'm not afraid, Jordan. What we're doing is right. Justice is on our side. And if I ever do meet Miguel Loayza face-to-face, he won't forget the encounter. He'll have to kill me, just to shut me up."

Jordan's green-eyed gaze swept her face, lingering a moment on her mouth, then returning to her eyes. "You're quite a woman, Spencer O'Rourke," he said softly. "Do you know that?"

She smiled. "And ye are quite a man, Jordan King."

Their eyes held a moment longer, then Jordan gruffly strode away. "See you soon—I hope."

After he was gone, Spencer busied herself with peeling a banana. She had eaten nothing since early morning and was herself half starved. But she could barely swallow the first bite, her nerves were too raw. It was one thing to feign bravery in front of Jordan and boast about what she would do if caught by Loayza's men, but quite another to actually ponder the frightening possibility. More than she feared for herself, she feared for him. If he got hurt, it would be her fault for embroiling him in this entire scheme. She could not bear to think of him getting hurt; every hair on his head had become precious to her.

Her heart thumped painfully, and she strained to listen for the slightest sound. There was none, and the light in the clearing was waning. She wondered how they would ever find the *batelão* in the darkness. In all likelihood, they would have to spend the night in the jungle and locate the canoe in the morning. She slapped at a mosquito and dreaded what the night would bring: more mosquitoes, the possibility of attack by larger creatures, and the greater possibility of getting lost or being discovered. Only if Jordan put his arms around her and held her through the darkest hours would she be able to relax and set aside her fears. How ironic! she thought, almost laughing aloud. Having spent all her time alone with him avoiding his embraces, she now hoped he'd try again. Indeed, she longed for his presence with a fierceness that made her tremble.

Oh, Jordan, please hurry. Free the Indians, and come back to me.

By the time Spencer heard the sound of footsteps, it was nearly too dark to see. A man came stumbling toward her, then another—and after them, came Jordan.

"Spencer, where are you?"

"Here, Jordan. Right here." Spencer rushed toward him. "I was so worried! What took ye so long?"

"The Indians. I opened all the cages, but only about half the poor wretches had the strength to crawl out of them and follow me. More are coming. You'd better look them over before it gets too dark."

"It's already too dark."

Spencer peered at the nearest man. She could smell him easily enough but could barely make out his features and the fact that only a scrap of cloth covered his nakedness. She grabbed a couple of bananas and shoved them into his hand. "Go!" she urged in Portuguese. "Into the jungle. Run and hide."

"Forget it," Jordan said. "They don't understand Portuguese. I had to use my poor Spanish and a word or two of the *'līngua geral,'* which I don't speak very well. I think the only thing they did understand was that I opened their cages and motioned for them to follow me."

"Well, at least we can feed them." As the Indians crawled or lurched into the clearing, she began handing bananas and mangoes to them. They took the food with shaking hands, sat on their haunches, and started gobbling it down, skins and all. "Dear Lord, they'll make themselves sick eating so fast!" Spencer commented with dismay.

She tried to make them slow down, but the men and women were so eager for food they ignored her efforts. Their arms and legs resembled sticks. Instead of walking upright, they moved sideways with crablike motions. Spencer despaired that any of them would be able to escape the area. They were simply too weak. Their muscles were atrophied, their bodies twisted and bent into unnatural positions, so that they resembled strange jungle creatures, instead of humans.

"Oh, Jordan! What shall we do? They'll never get away from here."

"We'll have to leave them, Spencer. We've done the best we can by setting them free. Some may escape. If the guards don't discover that they're missing until sometime tomorrow . . ."

A loud shout suddenly split the night. It came from the direction of the cages, causing alarm to ripple through the Indians. Inhuman as they seemed, the deformed creatures had no difficulty realizing what the shout meant. Grunting to each other and hugging the fruit, they moved crab-wise into the jungle. Jordan snatched Spencer's hand.

"Let's go, Spencer. There's not a minute to spare."

"B-but the medicines! If the soldiers find them, they'll know we're here!"

"Grab the medicines—and the fruit, too. What we can't carry, we'll toss in the underbrush."

As he spoke, Jordan hurried to follow his own orders. Spencer had to grab things by feel, rather than by sight. In the few moments since Jordan's arrival with the Indians, it had grown pitch black. With a growing sense of panic, she realized she had lost all sense of direction and had no idea which way they should run. Her only clue was the sound of the shouts coming from the compound. So long as the guards kept shouting, at least she would know which direction to avoid. Thrusting bottles into the two side pockets of her skirt, she dropped one or two and could not find them in the darkness. She also could not find the small canvas bag in which she had brought the medicines with her that morning. All day she had worn the bag slung over one shoulder, its compact size and minimal weight making it unnoticeable—but the soldiers would notice it soon enough when it grew light enough to search the area.

"My medicine bag!" she gasped to Jordan. "I canna find it!"

"Then we'll have to leave it. I see torches . . . and the dogs are barking. Can't you hear them?"

Spencer did indeed hear them. Through the close-packed trees, she detected a faint orange glimmer. Jordan's hand clamped around her elbow. "Try and make it to the *batelão*. I'll hold them off here."

"I'll not go without ye!" Hysteria made her voice rise, but she was past caring if the soldiers heard. "We can make it together! They won't find the medicine bag till mornin'. We've got all night before they think t' search the river for us."

"The dogs will find us . . ."

"The dogs will go after the Indians first."

"Then I'll stay and give the Indians a chance."

"No! I'll not go! Not without ye . . ."

To Spencer, the plight of the Indians ceased to matter. Jordan was the only thing that mattered now. Either they would escape together, or *neither* would escape.

"Damn it, Spencer! Why will you never listen to me?"

The barking of the dogs grew louder. Snatches of angry Spanish were clearly audible.

Spencer clung to Jordan's arm. "Please, Jordan! We can make it! *Please . . .*"

He hesitated only a second longer, then shoved her ahead of him into the jungle. "All right, run! I'll be right behind you. Run as if your life depended on it—which it does, and mine, too."

Spencer ran. She ran not only for herself, but for Jordan. She ran blindly, dodging things when possible and running into them when not. Jungle mud sucked at her boots. Vines lashed her face and arms. More than once, she tripped and stumbled. At one point, Jordan crashed down on top of her, squeezing the breath from her lungs and grinding her face into the spongy forest floor. They got up and ran farther, fleeing the barking, snarling dogs, noisy in the distance.

A long, agonized scream told them one of the Indians had been found. Shots rang out, followed by the frenzied yelping of the hounds. Spencer faltered, her burning lungs begging for air. Jordan took her by the arm and dragged her after him. She clutched at his shirt, tearing the fabric. He laced his fingers through hers, and they ran on, hand in hand. Without him, she would have given up. His hand in hers was her only link with reality. The rest was all a nightmare.

Finally they could run no longer. Gasping for breath, Jordan sagged against a tree trunk. Spencer did the same, hearing nothing but her own labored breathing. Her lungs sounded like a broken bellows, wheezing ineffectively. For several moments, she concentrated on gulping air.

"Dogs . . . silent," Jordan muttered.

Spencer listened. It was true. She could no longer hear the dogs.

"We've . . . outrun them," she agreed.

"For tonight. Tomorrow . . . another story. They'll find your medicine bag."

"And the medicines I dropped."

"Can't go back to the *batelão,* yet. Safer away from the river."

"Whatever ye say." With her back to the tree, Spencer slid down into a sitting position. She did not think she could go another step.

"Not here. Can't rest yet," Jordan said. "Just a little farther."

Groaning, Spencer got to her feet and followed him. They had not gone far when the ground suddenly felt firmer—drier, without the squishiness she associated with the jungle. Something crunched beneath her feet.

"Far enough . . ." Jordan sighed. "This is better. Not so swampy. Less chance of snakes."

Pulling her down beside him, he collapsed near a fallen log and leaned against it. His arms slid around her waist and pulled her closer. She did not resist; she hadn't the strength for it—nor the desire. "Rest. Sleep now, Spencer. We'll go on in the morning."

It was all the encouragement she needed. Laying her head on his chest, she closed her eyes and succumbed to exhaustion.

In the morning, Spencer discovered they had been sleeping in a boneyard. She opened her eyes and looked around, expecting to see only the usual jungle greenery. Instead, she saw a broad, shallow pit located only five or six feet from where they had collapsed. All around the pit were bones—arm and thigh bones, sets of ribs, and half-crushed, broken skulls.

"Saint Brigid, protect us," she murmured, quickly making the sign of the cross, a religious gesture harkening back to the days of her childhood when her father had been strict about her spiritual upbringing.

With his arms still wrapped around her, Jordan stirred. "What are you mumbling about?" he rumbled in her ear.

"Wake up, Jordan. We're lying at the edge of a burial pit. It's a wonder we didn't fall into it last night."

"A burial pit?"

Suddenly Jordan was wide awake. He moved away from her so he could see better, passed a hand over his eyes, blinked once or twice, and grimly studied the scene before them. The pit itself was brimming with bones, skeletons both large and small, tossed helter-skelter and stripped clean of all flesh and human semblance. Once a thin layer of dirt must have covered the pit, but the scavengers of the jungle had done their work—digging up the bodies and dragging them short distances into the surrounding jungle. There were no remnants of clothing or artifacts, and Spencer could not begin to guess how many dead had been buried here.

"It's hard to tell how long ago these people died," she noted. "In this heat, bodies must decompose quickly. However, since most of the bones are still intact, I'd say they died within the last two or three years, maybe less."

Beneath his deep golden tan, Jordan's face had turned an odd shade of white, tinged with green. "Let's get out of here," he grunted. "I'm not a doctor. I can't take this. I don't even want to know if they're Indians or not. Let's just assume they are. It had to be some sort of mass execution. I've never known Indians to just throw the bodies of their friends and relatives into a big pit."

Quickly and quietly, they departed the place, hiking several miles deeper into the jungle, maintaining a rapid, steady pace and saying not a single word. Finally, Spencer thought they ought to stop, find water, and eat the fruit they had brought with them. Hunger was making her grow dizzy and light-headed. If they were to keep up their strength, they had to eat.

"Jordan, wait . . . I need t' rest," she pleaded.

Instantly he was at her side. Lowering the machete he had been using to hack through vines, he used his free hand to tip up her chin. "Are you all right? No, of course not. I've been going too fast. I'm sorry, Spencer. I had to get away from there. All those skulls and bones, I felt sick to my stomach. Had I seen them last night, I never could have slept there."

She thought he had never looked so rattled; the experience had clearly unnerved him greatly. "Skulls and bones canna hurt ye, Jordan. The dead are simply dead . . . I learned that in medical school. It was very difficult t' obtain bodies for dissection, but we managed—rather, one of the staff doctors managed. I always wondered where he got them. We students used to laugh and joke about it, imaginin' him chasin' hearses or diggin' up coffins."

"I . . . I dinna think I could ever be a doctor," he said wryly, mimicking her brogue.

This humble admission, coupled with his lingering paleness, moved Spencer to pity and a sweeping tenderness. Thus far in their relationship, Jordan had only shown her his strong side, though he had not, she remembered, been too relaxed during Raymundo's surgery. Still, he was an amazingly strong, self-possessed, confident man, who radiated virility even when ill with fever. That he might be afraid of ghosts deeply touched her, so that she wanted to hug and hold him, soothing away his fears, as she might a little boy's.

"Everyone isna meant t' be a doctor," she whispered. "Ye have other talents—for example, tracking through the jungle. I havna the faintest idea where we are and could not find our *batelão* in a week of searching."

"Don't worry about the *batelão*. That's where we're headed—in a roundabout way. I want to approach it from the opposite direction entirely. As an extra precaution, I want to delay getting there until tomorrow. If the soldiers find the things we left behind, they'll start searching the river today. We should wait a couple of days before we even venture out on the river, and then we should only travel in the late evening before dark and the early morning, near dawn. We'll have to be very careful and take our time getting back to Paraîso."

Being alone with Jordan so long suddenly did not bother Spencer; if anything, she now relished the prospect. Somehow, the death and suffering they had witnessed at El Encanto had made her more appreciative of life—and of Jordan. Gone were the constraints of society and the inhibitions she had imposed upon herself. She now saw them as the petty things they were. It was glorious to be alive, breathing the sultry, humid air, and savoring a quiet moment with a man who had grown to mean more to her than any man she had ever known, including her father. No one controlled her, no one placed limitations upon her; she was her own person, free to experience whatever she wanted to experience—most particularly Jordan.

Gazing at him with newly opened eyes, she shyly took his hand. "As long as I'm with ye, Jordan, I find I dinna worry about anything."

For a minute, he looked startled by her change of attitude. Then a wide grin broke over his handsome features, and a sparkle lit his green eyes. "We aren't out of this yet, Spencer, my love. We're still a long way from safety."

My love. He had called her his love. She touched a hand to her disheveled hair, for once in her life wishing she was beautiful—or at least had a comb. She was a sorry mess, but then, so was he. They smiled at each other, at ease together for the first time since they'd met. All the horrors of El Encanto were still very much in Spencer's mind, and also, she knew, in Jordan's. But sharing them had brought them together, joined them in spirit.

When they got back to Paraïso, they would have to decide how to use what they had learned. But in the meantime, she would live every minute as if it were a precious, fleeting gift, which indeed it was.

El Encanto had taught her that. At El Encanto, life itself was a miracle. It was so fragile, so easily extinguished, so vulnerable to violence, cruelty, and greed. She must never again take it for granted.

Ahead of them in the jungle gloom, Spencer caught sight of a splash of pink and purple. Jordan got there first, and plucked the single, perfect orchid blooming in the bleak darkness. With a flourish, he presented it to her, and she tucked it into her knotted hair.

"For you," he said, his tone caressing. "The bravest, most beautiful woman I've ever known."

Chapter Fourteen

While Spencer waited in the cover of the jungle, Jordan prowled the secluded spot on the riverbank where he knew he had left the *batelão*. It wasn't there. He found the marks in the mud where he had dragged it onto the shore, but someone—Loayza's men?—had dragged it back into the river. That was the only possible explanation; the canoe had been discovered and confiscated, and Loayza now knew they were here.

Jordan wanted to pummel someone, preferably himself. They had left food supplies, extra clothing, hammocks, mosquito netting—everything they needed to survive—in the *batelão*, and by doing so had indicated who they were as clearly as if they'd left a note. Loayza would examine the items and realize that two people—a man and woman—were in the vicinity, had spied on El Encanto, and freed the caged Indians. He would then conduct a hunt to find and destroy them before they could reveal what they had seen at the rubber depot.

Jordan cursed himself for being so stupid. He ought to have hidden everything, not left it lying in the *batelão*. He ought to have done a better job of hiding the *batelão* itself. He did not know how he would face Spencer and tell her they were stuck in the jungle with only the clothes on their backs and in great danger of being killed, either by Loayza or by some mishap or even by starvation and disease.

Returning to Paraíso through the jungle was almost an impossibility—yet what other choice did they have? A machete, a Winchester, and the knife stuck in his boot were poor tools with which to fashion another *batelão,* even if he knew how to make one. And Loayza would be watching the river, knowing it was the only way out for them, expecting them to follow it on foot, if nothing else.

Jordan thought of Spencer's softened attitude toward him, the way she now smiled and willingly took his hand, and he felt even worse. He wasn't certain what had caused her change of heart, but he knew he didn't want it to change back. She was ripe and ready for him now, though he couldn't do a thing about it in their present circumstances. What bitter irony! Finally, at long last, she was offering him the prize of her sweet surrender, and instead of responding with strength and self-assurance, he was so tired and scared he felt like quitting.

Never had death seemed so close, so inevitable. He and Spencer were in a no-man's land, where the only law was the law of the jungle—kill or be killed. Civilization was so far away as to be nonexistent. He had known danger before, but never with such sharp clarity. None of the stories he had heard about El Encanto matched the terrible reality of the place itself. He did not know how he was going to keep himself and Spencer alive. He did not know how he was going to get them back to

Paraïso. Worst of all, he did not know how he was going to look into Spencer's blue-green eyes and tell her what a jackass he was.

"Jordan? Did you find the *batelão?* Where is it? I don't see it."

He spun on his heel. "Spencer! I thought I told you to keep well hidden. At this time of day, I don't want you anywhere near the river; one of Loayza's men could spot that bright red hair of yours."

"Your blond hair is as visible as me red," she sniffed, tossing her fiery locks back over one shoulder.

Though she had made an obvious effort to restrain the brilliantly colored mass, her hair, like her brogue, defied all efforts at subduing it. It tumbled in glorious disarray around her shoulders, giving her a wanton aspect to match the lushness of her bosom. Her demure white skirt and ruffled blouse were torn and stained, filthy beyond recognition. A streak of dirt marred one cheek, yet somehow she managed to be breathtakingly beautiful. Her eyes were the green of the jungle mixed with the blue of the sky, and every freckle dusting her nose suddenly seemed dear to him—he would not have minded counting each one, and kissing it as he did so.

Desire jolted him, pushing the matter of the missing *batelão* far to the back of his mind. Here and now, this very minute, he was still alive—very much alive, and this incredibly desirable woman was peeping provocatively through her lashes at him. Going to her, he took her hand and led her a short distance back into the jungle, to a spot where the ground was less damp but still soft and yielding, and there was room enough to lie down—if he got that far.

"Jordan, what's wrong? What's happened? Did someone take the *batelão?"*

Leaning his Winchester against a tree trunk, he decided to be brutally honest with her. He placed his hands on her shoulders, compelling her to look him in the eye. "Spencer, the *batelão*'s gone. Loayza's men must have found it. Now they know we're here, and our lives aren't worth a *cruzeiro*. They'll either find us and kill us, or we'll die trying to get back to Paraïso."

Emotions flitted across her expressive face—the same ones *he* had been feeling, he was certain. Then she did something that astonished him. She threw her arms around his neck and hugged him, burying her face against his shoulder. "Oh, Jordan, dinna look so guilty! It's not yer fault. Please dinna blame yerself. I got us into this mess. I'm the one responsible."

He could feel the press of her full breasts against his chest and the rapid beating of her heart. Her warmth surrounded and engulfed him. With a low groan, he crushed her to him. "Spencer . . . Spencer, I'm sorry. I should have known what would happen. I should have stopped you from—"

"No, no! Ye couldna have stopped me, Jordan. Oh, my darling, I dinna care about meself, but if any harm should come to ye because of me stubbornness . . ." She burrowed into him, freely offering herself to his embrace.

Tightening his hold on her, he lifted her off her feet so her mouth was level with his. "Spencer . . ."

he breathed against her lips. "If you don't want things to go any further than this, just say so, and I'll set you down and walk away. But dammit, woman, if you don't say no, this time I'm going to make love to you . . ."

She cupped his face between the palms of her hands. "Jordan, dearest, I've wanted ye for such a long time, but I kept fightin' it—denyin' what we both wanted. Only now, after seeing El Encanto, after realizin' how short, how precious life is . . . Jordan, teach me what to do. Show me how to please ye."

Jordan had never in his life had a woman beg him to tutor her in the art of love. The only women he had ever known sexually were whores or at least, well experienced . . . Oh, there had been one exception, a long time ago in his teens when he had kissed the daughter of a stablehand in the haymow of his father's barn. He and the young lady had engaged in some embarrassed fumblings, from which she had emerged weeping and scared and gone running out of the barn. He did not want to scare or frighten Spencer, so he took a firm grip on his galloping passion and determined that he would go slowly and gently . . . easing Spencer into the full flowering of womanhood.

"First, we kiss . . ." he said. "We kiss until we're drunk with kissing."

He touched his lips to hers, demonstrating instead of lecturing. Holding back, he kept the kisses gentle, tender, and coaxing, until she deepened them of her own accord. When her lips finally opened to him, he used his tongue to suggest what he wanted to do to her with another part of his body. She melted against him, never fighting, never turning away. When he paused to give her time to catch her breath, she gazed up at him with glazed, sleepy-looking eyes.

"Is this what it's like to be intoxicated? I feel like I'm floatin' . . ."

"Just relax. Let the feeling carry you away," he counseled, maneuvering her so she leaned against a tall tree whose silvery bark identified it as a prime hevea. At any other time, recognizing such an excellent rubber tree would have been an exciting discovery, but now he was much too excited by Spencer's responses to care about the tree.

Bending her back slightly, he nibbled along the column of her white throat and nosed her collarbone. When his hand cupped her breast, she gave a little moan. Deftly, he opened her blouse and slid it down her shoulders, encountering the same layers of gauze as he had the first time, when he tried to undress her. "Spencer . . . Your breasts are beautiful—full and perfect, as lovely as a man could want. Never again must you try and hide them. Everything about you is perfect, even your brogue."

"It's not that I'm *ashamed* of me bosom," she explained. "It's just I thought I was too big—too distractin'. I wanted men t' respect me for me medical skills, not be oglin' me for me body. As for me brogue . . . well, that's always been a hindrance t' me success."

"My love, you're neither all mind nor all body. Instead, you're both—a stunning combination. Be proud of what you are. Don't deny any part of yourself . . ."

As he spoke, he removed her clothing, caressing

each spot as he exposed it. It was like unfurling the petals of a flower, searching for the core of nectar. Spencer shyly helped him, thrilling him with her willingness. When she stood naked before him, he sought to take her in his arms, but she suddenly resisted.

"Now, ye . . ." she whispered. "*Ye* are beautiful, too. I thought so the first time I saw yer body. Ye are as perfect as a man can be."

Her words astounded him. Always before in his past experiences with women, he had set the pace and controlled the rhythm, deciding how fast to go, when each should undress, how quickly they should proceed. But Spencer would have none of that, he realized. She was a full participant, making her own demands, giving and taking at the same time. He wondered why he did not feel threatened or put off; even whores sometimes insisted upon darkness or hiding beneath a sheet, and he knew of men whose wives averted their eyes from the sight of their husband's nudity. But Spencer stood face-to-face with him in the filtered light of the jungle, and somehow it felt so right, as if this were the way it was meant to be—man and woman meeting and mating as equals, Adam and Eve in the Garden of Eden . . .

While Spencer watched, her eyes luminous and appreciative, he stripped off his clothes and tossed them in an untidy heap. Then he held out his arms to her. She came into them, pressing the palms of her hands flat against his chest, gently exploring him. "When I touch ye here, does it feel as grand as it does when ye touch me?"

In answer, he could only groan. Playfully, she

tweaked his nipples. Then she dipped her head and licked one. When he jerked helplessly, she lifted her head, mischief dancing in her eyes. "Oh, Jordan! Getting to know yer body is so much fun! I want t' learn everything there is t' know about it. I want to know it better than I know me own."

Fearing it would all be over before it got started, he entwined one hand in her unruly tresses and hauled her to him. "The first thing you must learn is that when you touch me, I can't always control what's going to happen. Therefore, it's best if I touch you, first. Let's start by discovering what you like, then we can go on to what I like, which frankly, my love, is everything."

"All right . . ." she murmured tremulously. "I already know I like it when ye kiss me and touch me breasts . . ."

With one foot, he pushed their clothing together to make a pillow for her head, then drew her down to the soft jungle floor. Mercifully, he saw no snakes, fire ants, or other obnoxious creatures, and he ceased to worry about them as the wonderful reality of Spencer O'Rourke flooded his senses. He discovered that she did indeed like to be kissed while he caressed her breasts. And she liked it even more when he kissed the creamy mounds and suckled the rose-colored nipples. She moaned and made soft, little mewling sounds when he licked her navel and stroked her thighs. As he gently probed between her thighs, she nipped his ear and reached for his groin. Though he tried to control his own rising passion, he found he could not. His body clamored to be joined with hers.

Her warmth and wetness told him she was ready,

but still he held back—afraid of hurting her, causing pain instead of pleasure. Her hands frantically searched his body. To keep from exploding, he gritted his teeth and thought of ice and snow. Suddenly, she rolled on top of him.

"Jordan, I dinna know how we're supposed t' do this. Medical texts are not terribly instructive on the actual details. All I know is I've *got* to have ye inside me."

On her knees, her magnificent breasts level with his mouth, she guided him into her with one hand. As he pierced her sweetness and tore her maidenhead, she stiffened slightly, then pushed him deeper inside. A rushing sensation assaulted him, spurring him to a greater urgency than he had ever felt before. It wasn't enough to merely pump his hips, thrusting upward. He again rolled them over, pinning her to the ground beneath him, in which position he could exert the full force of his passion.

As he thrust with wild abandon, Spencer met his thrusts with a matching passion. Her hands clawed his back. She arched against him. His name spilled from her lips. Intense heat radiated from her flesh, the contractions of her pleasure drawing him further into her, forging them together, making them one. A delicious explosion rocked him from head to foot; all his life force pounded through his veins, erupting finally in Spencer's body. Spent, he collapsed on top of her.

Only after he had rested several moments was he able to ask: "Sweetheart, did I hurt you? Are you in pain?"

He raised himself to look into her shining eyes. The look on her face was one he knew he would never forget: wonder, satiation, and brimming love. She did not say a word. She only smiled and drew him down to lay his head on her bosom, the softest, most wonderful pillow imaginable. He wanted to sleep forever locked in her arms, his body joined with hers, their spirits blended. For him, the jungles of Brazil had ceased to exist; he felt as if he had just come home.

Conscious of something tickling her big toe, Spencer opened one eye. One of the Amazon's magnificent, blue-winged butterflies was poised there gently fanning its incredible wings. She wiggled her toe, and it flew away, freeing her attention for more important matters. Jordan's arms and legs were still entwined with hers. He lay half beside her, his head nestled on her left breast, his eyes closed, his breathing deep and regular.

Raising up on one elbow, she gazed down at him, loving every inch of his long, sun-bronzed body. The miracle of what had so recently occurred between them was fresh in her memory, and she spent several moments reliving each glorious kiss, each intimate caress. Her body still throbbed with the pleasure of their joining, though there was a soreness, too, that she hoped would soon pass.

How amazing it all was! She had crossed that invisible boundary line separating girls from women, and life as she had known it would never again be the same. With her newfound carnal knowledge, she was aware of needs she had never before recognized and powers at which she had only guessed. For the first time in her life, she felt in harmony with her feminine self. That was reason enough to love the man beside her—he had given her this precious gift—but there were other reasons, as well.

Jordan King was a man worthy of a woman's love and admiration. He tried to subdue and ignore his ideals, but they matched her own. When confronted with gross injustice, he had joined her in trying to free the Indians—indeed, he had taken the lead. Pondering the complexity of their relationship, she wondered if this was not always the case between men and women: When it came to safeguarding morals and decency, women pointed the way, but men forged ahead and actually fought the bloody battles.

Together, she and Jordan made a powerful team, each contributing their own strengths and making up for the other's weakness. Looking down at him, noticing the wrinkle between his brows, she knew how much he hated their present circumstances and worried about their return trip to Paraîso. He blamed himself for the loss of the *batelão* and doubted they would ever escape the vicinity of El Encanto alive. It was up to her to give him hope; she must swallow her own misgivings and make the impossible seem possible. If anybody could get them back to Paraîso, it was Jordan. And if anyone could help him find the courage to deal with whatever problems were going to arise, it was she.

Leaning over him, she awoke him with a kiss. His hand came up and clutched her head, holding her in place, but before their mutual arousal could blossom, she reluctantly pulled away. "Jordan, hadn't we better get going, before someone finds us?"

He expelled an exaggerated sigh. "I suppose we must, though I'd much rather stay here and make love again. I want to be sure I wasn't dreaming—that it really was as wonderful as I thought."

"It was," she assured him. "But we mustn't linger any longer."

"Spencer . . ." He grabbed her hand before she could move away. "One day we're going to have to talk about what happened here. I just want you to know that to me it was very special, very . . . wonderful."

Was he trying to say he loved her and wanted to marry her? She did not know the rules of etiquette involving this sort of thing, but in the world she had left behind in the States, at this point, a man usually declared himself—unless he was a crass adventurer, out to get whatever he could from a woman. Still, this was not a normal situation, and whatever she did, she must not jump to conclusions. Marriage was something she herself had not fully considered.

"It was t' me, too, Jordan. And there will be plenty of time t' talk about it after we get back to Paraïso."

"If we get back . . ." His eyes darkened. All the warmth drained from his face. "I'll do my best to get us there, Spencer. Unfortunately, the odds are against us. Two Indians might make it, but two whites . . ."

"Shh . . ." She laid a finger across his lips. "Dinna talk about the dangers. At this moment, I'm the happiest I've ever been in me life. Dinna spoil it with dire predictions. We're alive and together; that's all anyone ever has. From moment to moment, life can change, tragedy can strike. All anybody has is the present. Let's make the most of it."

Once more he took her in his arms and kissed her, pressing her against his naked length so that their hearts beat in unison and they breathed together, as if their bodies were a single entity. *I love ye, Jordan,* she thought, certain his thoughts were similar. They were two halves of the same whole, inseparable and complete, capable of withstanding anything that came their way. When the embrace ended, they rose, dressed, and set off through the jungle for Paraíso.

Chapter Fifteen

Three days later, they knew they would never make it. Covered with insect bites, splattered with mud, starving and feverish, they clung together in a rain shower that washed away the sweat and grime but also made their teeth chatter.

"How far away do ye think Paraïso is?" Spencer muttered, leaning her head against Jordan's shoulder as they rested beneath trees so tall and leafy that even if it wasn't raining, no sunlight could have penetrated.

"I've no idea—but it must be miles and miles of trackless jungle, thick with vines but thin with game. Right now I'd welcome a bushmaster, though I don't know if I'd have the strength to shoot it, or if the Winchester would fire. Probably it wouldn't, so we better hope we encounter nothing dangerous."

"We'll make it . . ." Spencer soothed, repeating the same relentless litany she had been chanting for three days.

"No, we won't. It's time we faced it, Spencer. We've only been fooling ourselves."

"Have some more quinine," Spencer urged, sitting upright. "We mustna let delirium set in or we'll really be in trouble."

"We're *already* in trouble—deep trouble. I don't know what to do. If we don't obtain decent food soon and find shelter and rest, we're going to be too ill and weak to travel. Hell, we're already too weak."

"Pooh! I'm not tired. We can go a little farther today yet." Spencer struggled to rise, fighting the dizziness that made her head spin and her ears ring. "Maybe we'll find more tree grubs t' have for dinner—or we'll spot a monkey. Before it started raining, I thought I heard one chattering up ahead."

"Sit down, Spencer." Jordan pulled her back down beside him. "I'm sick to death of tree grubs, and the monkeys move too quickly. Before I can even aim, they're running away through the trees."

"How do the Indians catch them so easily?"

"Next time you see one, ask him. I'm used to hunting game from the river, where I can shoot the animals when they come to drink."

"Then let's go back to the river. There's always more game by the river. Dinna ye tell me that once before?"

"Yes, I did, but there's also the danger of Loayza's men. Still, it's our only chance. Maybe we'll get lucky and spot someone other than a boatload of bloodthirsty thugs paddling a *batelão* downriver."

Hope ignited in Spencer's breast. "Do ye think that's really possible?"

"Possible, but not probable. Before Arana grew so powerful, Colombians and stray Indians used to travel the Putumayo all the time. Then they learned it wasn't safe. That's why David Serrano built La Reserva so far back from the river. His place is on the other side, set back in the jungle about ten miles, where the rubber trees are thickest. I told him he was a fool to put his depot so far from the only avenue of transportation, but he said it was easier for the Indians to haul the rubber there from their *estradas,* and also safer from attack. Loayza can't line up his armed launches and blow him away with a few well-aimed blasts. However, Loayza didn't have much trouble marching his soldiers through the jungle and attacking anyway, so it didn't do Serrano any good to be so far from the river after all."

"If there's even a slim possibility of encounterin' someone other than Loayza, I think we should return t' the river," Spencer resolutely stated. She kept her eyes averted so Jordan wouldn't see her dwindling hope.

Jordan squeezed her arm. "Don't be ashamed of giving up, Spencer. We've made a good effort. I doubt anybody but you and me could have come as far as we did, cutting every step of the way through the jungle as we've had to."

"I'm not givin' up!" Spencer denied, but in her heart, she knew she was. The jungle had defeated them; by tomorrow, they would not be able to walk, and by the next day, they'd be delirious. It rained often enough to slake their thirst, but the need for decent food was desperate. Sometimes her mind wandered, and she had a hard time remembering where she was. Jordan was beginning to resemble a walking skeleton; he had grown hollow-eyed, gaunt-cheeked, and gray-tinged. In his weakened condition, a malaria attack was inevitable. If one occurred, he would never be able to fight it off.

His chuckle interrupted her grim thoughts. "Pardon me for suggesting you might be giving up. I've never known anyone with your persistence. If the devil himself came to drag you to hell, you'd dig in your heels and fight every step of the way. Pity the poor devil; his pride would take a sound beating, and in the end, he'd only lose. You walk with angels, Spencer O'Rourke. Whatever made you take up with a weak, spineless bastard like me?"

"Yer green eyes," she teased, glad to change the subject. "Eyes like yers can compel a woman t' do anything."

"I wish I had the strength to compel you to do my will right now. What a tragic waste! All this time alone together, and all I can do is *dream* of ravishing you. I have to horde my strength just to get on my feet and keep walking."

"Poor lad. No more complaints. If we make it t' the river, I promise ye me gratitude will take a physical form. This time, tis *ye* who shall be ravished."

"Is that so? Then how can I refuse? Anticipation is giving me new strength already. Take my hand, fair damsel, and let's see if we can find the damn river."

They were so weak it took them several minutes to get to their feet. Spencer had to hold tightly to Jordan's hand to keep from falling. Tears stung her eyes, but she turned her head so Jordan couldn't see them. No matter what happened, she wouldn't let despair overwhelm them. If they had to die, at least they'd be doing it in each other's arms. All things considered, it wasn't a bad way to go. She had seen deaths that were far, far worse. She thought of the Indians who had died—were dying—at El Encanto, stripped of freedom, dignity, and humanity. She shivered and forced herself to keep walking behind Jordan. By comparison, dying in the arms of your beloved wasn't a bad death after all. The only bad deaths were the ones where the dying person had never known love, tenderness, passion, or commitment. People who died in that state had never really lived.

"Stay here, sweetheart. Rest. I'll watch the river," Jordan rasped in Spencer's ear.

Spencer nodded, a supreme effort but easier than speaking. Hunger had made her so light-headed, she doubted she could get her words straight. They had made it to the river, slept side by side through the night, and were now going to begin a vigil of watching for traffic on the Putumayo. If none appeared, they would die. They had gone as far as they could go. She had reached the end of her strength, and Jordan's collapse could not be far behind.

Never opening her eyes, she leaned against a tree trunk and let her thoughts drift. It was peaceful and quiet, with only the sound of the water sweeping past and the distant cries of birds feeding in the shallows. If not for the hunger cramps in her belly, she'd be perfectly comfortable. Jordan had crushed some insects between his fingers and fed them to her last night, after first eating them himself to ascertain if they were poisonous. She had pretended she was eating nuts; the insects had been crunchy and bitter-tasting, but they had given her strength to get to the river. Now the only thing left to do was wait . . . and hope, only she was too tired to hope anymore, too tired to *think,* actually. So she rested, floating on a warm sea of apathy, no longer caring if she lived or died.

"Good God, there's someone coming!" Jordan suddenly croaked.

Spencer's nerve endings jolted alive again, thrumming in painful awareness of her cramped, shrunken stomach and throbbing head. "Who? Where?" On hands and knees, she crawled to the riverbank and joined him in peering into the early-morning sunshine illuminating the river.

"There . . ." he pointed. "A *batelão* coming this way. Keep your head down until we see who it is."

Adrenaline surged through Spencer's body imparting new vigor. With bated breath, she watched the canoe come closer. No one was paddling in the bow end, but someone had to be doing so in the stern. Like their own *batelão,* this one had a triangular-shaped roof of thatched palm to shield the occupants from passing rain showers. It also concealed them from view. Whoever was paddling the vessel could not be seen until the canoe came abreast of them.

"I only see one passenger," Jordan whispered. "A man. As he passes, I can easily pick him off, and the *batelão* will be ours."

"Ye mustna kill him!" Spencer grabbed Jordan's arm as he raised his Winchester. "He might be friendly."

"Or he might not—and he might not stop for us if we call to him. We've *got* to shoot him, Spencer. It's our only chance."

Grabbing hold of a vine, Spencer pulled herself upright. "You there!" she shouted in precise English, completely forgetting that the occupant of the *batelão* would likely not understand. "Stop that boat!"

The man ceased paddling and raised his head in startlement. His eyes scanned the riverbank, seeking the source of the sound. The *batelão* kept coming as the current swept it nearer to shore.

"Now you've done it," Jordan muttered, rising and aiming his rifle. *"Ola!"* he shouted, repeating her command in Portuguese.

To Spencer's great astonishment, the bedraggled-looking figure in the *batelão* responded in English. "Who's there? Whoever you are, hold your fire. I'm an *Americano, comprende?* Show yourself, and I'll get out my identification papers. You can examine them and see for yourself who I am."

Jordan shot Spencer a look of complete and utter bewilderment. "What the hell is another American doing all alone on the Putumayo?"

Grinning, she took his arm. "Let's find out, shall we? Maybe he's Saint Brigid's own emissary, sent t' rescue us in response t' me prayers."

"If that's true, I'll name our first daughter Brigid, though I hate the name."

Spencer grinned so hard her dry lips nearly split. "Better not promise that, or I'll hold ye to it."

Arm in arm, they staggered into the shallows to pull the *batelão* to shore. To their stunned surprise, they soon recognized it. It was their very own *ba-*

telão—the one they had left tied up on shore near El Encanto.

In no time at all, Spencer and Jordan learned the identity of the thief who had stolen their *batelão*. He was an American named Walter Ernest Hardenburg, a twenty-one-year-old engineer who had been working on the Cauca Valley Railroad in Colombia with his partner, William B. Perkins, when the thirst for adventure became so strong that the two of them had set out on a fateful voyage to see if they could reach the Amazon and Manaus.

Over a lunch of tinned peaches and sardines left stored in the canoe, Spencer watched and listened as the young man told his story. He was square-shouldered, with dark, receding hair, prominent ears, and wide-set, intense blue eyes. When he spoke, he used expressive hand gestures that struck Spencer as emphatically American and decisive, so unlike Latin gestures, which were profuse but somehow weak.

"You don't know how glad I am you folks are American," he said in a pleasant, deep voice. "When you first hailed me, I thought I was imagining things. What would a woman be doing out here in the middle of the jungle? I asked myself. I'd still like to know the answer to that question, if you're ready to tell me something about yourselves now that you know about me."

"We haven't heard everything yet," Jordan disputed, calmly spooning peaches into his mouth while he talked. He chewed a moment, then swallowed. "You've only told us the bare facts. Let me see if I've got everything straight so far. You and your partner, William Perkins, or Perky, as you call him, started out from Buenaventura on the Pacific Coast, crossed the Andes with great difficulty, then struck the Putumayo and successfully navigated it past the falls and rapids of its upper reaches with the help of two Cioni Indians. Along the way, friendly Colombians assisted you, you had many adventures, and finally, you ran afoul of Miguel Loayza. Loayza detained you at El Encanto until you convinced him you were en route to work with Percival Farquhar on the Madeira Railroad under construction south of Manaus. Perky is still at El Encanto, trying to get your instruments and supplies released, but you sneaked off in our *batelão* to warn a man you've never even met that Loayza intends to destroy him. Assuming I've got all that right, the next question is: Why would you do that, Mr. Hardenburg? Just why in hell would you do that?"

Spencer felt that Jordan was being unnecessarily accusatory and suspicious of their new acquaintance. Walter Hardenburg had already expressed his outrage at the depraved character of Miguel Loayza and the horrors he had witnessed at El Encanto. Though the young man had not seen everything she and Jordan had seen, he had seen enough to be thoroughly appalled.

"It's just as he said, Jordan," she started to explain, setting down her peaches before nausea could overtake her. "He overheard Loayza's thugs talking about eliminating David Serrano once and for all, and planning how the attack should take place. So when he stumbled upon our *batelão* while searching for unusual botanical specimens, he decided to risk trying to warn him. When he returns to El Encanto, Mr. Hardenburg's going to claim he got lost in the jungle."

"You misunderstand my question, Spencer," Jordan said impatiently. "What I want to know is why any man would go to such dangerous lengths to help a complete stranger. Such idealism is a rare commodity in these parts; I'm surprised to find it and want to know what's really on Mr. Hardenburg's mind."

"Well, sir," Walter Hardenburg said, balancing a tin of half-eaten sardines on his knees. "I'll tell you. I abhor violence and injustice. I was born and raised in Galena, Illinois, and where I come from, people take an interest in each other. They step in and help when disaster strikes or a tragedy befalls some member of the community. My own family has received such help, and on this trip, my partner and I were many times helped by both Colombians and Indians. This David Serrano is a Colombian, I understand, and though I've never met the man, I feel it's my duty to help him if I can."

"But what if Loayza suspects something and kills or tortures your partner while you're gone? Or what if he doesn't believe your story of getting lost when you return?"

"I'll make him believe it, Mr. King." Walter Hardenburg's blue eyes grew hard and steely. "I was most convincing when I lied to him about us being members of the prestigious Farquhar expedition. In truth, we hope to find work with Percival Farquhar, for we're both short of funds, but first I'm going back to Iquitos in Peru to protest the imprisonment of Dom Jesus Orjuela, the Colombian government official who was captured about the same time we were."

"Orjuela!" Jordan exclaimed.

Spencer was as surprised as Jordan to hear the Colombian's name, which she very well remembered. Don Jesus Orjuela was the Colombian emissary whose arrival David Serrano had been anxiously awaiting.

"You saw Dom Jesus Orjuela at El Encanto?" Jordan's skeptical green eyes nailed the young American.

"Of course. That's what I just said. When the soldiers took Perky and me prisoner, they locked us in a room in the main building with him. Orjuela told us who he was and how he came to be there and why. His launch was waylaid by the *Liberal*, and he's being held under military arrest."

"Military arrest! But he's a diplomat!" Jordan exploded. "He's supposed to be smoothing things over and preventing the outbreak of full-scale war between Peru and Colombia."

"So I understood him to say, though neither my Spanish nor my Portuguese are the best in the world." The young American sighed. "I tried to convince Senhor Loayza that he was courting a great deal of trouble holding a Colombian government official against his will, but he wasn't convinced. He said Colombia was a hostile country, at war with Peru, but their war is not yet openly acknowledged. That's when I threatened to protest his actions to the Peruvian government, and do you know what he did? He offered to have the *Liberal* take me back to Iquitos the next time it makes the run so I can protest in whatever fashion I desire. He doesn't fear a thing from his own government. The only thing he did fear was how mad Percival Farquhar would be if my partner and I never showed up to help build his railroad."

Jordan gave a loud snort. "No wonder. That railroad will help get Arana's rubber to market faster. That's why Loayza let you go—he knows his own boss will be mad as hell if anything deters that railroad."

Walter Hardenburg cracked a wry grin. "I guess I did make it sound as if *we* were the two most necessary people on earth to help design and build the Madeira railroad."

"Good thing you did or you'd be dead by now," Jordan dryly commented.

Spencer thought of something neither man had thus far mentioned. "You spoke of the *Liberal,* Arana's biggest launch," she said. "Where is it now? We didn't see it at El Encanto."

Hardenburg shrugged. "I've no idea. I can only hope it hasn't set out already to ferry soldiers down to Mr. Serrano's rubber depot. If so, then my efforts to warn him will be in vain. Even knowing I might not make it in time, I have to try. I couldn't live with myself if I thought that a man and all his family and workers were going to be killed and I did nothing to try and stop the slaughter."

"You're already too late to try and save his family," Jordan informed him. "Serrano's wife and son are slaves at El Encanto. Loayza captured them some weeks ago."

Hardenburg shook his head, his eyes glinting with fury. "One way or another, Loayza and this Arana must be stopped. They are a blight on all humanity."

"We quite agree with you, Mr. Hardenburg," Spencer said. "That's why we're here. We came to El Encanto to see for ourselves how bad conditions are. We plan to document what we've seen and take the information to people who have the power to do something about it."

Jordan frowned, warning her to keep silent, but she saw no reason to keep secrets from Walter Hardenburg. Clearly, he was on their side.

"That's an excellent idea," the young American responded enthusiastically. "When I get to Iquitos, I myself plan to confront this Arana if he's in residence there and tell him what I think of him for allowing his overseer to seize innocent bystanders and diplomats sent to avert bloodshed. I'll also protest the mistreatment of the Indians at El Encanto."

"You won't find Arana in Iquitos," Jordan grumbled. "His family home is there, and his three brothers also live there, but Arana himself spends most of his time in Manaus, wining and dining the rich and powerful. The man is the very image of elegance and sophistication. His friends are legion, and discrediting him will not be easy."

"However, we do intend to try," Spencer added.

"Of course you must try! We must both try. When I get finished in Iquitos, the Peruvian government officials will most definitely take action against him."

Jordan's frown deepened. "If I'm not mistaken, Arana's brothers are Peruvian government officials. The trip may not be worth your time."

"It will be worth it," Walter Hardenburg insisted. "When I make up my mind to fight something, I'm not a man to be easily put off."

"Have some more peaches and sardines," Spencer urged, thrilled with their new acquaintance. "And then we must plan what we're going to do next."

"I've already decided that," Jordan said, casting her a look of great annoyance.

Spencer could not understand the hostility radiating from him. They had found the *batelão* completely intact and discovered a willing ally for their cause. She was delighted, but Jordan seemed furious. What could be wrong? Then it came to her. Maybe he was jealous! She perused his murky green eyes and set mouth. Yes, that was it. He was jealous of Walter Hardenburg for so quickly winning her friendship. She smiled to herself, secretly pleased that Jordan cared so much. Of course, he had nothing to worry about. For all his youthful, puppy earnestness and determination to fight Arana, Walter Hardenburg was a mere child, while Jordan King was a mature, virile man. The young American could never make her heart soar or her senses vibrate—but Jordan didn't need to know that, at least not yet. It might do him good to be jealous for a time. It might fuel his flagging enthusiasm for battling Arana and also lead to a marriage proposal.

She smiled at Jordan, and when she spoke, was careful to enunciate each word. "Do tell us what you have decided, Jordan, though I warn you—if

Mr. Hardenburg and I do not agree, we'll outvote you, two to one."

Jordan's frown became a scowl. "If you do outvote me, you can both walk back to civilization. Need I remind you, you're sitting in *my batelão!*"

Chapter Sixteen

Jordan did not know why he was so angry, but he was. Watching Spencer and Walter Hardenburg eagerly discuss their mutual hatred for Don Julio César Arana made him feel old, like an adult charged with restraining two naive, idealistic children. Neither Spencer nor the young Walter had any idea of what they were talking about. Walter thought all he had to do to stop Arana was protest to Peruvian government officials who probably owed their jobs to Arana's influence. Didn't he realize what they were up against?

The detainment of the Colombian emissary, Orjuela, was proof positive that Loayza and Arana feared nothing and no one. Orjuela may have been captured with the full approval of the Peruvian government. These were deep, dangerous waters, wherein the lives of three meddling Americans were worth less than the cheap paper money Brazil kept churning out as an answer to inflation.

Nor did Jordan like the look on Spencer's face and her rapt attention whenever Walter Hardenburg opened his mouth. Jordan could easily imagine the young American being smitten by Spencer's beauty, bravery, and intelligence and fancying himself in love with her. There had been an instant attraction between the two, an almost spontaneous recognition of similar character traits. While he and Spencer were miles apart on almost everything, Walter and Spencer might have been cut from the same cloth.

"Here's what we're going to do," he said brusquely, employing great effort to keep from punching the young American in the nose. "Walter, we'll take you back upstream a short distance so you can return to El Encanto, catch the *Liberal* and make your protests in Iquitos. After we drop you off, Spencer and I will go back to Paraïso, stopping on the way at La Reserva to warn David Serrano of Loayza's plans. When you finish at Iquitos, you're welcome to visit us on your way to Manaus. You can't miss my place. It's right near where the Putumayo empties into the Amazon."

"That's a fine plan . . ." Walter Hardenburg said. "But aren't you going to go directly to Manaus with your depositions? I thought from what Miss O'Rourke said, that . . ."

"Doctor O'Rourke isn't the boss of this expedition, I am. She works for me. And I've got a rubber harvest to get out. When I'm good and ready, we'll return to Manaus and decide what's to be done with our depositions. Right now, I can't spare the time."

"But, Jordan!" Spencer protested. Her eyes blazed at the idea that she worked for him; probably she hadn't liked the rest of what he had said, either. "We should leave immediately for Manaus. While ye're gatherin' rubber, more Indians will die—maybe more Colombians, too. We should at least inform the newspapers in Manaus that war is imminent on the Putumayo."

"I'm not a damn journalist," Jordan spat. "I'm a humble *seringueiro* trying to get rich on rubber. I didn't come here to right all the world's wrongs. Brazil can't and won't do a thing to stop war between Peru and Colombia. Neither will they lift a finger to help the poor Indians. I was as shocked as anyone to learn what's really going on at El Encanto, but until I get my rubber to market, I can't do a damn thing about it. I certainly can't leave my own workers unprotected while I go running off to Manaus."

Spencer's crestfallen face told Jordan how unhappy she was with his decision, but her disappointment only served to make him more determined. "I never promised to return immediately to Manaus, Spencer. I've already delayed harvesting my rubber far too long, and I can't afford to delay any longer. I need money to feed my workers and their families and keep us all going through the next rainy season. Battling Arana will have to wait." When Spencer didn't say anything, but only stared at him with huge, upset eyes, Walter Hardenburg hurried to fill the awkward gap in the conversation. "I understand your concerns, Mr. King. When I get to Iquitos, I'll write to you. I should be able to find someone en route to Manaus who can carry a letter. I'll let you know what success I'm having with the Peruvian officials."

"That would be very kind of you," Jordan grudgingly acknowledged. "I'll give you my address in Manaus, and you must let me know how and where I can reach you. I'd like to continue our association and cooperate in whatever way possible to stop the injustices on the Putumayo. Unfortunately, I can't devote my entire life to the endeavor."

"Few men can, sir," Walter Hardenburg said. "Fortunately, I seem to be at a particular point in my life where I can spend the time to fight evil. Until Loayza decides to release our equipment, Perky and I cannot go back to work."

For a moment, Jordan feared Spencer might suddenly offer to accompany Walter Hardenburg to Iquitos, but then she busied herself cleaning up the remnants of their meal and never said another word—either to him or to Walter. They napped during the worst of the noonday heat, ate again when they awoke, and Jordan then felt refreshed enough to begin the journey upstream. They had not gone far, however, when the noisy chug-chug of a launch overtaking them warned they should seek immediate cover. They did so behind a screen of limbs from a huge tree that had toppled partway into the river.

"It's the *Liberal,*" whispered Walter as they crouched in the *batelão* and hid among the dying leaves and branches. "I wonder where she's been. Look how many soldiers are aboard."

Jordan studied the long, two-storied vessel which had a big, black, belching smokestack set almost square amidship. The ship itself was painted shiny white and had gleaming white rails and ample protection from the weather. Most of it was enclosed, with large windows overlooking the narrow decks. Aboard were at least a hundred soldiers, laughing, talking, and singing in what appeared to be a celebration. Only a few stood guard, though Jordan could imagine no one challenging the big guns mounted both fore and aft. If he needed any further proof of Arana's dominance on the Putumayo, here it was. The *Liberal* was big enough to rule not only this river, but the mighty Amazon itself. Thinking of his friend David Serrano, Jordan felt a tightening of his gut. If the *Liberal* had indeed paid a visit to La Reserva, nothing would be left. He decided that when he and Spencer arrived there, he'd make her wait in the *batelão* while he hiked the ten miles into the jungle to find David.

As soon as the big launch had safely passed, they resumed paddling upriver and continued until it grew dark. In the morning, they went a bit farther, and finally deposited Walter Hardenburg as near as they dared to El Encanto. The depot was not as far as Jordan had thought. He and Spencer must have done a lot of circling and backtracking in the jungle during their several days of wandering, and he felt even more inept and ashamed that he had not done a better job guiding her to safety.

"Good-bye, my friends," Walter Hardenburg said before slipping into the jungle. "You'll hear from me. Together we'll bring Arana to his knees."

For the first time since the preceding day, Spencer came to life. "Be careful, Walter! I'll pray ye come t' no harm."

Jordan grimaced. Now, when had she taken to calling him Walter? Had they been awake and talking last night, while he was asleep? What else had they been doing? He knew his jealousy was irrational, all the more so considering Spencer's state of exhaustion, but still, he couldn't help it. He did not like the idea of her even talking to another man, much less praying for his safety.

"Are you going with him, or staying with me?" he gruffly inquired. "Make up your mind."

"Why, I'm staying with ye," she answered in surprise.

"Good, then sit down and shut up."

As soon as she had done so, he began paddling away from shore. He could feel her eyes boring into his back, but he refused to turn around and look at her. If she was comparing him to Walter Hardenburg, he did not think he could bear it. He longed for the closeness they had shared in the jungle, when they feared they were going to die, but had no idea how to reinstate it. Jealousy was a new and frightening emotion for him. No female had ever meant that much to him, and such feelings deeply shocked him. Avoiding all contact with Spencer, he paddled doggedly downriver, putting as much distance as possible between her and Walter Hardenburg.

"Just how long are you going to continue ignoring me?" Spencer asked Jordan that evening as they were setting up camp in an abandoned storage hut whose gleaming metal roof she had spotted from the river.

For a few moments, Jordan didn't answer but continued hanging up their hammocks and arranging their belongings so they could make a fast exit if anyone came to check on them. *Bolachas* of rubber were piled in one corner of the rather large structure, but judging from the refuse left by foraging jungle creatures, no one had been there in a very long time. It was impossible to tell who owned the building and why it had been put there all by itself. No other buildings stood near it, and the only remnant of a dock in the river were two solitary wooden posts leaning into the water.

"I'm not ignoring you," Jordan finally said. "I'm very much aware of your presence. It's you who's been ignoring me . . ." He turned toward her, acting very matter-of-fact, and calmly continued. "I think we should stay here a couple of days and recuperate, don't you? It should be safe enough. This place probably belonged to a Colombian long since driven out of the area by Loayza. I doubt anybody's working the trees in this vicinity; I haven't smelled a rubber fire all afternoon."

Spencer realized she had not smelled one, either. Usually, the scent of coagulating latex hung over the river, though the rubber fires might be miles away. Somehow, the sulfurous odor always clung to the jungle, even after a heavy shower. She nodded. "Yes, it should be safe, and I *am* still exhausted. Besides, it looks like rain. Why does it rain so much when this isn't the rainy season?"

Jordan shrugged. "Who knows? Nothing about this part of the world makes any sense. All the rules are different here. You can't just apply American logic and expect to understand anything."

The conversation vibrated with hidden meanings, and Spencer mightily resented the tension that had risen between them. Determined to regain what they had enjoyed before they met Walter Hardenburg, she abandoned formality, threw down the things she had brought up from the *batelão,* and confronted Jordan. "Jordan, please tell me why ye're so angry. I dinna understand. And I . . . I canna bear it when ye look at me as though ye hate me."

At sight of her brimming tears, his eyes softened, and he reached for her. She flew into his arms like a child seeking forgiveness. He held her against his chest and buried his face in her hair. She gloried in his warmth and tenderness. Nothing mattered for the moment but getting close to him. In his arms was all the security and happiness she could ever want. Gradually, her senses began to register small but demanding details—the salty scent of his soiled, sweat-stained shirt, the feel of his chest muscles beneath his shirt, the hardening of the bulge at his crotch . . .

He drew back slightly. "Spencer . . ." His voice was a caress. "I don't want to fight with you. I'm not even sure what there is to fight about. What do you say we have a bath, then eat some dinner, and then . . . see what happens. Maybe we'll find we aren't upset with each other after all."

He was offering a truce before the war got started, neatly setting aside the important issues they ought to discuss—such as how soon they could go to Manaus and how long it would take to reach La Reserva. But suddenly, such matters did not seem so urgent. Of far greater urgency was the re-establishment of their relationship.

"I'd like that," she whispered tremulously, shivering in anticipation of what would surely occur later that night. "But how do ye intend t' manage a bath?"

"Nothing's impossible if you put your mind to it." Jordan sounded smug, his eyes gently mocking her own responses to life's many challenges, but she was too happy to be in his arms again to take offense. "See if you can find fresh clothing—and a hunk of soap," he directed. "And I'll start hauling water up from the river."

Barely a half hour later, as the jungle darkness

descended, they had everything ready: river water in assorted containers, a large metal basin to serve as a bathtub, a sliver of brown soap, and a relatively clean burlap bag to use for a towel. Jordan laid a section of palm thatching beneath the basin and hung a lantern nearby so that its light dimly illuminated that part of the hut. He also forestalled any complaints Spencer might have about insects or bats being drawn to the light, by joining and stringing up their mosquito nets, including the extra they had brought along, so that a sheltered bower now existed which could later be moved to cover their hammocks.

Spencer found herself giggling with excitement, but also nervous about disrobing in front of Jordan. It made no difference that he had already seen all there was to see of her; she still felt shy and extremely brazen to be contemplating a bath beneath his interested scrutiny. "Ye first," she urged. "I'll just turn me back, and ye can go right ahead."

"Both of us together," he corrected. "That way I can watch you while you watch me, and neither one of us will be embarrassed."

She accepted the challenge with outward equanimity but a wild inward fluttering. "All right."

Lifting the mosquito netting and stepping under it, she began to take off her clothes. Doing the same, Jordan matched her, piece by piece. First she disrobed the top half, keeping her blouse draped across her bosom. Then she forgot about her own emerging nudity in the pleasure of watching his. He had grown lean as a whipcord, but the leanness only served to emphasize the perfection of his proportions. He was still sleekly muscled, like a golden panther, and his chest and upper arms were blatantly masculine. The contrast of the tanned skin of his face, forearms, chest, and neck with the white flesh of the rest of him excited her unbearably. She liked seeing what no one else—not even the sun—was accustomed to seeing.

With a soft whooshing sound, her skirt and the rest of her undergarments pooled at her feet. His eyes touched her intimately, exciting her all the more. "I'd almost forgotten how beautiful you are . . ." he murmured, taking her blouse from her hands and tossing it aside. He grinned wickedly. "Almost, but not quite. I'm glad you quit wearing that silly bandage."

"I havna worn it since . . . we first made love," she admitted, feeling shy as a new bride. "I decided that as long as ye like me as I am, I should learn to like meself better. I'm not even fightin' me brogue as much as I used to."

"I *love* you as you are," he whispered, green eyes glowing. He slid one arm around her waist, and with his free hand, cupped one breast possessively. "You were made for my hand," he said. "See how perfectly you fit my palm."

Stepping over her discarded clothing, she allowed him to draw her closer. "I think perhaps we were made for each other."

He let go of her breast, took her hand, and pressed it down on his erect, swollen shaft. When she clasped him, he closed his eyes and swayed against her, growling in the back of his throat. Reluctantly, she released him. "What about our bath?" she gently reminded. "I'd hate t' think we went t' all this work for nothing. I do need a good washin', Jordan."

"Oh, all right . . ." he grumbled. "Come along, and we'll wash each other."

They made a delightful game of it—first soaping each other with the ridiculously small sliver of soap that kept slipping out of their hands, then taking turns standing in the basin while the other rinsed the soap away with dippers of tepid water. It was so warm in the hut they scarcely thought of drying themselves with the scratchy burlap. Instead, Jordan insisted upon noisily slurping the water droplets from her breasts, which made her laugh, and she returned the favor by delicately licking them from his chest.

"I wish I could wash me hair," she sighed. "It's the only part of me that isna clean, and I do so long t' be clean again."

Jordan's hands were on her hips. Earlier, he had lavished several dippers full of water on them; now, he was checking to be sure she wasn't still soapy. "But you can," he said. "I set aside two buckets of water solely for that purpose. Do you want to do it now—or later?"

His kneading fingers were working a magic that made all her bones seem to melt. "Later. I think it can wait until later."

He stopped what he was doing long enough to shove aside the basin and other paraphernalia from their baths. Then he pulled her down beside him on the woven mat. "Spencer . . . my beautiful Spencer. I don't think I'll ever get enough of you."

His hand explored her inner thighs while he bent over her and suckled her breasts. Helpless to resist him any longer, she spread her legs and surrendered to the spiraling excitement and pleasure such intimacies engendered. His hands and mouth knew exactly what to do to build the tension higher and higher. Before she lost control entirely, she pushed him away.

"What is it? What's wrong?" he murmured.

"Nothing, except *ye* are doin' all the work. Lie back, and let me love ye, Jordan, at least for a little while."

"I won't last long if you do," he warned.

"Ye won't have to," she assured him. "I'm ready now. I just want to enjoy ye more first."

She didn't say it, but she also wanted to test her power over him, to see if he wanted and needed her as much as she needed him. For the sake of his kisses, she was willing to set aside all her concerns, yet this very vulnerability struck her as a kind of weakness. For too many years, she had zealously guarded against wanting any man, convincing herself that medicine was enough and always would be—only now, she knew it wasn't enough and never again would be. Her desire for Jordan was a hunger demanding to be fed every day. A single feast would never appease her; each day, she would arise wanting him anew—wanting the sight, sound, and smell of him, the taste of him on her tongue . . .

With avid possessiveness, she explored his body, touching, tasting, and caressing to her heart's content. Growling impatiently, he took matters back into his own hands, rolled over on top of her, and very deliberately pushed his elongated shaft inside her eager, pulsating body. Poised above her, encased in her quivering flesh, he looked down into her eyes. "Tell me how much you want me, Spencer O'Rourke," he instructed in a voice raw with passion. "Tell me how much you want only *me* inside you, doing this to you." He arched his back, withdrew, and thrust deeply.

"I want ye as much as I want air t' breathe," she gasped. "I want ye *more* than air."

Her heart swelled to the point of explosion, thundering against her rib cage, as he began a slow, deliberate thrusting, never taking his eyes from her face. She lifted her legs and wrapped them around his waist. He thrust faster, deeper, harder, piercing her to the core. He poured himself into her, and she clung to him in mounting wonder and delight. In all the world, there was only the two of them, straining together in sweat-slickened rapture. The sounds of their mutual pleasure filled the hut, intermixed with the strange, eerie cries of the jungle night. In the far distance, Spencer heard the snarl of a hunting panther, followed by the shriek of its prey. Locked in Jordan's arms, she knew no fear, only a wonderful, pervasive joy and contentment.

After they had rested awhile, they made love again—this time lazily, taking their time, toying with each other's bodies until the sweet intimacies again drove them over the brink into stunning completion. Even then, they did not part but slept arms and legs entwined, bodies joined, hearts still thudding in unison. And Spencer knew she wanted to sleep that way every night from then on, fused body and soul to Jordan, so close that nothing, but nothing could ever come between them.

Chapter Seventeen

In the morning, a misty, damp morning following a quiet, predawn shower, Spencer and Jordan rose early, packed their gear in the *batelão,* and continued downriver toward La Reserva. Reluctant to do or say anything that might destroy their happiness, Spencer avoided controversial topics, and they spent the next two days in a special kind of bliss normally reserved for honeymooners. In her heart, Spencer felt married to Jordan, and she refused to allow any pricklings of guilt to intrude on their precious time alone together.

Jordan seemed to share her reluctance to discuss what they had seen at El Encanto, what they were going to do about it, or what their encounter with Walter Hardenburg had done to their fledgling relationship. Instead, he behaved like a newly married, very-much-in-love husband courting her at every opportunity, bestowing kisses and intimate caresses whenever they were near enough to touch, and going out of his way to find sheltered spots to camp. They tried making love in a hammock and wound up on the ground laughing, their contortions having dumped them unceremoniously on their behinds. Climbing back in again, they tried until they finally succeeded, but afterward, Jordan vowed he'd never do it again. He claimed his back was broken, and Spencer sympathized; her own was aching as a result.

They were amazed that Brazilians managed to have children, considering how and where they usually slept. Once, in frustration, Jordan dragged Spencer out of the swaying hammock, and made love to her standing up, with her back against a hard, unyielding tree trunk. They passed several idyllic days, taking far more time than they should have to make the journey downriver, causing Spencer to wonder if somehow, they *knew* what awaited them at La Reserva.

Barely had they tied up at David Serrano's wooden wharf when they broke into an argument that completely shattered the previous mood of oneness and fulfillment, revealing it as an impossibly fragile thing that could never survive the harsh glare of reality.

"I'm comin' with ye to La Reserva, and that's *that!*" Spencer shouted at Jordan. "Ten miles is nothing after what we've been through already."

"No, you're not. You're staying here—out of sight of the river but near it just the same." Jordan's mouth assumed a thin, stubborn line. Gone was the adoring, indulgent expression which had made him so dear and wonderful over the last few days. Now he looked like a spoiled, petulant bully, bent on forcing her to his will.

"You canna make me stay here, Jordan. I insist on coming with ye. If Loayza's soldiers have already destroyed La Reserva, I want t' see it. The destruction canna be any worse than the sights we saw at El Encanto."

"Why do you have to wade into everything with such . . . such *masculine* determination, Spencer? Where's your maidenly shyness? You *are* a woman, after all. If you're going to become my wife, it's time you started acting like a normal female."

This was the first time Jordan had ever mentioned marriage; in the joy of discovering each other, they had somehow put off discussing it, though the subject had crossed Spencer's mind. It infuriated her that he mentioned it now, in the midst of a shouting match. It also infuriated her that he took for granted that she wanted to become his wife.

"I dinna notice ye complainin' about me lack of maidenly shyness when we were stripping naked at every opportunity durin' the last few days," she retorted. "If ye dinna like me the way I am, I have no intention of ever becomin' yer wife."

"I do like you the way you are! I just don't want you to overdo it. You needn't embrace every ugly, sordid experience the world has to offer. Maybe I'd like to start protecting you from violence and ugliness."

"Be reasonable, Jordan. 'Tis far too late for me to start buryin' me head in the sand and pretendin' such things don't exist. I'm comin' with ye t' La Reserva. Shall we stop wastin' time an' get goin'? Maybe David Serrano needs me medical skills this very minute."

Jordan's lip curled downward in disgust. "Sometimes I wish you weren't a doctor. It isn't a very feminine thing to be. Frankly, I like the feminine side of you much better than I do the cool, professional one."

Spencer was deeply stung. She had her own conflicts about who and what she was. In loving Jordan, she thought she had resolved all those conflicts. Now she saw quite clearly she had only deepened them. If she married him, would he insist she give up the practice of medicine? Both her heart and her stomach turned somersaults at the mere idea of losing either Jordan *or* her career.

"I thought ye said I was both a mind and a body, a stunning combination, and I should be proud of meself. But ye dinna really mean it, did ye? Like most men, ye just want the body, without the mind . . ." Tears trembled on her lashes. Filled with anger at him and at herself, she brushed past him, heading for the jungle. "I'm going to La Reserva. Ye can do whatever the hell ye want. Just don't think ye can dictate to me."

"Spencer!" he shouted after her, but she tromped ahead, too angry to look at him. "Just wait a goddamn minute, will you? I have to get my machete—or do you intend to wither the vines blocking your way with one of those prune-faced glares of yours?"

"These wee vines won't stop me; nothing will stop me! If it's one thing I've learned, lad, it's how to manage on me own!"

They found La Reserva in worse state than they could ever have imagined. All the buildings had been burned to the ground and only the mutilated bodies of the workers and their families remained, scattered across the trampled clearing where the compound had once stood. The stench of decay and putrefication sickened her, but Spencer tore off a piece of her skirt, tied it across her nose and mouth, and forced herself to go from one body to the other, looking for someone who might still, against all odds, be alive. While she bent to this gruesome task, Jordan, white-faced and speechless with outrage, wrestled with nausea behind a tree.

Guilt made her do it; while she and Jordan had been climbing all over each other in the jungle, people had lain here dying from gunshot wounds, bashed-in heads, and machete chops. The soldiers must have had an orgy of killing and maiming. Many of the women had been raped, as evidenced by their grotesquely sprawled, naked bodies and the men tortured. The children simply lay as they had fallen as they tried to flee into the jungle. She searched for David Serrano, but did not find him among the dead. And there were no living. Maybe some had escaped, after all. A total of forty-two people had died during the attack, and she wondered how they would ever bury so many, and if she could bear to touch the stinking bodies. She dared not swallow and scarcely inhaled, for fear of being sick.

"Let's go," Jordan said at her side. "Let's get out of here. There's no one left alive. If any did survive, they've long since fled."

"We should bury them in a mass grave, at least—like those Indians at El Encanto."

"How could we dig a big enough hole? We haven't the tools."

"We could burn them. Cremation would be better than nothing."

"Still trying to be proper and do the right thing, aren't you?" Jordan said bitterly. "Do you want to stand around inhaling tainted smoke? Do you want someone else to see and smell it and come investigate?"

"I guess ye're right. There's nothing we can do—at least not here, not for these people. In its own good time, the jungle will dispose of this mess."

They trudged in silence back toward the river. Halfway there, Jordan embarked on a dismal, running commentary that demanded no response and may have been for his own benefit, rather than hers, though each word he spoke drove a wedge more deeply into her already wounded heart.

"You wouldn't listen to me when I told you what it was like out here, would you? Well, now do you believe me? This place is hell on earth. It's not fit for human habitation. The only humans who come here are animals . . . and the rest of us would do well to get out as soon as we can, before we become animals, too. Don't try and talk me into taking our silly, little depositions back to Manaus, Spencer. Do you know what will happen to us if we start making accusations? Arana will kill us. He hasn't any choice. We've seen too much. We *know* too much. We can't just walk into the office of some newspaper, plop our story into an editor's lap, then go our merry way. Arana won't stand for it. He'll find some way to discredit us, or else he'll get someone to slit our throats while we're sleeping in our beds one fine night. David Serrano will certainly never testify against him. I bet we never hear of David again. If he's still alive, which I doubt, he's probably somewhere in the jungle where he'll only die, anyway. No, Spencer. It won't do any good to argue with me. I'm going back to Paraîso, gather this season's rubber, maybe stay for one more season if I can stand it, and then, I'm getting out. By then, I'll have enough money to make a new start back in the States. I'm going to buy back my family's farm, Castle Acres, and breed fine race horses. I'm going to live like a gentleman, get married, and start a family. It's what I've always wanted, Spencer, why I came here in the first place."

He rambled on and on—telling her everything she had always wanted to know about his family background, his sisters, his hopes and dreams, and his plans for the future. But he never once mentioned what her place in his life might be, or what he hoped it would be. Perhaps he feared to probe the matter or was certain she would not go along with his wishes or no longer respected him because he refused to fight Arana. Or perhaps he did not ask her to marry him because he had finally realized they weren't right for each other.

Her own mind was too muddled to deal with any of these issues, least of all the personal ones. Every word he said about Arana was true. Arana would kill anyone who threatened his empire. She could easily imagine him or his brothers eliminating Walter Hardenburg. If the young American got too persistent in Iquitos, complaining about Loayza's actions at El Encanto, she and Jordan might never hear from him again, either, and would never know what had happened to him. What it came down to was that she and Jordan were the only two people in the world with direct, personal knowledge of Arana's and Loayza's crimes.

Too numb from shock and horror to sort it all out, she only knew that her "honeymoon" with Jordan was over, and already, he seemed to be regretting the interlude. Sadness and despair swept over her, mingled with grief for the victims of the attack on La Reserva. So many brutal, senseless deaths! And she had managed to walk through the area and examine the bodies with a cool detachment that, in retrospect, appalled her. Like Arana himself and Loayza, she had finally become accustomed to brutal death.

The remainder of the journey back to Paraîso passed quickly in strained silence. Jordan was so withdrawn he responded only in grunts and nods. Neither did Spencer feel much like talking. Upon their arrival, Jordan immediately plunged into problems that had arisen during his absence, and Spencer saw him only at mealtimes and often not even then. After three days of feeling sorry for herself and resenting Jordan's aloofness and involvement in his own affairs, she looked around and decided she had enough to occupy her time, without worrying how to deal with Arana *or* Jordan.

Paraîso had an ample share of sickly, malnourished Indians who drifted in and out of the compound, appearing one day, remaining for a short time, then disappearing again without a word of notice. Luiz put them to work when he could, and occasionally Jordan recruited a few of them to accompany him in *batelãos* to visit an *estrada,* from which he would return with a small number of *bolachas* in tow behind the canoes. But mostly, the Indians just sat and watched whatever activities were taking place.

Spencer tried to initiate conversations with the shy women and children who hid their faces behind their hands whenever she approached, but she had little success. Nor were the men disposed to speak with her. She drew numerous astounded stares and was certain the color of her hair amazed them, but no one dared mention it. In the evenings, the Indians gathered around campfires scattered amidst rude dwellings which they were able to construct in a single day. They were expert at palm thatching, and since she still had a problem with her leaky roof, she determined to learn from them how to fix it. Thatching would give her something to do until the Indians gained enough confidence to approach her with their medical problems.

Sadly, though she saw many who needed help, no one sought her out to get it. Luiz approached her once about an upset stomach and was effusively grateful for the stomach powders she gave him, but other than that, her idea of a clinic remained just that—an idea, existing in her head alone. She bided her time until an afternoon when Jordan had once again set off with Luiz and a few Indians to visit one of his distant *estradas,* then she approached a small group of women engaged in plaiting palm leafs into large sections of thatch.

Sitting down in their midst, she smiled and made a show of admiring their work. The women immediately stopped working and sat still as stones, their hands resting in their laps, their eyes averted. Knowing they understood little Portuguese, she made no effort to converse in that language, and instead decided to use English, since the "lĩngua geral" was still quite beyond her.

"You do wonderful work," she said politely, bending over and closely examining the carefully woven mat of the woman nearest her. She extended her hand to touch the mat, and the woman gave a frightened little shriek and snatched the thatching out of reach.

"Why are you so afraid? I won't hurt you." Glancing around, Spencer saw fear and trepidation reflected in the round black eyes of all the Indian women. Several of the children scooted behind their mothers and anxiously peeped out at her, and Spencer suspected that if she made another move, they would suddenly all get up and make a mad dash for the jungle.

For several moments, she sat very still, at a loss as to what to do next. There seemed to be no way to bridge the cultural gap between herself and these women. She was the only one among them with red hair, white skin, and blue-green eyes. She was also the only one fully clothed. The oldest females in the group wore only plaited grass skirts, covering from waist to thigh, and even the younger ones had wrapped only the bare essentials in lengths of gaily printed cloth that Jordan himself must have furnished in payment for services rendered by their husbands. The children were completely naked, except for the odd amulet or two suspended on thongs around their necks.

She noticed one woman looking intently at her boots sticking out from beneath her skirt. Slowly, she leaned forward, unlaced one boot, and removed it. All eyes stared at her foot as she wiggled her toes to show the group she was human, like they were: She realized she might make more headway if she also removed her clothes, but quickly discarded the idea as being too accommodating. They would have to accept her as she was, just as she was trying to accept them. Never once did she express shock or disapproval at their careless nudity, nor indeed did she feel shocked. The Indians were so much creatures of the forest that when they did don clothing, it looked out of place on them. Fortunately, Indian men concealed their privates in animal skin pouches, or she might have been embarrassed, after all.

For an hour or more, she sat wiggling her toes and trying to catch someone's eye so she could smile at them. But the women were careful never to look directly at her. After a time, they went back to thatching, but if she showed too much interest, they did as before—shrieked and pulled their work away. Spencer grew very frustrated; at this rate, she would never be able to entice the women to make use of her clinic. To stave off boredom, she examined each of the children with her eyes. Most of them showed signs of parasite infestation, and several had loose bowels. From time to time, they darted a short distance away to relieve themselves, squatting unconcernedly in the dust and not bothering to kick dust over the droppings afterward.

The lack of sanitation bothered Spencer. She saw there was much she could do to improve health conditions at Paraïso, beginning with teaching the people to go into the jungle to relieve themselves, and to dispose of their garbage and other refuse in burial pits, instead of tossing it on the ground. She put her boots back on and lamented the barefootedness of the Indians, who took no particular care to watch where they stepped. Probably, Jordan had no time to worry about the personal habits of the Indians, or else he didn't notice their lack of hygiene because he never bothered to sit among them, making observations.

When the women dispersed to begin preparations

for the evening meal, Spencer returned to her lonely hut, with a better idea of how to repair her leaky roof but no idea at all of how to establish communication with the Indians. She opened a tin of sardines, which she was beginning to despise, and had just started to eat when she heard a terrible scream. Loud shrieks, wails, and anxious shouts pierced the air. Dropping the tin can, she dashed out of the hut and headed for the direction of the noise. It was coming from the Indian encampment on the fringes of the compound where she had spent the afternoon.

It did not take long to discover what had happened. Two small boys had apparently been tussling over a miniature blow gun. One of them had fallen into the women's cookfire, burning his bare back, arms, buttocks, and legs. The mother of the burned child was shrieking and wailing, cradling the boy against her naked breasts. After that first chilling scream, the child himself was silent, his eyes round and wide with shock, the full extent of what he had done to himself not yet completely assimilated.

Spencer and the child's father reached the boy and his mother at the same time. While the father busied himself grunting and shouting at the cowering women, Spencer elbowed her way close enough to examine the burns. One look told her they were severe and involved a considerable amount of skin area. Even the hair had been singed off the back of the boy's head. Racing back to her hut, she made a mental list of what she would need to treat him. In a few minutes, she had gathered the items and was racing back again to the Indian camp.

By then, the boy had been carried inside one of

the palm-thatch structures, but there were so many people crowded into the hut that Spencer could not get through. She pushed and shoved. Docile creatures that they were, the Indians fell back, and finally, she got close enough to see the child lying on a mat on his stomach. His father bent over him, making grunting sounds in his throat. Off to one side knelt his mother, weeping silently into her hands as another woman tried to comfort her. Spencer went directly to the father and touched his arm.

When he looked up and saw her, the man recoiled in shock. For an Indian, he was a big man, with broad, squarish shoulders, an impressive physique, a large, round face, and the typically flattened Indian nose. He wore a necklace of jaguar claws, proclaiming him a good hunter and a man of importance. When he recovered from the surprise of seeing her in his hut, he seemed less in awe of her than any of the Indians she had thus far encountered. She cast about for some way to tell him she was a doctor, and finally decided to show him her medicines instead.

Holding up the basket in which she had hurriedly stuffed everything, she pointed to its contents, then motioned to the prostrate boy. The man frowned dubiously. Spencer desperately wished Jordan or Luiz were there to explain what she wanted to do. "I can help," she said. "I have powerful medicines to soothe his burns and ease his pain. But I must work quickly. Every moment we delay will make it less likely I can save him."

She knew by the man's expression that he understood not a single word. She tried the Portuguese word for doctor, but got no response. Then she remembered what Luiz had called her: a *macumbeiro*. Tentatively, she pointed to herself and said the word. The Indian's pudgy eyebrows lifted, his black eyes questioning. *"Macumbeiro?"* he repeated.

She nodded. Just then, another man pushed his way inside the hut. He was a scrawny old fellow, with no teeth, sparse hair, sagging skin, and fetid breath. He peered curiously into Spencer's face. Two feathers—a yellow and a red one—were entwined in his thinning hair. The boy's father stepped back respectfully, and with some difficulty the old fellow knelt down and peered at the already blistering flesh on the boy's back. Spencer winced when he touched it with bony fingers and made a clicking sound with his tongue.

He got up and said something in the guttural Indian tongue. The boy's mother began to wail again, while the father stood silently, his brown face blanching almost white. Spencer guessed that the boy had been declared a hopeless case. The old man removed a mottled snakeskin from around his waist and gave it to the father, indicating he should hang it over the boy's head. The father nodded, eyes bleak with sorrow, and the old man then departed the hut.

As he did so, the women outside set up a shrieking and wailing. Drums began to thud. In the cacophony of sound, Spencer could hardly make herself heard. *"Macumbeiro!"* she shouted at the boy's father, pointing to herself.

"Macumbeiro," the boy's father said, pointing past her to where the old man had departed.

Spencer tried other Portuguese words and phrases, but *macumbeiro* seemed to be the only one the father understood. She dug in her bag, pulled out a jar of ointment, and eagerly held it up, indicating she wanted to spread it on the boy's burns. The boy's father shook his head; he had already given up hope. Praying he wouldn't stop her, she pushed past him and knelt down.

Saving the boy might be beyond her capabilities, but at least she could do more for him than hang a snakeskin over his head. Sensing her presence, the child turned his head and looked at her. His big black eyes held wordless suffering and a stark terror that lanced her soul. To Spencer, he embodied all the suffering of the Indians she had witnessed since her arrival on the Amazon. A cold determination took hold of her; she would not let him die. Somehow, someway, she would keep him alive.

Chapter Eighteen

In the days that followed, Spencer learned that the boy's name was Abelardo and his father was the chief of the Huitotos of that area. She could not pronounce the father's name and in her mind simply called him Tom, because his name, whatever it was, began with a T. While Tom seemed resigned to his son's imminent death, he nonetheless appreciated Spencer's ceaseless efforts to save the boy. She battled shock, pain, infection, and all the other accompanying problems with every weapon in the arsenal of her pharmacopia. After three days, she still could not be sure of winning, but at least she had a sense of being needed.

Her insistence upon remaining at the boy's side soon won her the shy acceptance of all the Huitotos. They brought her food and fresh water, then sat quietly, watching her every move with intense interest. Even the old *macumbeiro* came and watched, clicking his tongue in resolute pessimism but curious to study her methods just the same. Her biggest problem was getting the boy to eat. He was in such pain he had no appetite, and the opiates she administered to ease his suffering only took the edge from it without giving him real surcease. Observing her dilemma, the old *macumbeiro* left the hut for a short time and returned with a gourdful of a milky liquid, which he then tilted into the child's mouth, spilling much of it in the process.

Spencer could only guess what was in the concoction but did not protest, assuming that anything in the boy's stomach at this point was better than nothing. To her amazement, the boy then fell into a deep, painless sleep, from which he later reawakened looking refreshed and expressing a desire to eat. While his joyful mother fed him broth and bits of monkey meat, Spencer regarded the *macumbeiro* with astonishment and a good bit of anger; if the old man knew of something that would help, why had he waited this long to offer assistance?

In answer to the unspoken question, the *macumbeiro* clicked his tongue, as if to say it was all useless anyway; the boy was still going to die. Spencer examined the smear of white in the gourd, tasted and smelled it, but could not identify the substance. Her perplexity pleased the old man. He pretended not to understand when she begged him to show her what he had put in the gourd. That night he brought more, then wandered outside and could be heard chanting outside the doorway of the smoky, dimly lit hut.

The next day, Jordan and Luiz returned with a greater number of rubber *bolachas* than they had ever before brought back at one time. On her way into the hut after a short respite from her nursing chores, Spencer spotted the two men and a handful of Indians unloading the harvest and storing it in a large grass-roofed structure near the riverbank. The mere sight of Jordan made her heart hammer and her knees grow weak, but she reminded herself of the distance between them and did not go to greet him.

An hour later, Jordan himself burst into the hut. "So this is where you are!" he barked. "When you didn't come to say hello, I thought something bad had happened to you. The least you could do is welcome me back to Paraïso after I was gone so long a time."

"You never told me how long you would be gone, so how would I know when to look for your return?" she coolly inquired in her most professional tone of voice. "In any case, as you can see, I'm quite occupied trying to keep this poor child alive."

"How bad is he?" Jordan asked, coming closer, filling the hut with his blond masculinity. "I heard about him as soon as we landed. Luiz has made great progress understanding the *"lĩngua geral"*, and the child's accident was the big item of news. Will the poor kid make it, do you think?"

"It's still too soon to tell. I hope so. I'm doing my best."

"I see you haven't let this opportunity go to waste. They're calling you the Great White Voodoo Woman."

"Voodoo Woman! Now where would they get the idea for *that* nonsense? I've been *trying* to tell them I'm a doctor, but they don't understand the word."

"They got the idea from you apparently. The first day you were here, you told Luiz you were a *macumbeiro,* and later you told the chief the same thing. Don't you know what the word means? It's someone who practices voodoo and black magic.

Brazilians, Colombians, Africans, Indians—everyone in this part of the world has a healthy respect for *macumbeiros.*"

"It's Luiz's fault. He wouldn't believe I was really a doctor, and when he asked if I meant *macumbeiro,* I said yes, thinking it was a pharmacist or midwife or something similar. Should I try and explain that I'm not a voodoo woman after all?"

Jordan waved his hand. "Don't bother. I can't see any real harm in it, and you'll get more respect as a *macumbeiro* than you will as a doctor. Just be careful not to slight or insult the old voodoo chief of the Huitotos. He's a real *macumbeiro.*"

"So I gathered. He's been giving the boy some kind of medicine that works better than what I've got. If the boy lives, the old man can claim it was due to him, and he may be right."

Wanting to tackle a more volatile subject, Spencer motioned Jordan away from Abelardo. While the boy was dozing, was as good a time as any to quiz Jordan on his plans for the future. "How is the harvest going? Will you soon be ready to take it down to Manaus?"

Jordan narrowed his eyes. "Not for a while yet. But it's going great. As long as nothing happens to prevent me from getting it to market, it should bring a healthy sum. I'll let you know when I'm ready to leave for Manaus."

Spencer's heart plunged into her boots. Apparently Jordan had not changed his mind about the futility of trying to fight Arana. The only thing that mattered to him was making a fortune on his rubber.

"Dinna worry about me keeping busy while ye're off in the jungle visitin' yer *estradas,*" she said acidly. "Someone has t' look after the Indians. I guess I'm the only one who cares."

His glance was level and not the least ashamed. "I admit I sleep better at night knowing you're here in Paraïso. Though I'd sleep even better if I knew you could handle a Winchester."

"Maybe I'll teach meself. We could be attacked and wiped out like they were at La Reserva."

"Spencer . . ." His voice dropped a note. Suddenly he sounded weary. "Do you think I would go away and leave you here alone if I thought Loayza intended to attack Paraïso?"

"I dinna know what ye'd do," Spencer retorted. "I've come t' feel I dinna know ye very well a-tall, or else I was mistaken in what I *thought* I knew."

He sighed heavily. "When I mentioned the Winchester, I wasn't thinking of you having to defend yourself against Loayza. It's all the other dangers—the jungle dangers—I was thinking of. Don't worry. I don't expect Loayza to come here. He can justify an attack on La Reserva as being an act of war on Colombia, but he could never justify attacking an American outpost. Arana would have Loayza's hide if he jeopardized sales to American companies by shooting and killing Americans. Besides, since it was Hardenburg who found our *batelão,* Loayza doesn't really know it was us who spied on El Encanto. If we remained silent about what we saw, he'd never know. We'd be relatively safe."

"That kind of safety makes me sick!" Spencer spat in a blaze of fury. Remembering Abelardo, she tried to speak quietly, but the effort was as futile as trying to contain her brogue. "Ye dinna know me very well if ye think I intend t' keep quiet about this forever just so you can collect yer damn rubber with a minimum of bother!"

"Stop jumping to erroneous conclusions, Spencer. I wasn't suggesting we keep quiet forever. But while you're plotting how to expose Arana when we finally get to Manaus, bear one thing in mind: As soon as Arana discovers what we know—and that we intend to stop him—the lives of everyone at Paraîso will immediately be endangered. This boy you're trying so hard to save might one day be lying dead with his head split open, because *you* refused to see reason and went off half-cocked."

"I dinna believe ye ever intended t' do anything about Arana, Jordan! I just dinna believe it. At the moment, he's not threatenin' ye personally so the only thing on yer mind is gatherin' yer harvest. I dinna know why I ever thought ye were so strong of character. Obviously I allowed me attraction to ye t' cloud me judgment."

Now, it was Jordan's voice that rose angrily. "Your judgment was already hopelessly clouded by your arrogance! Who are you to judge me? You haven't the least idea what's in my mind or in my heart. Don't you understand? I have responsibilities. To the people here, to my sisters at home, and last but not least, to myself. I've invested a big chunk of my life in this enterprise, and I can't afford to fail. Unlike you, I haven't some other profession to fall back on. If I don't succeed, I'll be a dismal failure who takes other people down with me."

"We're talkin' about gettin' rich on rubber, not performin' some noble service t' humanity! Dinna cloak yer slaverin' greed in the mantle of 'responsibility' t' others!"

"Then don't cloak your self-righteousness in

idealism! You think you're better than anybody else, don't you? More noble, more heroic. Well, you're a fraud, Spencer. The only reason you're so virtuous is because you've never been tempted. You've spent your entire life crusading, and its protected you from ever feeling anything, from wanting and craving things you can't have . . ."

"That's so unfair!" She swallowed hard to keep from sobbing. "I've had t' fight for everything I've ever gotten—that's true. But I *have* been tempted."

"By what? All you've ever really wanted is to be a man, and by God, you've almost achieved it . . . What, are those tears? How very human! So you aren't quite a plaster saint after all. You do have feelings."

"Get out of here, Jordan! Ye've awakened Abelardo . . ."

Abelardo did indeed begin to whimper. Jordan stood a moment looking down at the suffering child. Then he looked at her, and his eyes held a naked torment that mirrored Abelardo's.

"You push me too hard, Spencer," he whispered raggedly. "I'm only a man, not some hero in a romantic novel. But a mere man isn't enough for you, is it? Never in a million years could I meet your expectations."

She wanted to deny it—to protest that she did want him, and most of the time, he exceeded her expectations. But he turned on his heel and left, and she had to go back to taking care of Abelardo. Bitter tears coursed down her cheeks. The irony of it was that she could not have gone off and left the boy, even if Jordan had said he was ready to go to Manaus and fight Arana that very day.

* * *

Two weeks passed. Abelardo clung to life and began to get stronger. The least severe burns evidenced healing. Tender pink skin formed over them, and it was no longer necessary for Spencer to spend so much time with the child, though she enjoyed the time they did spend together and used it to teach him English and to learn Tupi. When she wasn't with him, she held open clinic in her own hut, which now boasted a brand-new roof, compliments of Abelardo's grateful mother.

The first person she invited to attend the clinic was the old *macumbeiro*. He walked around it on the outside, chanting, before he would set a foot on the inside. When he did enter, he proceeded to poke into every crate and box that held her medicines and supplies. Still hoping he might reveal more about the potion he had administered to Abelardo, she tried explaining the uses of her own powders and potions, but the language differences proved too great. Fortunately, the old voodoo chief showed no jealousy. From that day onward, he actually encouraged his people to come to her for medical aid.

It was an exceedingly odd relationship, Spencer often thought. After she had instructed the Huitotos in crude sign language on how to deal with their fevers, loose bowels, or injuries, they went to the old *macumbeiro* to receive some amulet or further instruction, which usually consisted of wearing a dead bat around their necks for a day or two, chanting something, or inhaling the smoke of some particular burnt object. On her own, it would have taken Spencer months, if not years, to gain the confidence of the shy Indians, but Abelardo's recovery and the old voodoo chief's acceptance cut through the barriers in the twinkling of an eye.

Pleased at the outcome of recent events, she went about her work with a quiet confidence and satisfaction that could have been called happiness, if she were not so miserable over her continued stand-off with Jordan. At night, lying alone in her hammock, she dreamed of him coming to her, taking her in his arms and stoking the fiery passion that still flared whenever she saw him. Did Jordan still want her? Did he feel the same way? She saw no encouraging signs that he was suffering as badly as she was.

Jordan was obsessed with getting rich. He came and went, bestowing nary a word to her between journeys. On the few occasions when he was in camp, he looked haggard, driven, and overworked. The stack of *bolachas* soon overflowed the storage hut, and each time he set out in the *batelãos,* he took as many Indians as possible to help transport the harvest back to Paraïso. Abelardo's father often went with him, and sometimes, the only Indian male in the compound was the old *macumbeiro.*

Between doctoring the Indians and teaching English to Abelardo, Spencer had plenty to occupy her time, but nothing could fill the emptiness that plagued her day and night. If she thought too much about Jordan—or Arana—she was likely to dissolve into tears of frustration. She told herself that Jordan had been terribly unfair to her during their argument. But in retrospect, she conceded that she had not given much thought to his concerns. She had expected him to drop everything to battle Arana.

Yet she couldn't simply forget about the

monster! If Jordan delayed too long, she would have to fight him on her own. Doing nothing was inconceivable. More and more, her hope centered on Walter Hardenburg. Maybe the young American's protests in Iquitos would prove effective. Maybe there would be a letter from him awaiting her in Manaus. Maybe Orjuela, the Colombian emissary, had already been released, and the outbreaks of violence and mistreatment of the Indians would soon end. And maybe, she thought in a moment of bleak humor, Arana would decide to get out of the rubber business and go into missionary work instead.

As the third week crept by, Spencer's only relief from the misery of her thoughts came in the brief, joyful moments when Abelardo's progress thrilled her. The child's recovery was proof that miracles could happen. Even the most severely burned areas showed no sign of infection, and there was every indication that new skin would eventually cover the raw, weeping flesh. The boy would always bear scars from the incident, but severe disfigurement was out of the question. From the front, his scars would barely be noticeable.

Despite his continuing discomfort, Abelardo's smile flashed often now, and it was an especially charming, beguiling smile. The boy was quick-witted, insatiably curious, and eager to learn. Spencer thought she had never before encountered such a bright, personable child. His merry brown eyes, plump cheeks, and straight black hair hinted of future handsomeness, and his sturdy hands and feet suggested he would be big like his father. If ever there was a born leader, Abelardo was one, destined to follow in his father's footsteps.

"Good morning, Doc-tor," he would say when she arrived to dress his burns.

"Good morning, Abelardo," she would respond, allowing no hint of her Irish brogue to sully the English she spoke to her avid student. "And how do your people say 'good morning'?"

Sometimes he would tell her, and sometimes not. Often, he just laughed and pointed at some object in the hut. "Walking stick!" he would crow triumphantly, much more interested in practicing his new vocabulary than teaching her the *"lĩngua geral."*

So the days passed, until finally, Jordan had enough rubber to make the journey downriver to Manaus. "How are you going to transport it all?" Spencer asked, when he told her the news that he'd be ready to leave in two days' time. It was early evening. They were standing on the riverbank watching Abelardo's father and some other Indians unload four *batelãos* heavy-laden with rubber from Jordan's last foray to his *estradas*.

"We'll load as much as we can onto the *Evangeline,* and the rest we'll tow behind her. One way or another, we'll make it," he said.

"But there's so much," Spencer protested doubtfully, thinking that even the *Liberal* would be loaded to the gunwales, trying to move so many *bolachas*. The *Evangeline* might sink under all the weight.

"If I can't take it all this time, I'll store the excess and take it the next . . . How's Abelardo? Will you be able to leave him?"

"I think so. He's healing so well that I don't anticipate any problems arising. If some do, the old *macumbeiro* will be able to deal with them. And Abelardo's mother has watched me change his dressings often enough that she should be able to do it, now, too. I'm more than ready to go to Manaus, Jordan. I've *been* ready."

Jordan's mouth tightened at the reminder. "I know you have, Spencer. But don't expect too much when we get there. I have a plan in mind, but it's possible nothing will come of it."

"What plan?" Spencer demanded, but Jordan only raised a hand, as if to calm her.

"Now don't get excited, Spencer. I shouldn't have mentioned it. You're like a cocked rifle, ready to go off. Get your finger off the trigger, sweetheart. Until I see if my plan has a chance of succeeding, I'm not saying another word about it."

"Blessed Saint Brigid! Ye can be so damned infuriating!" Spencer exploded. "Why won't ye tell me? All this time, I've been thinking ye dinna really care—but in reality, ye've been makin' plans without me!"

Jordan's glance was cool, his green eyes murky. "Haven't you learned by now, Spencer? No one tells me what I should or shouldn't do. No one controls me. I especially don't have to ask a hot-tempered Irish female for permission to 'make plans' about things that concern me every bit as much as they do her. Arana has been my enemy far longer than he's been yours. In as much as I have more to lose by taking him on, I should be the one who decides what methods we will use. Is that clear?"

Spencer was so angry she could scarcely see straight. If she stood talking to Jordan a minute longer, she feared she might do something completely illogical and possibly violent. "Perfectly clear, Mr. King," she managed to get out. Then, to keep from smacking him, she turned on her heel and stalked away.

Jordan stared after her a moment, wondering if he ought to have told her, after all, what he had in mind. Then he shook his head, clearing it of the ridiculous thought. Where Arana was concerned, Spencer simply could not be trusted to stay calm and reasonable. It was therefore better she knew nothing of what he intended. Probably his plan would be too tame for her anyway. Before he had a chance to try it, she'd be picking it to shreds. She had no faith in him whatsoever, and her lack of trust—indeed, her scorn—cut like a knife. Though he knew in his heart he was doing the right thing, his manhood felt sorely lacerated.

Watching her walk away, head high, back straight as a ramrod, he was tempted to dash after her, seize her, and kiss her into submission. That was what she needed—a reminder of who was boss. He did intend to deal with Arana, but in his own time, in his own way. How dare she suggest otherwise and insist that he prove himself to her?

He was still smarting from their last argument, and their present one had done nothing to soothe the sting. Every time she looked at him, accusation and reproach darkened her magnificent eyes. What he wanted to see was love, respect, approval, and desire—the normal emotions a man hoped to arouse in his future wife. Spencer displayed none of these; rather, she made him feel small, incompetent, and unworthy. If he didn't resolve this matter of Arana to her satisfaction, she would probably never marry him. Did he even want her for a wife?

Facing contempt across the breakfast table was something to which no man would willingly condemn himself for the rest of his life.

After a few moments of inner turmoil, he went back to helping the Indians unload the *batelãos*. Hard work was the only way he had discovered to keep his emotions in check. Work was his healing balm and saving grace. Being near Spencer and not being able to communicate, much less make love to her, as he longed to do, made hard work an absolute necessity.

Chapter Nineteen

Jordan loaded the *Evangeline* as heavily as he dared, then floated as many *bolachas* of rubber behind her as possible, attached by long tow ropes to the stern. He still had almost a third of the harvest left, which would have to be transported the next time. The harvest this season had been excellent, and he was pleased—especially since it wasn't over yet. There was still time before the rains came for his *seringueiros* to gather more, and he was sure they would make a great effort because he had promised them all bonuses if they did.

Another load like this one, and he could chance quitting the business altogether. Another year or two would guarantee the fulfillment of his dreams. But he'd be willing to sell out early just to get out of Brazil. The only man he wouldn't sell to was Don Julio Ceśar Arana.

Spencer came aboard at the last moment, and the look on her face told him it was going to be a long, silent journey—which suited him fine. It would be enough of a challenge keeping the unwieldy, overloaded vessel on course. Luiz was not accompanying him, but a few of the Indians were hitching a ride halfway to Manaus so he would have help for a portion of the trip at least. The second half was easier, anyway. The closer they got to Manaus, the less chance there was of encountering obstructions in the river or being attacked by unknown hostiles on shore.

As he stoked the engine and then cast off, Luiz and the remaining Indians waved and gestured good luck. Jordan saw Spencer waving at the old *macumbeiro* and Abelardo's parents who had come down to see them off. The *Evangeline* had never had such a well-attended departure. With a touch of jealousy, he realized it was due to Spencer. In the short time she had been there, she had made many friends, who hated to see the Great White Voodoo Woman leave. As the launch steamed out of sight of Paraîso, he could hear some of the younger women wailing in grief at her departure.

The journey passed uneventfully, with no dangerous or amusing incidents, save for a persistent manatee who kept trailing them and butting its head against the floating *bolachas*. Halfway to Manaus, the Indians departed, none of them having any desire to see the wonders of civilization. Another remnant of the tribe lived in that vicinity, and those who had accompanied them were going to visit relatives.

Jordan had anticipated at least a few difficult moments, but the trip seemed charmed—except for the hostility of his traveling companion. Spencer was coldly polite and infuriatingly professional. Never once did she lapse into her brogue, which struck Jordan as particularly ominous. At least when she was angry and saying "ye" instead of "you," and running her words together, he knew where he stood. Now, the gulf between them was so wide as to be unbridgeable. They arrived in Manaus in the shortest time it had ever taken for the *Evangeline* to make the journey. But to Jordan, the trip seemed endless.

At midmorning, they tied up at a noisy, stinking wharf near the marketplace, where the smell of rubber permeated everything. It came from cool, dark warehouses where newly cured, black-brown rubber lay awaiting shipment to Liverpool and New York. As always, Jordan felt overwhelmed by the city and its smells. After the vast green wilderness they had left behind, Manaus was a feast for the senses. Even Spencer was stunned into respectful silence. Her awed contemplation of the bustling docks gave Jordan a sudden inspiration.

Going to her side, he said: "I'm going to be tied up here most of the day, Spencer, but I'll make arrangements for you to get to my house. Why don't you rest and relax this afternoon? Tonight I'll take you to supper and the opera house. There's bound to be some sort of entertainment going on there. I think we need to immerse ourselves in the delights of civilization. We've been too long wallowing in the jungle."

Her blue-green eyes widened, as if she could not believe what she was hearing. A light came into them, and Jordan was reminded of one of his young sisters anticipating Christmas. "Oh, could we really see the opera house?"

"Of course, if I can get tickets." Silently, he vowed he'd get tickets if he had to pay a fortune for them. "Get out your prettiest frock, Spencer. Tonight, we're going to conquer Manaus."

Her face fell. "I . . . I'm not sure I have anything suitable to wear."

"Then *buy* something," he snapped. "When you get to the house, ask Chico where to go. He'll direct you to one of the shops where I have an account, and you can charge whatever you buy to me. Later, you can pay me for it, if you must. I have a feeling you won't accept charity."

"I won't!" Spencer said haughtily, lifting her chin and clipping each word. "Perhaps we shouldn't go out tonight, after all. Don't you have some plan to put into effect, anyway? I'd rather you spend the evening implementing your precious plan than taking me to the opera house."

As anger flared, he almost withdrew his offer but stopped himself just in time. Arguing with Spencer never got him anywhere. It was time to try wooing her with good food and fine wine in a romantic atmosphere. Given the right setting, maybe he could still convert her from hostile adversary to willing partner—maybe even eager lover, though he feared that was too much to hope for. "How about if we discuss my plan over dinner tonight? If we talk business while we enjoy ourselves, will you still feel that you're cheating on the world?"

Her face reflected her inner struggle. Happily, the less austere side won. "I suppose that would be all right—so long as you don't try to weasel out of the discussion once you get me alone with you."

"I've been alone with you on this boat for a week or more. Why are you so afraid of being alone with me over dinner in a public restaurant?"

She frowned. "I don't know. I just am . . . But

we will talk about Arana tonight, won't we? Do you swear to it?"

"I swear to it if you'll swear to a truce between us. No more harsh words and accusations. Tonight we'll act like . . . lovers."

At the word "lovers," her head came up, and she stared at him, obviously nonplussed and unsure of herself. Sensing dangerous waters, he quickly corrected himself. "I mean like old friends. We *are* friends, aren't we, Spencer? If I can't be your lover, I'd still very much like to be your friend."

"I . . . I'll do me best t' find somethin' suitable t' wear," she murmured distractedly, bypassing the question altogether.

Ears pricking at the sound of her brogue, he smiled down at her, pleased by the small crack in her armor. If he had his way, it would soon be a large gap—then he'd divest her of it altogether. Taking her hand, he kissed her curled fingers. "Until tonight, dear Spencer. Tonight, we'll discuss my plan for Arana and make everything right between us."

By late afternoon, Jordan had a good portion of his rubber unloaded. The rest he turned over to a responsible man who had overseen the storage of his harvest in the past. Checking the position of the sun, he decided he had better go after the opera tickets. If he hurried, he would also have enough time to begin putting his plan concerning Arana into action. By the time he reported to Spencer that night, he hoped to know exactly what was possible and what wasn't.

Obtaining the tickets was relatively easy; the star performer in town at the moment was a lesser name than many who played at the famed opera house. All of Manaus was not frantic to see her. He bought tickets from a vendor on San Sebastian Square, then turned down a small side street where poorer buildings were sandwiched between the sumptuous structures of the rich. Jungle smells lay trapped in the narrow alleyways, a potent reminder that even in the city, primitive dangers were not far away.

He searched until he found a modest, white-washed building with a red-tiled roof, not unlike his own house. A sign on the crumbling wall surrounding it read: *Journal de Povo,* which translated into *People's Newspaper.* Below it in smaller print was the name of the Chief Editor and Publisher, Roberto Ramalho.

Hoping to find Ramalho at home, Jordan entered the open gate and went immediately to the door. The *Journal de Povo* was one of many scandal sheets that circulated on the streets of Manaus and throughout the Amazon Territory as far away as Belém. Jordan had picked it precisely because it was a scandal sheet, as opposed to a respected newspaper with a staid board of directors wanting to approve every controversial story. However, it was the most serious and respected of the smaller publications, read by virtually everyone who relished a bit of gossip and wanted to believe it was true. The *Journal de Povo* rarely, if ever, stooped to publishing outright lies. Occasionally, it dared to take on public officials, wealthy rubber barons, and others whom most newspapers had the good sense to leave alone.

It was almost a one-man operation, and though Jordan had never met Roberto Ramalho, he respected him for his reputation as an "editor who could not be bought." This was the first time he had reason to contact the man, and he desperately hoped that Ramalho would be open to his plan, which involved the *Journal de Povo*. If he wasn't, Jordan would have little to discuss with Spencer over dinner that night or any night in the near future.

He banged on the closed wooden door, waited several moments, then banged again. A short, plump female wearing a full red skirt, white lace blouse, and matching kerchief over her hair finally opened the door and asked what he wanted. In his best Portuguese, Jordan explained that he had come to see Roberto Ramalho. The plump, black-eyed woman told him he would have to come back in the morning; the office was closed this late in the afternoon. Jordan persisted, demanding to know if Ramalho was home.

The woman admitted he was, but still denied him entrance. Jordan then slipped her a few Brazilian notes, and she grinned widely and threw open the door, urging him to enter. She led him through the cool, dark house to an inner courtyard, dominated by a bright-red-and-yellow parrot chained by one leg to a perch. Upon seeing him, the parrot began to scream: *"Bandido! Assassino! Ladrão!"*

Taken aback at being called a thief and a murderer, Jordan did not at first notice the other occupant of the courtyard: a tall, thin, bald-headed man with an elaborate mustache who sat drinking *cafězinho* in a corner and studying a folded newspaper.

When he saw Jordan, he looked up questioningly. Ignoring the raucous parrot, Jordan quickly introduced himself. "I'm Jordan King . . . Excuse me, Jordano Rei."

"Is all right to speak English. I speak pretty good," Romalho said, motioning to a wrought-iron chair across the table from him. "Sit down. *Cafězinho, por favor,*" he said to the woman, directing her to bring more refreshments. *"Pedro silẽncio!"*

At his command, the bird fell silent. The woman, too, scurried away, and Jordan sat down, pleased to note the keen intelligence and guarded interest in Romalho's golden-brown eyes. The Brazilian was studying him intently over his lowered newspaper.

"Why do you wish to see me, Senhor Rei? We have never met, though I know your name. You are one rubber baron who lives modestly in Manaus, while the rest spend money as though it grew on the same trees from which they make their fortunes."

Romalho spoke English with a slightly French accent, not so unusual considering the European influence in the city. The most popular newspaper in Manaus, Jordan suddenly recalled, was *Le Matin,* printed entirely in French and devoted to fostering "the gay spirit of Parisian life" in Manaus. Surprisingly, it was a copy of *Le Matin,* not the *Journal de Povo,* that Romalho held in his slender brown hands.

Jordan got right to the point. "I'm here because I have information which could prove very damaging to one of the leading citizens of Manaus."

Romalho's dark eyebrows lifted. He set down *Le Matin* on the small, round table and leaned back in his chair. "So you wish to discredit a competitor by giving this information to me. Is that not so?"

"Not quite," Jordan said. "What I really wish is to put the man out of business—not merely to discredit him. And there's no personal gain in it for me. If anything, I'm risking all I own by coming here."

Romalho looked surprised and intrigued. "This is some sort of personal vendetta between the two of you? He has harmed you in some way, or harmed someone in your family?"

"I believe he's responsible for the deaths of several of my *seringueiros*. More than that, he's killed hundreds of Indians, wiped out the rubber depot of a friend of mine, and slaughtered all of his workers and their families. His crimes are almost too numerous to list, and it's long past time that he be held accountable."

"Then why do you come to me, senhor? You should be speaking to the *comandante de polícia.*"

"The Brazilian police have no authority over this man. He is not a Brazilian citizen, and the crimes I've just mentioned took place outside Brazil, in territory currently being disputed by two other South American countries."

"Ah . . . the Putumayo rubber lands." Romalho sighed wearily and commenced twisting the ends of his mustache. "I know of whom you speak, senhor. But it would be wise not to mention his name aloud. In Brazil, even the walls have ears. I trust only Pedro, my parrot, but he, poor bird, trusts no one, not even me."

"You know who I mean?" Jordan asked in surprise.

Just then the woman in the red skirt, lace blouse, and white kerchief brought him a *cafẽzinho*. Jordan refrained from speaking again until she left the room. Then he leaned forward in his chair. "Have you received other reports concerning this man's activities on the Putumayo?"

Roberto Romalho regarded him sadly. "Wait here a moment, senhor. Drink your *cafẽzinho* while I fetch something that will be of great interest to you."

Jordan did as he was told, while Romalho rose and left the courtyard, returning a few moments later with a sheaf of papers in his hand. "Look at these, senhor. I presume you can read Portuguese."

"Well enough," Jordan said, accepting the large stack of dog-eared papers. It took him only a few stunned moments to determine what they were. "Why, these are eyewitness accounts of the same sort of crimes I came here to tell you about—all of them involving Arana and his chief henchman, Miguel Loayza!"

"Hush, senhor! I asked you not to mention names. I pay my servants well, but I could never compete with the mightiest rubber baron in all of Manaus. If the Peruvian were to threaten them—or to offer rewards beyond their wildest dreams—I have no doubt they would betray me. They are poor people, after all, and of the lower class. They could easily convince themselves they were doing the right thing."

"Sorry," Jordan said contritely, looking about to

make certain the woman in the red skirt wasn't hiding behind a potted palm or some other clump of greenery in the courtyard.

"But why have you done nothing about these?" He rattled the papers in Romalho's face. "How long have you been collecting them? The top letter is dated more than three years ago."

"Please do not excite yourself, senhor. Give me back the depositions and listen carefully. I will tell you how they came into my possession and why I am powerless to do anything with them."

"All right . . ." Jordan said, handing over the papers and sitting back. "Explain. I'm listening."

Roberto Romalho set the papers on the table and rested his hands on them, as if they were the most precious—or most terrible—things he had in his possession. "It was at least six years ago when the Peruvian's crimes first came to my attention. One of his own overseers came to me and told how he was forced to whip Indians, shoot, torture, and starve them, while he was employed up the Putumayo. I became very excited and planned a great exposé in my newspaper. But before I could print the first word, this man—my only witness—was found dead in the bed of a whore. He was examined by a *doutor* who claimed he died of heart failure, due to amorous exertions. Later, I learned that the *doutor* was the Peruvian's own personal physician. Of course, I could not print this story. My witness was dead and could not corroborate it. Also, the circumstances of his death suggested he was not a man of good character."

"But what about all those others?" Jordan nodded toward the stack. "Surely they didn't all die mysterious deaths."

"Alas, senhor, they did. Either that or they simply disappeared and were never heard from again. I have spent six years gathering these reports, begging reluctant witnesses to confide in me. Sometimes I had to pay them, not as a bribe, you understand, but so they could flee somewhere safe. Many of the letters are unsigned, because I could not convince the witnesses to tell their names—or else they could not write anyway. Many are written in my own hand and signed only with an X. Until today, I had no way to use them, because I had no one willing to come forward and say publicly what he was willing to tell me privately. I hope, senhor, that you will permit me to quote you directly in my exposé!"

"Not directly, no!" Jordan denied. "I came here to tell you in confidence what I myself have personally seen on the Putumayo. But what you do with the information—how you use it—is your business. I envisioned you printing an anonymous account which I'm even willing to help you write. Hopefully, it will spur some sort of investigation, if not by the authorities, then by the Peruvian's English and American investors. But my own name cannot be linked to it, or my employees may suffer dire consequences. As I said before, I've already lost several *seringueiros*. Living alone in the wilderness, they are easy prey: Protecting them is utterly impossible."

"I am so sorry to hear that, senhor, for all I can do then is add your deposition to these others. I cannot print your story, because I would have no way of proving it if I had to reveal my source."

"Do you publish the sources of all your stories? I've never seen such names listed in your newspaper, or in any other, for that matter. Why must you reveal who gave you the information?"

"Senhor, this would be no ordinary story. Most of what I print is gossip that does little harm and is quickly forgotten. With this, I would be accusing a man of heinous crimes—murder, enslavement, rape, and torture. No one in Manaus commands more respect than the Peruvian. I would be accused of slander. My own life would be in danger. I will try to protect you, of course, but I cannot guarantee your anonymity, especially if my story does result in an investigation. If you are unwilling to testify publicly, the investigation would come to nothing."

"That's not true. Investigators have only to go up the Putumayo themselves, and they will see everything I myself and others have described. They will see the boneyard, the caged Indians, the whipping post. If that's not enough, they can stop off at La Reserva, the Colombian depot where dead bodies still lie stinking in the sun."

"Such things can be cleaned up ahead of time, senhor . . . and rest assured, they *would* be. I would still be accused of being a liar. No, I will not print the story unless you agree to come forward and swear to its accuracy."

"Out of the question," Jordan said, but then he began to think about it. "Wait a minute . . . How long do you think you could keep my identity a secret?"

"If it is more time you wish, I could probably delay for several months. One story alone will not draw much attention, but if you hammer on a subject day after day, week after week, then soon it is all people talk about. It may be half a year or more before an investigation will come to pass."

"If you could delay several months, that might be all the time I need to settle my affairs here in Brazil. You see, I'm planning on getting out as soon as possible. Once I'm out, I won't be nearly so vulnerable. What I'd be willing to do is to give you a sworn, signed statement of what I've seen. Then you would have to promise to guard my identity until I've sold the last of my harvest and disposed of my land. After that, I don't care what you do. The Peruvian can't harm me so easily in my own country."

"Ah, but he can still harm *me*. However, that is not your concern, senhor. All my life, I have been waiting to fight this battle. The Peruvian may already know what I have in my possession. It would be strange if he did not; he seems to know everything else in Manaus."

"Then how will you protect yourself? You can't do so living here; a loud-mouthed parrot may be able to warn you of imminent attack, but he'd be worthless in an actual fight."

"If I print this story, I will not stay here, senhor. I have another place where I go to be safe, when I am making people angry. After so many years in this business, I have learned little ways to protect myself."

"I hope so," Jordan said. "Well, if we're agreed on how to handle this, I'll be on my way. In a day or two, I'll bring you my statement. Just remember, if you release my name before I'm ready, I'll deny everything I've written."

"I will not betray you, senhor. It took great courage for you to come here. I admire men of courage. See what I have been hiding in the folds of this newspaper—some courage of my own." Romalho lifted the copy of *Le Matin* and shook it. Out slid a small, snub-nosed pistol. It lay on the round table, within easy reach. "I keep my courage close to me at all times. One never knows when a jealous husband will protest a story I have written about his wife. Or an angry politician will threaten to break my neck for telling the truth about his self-enrichment at government expense. I am always prepared for the unexpected. You came to the right place with your story, senhor."

"I can see I have," Jordan agreed, impressed. "Excuse me for leaving so abruptly, but a beautiful woman is awaiting my arrival. I've promised to take her to the opera tonight. Is the performance any good?"

"Only fair, senhor. Perhaps if the ingenue paid more attention to the needs of the audience and less to her leading man, it would be better. That is a situation I hope to remedy in tomorrow's paper when I reveal what happens *between* their performances."

Jordan laughed, though he wasn't sure what was so funny. "You'd better keep your pistol handy, then. It appears your enemies are legion."

Roberto Romalho only shrugged his thin shoulders philosophically. *"Sĩm,* senhor . . . but so are my fans."

Chapter Twenty

"Oh, Jordan, the opera house was everything I thought it would be!" Spencer sighed, still awed by the building's sky-blue ceiling, where angels and pink cherubs cavorted among magnificent Venetian crystal chandeliers. An image of the reception foyer rose in her mind: rich golden drapes and tall vases of Sevres porcelain offset by soaring cream and coral pillars of Carrara marble. Carved jacaranda wood chairs, so heavy it would take two men to lift them, flanked the pillars of marble, creating a lush, fantastic setting.

It was incredible that such luxury existed within walking distance of the jungle. Indeed, the entire evening was incredible—like a fairy tale come to life. The restaurant in which they were enjoying a late-night supper could not compete with the opera house, but it, too, gleamed with cut crystal, touches of marble, and fine, polished woods. The lighting was muted, the food delicious, the service excellent, and the company stimulating. Toying with her slender-stemmed wineglass, still almost full despite Jordan's insistence that wine was the only suitable beverage to accompany the exquisite meal they had just consumed, Spencer gazed at

Jordan from beneath her lashes.

They had not yet discussed his plan concerning Arana, and she was waiting for him to begin. At the same time, she half wished they could postpone the discussion until another time. For a little while at least, she wanted to indulge the fantasy that she was wealthy, pampered, beautiful, and desirable, with no more on her mind than dazzling the handsome man opposite her as she herself had been dazzled by the opera house. The woman in the mirror at Jordan's house had been a stranger to her—a vibrant, voluptuous creature with high-piled curls and artfully-applied makeup, compliments of Lucia, Chico's sister.

Her gown had something to do with the transformation, too. It was pure froth—all white lace, ruffles, revealing bodice, and fabric so sheer it looked and felt like gossamer against her body. Never had Spencer imagined wearing such a gown or owning one, but the modiste in the tiny, elegant French salon where Chico had insisted she must go had practically bullied her into trying it on. Once she saw herself changed from ugly duckling into glorious swan, she had been unable to resist.

She would always count that moment when Jordan had first seen her in the gown as her greatest feminine triumph; his admiration was everything she could have wished for in a man. Even now, he was watching her with undisguised pride, as if she belonged to him, and he delighted in his ownership.

"I'm glad you're enjoying the evening, Spencer," he said quietly. "I'd like to give you many more such evenings. You belong in a setting like this;

I've never seen a woman look as lovely and glowing as you do tonight."

She lowered her eyes, both embarrassed and pleased by his obvious flattery. "It's the wine," she explained. "It makes me feel quite flushed. I should have refused it."

"You've hardly swallowed a drop," Jordan countered in a gently chiding tone. "One glass does not a drunkard make—nor a flushed beauty, either. No, Spencer, your loveliness comes from within. All it needed was a pretty gown to set it off."

"I'm ashamed to tell ye how much this gown cost. I may not be able t' pay for the whole of it right away."

Jordan's green eyes held hers, the intensity of his gaze hypnotic. "I'd rather you pay for none of it. I'd like it to be my gift to you."

"That would be inappropriate, Jordan. I'm neither yer mistress nor yer wife. What we shared in the jungle was . . . just something that happened."

"Then I hope it happens again," Jordan smoothly parried.

His tone was a throaty invitation, causing shivers of excitement to course up and down her spine. She realized she had better steer the conversation toward safer topics. It was past time to discuss his plan, if he really had one. If he did not, she'd be newly angry, and the wonderful evening would end in disappointment and frustration.

"Jordan, please tell me what ye intend t' do about Arana. Before I make plans of me own, I must know what ye have in mind."

"Just as I expected . . ." Jordan growled. "I knew as soon as I started talking romance, you'd want to talk business."

"Ye did promise me," she reminded him. "Ye said we'd discuss yer plan t'night."

"All right, we will." He laid down his napkin and pushed aside his wine glass, suddenly very brusque and businesslike. "This afternoon, I paid a visit to Roberto Romalho, the editor of a local newspaper everyone reads. Before I even mentioned Arana's name, he knew why I had come. He showed me a sheaf of letters, written by others over the past few years, saying almost exactly the same things you and I would write in such a letter. I became very excited and demanded to know why he hadn't printed them."

"What was his response?" Spencer asked breathlessly, hanging on Jordan's every word.

"He said he couldn't print them because everyone who wrote them is now dead or has disappeared. He has no witnesses and can't prove a thing."

"But if he printed them, people would demand an investigation, which would quickly prove the truth of them!"

"That's what I told him, but he refused to publish even my statement—the one I offered to write for him—unless I agreed he could make my name public, if he had to."

"What did ye say to that?" Spencer demanded, fearing she already knew the answer.

"I said I couldn't do it—at least, not now. Not yet. But once I close down Paraïso and return to America, I don't care if he releases my name. Arana can't touch me there, or if he tries, I can do a far better job of defending myself."

"Oh, Jordan, that's quite grand of ye! Just how

soon will ye be returnin' t' the United States?"

Her reaction caught him by surprise. He raised his brows and gave her a startled look. Had he expected criticism, instead of praise? If so, he had misjudged her. She very well realized the dangers of confronting Don Julio César Arana; he had warned her about them often enough. The lives of everyone at Paraïso would be endangered. In light of that, she was overjoyed that Jordan had agreed to the release of his name as a witness, even if he wanted to delay the release until it was safe. She was also ecstatic that a newspaper had agreed to print an account of what they had seen on the Putumayo.

"If I can bring in another load of rubber like the one I brought today, I'm willing to quit, Spencer. I've got enough money saved to make a new start—perhaps not on the grand scale I envisioned, but enough to manage. And once I'm settled in Kentucky with a means of making a living and a house in which to raise a family, I'll be ready to look around for a wife."

His hand reached across the table and descended upon hers, causing a jolt of electricity up her arm. Breathlessly, she waited for him to continue. "Do you think you might be interested in the position if it comes open?"

His proposal was so offhand and unexpected—so *qualified*—that Spencer did not know how to react. It was the first time he'd actually come right out and said he wanted to marry her, or almost said it. She was painfully conscious of all the "ifs" that stood in the way. *If* he got another big load of rubber . . . *If* they escaped Arana's wrath . . . *If* he succeeded in buying back his family's farm. Her head spun with the uncertainty of it, but at least he wanted her in his future. For now, she would have to be satisfied with that.

"Yes, Jordan . . . I'd most definitely be interested, *if* the position comes open."

"Let's toast our future then," he urged, lifting his glass.

She clinked glasses with him, and for the first time in her life, abandoned caution and drank deeply, all the while gazing into his jungle-green eyes. Almost immediately, the wine made her feel light-headed, as if she were floating. Her spirits soared. She wanted to ask him about the statement he was going to prepare for Roberto Romalho and whether or not she should prepare one of her own or simply sign his. She also wanted to accompany him to the editor's office when he delivered the deposition. But such matters could be discussed some other time; right now, it seemed far more important to enjoy this precious, wonderful moment when complete accord and harmony existed between her and Jordan.

"I think I'm intoxicated," she confided, giggling.

"I certainly hope so," he said. "I hope you are intoxicated with love—just as I am. Let's go home, shall we?"

The intimacy in his tone caused a flare of anticipation in her belly. Her mouth refused to form any words, so she simply nodded. He kept her hand tightly clasped in his as he led her from the restaurant and out onto the cobbled street. There, he hailed a carriage to take them to his house. Dimly, she realized what she was doing—brazenly going home to sleep with a man. Such behavior would be utterably unacceptable in Boston, but in Manaus, no one so much as raised an eyebrow. But then, no one really knew her here—except Jordan himself. And someday, he would be her own dear husband. They would marry and be deliriously happy. The impossible did not seem so impossible, after all. She giggled from sheer joy.

When Jordan leaned closer in the open-air carriage and began to kiss her, Spencer did not resist. Instead, she returned his kisses with unabashed enthusiasm. Between kisses, she rested her head in the crook of his arm and gazed up at the stars in the black velvet sky. In the jungle, the stars could not be seen. It was a shock to see them now—so brilliant and beautiful, lending an aura of enchantment to a night already infused with it.

"Jordan," she whispered. "I'm so happy tonight. I dinna remember ever bein' this happy—except once before, in the jungle with ye . . ."

"I know how you feel, my love. I feel the same." He nuzzled her earlobe, then took it between his teeth and gently nipped it. "I can't wait to get you alone with me."

Desire rose in a surge, swamping her with its intensity. She wanted this man, wanted him desperately. She had wasted so much time being angry with him, demanding he do things *her* way and meet certain expectations. She had been unfair and dictatorial. All this time, he had indeed had a plan, a very good one, and he had hastened to put it into effect immediately upon their arrival.

"Jordan, please forgive me for the way I've acted, the things I've said. I dinna have the right t' judge ye so harshly and accuse ye of bein' selfish and greedy."

"Ah, but you were right, Spencer. I *am* selfish and greedy. I want to protect what's mine, and I want to be rich, not so much for myself but for my family. I want to ensure that my three sisters will have a measure of financial independence. I want my wife and children to know security and freedom from want. I've known what it's like to wake up one morning and discover that you've lost everything and don't know where your next meal is coming from . . . Sweetheart, don't delude yourself that I'd ever, under any circumstances, jeopardize my family for the sake of some lofty ideal. I'm only willing to fight Arana if I can first take steps to keep him from harming me and mine . . ."

"I understand, Jordan. Really, I do. Yer father's irresponsibility cost ye dearly, and ye are determined not t' be like him. Ye *aren't* like him in the least. When ye take financial risks, such as this one, it's for a good reason . . . Oh, let's not discuss it anymore tonight! I just wanted t' tell ye how happy ye've made me—that ye did do something, and are committed t' carryin' it through. I've been so unfair, so needlessly critical . . ."

He cut her off midsentence with a deep, sensual kiss that stopped the breath in her throat and made her head spin. When the kiss ended, he whispered in her hair, "I think you're right, Spencer. Let's not discuss it anymore. Let's not even talk. Words only seem to create problems between us, and tonight, if you get mad at me again, I don't think I'll be able to stand it."

"Oh, Jordan . . . Jordan . . ."

She reached for him and shamelessly embraced him, though the carriage driver could have seen everything had he glanced over his shoulder. All too soon, the driver coughed and cleared his throat, indicating they had reached their destination. Jordan withdrew slightly, reached into his pocket, and tossed the man a handful of bills. When Spencer moved to get out of the carriage, Jordan leapt out ahead of her, and instead of helping her down, picked her up in his arms, cradling her against his chest.

"Jordan, I can walk!" she insisted. "I dinna drink that much wine."

"I prefer to carry you," he responded, nuzzling her neck.

He bore her up the path to the closed door, gleaming whitely in the starlight, and kicked it open. His face was shadowed, but his blond hair shone like a halo around his darkened face. Filled with wonder, she caressed it with her fingertips. He was so very strong and masculine. He carried her as easily as he would a child; even the steps to the second floor presented no difficulty. They passed quickly through the darkened house, arriving in his room moments later, where he finally set her, trembling, upon her feet.

"Let me undress you . . ." he begged, keeping his big body pressed against hers. "All night I've been thinking of wading through the lace and ruffles to unveil your beautiful body."

"All right," she assented. "But be careful . . . I'll want t' wear this dress again."

"You can wear it for our wedding. It's white and makes you look like an angel. All you'll need is something to cover that gorgeous red hair." His hands fumbled in her high-piled curls and dismantled them, so they spilled around her shoulders. "I've been wanting to do this all night, too."

Reminded of the last time he had undressed her, Spencer stood perfectly still and allowed him to remove the delicate gown and lacy underthings she had bought to go with it. Had she known when she bought them that his hands would be the ones removing them? She hadn't thought of it consciously, because she had still been angry and wary, but in her heart, she must have known. His quick intake of breath when he freed her breasts thrilled and delighted her; he still found her desirable, still wanted to touch and fondle her—anywhere and everywhere.

White lace slid down her hips and pooled at her feet. Its soft rustling sound pricked her senses, heightening her awareness of being alive in every nerve ending. She stepped out of the gown, and he bent and picked it up before she could do so. He laid it across the back of a chair, then returned to caress her quivering skin. He ran his hands up and down her nakedness, as if trying to memorize every contour. With shaky fingers, she began to undress him.

Though hampered by his kisses and caresses, she soon managed to get his clothes off. He slid his arms around her waist and pulled her closer. Their naked bodies touched along their lengths. Her soft breasts pushed into his hard chest, where the curly chest hair nubbed her nipples. Between her thighs, the jut of his manhood promised a deeper penetration than the one she already felt. Opening her legs, she straddled him, longing for his first, fierce plunge.

Lifting her slightly so her toes merely brushed the floor, he carried her to the bed and bent her backwards upon it. For several moments, he leaned over her, palming her breasts, playing with her erect nipples, darting his tongue into her mouth. She ate and drank of him, filling herself with his scent and taste. Too long starved for these sweet, arousing intimacies, she could not summon the maidenly inhibitions she thought she ought to feel.

Lying down beside her on the bed—so soft compared to the jungle floor!—he made long, slow, leisurely love to her. Not an inch of skin did he leave untouched; instead, he laved her everywhere with his tongue, licking and sucking, biting sometimes, pressing kisses in spots she had scarcely noticed before, which now throbbed with erotic delight. His hands parted her thighs. Then he lowered his head to plunder her with his mouth. In a haze of quivering want and need, Spencer denied him nothing. Her pleasure rose and crested, sweeping her toward dizzying culmination.

Then Jordan entered her. So quickly did he maneuver himself and thrust that she was caught unawares. She gasped and cried out. On his knees, he reached his hands under her buttocks and lifted her, tilting her hips to receive his full length. "You're mine, Spencer," he said huskily. "Mine . . . all mine."

Proving the truth of the statement, he began a rhythmic thrusting. Each one drove her closer to the edge of the universe. Her mind ceased functioning, and her body strained upward of its own accord. Deep within, she convulsed and spasmed, closing and squeezing upon him. He collapsed upon her and plunged in earnest, shaking the bed, the room, the house . . . the earth . . . the sky.

Clinging to him, crying his name, she sank into a spinning whirlpool of rapture and exquisite physical sensation, accompanied by a spiritual oneness that defied any efforts she might ever make to describe it. Waves of pleasure pounded over her. As they slowly receded, she lay beneath Jordan in a state of utter repletion, wanting never to move, never to be separated. She wished they were already married, bound by vows as well as flesh, joined forever in the eyes of the world and God.

It would happen someday, she told herself. She must be patient. Gently, she flicked Jordan's ear with her tongue. Easing himself to one side, Jordan did not release his hold. Instead, he fitted himself around her as she lay still sprawled on her back, as yet unable to move. He flung one leg across her lower half, rested one arm across her breasts, and snuggled his nose into the crook between her arm and shoulder.

"I love you, Spencer O'Rourke," he murmured. "I know I've said this before, but it bears repeating: I love everything about you—even your stubbornness and desire to control me, which you'll never do, of course. I don't know why you try so hard. It's the grand scheme of things that man should control woman, not the other way around."

"What?" she choked, jerking her head toward him, not sure she had heard aright.

"Go to sleep," he commanded. "I refuse to argue the point. I've heard all the arguments anyway—

from my sister Victoria. The two of you should get along famously." He yawned and tightened his arm and leg around her. "I think you'll like my sisters, and they'll like you. They always hoped I'd find someone who was good at bossing me around. Well, you can boss all you want, but remember one thing: I wear the pants in this outfit—at least, I did until you took them off a bit ago. You wear the white lace and ruffles. That's the way it should be; that's the way the good Lord intended."

His voice trailed off and ended in a shallow snore. He had fallen asleep in midsentence! But Spencer was suddenly wide awake, feeling as if her bed of pleasure had suddenly sprouted nettles. What was he trying to tell her—that she would have to give up doctoring in order to marry him? That he would demand to make all the decisions in their future life together? His arm and leg across her body began to feel heavier and heavier. She wanted his arm and leg across her. Then again, she didn't. She wanted his love and to become his wife, but she also wanted to remain her own person. There were deeper conflicts between them than just the matter of Arana; she had sensed them before but ignored them. Now she recognized them with great clarity and a deep, burgeoning dismay.

Did she really want to spend the rest of her life on a horse farm in Kentucky? What about the needs of the Indians and the poor Brazilians, such as Chico and all his relatives? Her time at Paraĩso had taught her she was needed here; her skills had found acceptance. In Brazil, she could live the life she had always dreamed of—a life of self-sacrifice but also great satisfaction. Without her medical skills, Abelardo would have died. And Raymundo, too. And had she not been there to goad him, Jordan would never have gone to El Encanto, seen the horrors there, and finally decided to do something about them.

In her short time in Brazil, she had made a difference, a real contribution. How could she turn her back on all that, return to the States, and become a . . . a mere *housewife?* In her own country, she could not even vote, and she had nearly starved trying to practice medicine. The more she thought about these things, the more gloomy she became. Her happiness ebbed away, leaving only emptiness in its place. Emptiness and bitterness. Had she been born a man, she would have none of these problems. In making her a woman, fate had dealt her a cruel, heartless blow. The proof of it was lying beside her. While she agonized over her future, Jordan slept, oblivious to the terrible decisions she must make—decisions and sacrifices only a woman would ever have to face.

Damn ye! she thought, wriggling out from beneath his arm and leg. She sat up in bed and looked down at his sleeping form. Enough starlight came through the open window to illuminate his face. He was smiling! As she watched, he clutched the pillow and pulled it closer, substituting it for her body. For him, everything was so simple. So black and white. So . . . *easy.*

Wrapping her arms around her knees, she rested her head on them and pondered her predicament until the starlight faded and dawn pearled the sky outside. Even then, she could not make the choice—Jordan or her freedom. The freedom to do what she wanted most, go where she wanted, and be who she wanted to be. Complicating matters further, there was the question of children. If she and Jordan had children, her freedom would become even more constricted. Yet she loved children and had always looked with longing upon women cuddling their babies. Dear Saint Brigid, what was she to do? What did she really want?

Chapter Twenty-one

"Jordan?" Spencer awoke with a start and groped in the bed beside her. Brilliant sunlight stabbed her eyes. The sound of a passing wagon rumbled through the open window.

Jordan was gone, and the angle of the sunlight told her the morning was half over. After being awake all night, she must have fallen asleep finally, and Jordan had risen and departed without awakening her. Hurriedly, she pushed back her hair, struggled into clothing—not her white gown, but a blouse and skirt someone had placed on the chair near the gown—and ran out to find Chico or Lucia.

Lucia was in the tiny kitchen off the courtyard, stirring a big pot of black beans. At sight of Spencer, the girl broke into a wide smile that was somewhat marred by the condition of her teeth. Like many Brazilians, she had never seen a dentist, and her teeth had been neglected. But her thin face was pretty, with its big dark eyes and fragile bone structure, and she had proven herself adept at anticipating Spencer's needs.

"I see you found the clothes I left for you in Senhor Rei's room," she said in Portuguese.

Spencer could not help blushing. Though the girl had helped her prepare for the previous evening and taken great pains to make her seductive, Spencer was embarrassed to have been caught in Jordan's bed. Seeing the blush, Lucia giggled. "I do not have to ask if you had a good time; you were sleeping so soundly you never heard me come in—and Senhor Rei left the house whistling this morning and looking very pleased with himself."

"He's gone out?" Spencer asked, disappointed to have missed him. "Did he say when he might be back?"

"He went to the docks, senhorinha, and won't return until this evening. He directed me to delay the big meal until tonight instead of preparing it for noon, as I would normally do."

"Oh, dear . . ." Spencer sighed, wondering if he would go see Roberto Romalho without her.

"Sit down and have *cafẽ con leite,*" Lucia invited. "Will you tell me how it was, last night? Was the opera house as beautiful as everyone says it is?"

The girl looked so wistful and envious that Spencer immediately sat down on a wooden bench drawn up to the table. Once again, she was reminded of the plight of Brazil's lower classes. Though the rubber boom had brought wealth to many, girls like Lucia might live all their lives in the rich city without ever setting foot inside the symbols of that wealth, such as the opera house. Over a cup of coffee half diluted with milk, the breakfast version of the *cafẽzinho,* Spencer described the wonders of the opera house and restaurant to a wide-eyed Lucia, after which Lucia expelled a long sigh.

"I would do anything to be able to wear a white gown and go to the opera house like you did last night. That is my dream—to have beautiful clothes and jewels, and to order anything I fancied in a restaurant. If a man offered me that, I would do whatever he asked."

"Don't say that, Lucia, because I don't think you really mean it," Spencer scolded, disturbed by the jealousy and longing in the girl's dark eyes. "Your self-respect is more important than jewels and riches. You would not do something wicked, would you?"

"I might," Lucia said with a toss of her long black hair. "One wicked thing would not make me a bad person. And if I felt guilty about it afterward, it would be worth it to have known what it's like to be rich."

"That's probably what all wicked people think," Spencer snorted. "But one wicked thing leads to another—and soon, you're trapped in wickedness and can't get out of it."

"Do not worry so, senhorinha. I am just talking. Pay no attention." Lucia dismissed the subject with a wave of her thin hand, gave the beans another stir, then asked if there was anything else Spencer wanted.

Spencer was glad to change topics. "Has the mail arrived yet?"

Lucia nodded. *"Sĩm,* senhorinha. Chico put it in Senhor Rei's basket before he went to market to fetch some fresh fish for supper."

"I'll check and see if any mail came for me," Spencer said, rising. "Thank you for the *café*, Lucia—and also for your help last night. I appreciate all you did for me."

Lucia's face was sad as she peered into the bean pot. "It was nothing, senhorinha. I enjoyed helping to make you look beautiful. It is probably the closest I shall ever come to experiencing the pleasures of a fine lady—unless I start selling my body, as some girls do."

"Lucia! You wouldn't!"

Lucia's big black eyes were suddenly wary. "No, I probably wouldn't, because Chico would beat me to death first. But I can think of no other way to gain white lace gowns and pretty trinkets."

It occurred to Spencer that perhaps Lucia thought that was what *she* had done—given herself to Jordan in exchange for luxuries she could not obtain otherwise. She went to the girl and touched her shoulder. "Lucia, despite the fact that you found me in Jordan's bed this morning, it isn't what you suspect. Jordan has asked me to marry him, and I've all but said yes. As for my white lace gown, I bought it myself. I do not permit men to give me expensive gifts."

Lucia shrugged her shoulders. "Ah, but senhorinha, you are a *doutor,* not an *empregada,* like me. If I found the right man who wanted to take care of me, I might defy my brother and run off with my lover. It would be much better than being poor all my life."

"But Lucia . . ." Spencer started to argue, stopping only because Chico suddenly burst into the courtyard, his black slippers flapping, a large basket under one arm.

"Lucia, the fish is excellent. Senhor Rei will be pleased." Noticing Spencer, he paused, his wrinkled, nut-brown face frowning in concentration. "Good day, *Doutor.* How . . . are . . . you . . . today?"

"I'm fine, Chico." Spencer smiled in acknowledgment of his fractured English. She remembered how difficult it had been to converse with him the last time she had been in Manaus; now she understood nearly everything he said—English *or* Portuguese. "Please excuse me while I check the mail you brought in earlier. Lucia and I will continue our discussion another time."

With a last meaningful look at the silent girl, she exited the kitchen and headed for the front room where Jordan's mail basket was kept on his desk. A large stack of mail stood beside it, and the basket itself was overflowing—evidence of how much time had passed since Jordan had last read his correspondence. Spencer started through the basket first, separating what appeared to be bills from personal letters. There were several that must have been from his sisters and absolutely nothing addressed to her. Not that she expected any, since she had not taken time to inform friends and acquaintances of her sudden departure for South America so many months ago.

She was about to give up when she finally came across a letter addressed to both her and Jordan. In the corner was the name of the sender: W. Hardenburg. Greatly excited, she tore it open and scanned the two meager pages filled with neat, economical writing.

"Dear friends," it said. "I must write this quickly because the bearer of my message is leaving Iquitos immediately. He has just received word of a family member taken ill in Belém, and though he will not be lingering long in Manaus, he has promised to deliver my letter personally to you so that you may know of my progress or lack of it in dealing with an important matter we discussed the last time we were together.

"For safety's sake, in case this letter should fall into the wrong hands, I cannot be more explicit. But you will know whereof I speak. I have achieved no success in persuading Peruvian government officials to intervene on behalf of the diplomat being held prisoner on the Putumayo. Nor have I been able to convince them of the atrocities we all have witnessed. These men constitute a brick wall built to protect the names and families of the powerful.

"When I encountered no cooperation there, I approached the American Consul, whose only response was to congratulate me on escaping death at the hands of paid assassins, who regularly attack critics of you know who. The only thing he would do for me was to submit a claim for my impounded equipment to the U.S. minister in Lima. I am deeply discouraged, but more determined than ever to persevere until something is done. I have wired the Booth Steamship Company in New York for money owed me from my fifteen months on the Cauca Valley Railroad so that I may remain here a bit longer to pursue this matter. I understand there was once a newspaper editor here in Iquitos, brave enough to raise his voice against these injustices and oppression. He had located witnesses to support his one-man campaign. Unfortunately, the poor fellow was found dead in an alley with his eyes sewn up with cobbler's thread and his ears blocked with beeswax . . . Never fear, I shall be most careful in conducting my own investigations, but eventually I hope to locate some of these witnesses to corroborate and expand upon what the three of us have seen . . ."

Spencer's hands shook as she read the rest of the letter. It dealt with Hardenburg's success in finding employment in Iquitos. The American was going to teach English to interested students for ten pounds a month. He was also going to design a new hospital for the sum of thirty pounds. While these facts were interesting, they did not compare with the information about the newspaper editor. Roberto Romalho must be warned, so that he, too, would not wind up dead in an alley. And she and Jordan must be very careful that no one learned of their campaign against Arana until they were safely out of Brazil.

The rest of the day passed in a fever of anxiety as Spencer waited for Jordan to come home. While she waited, she composed her own statement, detailing everything she had seen on the Putumayo and everything she believed to be true about Arana's activities there. At the end of the statement, she wrote: "I swear to the accuracy of the above information. To the best of my knowledge, every word of it is truth."

Then she signed her name and carefully blotted it. Jordan arrived home late in the evening, looking bone-weary. But he grinned at her when he came in the door and caressed her with his eyes. "Well now, after a day spent haggling over rubber prices in the marketplace, you're a welcome sight."

Too anxious to wait any longer, Spencer plucked at his sleeve. "Jordan, we've had a letter from Walter Hardenburg. I think you'd better read it right away."

His brow dipped in annoyance. "Can't it wait until after I've bathed and eaten? I'm too damned tired to read it right now."

"You haven't been to see Roberto Romalho yet, have you?" she questioned.

"No, not yet. I haven't even had time to draft a statement for him. I've been too busy selling my rubber."

"Thank God for that. All right, we'll eat first and then you can read Walter's letter."

"Why is it I always feel I'm in competition with that wet-behind-the-ears engineer?" Jordan complained, brushing past her.

"Maybe it's because ye are!" she responded tartly, once again wishing Jordan felt the same urgency she did about the issue of Arana.

They ate dinner in tense silence, and Spencer regretted having been so impatient. It was just that she was so worried. She wished they could go immediately, that very night, to see Roberto Romalho and tell him what had happened to his counterpart in Iquitos. After he had eaten, Jordan yawned, stretched his legs, and reached his hand across the table. "Well, where's the letter?"

Silently, Spencer handed it to him and watched intently as he unfolded and read it. "At least the damn fool hasn't gotten himself killed yet," he said when he had finished. "But I don't give him much chance for a long life."

"Is that all ye have t' say?" Spencer's pent-up

anxiety exploded. "Dinna ye think we ought t' warn Roberto Romalho what he's up against? Why, just the fact that he has those statements in his possession puts his life in danger."

"Are you just discovering that?" Jordan demanded incredulously. "What do you think I've been telling you all along? The man already knows he's in danger. Doesn't your worry extend to me? Or will the loss of me mean less to you than the life of a newspaper editor you've never even met?"

"Of course, I'm worried about ye! It's just that . . . well, I guess I dinna realize the hazards involved for any newspaper editors who might agree t' help us. That poor man in Iquitos had his eyelids sewn shut and his ears sealed; that's a clear enough message for anyone to keep his mouth shut or bear the consequences."

Jordan blinked and shook his head. "My God, I don't believe you! Now, you're saying what I've been saying all this time. We have to use caution. We can't just rush in and right all these wrongs in a single day. Why did it take a letter from Hardenburg to teach you that? Why couldn't you accept it when I said it?"

"I dinna know!" Spencer wailed. "I guess I thought ye weren't as eager as Walter and meself."

"Will you stop calling a man you only knew for a couple days by his first name? I couldn't get you to call me Jordan for weeks after we first met!"

"Oh, Jordan, I'm sorry! Please dinna be jealous. Please dinna quarrel. There isn't any need for ye t' be jealous. I respect Walter Hardenberg, yes, but he's the not the man I want t' marry someday or crawl into bed with every night!"

At that Jordan quieted, leaning back in his chair and staring at her morosely. Then a flicker of his rakish grin began to play about his full, sensuous lips. "Do you really want to crawl in bed with me every night?"

The look in his eye told her that if she wasn't careful, she would wind up in his bed again before they had finished this discussion. "What I want t' do," she said stiffly, "is go with ye t' see Roberto Romalho as soon as possible, preferably tomorrow morning. There's no need for ye t' write a statement of yer own. Ye can just sign mine, or if ye dinna want t' do that, mine alone should suffice."

The anger leaped back into his eyes. "Thank you, no, but I prefer to write my own statement. Actually, I had envisioned you signing mine, if you had insisted upon sharing the danger. Of course, this way will be even better. Now, Romalho will have two statements, and Arana will have two targets for his wrath. Never mind that I had hoped to protect my future wife. Obviously you scorn my protection, which causes me to wonder what else you scorn about me. Will I ever measure up to your lofty standards, Spencer?"

"Jordan . . . ye do measure up. I told ye that last night. Or if I dinna, I meant to."

"I'm not sure any man can be what you want, Spencer, least of all me. That's getting to be an old argument between us, isn't it?" He pushed back from the table and rose. "Don't wait up for me. I'll be busy in my office writing my statement. And in the morning, I'll be ready to accompany you to Roberto Romalho's—or to hell and back, if that's what you prefer."

Spencer dearly wished she could turn back the clock to the previous night, when Jordan had looked at her with desire and love in his eyes. But there seemed to be no way to reach him—not when he was jealous, hurt, and angry. Why did they keep striking sparks off each other, taking things the wrong way and mistaking each other's motives? If it wasn't one thing coming between them, it was another, driving them farther apart. It was almost as if Arana's poison had the power to infect and destroy their love, turning the sweetness to bitter bile. Unable to think of anything more to say, she simply sat while he left the room.

All the way to Roberto Romalho's house, Spencer wrestled with a sensation of dread, coiling like a serpent in the pit of her stomach. She had not slept well, all alone in Jordan's big bed. He hadn't joined her there, and despite the intimacy of the night before, she felt like an interloper. Finally, she had sought the hammock in one of the smaller bedrooms, where fitful sleep had at last been possible. The hammock was where she belonged anyway; at this rate, she and Jordan might never marry, and she certainly wasn't going to share the bed of a man whose intentions were still in doubt—just as hers were. By now he had probably changed his mind about wanting to marry her.

Jordan walked slightly ahead of her through the bustling, cobbled streets of Manaus, which for once held little allure or fascination. She scarcely noticed where they were going; all her attention was concentrated on what they would find when they got there. Somehow she knew it would not be pleasant; either Roberto Romalho had already changed his mind about helping them, or he soon would when he heard what had happened to the editor in Iquitos.

Jordan suddenly stopped walking, and Spencer almost ran into him. "This is it . . . I think." He nodded toward a whitewashed house behind a crumbling stone wall. "But there's a mourning wreath on the door that wasn't there the other day."

Spencer looked where he was nodding and saw a round black wreath hanging upon the closed door. At the same moment, she noticed a wagon across the street. An elaborately carved wooden coffin was being unloaded from it.

"Jordan, look . . . I think those men are going to take that coffin into Senhor Romalho's house!"

As they both turned to watch, two men lifted the long, polished box, balanced it on top of their heads, and began carrying it in their direction. Jordan stopped them as they approached the gate. "What's going on here?" he inquired in Portuguese. "Did someone die in that house?"

"Sĩm, senhor. The editor of the *Journal de Povo* was shot and killed last night. We are delivering his coffin. He will be buried tomorrow. If you are friends of his, you can probably pay your respects tonight."

"Oh, my God . . ." Jordan said, while Spencer gasped in speechless horror. "What happened? Who did it? Does anyone know?"

The first man shrugged. "I heard it was a robbery, though hardly anything was stolen. You can read about it in the newspapers. They will all be carrying the story; Senhor Romalho was a well-known man. Now, if you will excuse us . . ."

The two men started past Jordan and Spencer, but Jordan dashed ahead of them to the door, then pounded upon it like a madman. The two coffin-bearers stared in astonishment. Spencer herself did not know what to think.

"Open this door!" Jordan cried, pounding and thumping.

The door was finally opened by a plump, weeping, disheveled woman in a wrinkled red skirt, white blouse, and kerchief on her head. "What is it? What do you want?" she cried. Seeing the two men with the coffin, she stepped back. "Oh, the coffin is here. Come, bring it in. You can take it to his bedroom where I've laid him out."

She scarcely seemed to notice Jordan—until he rushed past her into the house. "Wait a minute! Where are you going, senhor? Aren't you the man who was here the other day?"

The coffin-bearers exchanged looks of puzzlement. Spencer didn't know what else to do, so she, too, hurried past the startled woman and entered the house. "Senhora! Stop! Who are you?" the woman shouted behind her.

"A friend of Senhor Romalho," Spencer lied, craning her neck to see where Jordan had gone.

"But he is dead!" the woman shrieked. "I found his body in the courtyard late last night. There were noises—Pedro screeching, Senhor Romalho shouting, then the sound of a gunshot. I was so afraid I hid in bed with the covers over my head. When all was silent, I crept out and went to look.

It was too late to help him. He was already dead. His blood had splattered all over the tiles on the floor . . ." The woman dropped her face into her pudgy hands and gave way to unrestrained sobbing.

One of the coffin-bearers cleared his throat. "Excuse me, senhoras, but this coffin is very heavy. Do you mind if we bring it into the house and set it down?"

"Yes, yes . . . Come ahead . . ." Spencer directed, leading the distraught woman out of the way.

The two men removed the coffin from their heads and maneuvered it through the doorway. "Where is the bedroom?" one of them asked.

"Through the courtyard. Turn left," the plump woman sobbed. "It is the second door. He's inside on the bed."

"Obrigado, senhora."

After thanking her, the men again hefted the coffin and started forward, while Spencer put her arm around the weeping woman. "Such a terrible thing! I'm so sorry . . ." She led her into a small front room and over to a chair. "Here, sit down. Can you tell me more about what happened?"

"Oh, it was awful! Whoever killed Senhor Romalho also killed his parrot, Pedro. They poked out the bird's eyes and tied its beak shut. The *polícia* say the motive for the murder was robbery, but I do not think so. I think it was someone who was angry about something Senhor Romalho printed in his newspaper!"

Spencer soothingly patted the woman's arm. "Exactly what was taken, senhora?"

"That is what I do not know. It was a small

black box containing only papers. Senhor Romalho kept it hidden in his bedroom beneath the bed. What was in the papers, I cannot say. He never told me, and he never took them out—except the other day when that man . . ." She stopped weeping and peered worriedly at Spencer through her tears. "Where is that man—the one who ran through the house when I opened the door? What does he want? Why have you come here? You are with him, are you not?"

"Sĩm, senhora. I am with him. But we mean no harm. We came here to meet with Senhor Romalho and give him information concerning an exposé he was going to write. Only it looks as if we're too late. Someone else found out about it first."

"Oh, I knew this would happen someday!" Choking on her tears, the woman wrung her hands together. "Senhor Romalho was always making enemies. That's why his family lives in a secluded place downriver, instead of here in Manaus. His wife and children are coming this afternoon, and I must have everything ready—the food, the house, the body, the burial arrangements . . ."

"I can see you have a lot to do," Spencer sympathized. "So I'll go find my friend, and we'll leave you in peace. I think he was greatly upset to learn of Senhor Romalho's death."

"Who is not upset, senhora? Roberto Romalho was a good man. Now he is dead and his parrot with him . . . A robbery! Only a fool would believe that! Be careful, senhora. If you know what was in that black box, your life could be in danger, too. I'm so glad Senhor Romalho never told me anything about his work. I had to buy his newspaper and have someone read it to me, if I wanted to know what was happening . . . He always told me I would be safe only as long as I was ignorant. And I *was* safe. They didn't bother to kill me . . . Oh, but it's sad! So sad!"

Wild-eyed and angry, Jordan suddenly appeared in the doorway. "I can't find those statements," he snapped in English. "Ask the woman if she knows where they are."

"Whoever killed Romalho has them," Spencer informed him. "They're gone. They were in a black box underneath his bed. It's the only thing that was stolen."

"Then we might as well leave. There's nothing to be gained by remaining here."

The haggardness of his face and the dull gleam in his eyes frightened Spencer. She had never seen Jordan look so dangerous, so ready to explode. Not even that day when he had confronted Arana in the dining room of the hotel.

"What shall we do now?" she questioned in a trembling voice, absolutely certain Jordan intended to do something.

"We pay a visit to Arana," Jordan snarled. "I think it's long past time, don't you?"

With her heart in her mouth, Spencer couldn't answer. She merely nodded and followed Jordan as he stalked from the house.

Chapter Twenty-two

"Jordan, wait!" Spencer cried breathlessly, unable to keep up with his long strides. She had to repeat the plea before he heard it, and he was scowling when he finally swung around to face her.

"Jordan, slow down," she panted, gulping air.

"What do you want?" he barked impatiently. "If you're tired, I'll go ahead without you. This isn't your battle, anyway. It's mine. It's been mine from the very beginning."

"Jordan, please . . . Do ye think it's wise t' go see Arana when ye're this . . . this furious?"

"Isn't this what you wanted, Spencer? For me to be furious? Correct me if I'm wrong, but you did want more eagerness on my part, didn't you? Well, I'm eager now, damn it! So don't try to convince me to be cautious and reasonable. When you're dealing with a monster, reason has no place. That day in the hotel when I had the chance, I should have strangled Arana with my bare hands."

He held his hands out in front of him, as if assessing their ability to commit murder. Spencer grasped his long fingers and held on tight. "Jordan, I'm so afraid! If ye do something rash, he'll kill ye outright."

Jordan's eyes swept her face. He expelled a heavy sigh. "Give me credit for a few brains, Spencer. All I'm going to do is go see the man."

"But what will ye do when ye see him? What will ye say?"

"Before I get there, I'll think of something. Are you coming with me? I'd rather you didn't, but by now I know better than to insist you go home."

"I'm coming," Spencer asserted, linking her arm in his.

"Then quit arguing and come."

He half dragged her down one street and up another. Spencer glimpsed a street sign and saw that they were now on Marshal Deodoro Street. The heat was intense, the late-morning sun unmerciful. She felt faint and had to clutch Jordan's arm to keep from stumbling. "Get rich! Get rich quick! Buy a ticket—it's a faster way to get rich than rubber!" a lottery-ticket seller bawled in her ear.

Somewhere off the street, behind one of the high, white walls, came the uncertain scraping of a cello or a violin—probably a child practicing scales. A bottle-green streetcar clanged past. Spencer's brain registered these sounds as if from a distance; a greater reality riveted her attention. They were going to see Arana, the man responsible for the terrible things they had witnessed at El Encanto, the man who had probably ordered Roberto Romalho's death.

Finally, Jordan paused before an unprepossessing building that looked more like a warehouse than an office. Spencer was about to ask if it contained Arana's offices when she saw a small brass plate beside the closed door. It read: "J.C. Arana Brothers, Manaus," and beneath that, a line of block print spelled out "Peruvian Amazon Rubber Company."

Jordan opened the door and pulled her inside after him. It took a moment for Spencer's eyes to adjust to the tranquil half-light. Electric fans whirled noiselessly in the thick air, drowned by the muted clack of typewriters on desks that were out of sight. A man in a glass-sided cubicle looked up from a stack of papers, saw them, and frowned. He came out of the cubicle adjusting the wire-rimmed spectacles perched on his nose.

"Bom dia. How may I help you?"

"Just direct us to the office of Don Arana. He's expecting us," Jordan clipped in a commanding tone.

"Your name, *por favor,* senhor?"

"Tell him Roberto Romalho's brother wishes to see him," Jordan said imperiously.

At the mention of the editor's name, the short, bespectacled man paled. "Of course, senhor. Follow me, please. I must announce you first. Then if Don Arana still wishes to see you, you may enter his office."

"What are ye doin'?" Spencer hissed as they trailed through the building in the little man's wake.

"Testing. Just testing . . ." Jordan hissed back.

They came to a massive door built of solid mahogany, the first evidence of luxury in the otherwise plain, utilitarian building that was divided into many little cubicles where men in shirtsleeves sat at typewriters or leaned over desks, shuffling mountains of paper and checking long columns of figures. Despite her hatred of the man they had come to see, Spencer was impressed. The offices of the Peruvian Amazon Rubber Company smacked of quiet efficiency. Obviously, it was well run and enormous. No wonder Don Julio César Arana's name evoked respect. An Englishman or American viewing it for the first time would consider it comparable to any big, successful business back home.

"Wait here, *por favor,*" the little man said, turning to them in front of the big door. He knocked first, then scurried inside, closing the door behind him to block their view of the interior.

Several moments passed while Spencer watched Jordan, and he watched her. Jordan's face was contorted with anger, his eyes twin pools of fury. Suppressed violence emanated from him, causing a wave of nervous heat to wash over Spencer's body. Though it was cool in the fan-washed gloom, she could hardly breathe from the tension. Fortunately, they did not have to wait long. The door opened again, and the little man stepped back.

"Don Arana will see you, now."

Jordan thanked him. *"Obrigado,"* he gruffly murmured and stepped inside.

Spencer followed, her eyes scanning the room and coming to rest on the swarthy, black-bearded Peruvian seated behind the massive desk. Don Julio César Arana was even more elegant than she remembered, with an innate dignity that set him apart from lesser men. His white linen suit was immaculate, his hair and beard perfectly trimmed. A fine Havana cigar jutted from his clenched white teeth. When he saw her, he rose to his feet, though he had apparently not meant to do so just to welcome Jordan.

His hand shot out in greeting, but Jordan did not take it. Instead, he glared down at the well-manicured appendage as if it were disgustingly offensive. After an awkward moment, Don Arana lowered his hand.

"Ah, Senhor Rei . . . I knew you were misleading my manager; Roberto Romalho has no brother that I know of."

"However, I see you took precautions—just in case I *was* his brother." Jordan nodded toward the desktop.

For the first time, Spencer noticed the gleaming, brass-trimmed pistol lying in plain sight on the polished wood. At her sharp intake of breath, Jordan darted her a triumphant glance, as if to say, See? I told you so. At the mention of Roberto Romalho's name, Arana knew he would need a pistol to defend himself.

"I always take precautions, senhor, especially when I know someone is lying." Don Arana picked up the pistol and rubbed his fingers along its shining barrel. "Since you don't seem to be armed and are accompanied by a member of the fairer sex, I presume this is unnecessary."

He opened the top drawer of his desk, dropped the pistol in it, and closed it with a nudge of his hand. "Now, are you going to introduce me to your companion? Or haven't your manners improved since the last time we met?"

"Sorry to say, they haven't. And I really don't want you to know her name."

"Then why have you come, senhor? Have you decided to sell your land to me, after all?"

Jordan's fists clenched at his sides. "My land is the last thing you'll ever get, Arana. Though, in fact it is for sale. I'll sell it at to anybody except you. And if you terrorize potential buyers, I won't sell it all. When I return to the United States, I'll leave it sit. But first, I'll destroy every last hevea tree on it. I'll cut them down, burn them, do whatever is necessary to make sure your dog Loayza can't move in and take over after I'm gone."

Don Arana's nostrils flared in anger, but his voice remained silky soft. "Now, why would you do anything so foolish as that, Jordano?"

"Don't call me Jordano! Only my friends ever call me that. One friend, in particular, always called me Jordano—David Serrano. Ever hear of him?"

Arana spread his hands on the desk. *"Nõn,* that name means nothing to me. I have never heard it before. This man is a Brazilian?"

"Colombian. And don't say you don't know his name—you ought to know it. You ordered his depot destroyed, his wife and son enslaved, and the man himself to be killed. No one's seen him since . . ."

"False accusations again, Senhor King. You can prove nothing. Why do you waste my time, coming here with your ridiculous claims?"

"You would not have thought my claims so ridiculous had you read about them in the *Journal de Povo*. With Romalho dead, you may think yourself safe, but you aren't, Arana. I'll find another newspaper willing to take a chance on printing the truth about you. You can't eliminate every honest editor in Brazil and the United States. Eventually, your story will be told—and once your investors know what kind of man you are, you'll be finished. Done. Destroyed. Neither your British nor your American buyers will consent to purchase rubber collected at the expense of human lives."

Arana's black eyes glittered as he studied Jordan from beneath heavy black brows. "Two can play at the dangerous game of destroying reputations, senhor. It may interest you to know that I have in my possession certain documents—sworn statements—that your father, Alexander King, obtained Paraĩso in a devious manner, by cheating at cards."

"That's a lie!" Jordan shouted. "My father never cheated a living soul! He was a fool, yes, but he never cheated people."

"Do you know that for a fact, senhor? I think not. I also possess documents attesting to certain flaws in your own character—flaws that make my shortcomings seem paltry by comparison."

"Then you might as well *eat* those documents, Arana. Your lies can't hurt me at home in the United States. Your influence stops at my country's boundary lines."

"Does it, senhor?" Arana's mouth smiled, but his eyes did not. Instead, he resembled a cat about to pounce on a mouse. "Since we last met, I have used my supposedly limited influence to obtain a great deal of information about you. Shall I tell you the names of your sisters—where they live, the school they attend, what they look like? The eldest is Victoria, a rabid supporter of granting women the right to vote. What lunacy! If something should happen to her one dark night, people would blame it on her propensity to meddle in the affairs of men. I assure you, they would never trace her untimely demise to me."

"Why, you bastard!" Jordan roared, throwing himself across the desktop at Arana. His sudden attack toppled the Peruvian backwards, and they both crashed heavily to the floor. Jordan's outstretched hands found the Peruvian's throat. As he started to throttle him, Spencer screamed.

"No, Jordan! Dinna kill him!"

The door flew open, and four large men dressed in black suits burst into the room. They seized Jordan and dragged him off Arana, then began to pummel him in the chest and stomach with their fists. Spencer screamed again and leaped upon the nearest attacker who seemed bent on murdering Jordan before Spencer's very eyes. She clawed at the man's eyes with her nails, but only succeeded in raking his cheek. With balled fists, she hit him as hard as she could. Another man grabbed her from behind and lifted her off her feet, holding her out in front of him, as if she were a spitting cat.

"Ho, ho, Don Arana!" he crowed in Portuguese. "What shall I do with this little tigress?"

"Put her down," Arana said. He had gotten to his feet and was straightening his mussed white suit. "And release Senhor Rei. They know they are outnumbered, and we could easily kill them. Perhaps now they will listen to reason."

"There's nothing you can say to change my opinion of you, Arana," Jordan snarled. Breathing raggedly, he rubbed his jaw and wrapped one arm protectively around his ribs, as if in great pain. "You've overpowered me today, but one day, I'll have the upper hand."

"That day will never come, senhor. You cannot fight me; the price is too high. I know everything there is to know about you—including what you had for breakfast this morning. I know you spent the evening before last at the opera, enjoyed a fine dinner at one of our excellent restaurants, then took this lady to bed with you. My spies are everywhere; I am watching everything you do. I tell you this: If you persist in harassing me, I will take action—perhaps against one of your sisters, or perhaps against your whore." He shot Spencer a contemptuous glance. "But you will never be able to prove anything, no more than you can prove that it was I or my men who destroyed La Reserva or killed Roberto Romalho."

"Damn you to hell, Arana! You would threaten the lives of innocent, helpless women?"

Arana's face was impassive, his eyes cold. "I will stop at nothing to protect what is mine . . ." He motioned to one of his bodyguards. "Throw them out on the street, Lizardo. They have already taken up too much of my time."

"Let me take a look at yer ribs," Spencer suggested, when she and Jordan finally arrived at his house.

"Leave me alone . . . I'm fine," Jordan said, brushing past her and going into his office.

Spencer doggedly followed. "I would like t' examine ye and see if ye're hurt!"

"Damn my aunt Milly's corset! I said I'm fine, and I am! Will you just get out and leave me alone?" He rummaged through his bottom desk drawer, took out a bottle of brandy, and set it on the desktop. "On your way out, tell Chico I want to see him."

"Why?" Spencer demanded. "Ye are hardly in a mood t' see anyone. And I doubt that drinkin' will help the problem."

She reached for the bottle, but Jordan snatched it out of her grasp. "Chico!" he roared. "Get your deceitful, lying ass in here!"

"Surely, ye dinna intend t' accuse Chico of spyin' on ye for Arana . . ." Spencer began, but Jordan advanced upon her, clutching the bottle as if he meant to break it over her head.

"Get out of here, Spencer! I asked you to leave me alone, and now, I'm not asking—I'm telling. Get the hell out of here!"

Stepping backward, Spencer almost ran into Chico as he flew through the open doorway. "You . . . call . . . me, Senhor Rei?" he inquired in his faltering English.

"Shut the door after the lady leaves, Chico. You and I have something to discuss."

Chico's expression conveyed his puzzlement, both at Jordan's anger and his wish for privacy. "Senhorinha?" He stood by the door, waiting for Spencer to depart.

She glanced from him to Jordan, and back again. Maybe Chico had spied on them for Arana, but she doubted it. The little house servant was devoted to Jordan. If he was feigning surprise at Jordan's angry summons, he was doing an excellent job of it.

"If ye need me, I'll be in the kitchen with Lucia," she said.

"We won't be needing you," Jordan snapped.

As the door closed behind her, Spencer could hear Jordan's voice rise in accusation. "All right, Chico. Suppose you tell me how much Don Arana is paying you to spy on me?"

"Spy on you! Senhor, I would never spy on you . . ."

Unable to bear it, Spencer hurried to the courtyard. Once there, she leaned against a palm tree and took several deep, soothing breaths. Not until she had regained control of her raging emotions did she proceed to the kitchen, where Lucia was on her hands and knees scrubbing the tile floor. The girl looked up, saw Spencer, and quickly averted her eyes. Staring at her bowed head and the guilty hunch of her shoulders, Spencer *knew.* "It was you, wasn't it? Not Chico. You told Don Arana all about me and Jordan—about how we went to the opera and the restaurant, about how we spent the night . . ."

Lucia ceased scrubbing the floor, but never raised her eyes. *"Sĩm,* senhorinha. I told him—not him directly, but one of his men. The man started coming here before you returned from Paraĩso. He asked many questions, but I told him nothing—not until early this morning. This morning, he offered me enough money to buy three white lace gowns, and he promised more money, if only I would answer his questions. I could not see the harm in it, senhorinha. After all, I only told the truth."

Spencer felt such a spurt of raw fury she could not contain herself. She ran to the girl, seized her by the shoulders, and began shaking her and screaming in English. "How could ye do it? How? Blessed Saint Brigid, how could ye betray Senhor Rei like that?"

Lucia dropped her scrubbrush. As Spencer shook her, the girl's head snapped back. Her long black hair flew in every direction. "Stop!" she cried. "Stop it, senhorinha, you're hurting me!"

Appalled at her violent behavior, Spencer stopped. Her breath was coming in great gasps, and her head was throbbing. It took her several moments to calm down enough to be able to translate what she wanted to say into Portuguese. Even then, her words came out thickly accented—Portuguese but with a brogue. "Leave this house at once, Lucia. Dinna come back. If ye do, I'll . . . I'll thrash ye within an inch of yer miserable life."

Sullenly, the girl rose to her feet. "I'll get another job," she dared to say. "Don Arana will give me a job."

"No doubt he will," Spencer agreed. "Ye are the kind of person he's looking for—someone who has no morals, no honor. Someone who'll do anything for money."

The girl straightened her shoulders and glared at Spencer. "Are you going to tell Chico what I've done—or the rest of my relatives?"

"No, I'll leave that to ye. Ye can make yer own explanations for why ye left here."

Lucia tossed her head. "I'll just say I got a better job."

"I don't care what ye say—so long as ye leave at once."

"I'm leaving, senhorinha." She stepped carefully across the slick tiles, not bothering to take her brush and bucket.

When she had gone, Spencer sank to her knees. It had been some time since she had scrubbed a floor—not since Boston, in fact. But if she did not do something, she might start weeping and never be able to stop. She rolled up her sleeves, picked up the brush, dipped it in the soapy water, and began scrubbing the tiles. She scrubbed until her arms and back ached. She scrubbed until her hands turned red.

Chico came into the kitchen, looking for Lucia. He, too, looked on the verge of tears. "Where . . . is . . . Lucia?"

"She's gone, Chico. She found a new job, and she's gone t' take it."

"A . . . new . . . job?" The effort of speaking in English proved too much, and he switched to Portuguese. "I need a new job, also. Senhor Rei has sent me away."

Kneeling upright, Spencer leaned back on her haunches. "Don't go yet, Chico. Wait until tomorrow. By then, Senhor Rei will be himself again. He'll realize ye could not have done the things he accused ye of doin'."

Chico paced back and forth distractedly, his black slippers flapping. "I don't know . . . I just don't know, senhorinha. I have never seen him so angry. Nor have I ever seen him drink like that." He turned to her and threw up his hands. "He drank more than half that bottle of brandy while I was in his office trying to explain that I did nothing to harm him."

"Ye see why ye must stay then, Chico. When he finally comes t' his senses, he'll need ye."

"Não, Doutor. It is you he will need. I am only his houseservant."

"He'll need both of us, Chico," Spencer corrected. "Right now, Jordan King needs all the friends he has in this world."

"He has big troubles, *sĩm?"*

Spencer nodded sadly. "Yes, Chico, his troubles are the biggest I've ever seen."

Chapter Twenty-three

Jordan awoke to a splitting headache and a muscle cramp in the back of his neck. Cautiously, he lifted his head. It felt heavy as an anvil. Looking around, he discovered that he was in his office, half sprawled across the top of the desk. The empty whiskey bottle beside him gave silent evidence of what he had been doing before he passed out. A muted light spilling through the unshuttered window suggested dawn, but all he could think of was finding his way upstairs and collapsing into bed before he got any sicker.

Oh, God, he thought. Why had he drunk himself into such a stupor? It had been years since he'd indulged like this. His last grand binge had taken place on the day Castle Acres had been auctioned off to the highest bidder. Bitter and frustrated, he had tackled a bottle of Irish rye whiskey; it had helped to dull the pain—but only until he regained consciousness. Then the pain had returned in full, stunning force.

So it was now. Since yesterday, nothing had changed. Arana had skewered him as neatly as an Indian might skewer a monkey for his supper. The man had bested him, beaten him soundly, made threats Jordan dared not ignore. He could not risk the lives of his sisters—or Spencer—to continue this battle. Arana had already won. The best he could do now was cut his losses and get out. Maybe Walter Hardenburg would have better luck; maybe Hardenburg had less to lose. Or more to gain. If Hardenburg stayed and Jordan got out, Spencer might find consolation—and love—with the young American.

Jordan groaned. Never had he felt so miserable, so defeated. Not even the loss of Castle Acres had unmanned him like this. At least then, he had still been determined to fight and regain what he had lost. Not now, however. Arana had stolen his pride and sense of self. His hands were tied, leaving him sickeningly helpless. If he did anything to stop Arana, the Peruvian would exact a terrible revenge—one Jordan couldn't bear to live with.

The sound of a door opening scraped his lacerated senses. Burying his head in his arms, he sought to block out all sound and feeling. Someone touched his arm. "Jordan, are you awake? Are you all right?"

Spencer's tone was calm, her English perfect. Jordan wished he could hide from her forever. He did not want to face her, did not want to see the contempt in her eyes when he told her he was through trying to fight Arana. "Get out, Spencer. Leave me alone. I don't want to talk to you."

"You don't have to talk. Just listen. It wasn't Chico who spied for Arana. It was Lucia. She did it for the money—so she could buy pretty gowns and live a different life than the one she's always had. I sent her away, though I've come to feel guilty about it, because I understand why she did it. To her, it didn't seem so wrong. She doesn't know what's at stake."

Jordan raised his head but still did not look at Spencer. In the morning, she was always so fresh—so pure and radiant. This morning especially, he could not stand to look at her. Instead, he looked at the empty brandy bottle—symbol of his weakness and despair.

"What is at stake, Spencer? What exactly are we trying to save? Romalho had many enemies, not just Arana. One of them would have killed him sooner or later. He himself lived in constant fear of retaliation. As for the Indians, their fate was sealed the moment the first white man discovered rubber trees growing along the Amazon. Arana has hastened the demise of the Indian, but he hasn't caused it. If Arana died today, some other greedy despot would come along tomorrow—doing the same thing, destroying and enslaving Indians, killing anyone who got in his way. This thing is too big for us, Spencer. You can't stop people from being greedy. I'm not sure Arana's investors don't know what's happening on the Putumayo. They probably do. So do his buyers. The truth is: None of them care. You're the only one who cares, Spencer. You and Walter Hardenburg."

"That's not true. You care, Jordan. I know ye do . . ."

"You know nothing of the sort!" With a sweep of his hand, Jordan knocked the brandy bottle off the desk. It crashed to the floor and splintered into a dozen fragments.

"Jordan . . ." Spencer began, but he cut her off.

"Go back to Boston, Spencer. It's over. Finished."

"But what will ye do?" Spencer asked in a quavering voice, her brogue thickening along with her obvious distress.

"Return to Paraíso and get out the rest of my harvest. Then, before I leave there forever, I'll do what I told Arana—destroy my trees."

"Ye would actually burn down the jungle?"

"No," Jordan sighed. "I won't do that. But I'll cut the trees so deeply they'll eventually die. If they somehow manage to survive, it'll be years before they produce anything. I've learned a few things while I've been here. If you aren't careful how you cut a hevea to milk the latex, you can kill the tree itself, and your land will soon be worthless. That's what I want. To destroy the value of Paraíso so that neither Arana nor any other greedy bastard will want it. The only ones who'll appreciate the place will be the Indians."

"Jordan, dinna be hasty. I know that right now everything looks bleak to ye, and it would be dangerous to challenge Arana, but . . ."

"But nothing, Spencer. I've made up my mind—about a lot of things. If you still want to fight Arana, I'd advise you to join forces with Walter Hardenburg. He's really a better man for you than I am. You've got more in common with him. The sooner you disassociate yourself from me, the better—for both of us."

"Jordan, please look at me . . ."

He could not resist the plea in her voice. Slowly he raised his eyes to meet hers. She was, as he had expected, fresh and beautiful—except for her tear-filled, reddened eyes. Her tender pink mouth was trembling, her control in danger of slipping. "Walter Hardenburg may be a better man for me than ye are, but the trouble is . . . ye are the one I love. What am I supposed t' do about my feelings for ye?"

And mine for you? he silently echoed. But to Spencer, he said, "I don't know, Spencer. I can't deal with that right now. Don't you understand? I don't know who I am anymore. I've lost my self-respect. Until I somehow regain it, you're the last person in the world I want to be near."

Her tears began to fall, and she wordlessly nodded—as if she understood. But how could she? How could she possibly know that a man always wanted to be strong in front of his woman, that he wanted to appear invincible, capable of handling any crisis, and protecting her against all harm? He wanted to be able to look in her eyes and see the reflection of himself the way he had always dreamed of being; certainly, he did not want to see the real man, the one with doubts, fears, and insecurities. Spencer had seen him at his worst, cowed and beaten, on his knees before a stronger adversary. If she did not scorn him, he scorned himself enough for both of them.

"Get out, Spencer," he repeated listlessly. "There's no hope for us. If we married, you'd only be disappointed, because in all likelihood I'll just wind up a drunkard like your father . . . Which reminds me. If Chico's still here, tell him to bring me another bottle of brandy."

Immediately, Spencer's face hardened. She straightened and folded her arms. "Ye self-pitying drunk! Dinna order me about! Tell him yerself. I've better things t' do—such as packin'."

With a last loathing glance at him, she left the room.

Two days later, Jordan was ready to return to Paraïso. After recovering from his hangover, he had made arrangements for his rubber to be sold, reprovisioned the *Evangeline,* and smoothed things over with Chico. He had even taken time to look up Raymundo, who was making good progress learning to maneuver on crutches and was happily awaiting a special device Doctor Jorge had invented to support his ruined leg so that, in time, crutches would not even be necessary. Not wanting to leave Chico, Raymundo, or Luiz without employment when he returned to the United States, Jordan had secured work for them with another rubber baron, a friendly, benevolent Brazilian, whose holdings were far from the Putumayo. Everything was falling into place for his departure from Brazil. This was his last journey to Paraïso; the next time he came to Manaus, he would not be returning to his rubber plantation.

As he made ready to cast off, he stole several anxious glances at the long, bustling wharf. Though he had not seen her for the last two days, he had kept hoping Spencer would at least come down to the dock to say good-bye. She had been avoiding him, and this was his last chance to tell her how sorry he was for letting her down, for being rude, for throwing her love back in her face . . . all things he wanted to say and did not know how. Whenever he thought of her, which was at least once every minute, he experienced a deep wrenching sensation in his gut. Saying good-bye would be like tearing his heart out, but he had not changed his mind about the way he felt. Ending it now was for the best.

With no one to help him, it was difficult to get the launch underway. Jordan dashed back and forth from engine house to bow to stern. As he rounded the corner of the engine house on his way to cast off at the stern, he saw a slim figure dressed all in white tossing a coiled loop of rope onto the dock. The bright red hair, freckled face, lush bosom, and determined slant of shoulder were achingly familiar, momentarily robbing him of speech. Then he exploded.

"Good God, what are you doing here?"

"Helping ye cast off," Spencer tartly replied. "Hadna ye better mind the steerin' before we crash into something?"

Still dazed—reeling from the shock of seeing her on the launch—he dashed back to the wheel and guided the *Evangeline* past the other launches and *batelãos* jamming the harbor. For the next twenty minutes, he had no time to ask further questions. Maneuvering occupied all his attention. Amazingly, he suddenly became acutely aware of his surroundings—the fleet of ocean liners and steamboats crowding the floating wharves . . . Brazil's green-and-yellow flag snapping from the masthead of one, the red St. Andrew's cross of the Booth Steamship Company adorning another . . . the black-topped, white-starred funnels of the Italian Liguria Brasiliana line, and the yellow shield and blue anchor designating the ships of the Hamburg Amerika line.

Jordan noticed them all, as if he had never seen them before, as if a blindfold had suddenly been snatched from his eyes. The incredible blue of the sky overhead hurt his eyes, and the smoke smudges on the horizon upriver made them water. He blinked against the radiance of the sunshine bathing everything in glorious, golden honey. *What was Spencer doing aboard?* He had told her to go back to Boston. She had been angry and packed her things. For two days, he had been tripping over them in the hallway.

When the *Evangeline* finally cleared the congested area near Manaus, Jordan shouted, "Spencer! Come here and tell me what in hell you're up to now!"

She came, all nonchalance and casualness, as if her presence was nothing out of the ordinary. Only her brogue betrayed her anxiety. "I should think it would be obvious, Jordan. I'm goin' back t' Paraîso t' nurse the Indians—t' check on Abelardo particularly."

"And how long do you intend to stay there?"

"Why, as long as ye do. After that, when we return to Manaus, I'll make up me mind what t' do then."

"Spencer, this is insane and ridiculous. I told you how I felt."

"Dinna worry, Jordan. I dinna intend t' force me affections upon ye. I'll stay out of yer way. I won't bother ye in the slightest. We'll keep our relationship strictly on a professional level—as employer and employee, though I'm not yer employee, as ye very well know."

Despite himself, Jordan had to smile. Their conversation had the ring of familiarity. She sounded exactly as she had when he first met her—like a stiff-necked virgin, a gauze-bandaged prude. "If we couldn't manage it the last time, how do you expect to manage it this time?"

"Manage what?"

"Keeping our relationship on a professional level."

"Dinna belittle me, Jordan!" Her color rose, and her blue-green eyes shot sparks. "Dinna mock me feelin's for ye! I'm not a child who canna control meself, and I dinna come along on this trip t' try and trap ye into marriage. I came for the sake of the Indians. I feel a responsibility to them, even if ye don't. Indeed, I may stay at Paraīso after ye leave. I'll stay as long the Indians want and need me."

Jordan let go of the wheel long enough to grab her arm. "You will not stay at Paraīso after I'm gone! You will not sacrifice your life to some foolish ideal!"

She yanked her arm away. "Ye will not tell me what I may or may not do!"

Jordan gripped the wheel with both hands, so rankled he could have broken it in two. "All right, Spencer. Have it your way. Do whatever you want. You will, anyway, no matter what I have to say about it. When I'm ready to return to Manaus, I'll go—with or without you. I may be a coward, but I'm not a fool. You can stay and get killed if you want to, but I decline that dubious pleasure. Whatever life I have left, I'm going to live, damn it, and make the most of it. Martyrdom doesn't appeal to me."

"I'm not tryin' t' be a martyr! I'm . . . I'm just tryin' t' live so I can hold up me head—so I dinna need a bottle of brandy in which t' drown me guilt and frustration!"

Her last remark cut to the quick; he could not believe how much it hurt. "Maybe if you did indulge in brandy occasionally, you'd be more human, Spencer. It must be terribly difficult being perfect, a constant strain on your physical and mental resources."

"As I said," Spencer stiffly responded. "I'll stay out of yer way."

"You'd better," Jordan retorted.

The long journey passed in chilly, brooding silence. Spencer hated it and wished she had not yielded to the impulse to come. Her only conversations with Jordan were guarded and stilted, making each day a trial to be endured. When she had boarded the launch in Manaus, she had not perceived it would be this difficult. Nor had she realized how much she would suffer, being near the man she loved, but being unable to touch, caress, or even talk to him. In the back of her mind, she had nurtured the hope that once they were alone on the river again, she would find a way to mend things.

Battling Arana no longer seemed so important, possibly because she herself could see no way to continue the fight without someone getting hurt. She had thought about taking her own statement to some newspaper editor and trying to convince him to print it—and had considered directly approaching Arana's investors and buyers. Both plans had one serious flaw. Arana would blame Jordan and retaliate by attacking Paraîso. So she had done the only thing she could—boarded the *Evangeline* to return to Paraîso where she could still do some good for the Indians. What she would do when Jordan finished harvesting his rubber, she had no idea.

The days slid past with monotonous regularity. It was all familiar, like a dream she had dreamed before. She knew what lay around each bend, and though it was different, it was also the same. They lost two days because of engine trouble, then made it up by traveling at night. Camping ashore one evening, Spencer got chased up a tree by a caiman, a ten-foot-long "croc," which Jordan then shot and killed. Another evening, she surprised a bushmaster, but instead of attacking, it simply slithered away, leaving her trembling and longing for Jordan to take her in his arms and comfort her.

One dark night, when Jordan fell asleep on deck without hoisting his mosquito netting, he got bitten on the earlobe by what might have been a vampire bat. Spencer stopped the bleeding with pressure, disinfected the bite, bandaged it, and scolded him soundly. With a trace of his old rakish grin, Jordan suggested he might feel better if she kissed the injury. Heat rushed into her cheeks, and she stepped back from him, instantly and painfully aware of his physical proximity. "Pay no attention to that last comment," he murmured, reddening. "For a moment, I forgot myself. The last thing we need is a renewal of intimacy between us."

She agreed—yet intimacy was always on her mind. She had only to watch his muscular, golden forearms as he worked at some task and a flush would consume her flesh, filling her with yearnings. She was shamed by her desire for him, especially since he had made it clear he did not want her, at least not for a wife. Had she been willing to resume intimacies without that assurance, she had no doubt he would take advantage of the situation. Hunger often simmered in his eyes, but as long as conflict lay between them, she dared not risk appeasing either his hunger or her own. They had to remain separate and apart, pretending an aloofness neither felt.

She was glad when they finally reached Paraïso; the Indians were delighted by her return. Abelardo greeted her with a hug, and the women crowded around like old friends, eager to welcome her back into their midst. In her absence, several children and old people had sickened with a mysterious fever, and one man had cut his hand. The wound had festered. She plunged into her work with a vengeance—as Jordan did into his. Each day, he left early and returned late, if he returned at all, and the pile of rubber *bolachas* soon overflowed the storage hut again.

When Jordan wasn't visiting his *estradas*, he drilled the docile Indians on what to do in case of an attack. He tried to teach them how to load and fire the extra Winchesters he had brought back from Manaus, but Spencer could see it was a lost cause. The Indians were in awe of the rifles, and whenever one went off, they screamed and ran for cover, as if malevolent spirits had just been released. Abelardo's father refused to touch one, and only the younger men could be persuaded to actually pull the trigger. As soon as they had done so, they, too, threw down the weapons and dove into the jungle. Jordan would patiently entice them out again and repeat the entire procedure, but the Huitotos had no stomach for warfare. Their gentle natures put them more in tune with prey than predators, and no amount of conditioning could turn them from meek rabbits into ferocious lions.

As the rainy season bore down upon them, Spencer wondered how soon Jordan would be ready to return to Manaus, for the last and final time. She dreaded the decision she must make—whether to go or stay—and dreaded even more the possibility that she might lose Jordan forever. She could not imagine life without him, even life such as it was, with no gaiety, no laughter, no shared moments of mutual happiness, no physical closeness. Still, as long as she was near him, as long as she could still see him, she clung to hope. If he returned to Manaus without her, she would probably never see him again. And after he left, what incentive would there be for the Indians to remain at Paraîso?

The Huitotos would likely leave; they'd simply fade into the jungle one day, never to reappear. By now, Spencer was familiar with their simple pattern of existence. As long as food was plentiful in one place, they remained there, hunting, fishing, amusing themselves as best they could . . . but as soon as the food supply dwindled, they moved on to a better place. When Jordan was no longer at Paraîso to fill the big stew pot with meat or else organize others to do so, the Indians would have no reason to stay. In exchange for their labors, he had furnished them with all the necessities. Spencer could no longer fool herself about her own importance to the Huitotos; when the necessities ceased to be available, the Indians would leave without sparing her a second thought.

She decided to tell Jordan she would be returning to Manaus with him whenever he was ready. She also decided to risk rejection and damaging her pride again by opening her heart and once more telling him how she felt about him. Surely, he had had enough time to recover from the blows Arana had dealt his male ego—and to ponder his own loneliness. Surely, like her, he lusted after the brief but spectacular joy they had once known together.

Besides, she had always believed in fighting for what she wanted—and Jordan was what she wanted most. So one night after he had retired to his house, she brushed her hair until it crackled, fluffed it about her shoulders, and donned clean if wrinkled clothing. Despite the way she had beguiled him the night they had gone to the opera, she did not find it easy to think in terms of seduction. But seduction was precisely what she intended. It was the only way she knew to reach him. Tonight, she vowed, she would force Jordan to admit his love, as he had done that night. She would then convince him that nothing—not even Arana—was more important than what the two of them could have together.

It had taken her a long time to realize it, but loving Jordan, and being loved in return—indeed, love itself—was the most precious, valuable commodity a person could possess. Nothing could outshine it—not the satisfaction of stopping Arana nor the exhilaration of saving a human life. She hoped she would not have to sacrifice everything, particularly her profession, but if it proved necessary, she'd make the sacrifice. Willingly. With her eyes wide open.

Please, Saint Brigid, she prayed. *Just let him love me as much as I love him.*

Chapter Twenty-four

Keeping the lantern lit, Jordan lay down on his bed in the airy bedroom of his house on stilts. He was exhausted, but knew from experience that sleep would be long in coming. The evening hours when he was finally alone, with no urgent tasks to occupy his mind and body, were always the worst. During those hours, he could not keep his thoughts from turning to Spencer. She was so close, yet so far away. He pictured her lying on the bed beside him, her unruly hair spread in a brilliant cascade of flame across the white sheets. He envisioned the swell of her magnificent breasts straining against the thin fabric of her blouse. And his fingers itched to remove her clothing and bare her soft white flesh to his eyes and mouth.

He sighed with frustrated longing. Her presence at Paraïso was a torture to him, and he traveled through his days as if pursued by demons. But there was really only one demon—Demon Desire, who sat on his shoulder wherever he went and whispered into his ear what he fool he was to deny himself the pleasure of loving her. He could pressure her into his bed again; he knew he could. She had said she loved him, and a woman in love was easy prey. But he could not stand the thought of turning that love into scorn and hatred, which it would become in time, when he continually failed to meet her expectations.

He knew himself unworthy of her—but that did not stop the fantasies from coming, or quell the passion that fountained in him whenever he thought about her . . . Spencer Kathleen O'Rourke. Even her name filled him with desire. Who would ever have guessed that the thin, unappealing spinster who had pursued him into the lobby that day at the hotel would one day have the power to plunge him into such relentless agony?

A timid knock came at his door. Expecting it to be Luiz with some problem, he shouted his annoyance. "I'm not here! Go away. Whatever it is can wait until morning."

The knock did not repeat itself, and he was struck with remorse. Maybe the problem was serious and ought not to wait until morning. Rolling off the bed, he trotted to the door in his bare feet and yanked it open. In the inky darkness of the veranda stood Spencer, ethereal in virginal white. Several moments passed before his shock receded enough so he could speak.

"Spencer, what is it? It must be something awful for you to come knocking at my door in the middle of the night. I can't remember the last time you were in this house . . . Wait, it was when we had dinner with David Serrano."

Fearing she might suddenly turn and bolt, he snatched her hand and led her into his room. She came shyly, nervously, her eyes glancing everywhere but at him. Abruptly, he noticed her hair, spilling in wild abandonment down her back. The top two buttons of her white, ruffled blouse were unbuttoned, and he grew alarmed. Spencer always buttoned up tight and wore her hair skinned back so she looked like the headmistress of a female boarding school. What could be wrong?

"Is it Abelardo or one of the other Indians? Did someone get hurt?" His heart pounded at her nearness. He wished she had come for some other reason than to be the bearer of bad tidings.

"Nothing's wrong, Jordan," she finally whispered, then continued in a stronger voice. "No, that's not true. Everything's wrong. I . . . I came t' tell ye I'd be returnin' with ye t' Manaus, not stayin' here, as I thought I might. I also came t' say . . . t' say . . ." She faltered and looked down at the floor.

Releasing her hand, he tilted up her chin so she had to look him in the eye. "To say what, Spencer?"

Her blue-green eyes were wide and glistening. Gazing into them, feeling his own emotions tumble, he knew what she had come to say; the unspoken words vibrated in the air between them. They trembled on the tip of his own tongue and ricocheted through his head: *I love you. I will always love you. No matter what.* For either of them to speak aloud might break the spell. Forestalling further speech, he kissed her gently on her slightly open mouth. It was all the encouragement she needed; her arms slid around his neck, and with a little moan, she pressed herself into him. He inhaled deeply, savoring the scent and feel of her. Now that she was in his arms again, he knew he could not let her go—at least not tonight, not before he had loved and cherished her in the only way he was capable of doing, with his body, if not with the rest of him.

She made him feel strong and manly, restoring what he thought he had lost. Suddenly, he was full and whole, brimming with virility and passion, scarcely able to control himself. "Spencer . . . Spencer . . ." Her name tore from his throat.

"Jordan, I canna help it! I had t' come here. I need ye so," she cried brokenly. "I've tried t' stay away. Honestly I have . . ."

He hushed her with a long kiss, then admonished: "Don't humiliate yourself when there's no need, my love. Do you think I don't need you? Do you think I don't dream of doing this to you . . . ?" He touched her full breasts. Her heart was thudding beneath the fabric, her nipples hardening into buds. "Good God, Spencer! All the way back to Paraíso on the *Evangeline,* I suffered for want of you . . ."

"And I for ye! We've wasted so much time, Jordan, each of us pullin' in opposite directions, when all I ever really wanted was to be with ye! I'll do whatever ye want, Jordan! I'll give up medicine! I'll forget about Arana! I'll obey orders from now on, without questioning everything ye say!"

"Sweetheart . . . Don't make promises you can't keep. You wouldn't be you without your ambition and stubbornness, your determination to root out evil. I don't want you to change and try to become something you're not."

"But can ye accept me the way I am?"

Jordan cupped her face in his hands, tracing her cheekbones with his thumbs. "A better question would be: Can *you* accept *me?*"

Tears shimmered on the tips of her lashes. "Yes, oh, yes, Jordan! What I canna accept is the thought of losin' ye!" She laughed through her tears. "Does that make any sense?"

"Perfect sense," he assured her.

They clung together, weeping and laughing, their hands greedily touching and caressing, rediscovering the shape and feel of each other's bodies. As passion accelerated between them, Jordan shifted his weight and nudged Spencer backward toward the bed. They fell upon it in a tangle of arms and legs. This time, Jordan could not restrain himself and take care removing Spencer's clothing, as he had done with her white lace gown. Nor did Spencer hold back. With eager hands, she ripped off his shirt and trousers.

When they were naked, they rolled together. First, he was on top, thrusting into her, unable to wait a second longer. Then she was on top, straddling his mid section, splaying her hands on his chest, tilting her pelvis to take the full length of him. Growling his desire, he rolled again, then had to grasp the bedpost to keep from falling on the floor. Holding on to him, Spencer giggled—a deep, throaty sound. She clasped him to her, pumping her hips, cradling him between her white thighs. The bed creaked and groaned.

Jordan lost all sense of time or place. There was only Spencer, spread beneath him, enfolding him in warmth and wetness. The heat of her flesh singed like fire. He reared and plunged, desperate to make her feel what he was feeling—the wondrous rapture, the exquisite burst of pleasure. She tensed and cried his name. Letting himself go, he drove home to the final ecstasy.

Afterward, there was no question of her leaving his bed and returning to her hut. Kittenlike, she cuddled against him. Jordan swore to himself that he would never again allow her to sleep anywhere else but in his arms. She belonged where she was—in his bed, in his house, wherever they might be. He would do whatever was necessary, make whatever compromises he must, to keep her beside him for the rest of both their lives. Thus decided, he closed his eyes and fell deeply asleep.

Spencer awoke, as she always did at Paraïso, with the first, filtered light of dawn. Once again, she discovered herself pinioned by Jordan's arm and leg, entrapped by the weight of them, but she made no move to escape. More than an arm and leg held her bound to Jordan's bed; she would not repeat the mistake of thinking she could live without him. Somehow, they would work things out. Jordan had said he accepted her the way she was. It was promise enough he would not demand harsh sacrifices. She wriggled closer to him and sighed her contentment.

His arm moved slightly, then his hand found her breasts. She lay perfectly still while he lightly fondled her, and her body quickened to his touch. "Let's stay here all day," he suggested in her ear, teasing a nipple to a hardened peak.

" 'Tis a temptin' idea, but we canna," she sighed. "I'm goin' t' teach the Indian women how t' purify water today, by boilin' and strainin' it t' remove the dirt and parasites. They might not get so many fevers if they were more careful about their drinkin' water."

"Forget the Indians just for today," Jordan urged.

"What about yer rubber? If we're going t' make it back t' Manaus before the rainy season, hadna ye better hurry and finish collectin' yer *bolachas?"*

"My rubber is almost all collected," Jordan informed her. "And I've destroyed most of my trees and let my tappers go."

"Where did they go? Are they here at Paraīso?"

"You haven't noticed them? Some struck off on their own in *batelãos* to find work at other plantations, but others have returned here. They're sleeping inside the storage hut, where they can keep an eye on my harvest."

Spencer was ashamed to admit she had not noticed more than a small influx of skinny brown men. She had kept too busy with the Indians and actually avoided those areas where she might be likely to run into Jordan. "Will they help us get the rubber t' Manaus?" she asked. "Ye have more now than ye did the last time. I dinna know how we'll get it all transported."

"It'll be hard work, but we'll make it. Between the Indians and my tappers, we should have no trouble. I just wish I'd been more successful teaching the Indians how to handle Winchesters. I'd like to use them as guards, too."

Spencer did not like the sound of that. "Do ye really think it will be necessary? Ye had no trouble the last time."

His hand ceased to fondle her, and he turned over on his back. She rolled over to face him. He was frowning now, looking deadly serious. "From now until I get my harvest to market will be a dangerous time, Spencer. If Loayza or anybody else has a notion of stealing my rubber, now is the time they'll try. It's the end of the gathering season, and all the *seringueiros* will be heading toward Manaus with their harvests. I don't want to alarm you, but we must take precautions against the dangers we're facing. In fact, this morning would be an excellent time to test your skills with a Winchester."

"Oh, no, Jordan . . ." she protested. "I could never shoot anyone; I'm too much like the Huitotos. Guns and rifles scare me."

"Get up, my love!" Jordan swatted her bare buttocks. "Why didn't I think of this before? I did think of it. I just didn't do anything about it. You've got to learn to fire a rifle."

That very morning, after breakfast, he taught her how to load and shoot a Winchester. Every time it recoiled, it knocked her down, until eventually she learned to brace herself. But aiming it was another matter. They persevered, and finally, after several hours practice, she could at least manage to shatter a limb in the tree at which she was aiming, though it wasn't the limb she wanted.

"All right," he said. "Now we're going hunting. The first beast we see in the jungle, you're going to kill with a single shot."

"Jordan, I canna!"

"Oh, yes you can. If you haven't the guts to shoot a monkey, how in hell will you ever shoot a man?"

They prowled the fringes of the jungle, searching for game, which had become scarce in the vicinity of Paraïso. Jordan then took her downriver in the *batelão* and stealthily tied up near shore.

"Remember, first thing that moves, you fire at it," he whispered.

"What if it's an Indian?" she countered indignantly. "Canna I identify my target first?"

"There are no Indians skulking around here. We're

still on my land, and any Indians in the area are already at Paraîso, waiting for you to bag meat for the stew pot."

Spencer frowned at Jordan and reached for the long Winchester lying beside her on a heap of fishnet. She wished that's what she was doing instead—fishing. Hunting did not appeal to her.

They crept a short way into the jungle gloom. It was late afternoon, when animals began approaching the river to drink. Crouching down in the tangled undergrowth, they watched and waited. Spencer brushed away a cloud of mosquitoes and longed to return to Paraîso. Soon the mosquitoes would become unbearable, and it didn't look as if any game was going to pass them here.

"Over there," Jordan suddenly whispered in her ear. "Get ready."

A slight sound reached Spencer's ears—the merest whisper of a footfall and rustle of vine. She lifted the Winchester and aimed in the direction Jordan had indicated. All her muscles tensed, but she kept her finger steady on the trigger. She only hoped the animal wasn't a deer; it would be easier to kill an ugly tapir than a fragile, delicate doe.

The animal's approach was clearly audible now. Spencer wondered why it could not smell them, then realized that the slight breeze was blowing into her face. She and Jordan were downwind of it. A parrot screamed overhead. At almost the same moment, the vines and thick undergrowth parted, revealing yellow eyes and a tawny head. Spencer pulled the trigger before the creature's identity fully registered. The resultant boom almost drowned out the yowl that followed—almost, but not quite.

"Good God, it's a jaguar!" Jordan cried beside her. "And you didn't kill it! Give me the damn rifle—quick!"

He grabbed it from her hands and recocked it, while Spencer cowered in the underbrush. Peering out, she saw a spotted, yellowish-brown cat, hardly bigger than a house cat, yowling in pain and terror. Stretched out on its stomach, it pawed its head, where a reddish crease between its ears marked the path of the bullet from the Winchester.

Jordan stood upright, aiming down at it, from which vantage point he couldn't miss. Spencer sprang to life. Leaping to her feet, she knocked aside the muzzle of the rifle before Jordan could fire it.

"What in hell are you doing?" Jordan yelped. "Don't you know a wounded jaguar is the most dangerous animal in the jungle?"

"Jordan, it's just a baby! Look at it! It's scared and hurt."

They both looked at the writhing little cat pawing its head and whimpering. The jaguar was paying them no attention whatsoever; its attention centered upon the searing pain between its ears.

"It is only a cub," Jordan said. "I'm not surprised. A fully grown one would never have been so careless as to blunder into us. In any case, we better put it out of its misery and get back to the *batelão*. Your shot probably scared its mama away, but she'll be back—searching for her baby."

"Oh, Jordan, do we have to? If we took it back to camp with us, I could treat it before we let it go."

"Are you crazy? This is a *jaguar,* not a kitten."

Spencer scarcely heard him. She was bending over the whimpering baby, trying to see how serious the wound was. As she reached out her hand, the jaguar spat and swiped at her with his paw. Jordan's arm around her waist pulled her back.

"Damn my aunt Milly's corset! Do you want to get torn apart? Even a cub can do plenty of damage."

"We need somethin' t' wrap it in and restrain it . . . I know! That fishnet in the *batelão!* Hurry, Jordan. Will ye get it? If we can catch it before the shock of its injury wears off, we should have no trouble takin' it back to Paraïso."

Jordan stared at her. "You're serious, aren't you? You actually intend to rescue this critter."

She gave him a melting glance. "Please, Jordan . . ."

He sighed heavily. "Here I go again . . . doing something I know is crazy."

Jordan returned to the *batelão* and fetched the fishnet. They threw it over the spitting baby and quickly gathered up the ends so the cub was helpless—or so they thought. Climbing into the *batelão* for the return trip upriver, Spencer set the cub on her lap, then gave a startled cry as it managed to dig its sharp claws into her knees. Gingerly, she moved it to the bottom of the canoe, where it lay alternately snarling and whimpering.

Their arrival at Paraïso caused a sensation among the Indians and rubber tappers, especially when Jordan told them it was Spencer who had wounded the jaguar. They all gathered around, eyeing the net-wrapped creature with great interest. While Jordan held the creature immobile, Spencer stuck her fingers through the netting and disinfected the powder burn. Then she swabbed salve on the raw, reddened flesh. She was at a loss as to what to do next. She couldn't leave the poor thing trussed up. Abelardo solved the problem by producing a cage in which his father had confined a large parrot for his amusement during the time his burns had kept him immobile.

Thanking the boy, Spencer dumped the jaguar out of the net into the cage and firmly closed the door on it. She secured the door with a stout thong. Abelardo was delighted to accept the task of finding food for the cub. Proudly, he carried the jaguar to the clinic, and spent the rest of the evening trying to win its trust and affection.

Preoccupied with Jordan, Spencer forgot all about the jaguar and spent the night in his bed in his arms. The following day, Jordan left to visit one last *estrada*. While he was gone, Spencer practiced her shooting, conducted health and hygiene classes for the women, and nursed the jaguar. Abelardo devoted himself to the little creature, and within three days had it remarkably tamed. Though it would allow no one but him to touch or stroke it, the yellow cat with the black spots permitted the boy to hand-feed it scraps of meat and carry it around the compound in his chubby arms. The sight of the child crooning and talking to the little jaguar delighted Spencer, reminding her that she was responsible for the boy's recovery from his terrible burns and for his growing facility with English.

Since she and Jordan would soon be leaving Paraĩso forever, it pleased her to know that her time here had not been in vain. She had accomplished a few worthwhile things. On the morning of the day she was expecting Jordan to return, Spencer was in the clinic, examining a sick baby one of the Indian women had brought to her. Abelardo, jaguar in arms, was helping to translate the woman's description of the baby's ailment.

Suddenly, a terrific explosion rocked the hut, followed by the rat-tat-tat of gunfire. Spencer ran out, Abelardo close on her heels. The first thing she saw was Jordan's house afire. Flames shot from the unshuttered windows. One entire wall had collapsed. Even more horrifying, was the sight of armed men in green uniforms racing into the compound from the jungle's edge. Everywhere, Indians were screaming and running. Babies howled, and camp dogs barked. Paraîso was under attack—and Jordan wasn't there to defend it.

Staggering back into the clinic, Spencer grabbed the Winchester she had been practicing with earlier. As she picked it up, she remembered she had used up almost all the ammunition she had brought with her from the house. To get more, she would have to return to the burning structure or traverse the entire compound to reach the small storage hut where Jordan kept additional supplies of ammunition. Her mind raced; without Jordan, defending Paraîso would be impossible. Her best bet was to take Abelardo and flee into the jungle—saving her few precious bullets until she really needed them.

"Abelardo, come!" she cried to the boy. He clutched the yowling cub whose claws were digging into his arms. "Put the jaguar down, and come at once! Those are wicked men; we must run and hide!"

The Indian woman whose child she had been examining began to wail and scream. Her baby was already crying. Spencer grabbed the woman's hand and began dragging her toward the jungle's edge. Images of the devastation at La Reserva danced in her mind. If she couldn't save all of the Indians, she could at least save these three. The rest were on their own; by herself, there was nothing she could do to save them.

As she fled the hut, she saw Indians and rubber tappers running in every direction. Most were wild-eyed with terror, but some of the tappers had managed to grab guns. Several Indians—Abelardo's father among them—had seized blowguns or machetes and were attempting to hold off the attackers so their women and children could escape to the jungle. As long as anyone was trying to resist, Spencer could not abandon them. She shoved the Indian woman and her crying baby toward the jungle and motioned to Abelardo that he should accompany the woman. Still clutching the cub, the boy stubbornly shook his head. He, too, had seen his father and wouldn't leave without him.

The green-clad soldiers raced through the compound, mowing down the fleeing Indians with gunfire, or else clubbing them over the heads with rifle butts. Spencer crouched on one knee and aimed her carbine at the horde of invaders. None would stand still long enough to be shot. Not so the Indians. All around her, Indians were dropping like flies. In a matter of minutes, she realized the futility of resisting; they were sadly outnumbered. She saw Abelardo's father fall and heard the boy scream.

When Abelardo started running in his father's direction, Spencer scrambled to her feet and sprinted after him. Upon reaching him, she tried to push him in the direction of the jungle, away from the fighting. With a great shout, a half-dozen soldiers broke free of the melee and pursued her. Grabbing Abelardo's arm, Spencer dragged him after her and was almost to the jungle when the soldiers finally caught up with her. Green-clad bodies surrounded them. Grinning faces leered in her face. Shielding Abelardo with her body, Spencer aimed her Winchester at the nearest one.

Laughing, he stepped forward, daring her to fire. Without a moment's hesitation, she squeezed the trigger. There was a hollow click. The soldiers laughed and jeered. As she backed away in stunned horror, the men stalked her. Hands fumbled at the fastenings of trousers. One man licked his lips. Another's mouth twisted into a feral grin. Spencer heard Abelardo's quick sob of fear. The jaguar made a hissing sound.

In vain, Spencer searched for a means of escape. There was none. Her worst nightmares were about to come true. Like the poor women at La Reserva, she was going to be raped and killed.

Chapter Twenty-five

Jordan knew Paraïso was under attack before he heard the explosion and sounds of gunfire. As he and the men he had taken with him to collect rubber paddled their laden *batelãos* toward home, they came upon the *Liberal* tied up to shore out of sight of the compound but within easy hiking distance. The launch appeared deserted, and Jordan had no trouble guessing where the occupants had gone.

Immediately, he guided the *batelãos* past the launch and paddled as hard and fast as he could for Paraïso's wooden dock. He arrived to find the attack in full swing, with soldiers running amok through the compound. There was no organized resistance to the invaders and only minimal self-defense, a situation Jordan immediately sought to remedy. The men with him were his most dependable rubber tappers, and they quickly followed orders to fan out and begin firing upon the soldiers.

As soldiers started to fall, the Indians took heart, and many more fought back. This so shocked the soldiers that the attack lost its impetus. Jordan concentrated his fire on the apparent leaders. When these men toppled, the less disciplined among their followers headed for the jungle, as eager as the Indians to escape the sweep of bullets. Jordan raced shouting through the compound toward the clinic where he expected Spencer to be at this hour. The smoldering clinic roof threatened to burst into flame at any moment, and his stomach muscles clenched with dread.

Beyond the hut, near the jungle's edge, he glimpsed Spencer's red hair shining like a beacon. Ringed by soldiers, she was attempting to hold them off with her Winchester. The gun's empty click signaled a lack of ammunition. There was a moment's pause while the men closed in on her. Lifting his own rifle, Jordan sighted down the barrel. As a soldier reached for Spencer, Jordan shot him. The man pitched forward and sprawled on the ground. The rest of the soldiers dove for cover—except for one man. Braver than the others, he seized Spencer's arm, twisted it behind her back, and maneuvered her in front of him to form a shield.

With his free hand, he withdrew a long-bladed knife and held it to Spencer's throat. Jordan stopped in his tracks. Grinning triumphantly, keeping Spencer between himself and Jordan, the soldier backed toward the safety of the jungle. Furious, Jordan sucked in his breath. Was there nothing he could do? The soldier would either escape with Spencer or slit her throat or both.

Behind the two figures, a third figure moved. It was Abelardo, clutching the jaguar cub to his chest. "Abelardo!" Jordan yelled. "Toss the cub onto the soldier's back!"

For the space of a heartbeat, nothing happened. Jordan realized he had unthinkingly spoken in English, while the Indian boy knew only Tupi and what few words of English Spencer had managed to teach him. Yet Abelardo did exactly as commanded—tossed the cub onto the soldier's back. The little creature promptly yowled and dug in with all four claws. Uttering a startled shriek, the soldier let go of Spencer and sought to dislodge the spitting jaguar.

His screams unnerved the last remaining soldiers in the compound. To a man, including the soldier grappling with the jaguar, they bolted for the jungle. Shouting triumphantly, sure now of victory, the rubber tappers and Indians pounded after them in hot pursuit. Jordan tried to call the pursuers back, but it was no use. More gunfire issued from the jungle depths. Several screams indicated hits. Then an ominous silence descended, broken only by the moans of the wounded and the beginning wails of grief from the women and children.

Jordan flung his arms wide, and Spencer dashed into them, throwing her own arms around his neck and weeping in delayed fear and shock.

"Hush, sweetheart . . . it's over now. They've gone—at least for the moment."

"Oh, Jordan!" Spencer sobbed against his chest. "The soldiers killed so many! If ye hadna come when ye did, they would have killed us all. It was La Reserva all over again!"

"I know, love." Jordan soothingly stroked her back and shoulders. "They came for the rubber. Loayza probably thought stealing it would be an easy matter. I doubt he expected the Indians to oppose the soldiers—nor would he have anticipated so many tappers being here at one time. That's quite unusual, and even more unusual for tappers or Indians to resist. In most cases, they just flee. We must thank them for helping to repel the attack—and convince them to stand by us should a second attack be mounted."

Spencer withdrew slightly and fixed worried eyes on Jordan's face. "Surely they'll not be back! By now, they ought t' have learned their lesson."

"I'd like to believe that's true, Spencer, but I can't," Jordan said gently. "If anything, they'll return with reinforcements—enough to crush us. The rubber is too great a temptation, especially now when they've seen how much I have."

"Then we'll have t' get ready for them. We'll have t' organize a method of defense."

"If any defense will work." As he glanced at the bodies littering the cleared area around Paraîso, bitterness consumed Jordan. "I haven't seen such a scene of devastation since La Reserva."

As if to underscore his words, the wailing that had begun sporadically suddenly gained strength and threatened to drown them out. Timidly, their faces still terrified, women and children crept out of the forest. They went from body to body, discovering who among their menfolk had been killed. A large group gathered around the body of Abelardo's father; he was the tribal chieftain, the most important man in the tribe. While Jordan had been comforting Spencer, Abelardo had joined the group, but the boy's mother, Jordan noticed, was nowhere in sight.

"Before we organize a new defense, we'd better see to the wounded," Jordan said. "And douse the fires."

Spencer nodded. "I'll check the clinic t' determine what medicines and surgical instruments I still have left. Bring the worst ones t' me, there. We'll put them on pallets until I can examine them and determine the most critical cases—those I must deal with first."

Jordan pressed a kiss onto Spencer's forehead, marveling at her ability to grapple with unpleasant realities. Already, she had recovered from her fright and was thinking ahead to business. He only wished he himself were half as efficient and self-confident. The Indians and tappers had repelled the attack this time, but next time they might not be so lucky. What he needed was a couple of cannons to hold off the attackers. Unfortunately, there were no cannons available.

Spencer worked unceasingly throughout the day to clean and bind wounds, remove bullets, and alleviate pain. By early evening, she had done what she could for the injured, and the dead had all been removed to a shallow mass grave Jordan and the *seringeiros* had dug at the edge of the jungle. Only two bodies remained unburied—those of Abelardo's father and mother, both of whom had been killed during the attack.

Because the chief had been such an important personage, the Indians wanted to take these bodies into the jungle to bury, hide in a tree, or do whatever Indians did with important personages. The old *macumbeiro* had stepped into the leadership role and was making all the decisions for the Huitotos. He had decreed that the remnants of the tribe must leave that very night to take their fallen chieftain to a place of honor and safety.

Spencer knew that the Indians rarely, if ever, traveled the jungle at night. She suspected that the *macumbeiro* wanted to remove the tribe from Paraïso before another attack wiped them out entirely or enslaved those who were left. Even the wounded were to be taken along and, of course, Abelardo. In her heart, Spencer wept for the boy's double loss, but she refrained from shedding tears in front him. She couldn't openly indulge her grief when the boy himself resisted weeping. Only his huge black eyes betrayed his pain and shock. Not only had he lost both parents, he had also lost his cherished friend; the heroic, little jaguar had disappeared, leaving Abelardo bereft of even the minimal comfort the animal might have given him.

It was a sad, depressing evening, all the more so because Jordan was deeply upset by the pending departure of the Indians. In vain, he pleaded with them to remain and help defend Paraîso. Luiz haltingly translated, but the Indians refused to listen. With curt words and gestures, the old *macumbeiro* declared they must go. Deep in the jungle, he pointed out, the Indians could find food, shelter, and safety, but here at Paraîso, there was only death and danger.

Sharing Jordan's disappointment, Spencer joined him to watch the departure of the Huitotos. Dry-eyed and stoical, submerging their grief, the women gathered together their few pitiful belongings and dismantled their grass huts. Docile as cattle, they stood with their bundles, awaiting the *macumbeiro*'s signal to depart. Even the women who had lost husbands, brothers, or children that morning showed no emotion; their eyes never strayed to the shallow mass grave but remained fixed upon the ground in meek subservience, while the *macumbeiro* completed a ritual involving the sprinkling of ashes over the leaf-wrapped pallets containing the bodies of Abelardo's parents.

Standing beside Jordan, Spencer spotted Abelardo

standing off by himself, watching the ritual impassively. She motioned to him, and he hurried over and slipped his warm hand in hers. Looking down at him, she blinked back tears and whispered, "I am going to miss you, Abelardo. I'll miss teaching you English."

His dark eyes glistened in the light of the palm torches illuminating the darkening compound. "I do not want to go, Doctor," he said. "I do not want to leave you."

At a loss for words to comfort him, Spencer squeezed his hand. Beside her, Jordan shifted his weight, but otherwise stood rigid as a stick. She had no words for him either but felt she ought to say something. "Jordan, I'm so sorry. I wish there was some way t' convince the Indians t' stay."

He grimaced, his face bleak. "So do I. They won't listen to a word I say. Their minds are made up."

"Ye canna blame them, Jordan. The Huitotos aren't fighters. They see no point in risking their lives t' defend a pile of rubber."

Jordan's eyes sought hers. His mouth curled contemptuously. "Are you saying we ought to quit and simply hand the rubber over to Loayza?"

"No," Spencer denied, though the thought had crossed her mind. "I'm only saying we mustna despair. We still have the tappers. They did a fine job today, and they'll do as well the next time, too," she asserted, hoping it was true.

Before she could say more, Luiz came up to Jordan. From the overseer's expression, Spencer knew he had additional bad news to impart. "Senhor Rei, I have been talking to the *seringueiros* . . ." he began hesitantly. "Now that the Indians are leaving, they wish to leave also."

Jordan stiffened. "What do you mean—leave?"

"They are down on the dock, senhor, arguing over how many *batelãos* to take. They say that if the soldiers return, we will all be killed. There are not enough of us to defend the rubber. So they wish to depart Paraíso this very night. Their fear is great, Senhor Rei. Otherwise they would not consider traveling the river in darkness."

"Damnation!" Jordan swore. "Is everyone around here a coward? Run down to the dock and tell them to wait a few minutes, Luiz. I'll come myself as soon as I can. I want to try one more time to convince the Indians to stay."

"Who will translate for you, senhor? You do not speak Tupi well enough for the Indians to understand."

"Abelardo can translate," Spencer suggested. "A plea from the son of the dead chieftain might be more persuasive anyway, especially since he himself doesn't want to go."

Jordan darted her a grateful glance. "Go on, Luiz. Tell those men if they take my *batelãos* without my permission, that's stealing. They can wait a few more minutes; I'll be there shortly to talk to them myself. If they agree to stay, I'll give them handsome bonuses."

Avoiding Jordan's direct gaze, Luiz shrugged his thin shoulders. "If you insist, senhor, but I doubt it will do much good. I myself have a wife and children to think of. What benefit is a bonus if I never have a chance to spend it? I cannot enjoy money if I am dead or a slave at El Encanto."

So Luiz wants to leave, too, Spencer thought. Poor Jordan! He might lose his rubber to Loayza, after all.

"Follow orders, Luiz," Jordan snapped. "If you're any kind of man, you'll stand by me during this crisis."

"Sĩm, senhor," Luiz responded, but he still would not meet Jordan's eyes.

After the overseer left, Jordan bent down and gazed into Abelardo's big, black, guileless eyes. "Abelardo, do you think you can convince the Huitotos to remain here at Paraĩso? I need help to defend my harvest from the soldiers. The next time we're attacked, we'll be better prepared. I'll keep working with the men to teach them how to fire rifles . . . and they won't have to stay here long. Very soon now, I'll be leaving for Manaus. Then I'll need men to help me transport the rubber downriver—lots of men. I'll pay well for their labors."

"I will speak to them, senhor," Abelardo said earnestly. "When the soldiers come again, I want to kill the ones who killed my . . . my . . ." He turned to Spencer, his mouth quivering, his eyes bright with unshed tears.

"Parents . . ." she supplied.

"Parents . . ." he grimly parroted. "Abelardo will not run away. Abelardo is son of chief. He will stay and fight." His round face flushed. His young mouth tightened. Without another word, he turned and walked toward the old *macumbeiro* and his people.

Spencer's throat swelled with pride and admiration. "There's one Indian who's on our side," she said, but in the next moment, her worries resurfaced. Another attack *could* wipe out the Huitotos, including Abelardo—but short of abandoning the rubber, what else could Jordan do but fight?

In silence, they watched Abelardo argue with the

old *macumbeiro*. The voodoo chief did not look pleased to be challenged by the youngster. He waved his hands and made angry, threatening motions. Abelardo stood his ground, the scarred pink flesh of his back gleaming in the torchlight. Then the old *macumbeiro* motioned to the four men waiting to pick up the pallets of Abelardo's father and mother. He grunted orders, and the men bent down and lifted the pallets, hoisting them to shoulder level. The women picked up their bundles, and several lit torches from the ones already burning.

"It isn't working," Jordan growled. "Thank Abelardo for me when you say good-bye to him; I've got to get down to the docks and stop the *seringueiros* from jumping off this fast-sinking ship."

"I will, Jordan," Spencer murmured.

Her heart was a leaden lump in her breast as she watched the Indians begin trekking after the old *macumbeiro*. Abelardo rejoined her, his young face mutinous. Spencer enfolded the boy in a tearful hug. "Ye tried, Abelardo! I'm very proud of ye. I'll never forget ye. One day ye'll be a great, brave chief, a credit t' yer people . . . I'm just so sorry I won't be here t' see ye when ye've grown to manhood."

"Abelardo not going with them," Abelardo said. "Abelardo stay here. Become white boy. Speak English. Shoot rifles."

"But, dear boy, ye canna! I mean, you *can't!* These are your people. You belong among the Huitotos!" Spencer pointed to the departing Indians. "Hurry now, before you're left behind."

Abelardo stubbornly shook his head. "Not go. No more live in jungle. No more run from bad men. Abelardo be like Senhor Rei. Be strong. Fight enemies. Collect rubber and buy many rifles."

"Abelardo, you can't stay here! Why, you . . . you're an *Indian*."

"No more," Abelardo insisted. "Father dead. Mother dead. Need new mother. New father. Abelardo pick you. Pick Senhor Rei. Abelardo no more Indian. Abelardo white boy now. Speak only English. Forget Huitotos."

Folding his arms, Abelardo sat down on the ground at Spencer's feet, leaving her to wonder how she could have been so blind and stupid. She had encouraged him in this folly. She was to blame for it. She had taught him English, answered all his questions, fed his inquiring mind, and shown him the white way of doing things. As if he were damp clay, she had molded him into something different, destroying his identity in the process. Now, he no longer wanted to be Indian—*wasn't* Indian. He no more belonged among the timid, shy Huitotos than she herself.

"Abelardo, dear child, are ye sure this is what ye want? I . . . I dinna—don't know how to be a mother! I've never been one. Frankly, I'm not sure I'll be very good at it."

"Abelardo sure." The boy jumped to his feet and threw his arms around Spencer's waist, startling her with his sudden outpouring of emotion. He clung so tightly she could not dislodge him. His shoulders shook; his whole body trembled. With his face buried in her stomach, he sobbed broken-heartedly. Helpless to do anything else, Spencer wrapped her arms around him—taking care not to hurt his tender, scarred flesh. For a long time, she stood perfectly still, holding the weeping child, accustoming herself to the idea of becoming his mother. It meant bonding to him in a way she had never bonded to anyone, except perhaps Jordan.

Gradually, an odd exhilaration crept over her. So this is what motherhood is like, she thought, so piercing and bittersweet—so unexpectedly joyous!—but also wrenching and sad. Frightening, too.

Shyly, she squeezed the small, determined body, telling him in the only way she knew how, that she accepted him, would not reject him. In that brief but earthshaking moment, Abelardo became her son, and she knew she would always fear for him, dote on him, worry about him. He would never be far from her thoughts. Never had she suspected she could feel so attached to one little boy; Abelardo belonged to her now, and she to him. In all the world, he had no one else to look after him. The Indians had all departed, abandoning them both without a backward glance . . .

A new thought occurred: What would Jordan say when he found out he had become a father without his knowledge or consent?

As he stood on the wooden dock, lit only by a single solitary torch, Jordan cursed and swore. All but one of the *batelãos* were gone; the *seringueiros* had not waited to hear what he had to say. Even Luiz had not waited. Apparently the cowardly overseer had decided to cast his lot with the rubber tappers and escape while he still had the chance. Looking downriver, Jordan could see the bobbing lights from the torches and lanterns the men had taken with them. They looked like fireflies winking over the black expanse of water. If he shouted, the men might be able to hear him—but what was the use? They were all cowards, so afraid of Arana's name and reputation they couldn't stomach the thought of battling him—or battling Loayza and the soldiers, which was the same thing.

Jordan's fury boiled. Despair clogged his throat. Now there remained only himself and Spencer to defend the huge pile of rubber and transport it to Manaus. The task was clearly impossible. All that backbreaking labor! All the expense! All the lost years of his life wasted on this futile, discouraging enterprise! This one last load of rubber represented his freedom, his chance to leave Brazil forever. His entire future rested on getting it to market. Without it, he couldn't put his plans into effect. Even with it, he'd be forced to scrimp and save, buy inferior breeding stock or be unable to restore Castle Acres to its previous efficiency. Without it, he dared not leave. He'd have to return to Manaus, hire more men—including guards and gunmen—and stick it out another year in hopes of augmenting his fragile profits.

Worst of all, he'd have to say good-bye to Spencer. No way in hell would he permit her to come back with him to Paraïso for another season. It was simply too dangerous. Nor did he want her waiting for him in Manaus where her obsession with Arana would only get her into trouble. He must put his foot down and insist she return to the United States. If she really loved him, she would do as he asked—return to Boston and wait for him. If he was lucky, in a year or possibly two, he could join her with enough money to give them a decent start.

One part of him recognized he had no choice in these decisions; he must do what circumstances required. But another part railed against the injustice of it all, making him sick with rage and disappointment. He had come so close—so tantalizingly close!—to modest victory. Now he had to relinquish his hopes and tell the woman he loved that they'd be fortunate to reach Manaus in one piece, and when they did get there, they faced a long separation and additional perilous uncertainties.

Jordan eyed the single, lone *batelão* left behind by the *seringueiros*. Shallow-drafted *batelãos* could negotiate the river at night, but the *Evangeline* could not. It was probably for that reason that Luiz had left the canoe—so they could depart tonight, like the rest of the defeated cowards. Perhaps they should, Jordan thought. It would be safer if they left tonight. Loayza wouldn't waste any time returning for the kill; the man knew Indians and rubber tappers. He'd built a career on the art of intimidation and violence. Counting on how scared everyone must be, waiting for the next attack, Loayza would strike hard and fast—and this time, he'd bring along more than enough soldiers to wipe out Paraĩso.

His mind made up, Jordan ceased brooding and went to tell Spencer to gather her things. They were leaving immediately.

Chapter Twenty-six

"What do ye mean—we're leavin' t'night?" Spencer gasped. "What about yer rubber? What about the *Evangeline* and Paraïso itself? If there's no one here t' defend it, Loayza will destroy the entire depot."

Jordan had just given her his shocking news, and she could not accept it. The departure of the Indians was at least understandable, but the flight of the rubber tappers amazed and disappointed her. It seemed incredible they had come to this—fleeing under cover of darkness, sacrificing everything Jordan had built at Paraïso. To abandon his harvest meant he was also abandoning his future. She knew what the rubber represented—not only his future but hers. Now that he had actually decided to toss it aside, she was adamantly opposed to the idea.

"I meant just what I said, Spencer. We're packing only what we can take in a *batelão* and getting the hell out, while we still can . . . What's Abelardo doing here? I thought the Indians left already."

"They did. Abelardo dinna want t' go with them. He . . . He wants t' be a white boy, t' stay here and live with *us*."

"Are you stark, raving mad?" Jordan shouted.

"He can't stay with us. He's an Indian, for God's sake. If we take him back to Manaus, civilization will destroy him as surely as Loayza will destroy Paraĩso."

Spencer slid an arm around the boy's shoulders and pulled him closer. "I dinna see why that should be true. We can teach him everything he needs t' know. We can adopt him, Jordan. He can be our son. We can educate him t' belong in our world; I've no doubt he'll be a great success."

"Damn my aunt Milly's corset! You must be mad! While I'm facing financial ruin and the loss of my life, not to mention yours, you're off adopting savages and embroiling me in your ridiculous schemes."

"Abelardo is not a savage!" Spencer cried, amazed at her own protectiveness and Jordan's callousness in front of the boy. "If ye dinna want him, I do! Ye canna have me without takin' him . . . I admit t' some initial reservations about adoptin' him, but I've come t' think it's a grand idea. Besides, I canna go off and leave him t' be killed . . . and if you can, ye are not the man I thought ye were."

Spencer knew she had gone too far when Jordan's face turned livid in the torchlight. He took a deep breath before continuing. "Spencer, now is not the time to argue over your impossible expectations. I'll only say they've plagued and disheartened me all along. Of course I won't leave the boy here to die. I just hadn't thought of becoming a father overnight . . . The soldiers will probably return in the morning. By then, I want to be far downriver, hidden behind a screen of vegetation on shore. The *Liberal* may come after us, but if we're careful, she won't find us."

"Why aren't we takin' the *Evangeline?* Wouldna the launch be much quicker and safer than a leaky *batelão?"*

"It would be quicker, yes, but not safer. In the dark, we might run aground or rip open her bottom on some obstruction. The waters near Paraîso are too dangerous; I can't risk it."

Spencer felt dangerously close to weeping. Nothing was working out as it should. Answers to their problems were farther out of reach than ever. Surely it made no sense to leave Jordan's harvest; he had worked too hard to obtain it. "The rubber, Jordan . . . I know what it means to ye. Isn't there anything we can do t' save it?"

"I don't know what. If we worked all night, we couldn't load it all. And the *Liberal* would only overtake us and get it anyhow. Two of us—pardon me, three—can't stop a boatload of soldiers. Don't you think I'd defend my harvest if I could? Had the *seringueiros* stayed, we'd at least have had a fighting chance."

"Couldna we . . . disable the *Liberal* in some way? The launch must be somewhere nearby; where else did all those soldiers come from?"

"It is near here. This morning, the tappers and I had to sneak past it. That's how we knew Paraîso was under attack."

"Then wouldna she still be there—anchored in the river or tied up near shore?"

"I suppose so, but we can't just walk up to her and disable her."

"Why not?" Spencer pressed, determined not to give up until all avenues had been explored. "In the dark, they wouldna see us. Of course, I dinna know how t' go about disablin' a launch, but ye do."

Jordan waved his hand dismissingly. "Oh, there's dozens of ways—if I could get to the engine, which I already know I can't . . ." He paused a moment, considering. "But maybe I wouldn't have to go aboard. Maybe I could do something to the launch's propeller, remove a vital part, so the propeller would fall off when they started the engine . . . On second thought, what good would it do? There's no one to help us load rubber onto the *Evangeline* anyway."

"I can help, Senhor Rei," Abelardo volunteered. The boy's face was swollen from crying. His eyes were red. But his young voice brimmed with confidence. "Abelardo strong. I can lift rubber."

"So can I!" Spencer cried. "We can work all night loadin' rubber and leave at dawn. We may not get all of it loaded, but we'll get some. All ye have t' do is figure out how t' disable the *Liberal* without gettin' caught."

"It's out of the question," Jordan snapped. "The whole idea is preposterous. We'd be taking all kinds of unnecessary chances."

Spencer seized his hands. "Dinna give up, Jordan! Please dinna give up. It just might work. We can at least try . . ."

She clung to his hands, willing him to regain hope. He shook his head, looked at Abelardo, and grunted. He shrugged his shoulders. But a little gleam came into his eyes. "I suppose it's not impossible . . . But three *men* couldn't load enough rubber to make the risk worthwhile."

"One man, one boy, and one woman could . . . if they were properly motivated."

"And you think we are . . ."

"I think I'd do anything if it meant we could start a new life together, Jordan. Isna that what we'll lose if we dinna try—precious time that could be spent lovin' each other and buildin' a home for little Abelardo?"

"A wife and son . . . A family . . . my own family . . ." Jordan murmured wistfully. His face softened. He lifted one hand to stroke back a tendril of her unruly hair. "Not next year or the year after, but as soon as we reach Manaus . . ."

"Yes, Jordan. This year, this rubber season . . . 'Twill be our last. We will make enough money from this harvest t' enable us t' quit. And there's an added bonus: We'll whip Arana. This one time he'll not succeed. When the soldiers come after the rubber, they'll find it gone—or most of it. Think how angry and disappointed they'll be!"

Jordan grinned sardonically. "You always know my weak points, don't you? You always know just what to say."

"Then we can do it? Ye're sayin' yes?"

"How can I say no? I just remembered something you forgot to mention: with or without the rubber, when I leave here, it will be for good . . . I've destroyed the rubber trees. I can't come back and spend another year or so building my fortune. What trees are left won't produce enough rubber to support a rabbit. This harvest will be the last harvest for a long time to come."

"We can do it, Jordan! I know we can."

Jordan drew her into his arms and hugged her. "I hope you're right, my love. Give me a kiss for strength and courage; then let's get started."

They gathered together all the lanterns and palm torches they could find and lit a path from the rubber storage hut to the dock where the *Evangeline* was tied. The distance was well over a hundred yards, but had the advantage of being downhill. However, once they got the *bolachas* to the dock, they would have to lift them into the boat. Spencer questioned why Jordan had placed the storage building so far from shore, and his answer made her feel stupid for asking.

"Because of the danger of flooding," he explained. "When the river rises, it carries away everything within reach. If my hut weren't on a little hill, I'd have had to build it even farther away . . . I never once worried about the distance, because I always had plenty of hands to help carry the *bolachas* to the *Evangeline* . . . Ready to haul rubber?"

Spencer nodded. "Why dinna ye leave Abelardo and me t' get started, and go disable the *Liberal?* Or do ye want me t' go with ye? I do hate for ye t' go alone."

"I'm not going until just before dawn," Jordan informed her. "Then I'll take the *batelão* and see how close I can get. As for you or Abelardo accompanying me, forget it. This is one job I want to do alone—and if I'm not back by a certain time, you'll have to leave without me."

"Leave without ye!"

"You'll have to," Jordan calmly insisted. "If not to save yourself, then to save Abelardo."

"But I canna run the *Evangeline* by meself!"

"You'll have to learn—and fast. Remember, Spencer, this whole scheme was your idea."

She remembered—and trembled with anxiety. Now that her brave words had to be matched by brave actions, it was hard to maintain her enthusiasm and confidence that they would succeed. As she reached for the first *bolacha,* her hands shook. To her dismay, she discovered she could not lift the thing.

"Wait a minute," Jordan said. "I'll heft this first one on to your shoulder. Watch how I grab hold and lift it, taking the strain with my legs. You'll soon get the knack of it."

He demonstrated his instructions and laid the heavy, rounded, oblong of rubber across her shoulder. She staggered beneath its weight and almost fell. "How heavy is one of these things?"

"Not over a hundred pounds. Some may be more, but most are less. Don't think about the weight. Think about your balance. Walk straight and keep your head up and your shoulders back. Otherwise, you'll stumble."

She tried to do as he suggested, but the *bolacha* seemed to weigh more like two hundred pounds. She didn't know how she would make it down to the river with her first one, let alone be able to carry a second, a third, a fourth . . . Jordan selected the smallest *bolacha* in the pile for Abelardo, but when he went to lay it across the boy's shoulders, Abelardo grinned and pointed to his head. "Carry Indian style," he said. "Abelardo has strong neck. Carry anything."

Jordan placed the *bolacha* on the boy's head, and true to his boast, Abelardo easily balanced it and set off down the path. "His burns didn't affect his strength much," Jordan commented. "But then, Indians have remarkable strength. Remember those poor souls at El Encanto? They'd been beaten and starved, but still could carry heavy burdens. Even the women and children. I guess that's why Arana enslaves them; they can do the work of a mule, don't cost anything to feed, and can be forced to labor until they drop."

"Get out of me way," Spencer shakily ordered. "I want t' keep up with Abelardo."

The reminder of what the Indians had managed to accomplish at El Encanto, coupled with Abelardo's ease in managing the rubber, gave Spencer a strength she had not known she possessed. Compared to the Indians, she had led a greatly pampered life—with constant access to nourishing food and medicines to make her well whenever she got sick. Just because she wasn't accustomed to hard labor did not mean she couldn't do it; she intended to do it or die trying.

Down the beaten track she went, with Jordan close on her heels. They deposited their *bolachas* on the dock, then returned for another . . . and another, and another. The work soon assumed a rhythm: hoist, balance, trudge, dump, return. Then do it all again, and again, and again. Spencer's muscles burned. Her head throbbed. But she was gratified to see the huge pile of *bolachas* slowly but surely begin to diminish.

When they had a big enough pile on the dock, Jordan commenced tossing the *bolachas* into the stern of the *Evangeline*. Thump! Bump! The loading had its own rhythm. Then Jordan jumped into the launch and rearranged the rubber to allow for more space. Afterward, he rejoined Spencer and Abelardo. Every aspect of the night's work was grueling and difficult, made more so by the knowledge that they would have to leave behind whatever they could not get loaded. Then Spencer had an idea—using a square of boat canvas to drag the *bolachas* down the hill to the launch.

At first Jordan scoffed at the suggestion, but he fell silent as Spencer and Abelardo succeeded in dragging four small *bolachas*, twice what they could have carried on a single trip. The dew-wet grass and downhill slope made dragging the rubber far easier than lifting and carrying it. Jordan got his own piece of canvas and managed to drag three large *bolachas* at one time by himself. Thus encouraged, they experimented and discovered that if they combined their efforts and tugged on ropes attached to canvas sheeting, they could manage six to eight *bolachas* in a single trip. The weight of the rubber on the downhill slide gave it a forward impetus so that they had to drag the canvas from the sides or risk being run over.

As the launch slowly filled with rubber, Jordan began hammering spikes into the *bolachas* so they could be tethered behind the *Evangeline*. He was much elated by their progress—until he realized what time it was. Consulting a pocket watch, he told Spencer he must leave at once to sabotage the *Liberal*, or dawn might find them with all their rubber loaded but no way to defend themselves against attack.

As she examined the rubber still remaining on shore, Spencer doubted the *Evangeline* could manage to take it all. But she did not argue or try to prevent Jordan from leaving. Stopping the *Liberal* was their only hope for getting any of the rubber to market. Nevertheless, she hated saying good-bye to Jordan and greatly feared for his safety. He dared not take even a lantern to light his way and scare off water snakes, crocodiles, or other dangerous beasts.

"Don't worry," he assured her. "I know this stretch of river like the back of my hand. The *Liberal* is just around the next bend. While I'm gone I want the two of you to get those ropes and braided vines still stored in the hut and start tying them around the spikes I pounded into the *bolachas* on the dock. Then all we'll have to do is toss them into the river and tie them to the big rings on the stern. I've got enough wood aboard for a day or two of travel before we have to forage for more fuel. That's enough to get us out of Loayza's reach; he'll have to figure out a way to fix the *Liberal* or else he'll have to hike all the way back to El Encanto to get another launch."

"Oh, Jordan, be careful!" Heedless of Abelardo watching their every move, Spencer flung her arms around Jordan and shamelessly embraced him. "If something happens to ye, I dinna know what I'll do!"

"Don't lose your nerve now, Spencer. Think about the future. Start planning our wedding. I want to get married as soon as we can." He squeezed her tightly, his hands spanning her buttocks and molding her body to his. Passion flared between them, and they shared a long, breathless kiss that echoed previous sweet, tender, passionate kisses. All too soon, Jordan pulled away and gruffly patted her shoulder.

"If anything does happen to me, Spencer, save yourself and Abelardo. He's a fine, brave boy. I'd love having him for a son. Raise him as our son.

Take him back to the States and tell everyone we got married here and adopted him. They won't challenge you. If they do, tell 'em to go to hell."

"But the launch!" Spencer wailed, choking back tears. "I'm not sure I can operate it—especially not loaded down as it is."

"Come quick into the engine house," Jordan said. "I'll give you a five minute lesson on operating the launch, and then I'm going. For a girl as smart as you, five minutes should be more than enough."

He took her aboard the *Evangeline*, pointed out this and that, warned her to beware the pressure in the boiler building too high, then finished with a briefing on how to avoid snags in the river and what to watch for. It took all of Spencer's concentration to focus on what he was saying instead of worrying about where he was going. Exhaustion blunted her faculties so that the simplest direction seemed absurdly complicated. Jordan took her in his arms and hurriedly kissed her one last time, then climbed down into the waiting *batelão* and cast off.

"I love ye, Jordan!" she called after him, tears coursing down her cheeks. "Just remember how much I love ye!"

"Me, too!" he shouted back. "I mean I love you . . . Oh, what the hell, you know what I mean!"

Beside Spencer, Abelardo stood waving also. "Good-bye, Senhor Rei!"

"Good-bye, Abelardo! Take care of Spencer, son, and do what she tells you."

Within seconds, the darkness swallowed him. Spencer strained to hear the soft slurping sound of his paddle dipping into the inky-black river—where piranhas might be waiting to devour him when he slipped into the river to disable the *Liberal*. Morbid imaginings sent a chill down her sweat-soaked back. Grimly she fought them down, reached for Abelardo's hand, and went back to work.

By the time dawn pearled the eastern sky above the jungle treetops, Spencer had the *Evangeline* ready to go. She and Abelardo had shoved all the tethered *bolachas* off the dock into the water and had managed to drag one last load of rubber down the hill. Grunting and groaning, they loaded it into the stern of the launch. The *Evangeline* now sat so low in the river that all they had to do was roll the *bolachas* to the edge of the dock, and they fell into the boat. Spencer and Abelardo were both so tired they could scarcely move.

A small pile of the rubber would have to remain behind. Spencer could see no way to transport it. There simply wasn't room; the launch could hold no more. If it could pull all the *bolachas* bobbing in the water, Spencer thought she would be more than content. She only hoped Jordan would be satisfied with the results of their efforts. She hoped he was still alive. Scanning the river, she saw no sign of him, and it was already past the hour he had told her to depart.

"I'd better see if I can get this old tub started," she told Abelardo. "We'll take her out to the middle of the river and wait there for Senhor Rei. That way, if the soldiers come, we'll have a head start."

"What is tub?" Abelardo furrowed his brow, looking greatly perplexed.

Realizing the boy had never in his life seen a bathtub, Spencer explained. While she talked, she worked, following Jordan's last minute instructions. Getting the launch underway was surprisingly easy; she had half expected the *Evangeline* to be temperamental, as it often was when Jordan himself was handling it. However, this time the old boat seemed to know exactly what was required of it. The engine came to life with a cough and a sputter, then began humming contentedly.

They were halfway into the middle of the river when Spencer heard rifle fire and saw soldiers pouring out of the jungle. Green-clad bodies over-ran Paraïso like a gigantic wave rushing inland from the sea. Within minutes, every hut was either afire or flattened to the ground. Too busy getting the hang of steering the launch, Spencer had no time to watch the destruction, but she did manage several backward glances. She knew the precise moment when the soldiers caught sight of them; a roar went up, punctuated by more gunfire.

Bullets splattered the water beside the launch and thudded into the floating *bolachas*. Spencer screamed for Abelardo to take cover. The boy hunched down in the middle of the rubber on deck. Shoving the throttle forward as far as it would go, Spencer headed for the safety of the opposite bank. The heavily laden *Evangeline* steamed slowly into the center of the river. When it got there, Spencer pulled the throttle back to idling speed and craned her neck, trying to catch sight of Jordan's *batelão*.

If he didn't come now, she'd have to leave him. He had warned her to leave if he wasn't there in time. He could be dead, wounded, or already captured. She had no way of knowing if he had succeeded in disabling the big launch. If he had, she could spare a few more minutes to wait for him. If he hadn't, it didn't matter anyway. The soldiers would return to the *Liberal*, and she'd soon be caught.

As she waited, Spencer begged Saint Brigid to perform this one last favor. She promised her protectress never again to ask for anything. Meanwhile, the soldiers raced up and down shore, cranking off their carbines in the direction of the *Evangeline*. When they realized the launch wasn't going anywhere—nor were their shots doing much more than peppering the *bolachas*—they quit firing. A slender man in civilian clothing walked out on the wooden dock. Spencer recognized him by his white linen suit and luxurious mustache. She had seen him only once at El Encanto, but she would have known him anywhere; he was Miguel Loayza, the only man in the world whom she hated every bit as much as Arana.

Brazenly, he stood at the end of the dock, watching the *Evangeline*, certain no one would dare shoot *him*. Spencer debated whether or not to abandon the wheel long enough to fetch the Winchester Jordan had left in the engine house. She darted an anxious glance toward the bend in the river around which Jordan's *batelão* must come . . . *It was coming!*

Low in the water, the long canoe skimmed toward the *Evangeline*. In the bow, Jordan was paddling furiously. As the soldiers noticed him, rifles spat from shore. As yet, Jordan was too far away to make a good target. He'd make a better one as he drew closer, Spencer realized. She maneuvered the *Evangeline* around to face him, intending to go meet him. The sooner he came aboard, the sooner they could face Loayza—together. Jordan's expression would tell her whether or not they stood a chance of escaping.

She squinted her eyes. Was he smiling? No, he was scowling. Her heart sank. At least, they had each other. Whatever awaited them—shame, defeat, and death—they would not face it alone. They had each other, and they had Abelardo. Most of all, they had their magnificent, wonderful love. It was more than the Aranas and Loayzas of the world had, could ever have, or even understand. No wonder they resorted to theft and murder to fill their empty, thwarted, frustrated lives!

It's all right, she wanted to tell Jordan as his canoe scraped along the side of the *Evangeline*. Whatever happens, *it's all right*.

"Senhor Rei is here!" Abelardo crowed triumphantly. The boy's tone implied that everything would surely be fine now that his hero had returned. Eyes shining, he crept up beside her.

"Spencer?" Jordan shouted up to her. "You disobeyed me again! Why in *hell* did you wait?"

Spencer quickly showed Abelardo how to hold the wheel and throttle so the launch would remain stationary. Then she went to greet Jordan. Her heart answered his question before her lips could frame the words. *I could never leave ye, Jordan King. I'll be beside ye always, even unto death.*

The crack of gunfire from shore reminded her that death was stalking all of them. Tossing her hair out of her eyes, she reached down to grasp Jordan's hand and help him come aboard.

Chapter Twenty-seven

With a muttered oath, Jordan swung into the *Evangeline.* He was furious over the needless risk Spencer had taken. The *Liberal* wasn't going anywhere in the near future so he had plenty of time to make his way downstream in the *batelão.* Very likely he could have caught up with Spencer in a day or two; why had she endangered her life and Abelardo's by dallying until the soldiers attacked?

As he glared into her eyes, the question trembling on the tip of his tongue, he read the answer: She loved him too much to abandon him to a perilous, uncertain fate.

"Oh, Jordan!" she cried. "I'm so glad ye're here. If I have t' die, I dinna want t' do it without seeing ye one more time." She shot him a wry brave grin that wrenched his heart.

"You're not going to die," he growled, covering his own emotions with bluster. "At least not yet. Fetch the Winchester while I try to get us out of here."

"But they'll come after us, Jordan! Should I cut the tethers t' the *bolachas*? We can go faster if we dinna have t' tow them."

"Don't cut a damn thing! Loayza doesn't know it

yet, but he can't come after us. That's what took me so long. I had to wait until the soldiers left the ship and started hiking through the jungle toward Paraïso. There were too many of 'em, and they had posted guards. I was afraid someone would see or hear me."

"Then ye did it!" Roses bloomed in Spencer's cheeks. Her eyes lit like candles. To forestall her from throwing her arms around him, he held up his hand.

"Yes, but this is a hell of a time to gloat. We can do that later, after we escape their gunfire."

Another hail of bullets rained down upon them; Spencer only just then seemed to notice the danger. "Oh, all right. I'll get the Winchester."

She whirled and dashed toward the engine house, while Jordan hurried to the wheel. "Good job, son," he said to Abelardo, giving him a quick pat on the shoulder. "I'll take over now. You get up near the bow and watch for snags. But don't poke out your head too far or you might catch a stray bullet."

"Do not worry, Senhor Rei. Abelardo will be most careful." He flashed a cheeky, man-to-man grin. "The soldiers will not catch us. Abelardo will find safe waters."

Jordan had to grin at the boy's confidence and courage. The more he saw of the child's character, the more he thrilled to the idea of becoming his adoptive father. A loud shout from shore shattered his musings. Narrowing his eyes, Jordan spotted Miguel Loayza on the dock. The man was waving a speaking trumpet such as captains of rubber launches often used to hail each other on the rivers. Arana's chief henchman obviously wanted to talk to him.

"Spencer, forget the Winchester and bring me the trumpet hanging on a hook near the engine-house door," he called.

A moment later she reappeared, carrying both, and handed him the trumpet. "Is this what ye want? Ye aren't goin' t' *bargain* with Loayza, are ye?"

"If I thought it might help a few Indians, I'd bargain with the devil himself." He lifted the trumpet to his mouth. "What do you want, you bastard?"

Miguel Loayza, his linen suit blinding white in a shaft of early-morning sunlight, moved to the very edge of the wooden dock. "Jordano Rei!" he called in thick Peruvian Spanish. "Surrender, or we shall be forced to kill you!"

Knowing the man spoke English, but not very well, Jordan answered slowly in his own language. "Go ahead and try. Your soldiers aren't particularly good marksmen. Next time you send to Peru for a batch, better warn them to practice before they come out here."

"They are good enough to have killed many of your workers," Loayza responded. "And soon they will kill you. You will not get far. Before this day is over, the *Liberal*'s guns will blow you out of the water."

"I don't think so." Jordan smirked at Spencer, enjoying himself immensely. "Not unless you can fashion a new propeller in less than a day. Yours is somewhere at the bottom of the river."

"What did you say, senhor?" Miguel Loayza lowered the trumpet, his expression stunned and disbelieving.

Jordan repeated the information and could not resist a final jab. "You've got a long walk ahead of you to get back to El Encanto. But don't worry. When we reach Manaus, we'll tell your boss what happened and why you didn't get my rubber after all."

"You will not escape with that rubber!" Loayza screamed, his face reddening. "And now that we have Paraĩso, we will keep it in the name of the Peruvian government. Your tappers killed many Peruvian soldiers; Paraĩso is now a spoil of war."

"Hell, you can *have* Paraĩso!" Jordan gleefully shouted. "But you won't get any rubber off it until you're an old, old man. I destroyed all the rubber trees."

"You did *what?*" Loayza's eyes bulged like a frog's. His luxuriant mustache quivered. "You cannot have destroyed all the trees, senhor. That would be the act of a madman."

"I never claimed to be sane," Jordan retorted. "On my land I can do any damn thing I please, and it pleased me to destroy the trees. You finally got Paraĩso, Loayza, but it won't do you or Arana any good. I'd love to see the look on your boss's face when you tell him *that.*"

"He will hear of it! And he will destroy you, senhor!"

"Let him try, if he can find me—and while he's trying, tell him to watch out he doesn't lose everything he's got in the effort. When I get through talking to his English and American buyers, they may decide they don't want his rubber anymore."

Spencer stiffened. "Why are ye tellin' him that, Jordan? Now, he'll know t' prepare for an investigation."

Jordan lowered the trumpet so Loayza could not hear his answer. "Which means he'll cease torturing and starving Indians. I'd rather he stopped today than a year from now, wouldn't you? I want him to worry about an investigation and mend his ways accordingly. Rest assured. You and I and Abelardo have seen enough to burn the ears of any investigators."

"You cannot ruin Don Julio César Arana, senhor!" Loayza screamed shrilly. "He is too big—too powerful. No one will believe your accusations."

"Then they'll have to come to El Encanto to check them out, won't they? They'll want to see with their own eyes how you treat the Indians on Arana's behalf," Jordan goaded. "In fact, I may be able to convince your boss's investors to leave Manaus immediately to see what sort of job you're doing as overseer on the Putumayo. Why, they could reach El Encanto before you do. On your long hike back, you might get caught by the rains and be unable to travel on foot. In the meantime, they could hire a launch and arrive there ahead of you."

The slim, dapper figure on the dock began to curse and swear. He shook his speaking trumpet in Jordan's direction. Jordan laughed. "In as much as I'll probably see him before you do, have you any messages you want me to give your boss?"

Another string of obscenities erupted. Looking less than human, Miguel Loayza hurled his speaking trumpet into the river and stamped his feet in fury.

"Why, he's nothing but a little boy-bully having a temper tantrum," Spencer said in wonder.

"Most monsters are little-boy bullies at heart." Jordan's amusement abruptly faded. "I thought I'd feel more satisfied whenever I fantasized giving him his comeuppance, but all I feel is contempt. Miguel Loayza is a damned sorry excuse for a man; I wonder if Arana will behave with the same lack of dignity when he finally gets caught with his pants down. I hope I live to see it."

"We'll see it," Spencer said firmly, linking her arm through his. "We've just won our first victory—and helped the Indians besides. I do think Loayza will get rid of the cages, the whipping post, and a few other things as soon as he gets back to El Encanto. 'Twas a good idea after all to threaten him, Jordan."

He grinned down at her. "I always have good ideas, my love. And my next idea is to get the hell out of here."

As he spoke, soldiers were spilling out onto the dock, joining the half-hysterical Loayza. The overseer pointed to the launch, and the soldiers obediently recommenced firing. "Get your heads down!" Jordan barked, giving his full attention to fleeing the reach of the gunfire.

The trusty *Evangeline* responded to his efforts and was soon chugging down the placid river, leaving Miguel Loayza, the soldiers, and Paraíso far behind.

Three weeks later, Jordan and Spencer spoke their marriage vows in a small chapel attached to one of Manaus's large, ornate churches. It had taken some persuasion, including the crossing of his palm with money, but the old priest had eventually agreed to waive certain requirements relating to the posting of banns and other prerequisites which would have meant a long waiting period before they could be married. Neither Spencer nor Jordan wanted a lengthy engagement; their love demanded the full expression of their passion for each other. In as much as they had already tasted the joys of married life, the priest relented and agreed to marry them at once.

However, he insisted that they live apart for at least a few days before the ceremony itself, during which time Jordan was occupied with storing and selling his harvest, and Spencer threw together plans for a simple, early-evening service. By the time they met at the marble altar in the chapel, they were both filled with yearning, physical and emotional, for each other's company. During the voyage home, Abelardo's presence had denied them privacy, so they stood at the altar and shamelessly devoured each other with their eyes. The priest intoned the words, and they made the promises that bound them together for life.

Afterward, they kissed and hugged Abelardo, Chico, and all of Chico's relatives—excepting his sister, Lucia, still in disgrace—who had gathered to witness the ceremony and wish them well. They then stepped into a small antechamber, where a solicitor and judge were waiting with papers to make Abelardo's adoption legal. Once this was done, they kissed and hugged everyone again, especially Abelardo, who was going back home with

Chico, while they themselves retired to dinner and a luxurious suite at the Grand Hotel Internacional. Their honeymoon would be short and sweet—a single night, and they wanted to be completely alone.

A beautiful carriage pulled by two white horses bore them to the hotel in style. In the white lace gown she had worn to the opera house, Spencer snuggled against Jordan's side, bursting with happiness and eagerness to have him to herself at long last.

"Are we dining in our room?" Jordan asked, nuzzling the lace mantilla covering her hair. "I confess I'm starved—and not just for food. I can't decide which I want first—you or my dinner."

"I feared ye might feel that way." Spencer giggled. "So I made plans for us t' begin the evenin' in the dinin' room, where the elegant meal I ordered won't go t' waste. I want t' sit again at the table where I first saw ye and felt the flutterin's of me awakenin' lust."

"You felt lust for me the first time you saw me?" Jordan asked incredulously. "*You,* the prim spinster?"

"Well, at the time I dinna know it was lust. But I did feel shivery all over just lookin' at ye, even though I thought ye were terribly rude and boorish, burstin' into the dinin' room with yer muddy boots and yer black, angry scowl."

"I never saw you," Jordan said. "All I saw was Arana . . . and I still think I should have killed him that day and saved myself a lot of future bother."

"Dinna not talk about Arana tonight," Spencer begged. "Tonight I want t' forget that man exists and is still walkin' the streets of Manaus, flauntin' his wickedness and grinnin' because no one knows about it but us."

"Sounds good to me." Jordan tilted her face toward his, love shining in his eyes. "Do you know how much I want to ravish you, Mrs. Jordan King?"

"No," Spencer whispered, flushing at the sweet prospect. "Tell me, Mr. King. I want t' hear every detail."

So he whispered endearments and erotic suggestions into her ear all the way to the hotel. By the time they arrived, she herself no longer cared about the elegant meal awaiting them; all she wanted was to get to their suite as fast as possible. By mutual unspoken agreement, they entered the hotel, intending to bypass the dining room altogether. But as they passed the arched entranceway, where the tinkle of crystal and murmur of voices floated out to them on flower- and food-scented air, a man almost ran into them on his way out of the dining room.

"Excuse me," he said in Spanish, drawing back and adjusting his finely tailored white dinner jacket.

When she saw who it was, Spencer gasped. Before she could react to stop him, Jordan grabbed the man by his lapels and snarled into his face. "Damn my aunt Milly's corset, if it isn't you again, Arana! What an unpleasant surprise!"

The swarthy, heavyset Peruvian did not move a muscle other than to snap his fingers at a passing waiter. Staring coldly into Jordan's furious face, he said calmly, "Take your hands off me, fool, or I shall have you thrown out of here. The management of this hotel will never stand for its most valued patron to be threatened in public a second time by the likes of you."

Reluctantly, with a glance at the waiter signaling others to join him, Jordan released Arana. "You're lucky it's my wedding day, Arana. Otherwise I'd be inclined to do something violent."

Arana cocked an arrogant eyebrow. "Why is that, senhor?" he smoothly inquired. "I have done nothing to injure you. Have you not recently returned to Manaus with an excellent rubber harvest? I had heard you did; why then are you so testy? Have you marital problems already?"

His glance at Spencer was mocking; she put a hand on Jordan's forearm to keep him in check, then spoke calmly and precisely. "My husband's only problem is the deliberate, wanton destruction of his plantation, Don Arana. In light of that, the sight of you arouses him to fury, as it must arouse everyone who knows your true character—the one you strive so hard to conceal."

Don Arana's thick lips smiled charmingly, but his eyes were the cold, calculating eyes of a reptile preparing to strike. "Ah, senhorinha, I am so sorry to hear about Paraïso. Clearly something will have to be done about the vicious mercenaries who no doubt did it. Perhaps I shall form a committee to look into the problem. As for myself, if you know of anyone whom I have personally injured, please inform me and I shall see that the wrong is righted. Don Julio César Arana is ever ready to correct his mistakes and errors, especially the ones he knows nothing about."

"You bastard! You damn well do know about them!" Jordan hissed. "I can't believe you're still playing this same stupid game of innocence, saying one thing in public but quite another in private."

Spencer hung on to her husband's tensed arm. "Someday, Don Arana, the whole world will know about your crimes—if not from us, than from others. You can't keep your sins a secret forever."

He gave a curt bow. "Ah, but I can try, senhorinha. A man in my position has many detractors—all of them liars. I only wish there was some way to convince you of my sincerity . . . Perhaps, since you are celebrating your wedding, you will accept a small token of my congratulations. I shall have a bottle of the hotel's finest champagne sent directly to your room."

"You do, and I'll break it over your damn head!" Jordan bellowed.

His outburst drew the attention of everyone in the dining room and lobby. Five waiters immediately converged, ready to lend their assistance to Arana, should he need it. Spencer saw no good in prolonging the distasteful encounter; it had already ruined their wedding day. If Jordan were goaded into attacking Arana, their wedding night would also be ruined. Arana's defenders might beat Jordan to a pulp.

"Come, darling," she said, tugging on Jordan's arm. "I canna endure another moment in this monster's odious company."

"We're not staying here," Jordan snapped. "I won't sleep under the same roof where this sneaky bastard eats, sleeps, and spins his web of trickery, lies, and deceit."

"Let's leave at once," Spencer pleaded.

Arana shot her another mocking glance. "Listen to your wife, senhor. She is as wise as she is beautiful. What a pity she has chosen to waste herself on a brutish lout of an *Americano*." He shook his head and made a tsk-tsking sound.

Spencer had to cling with all her might to keep Jordan from attacking him. "Please, let's go!"

Without another word, Jordan spun on his heel and all but dragged her out of the hotel.

"Jordan, please forget about Arana." Dressed in a long, filmy white nightgown fastened with pink ribbons, Spencer sat next to Jordan on the bed in his bedroom at the house, where they had returned after leaving the hotel. "I'm glad we dinna spend our wedding night at the hotel anyway. 'Twill be much nicer here. I dinna know why I made plans t' go there in the first place. Had I anticipated such an unpleasant meetin' with Arana, I would never have done it."

Jordan quit glaring down at his clenched fists and turned to her. "Don't blame yourself that he ruined our wedding day, sweetheart. You couldn't have known he'd be there—I'm sorry I allowed him to upset me. Sad to say, he'll always upset me. Every time I see him, I want to wrap my hands around his throat and squeeze the life out of him. When I think of all the misery and suffering he's caused . . ."

Spencer slid her arms around Jordan's waist. "Hush, darling. Dinna think about it—at least not t'night. Ye mustna give him the power of comin' between us in our marriage bed; he canna intrude if we refuse t' let him."

Jordan gathered her into his arms, his eyes a brilliant green. "You're right, my lovely wife. But I hope I will one day witness his downfall. I hope I'm a part of it. I sure as hell intend to be. Among the things he's destroyed is a large chunk of my manhood. It galls me that he should so easily get away with his crimes."

Spencer lowered her hand between Jordan's thighs and fondled him intimately. "Yer manhood feels quite intact t' me," she whispered suggestively. "Shall we see if it's in good working order?"

Pushing her back on the bed, he leaned over her. "You do know how to distract me, don't you?"

A bubble of laughter burst from her throat. "I hope so, Jordan. I surely hope so."

Entwining his fingers in her loosened curls, he gazed down into her eyes. His blond hair made a halo about his head, and she thought him the handsomest man she had ever seen. Before she could tell him that, a low growl rumbled in his chest. "Spencer Kathleen King, I love you. I love you with the whole of my heart, mind, and body. I swear to be true to you till death do us part."

"Ye're repeatin' yerself," she teased. "Ye already said that once t'day."

"Ah, but this time I have no witnesses," he responded with a twinkle in his eye.

She decided now was as good a time as any to mention one of the slight worries she still had about their future life together. "Does yer devotion to me mean that ye accept my dedication to medicine? Ye'll let me continue t' practice me profession after we return to the United States?"

Jordan blinked in surprise. "Did I ever say you couldn't? My sister Victoria would box my ears if I ever dared forbid you to do something that means so much to you. She'd call me an unfeeling monster and liken me to a primitive caveman."

"We never settled the matter the last time it came up," Spencer demurred. "If ye insist I be a traditional wife and stay home, I . . . I'll not be happy about it, but I'll obey."

Jordan looked astounded. "You'd give up doctoring for my sake?"

"Well, as I said, I'll not be happy about it, but I'll do it. I love ye, Jordan. Ye mean more t' me than anything. Without ye, I'm only half alive."

Jordan pressed his lips to her throat, muffling his response which still came quite clearly. "Sweetheart, my precious love, I thought you knew by now I feel the same." He drew back a moment, his face alight. "You are the reason I want Castle Acres so badly. If I had to choose between you and my dreams, I'd choose you without a single hesitation. I know I must seem obsessed by the idea of regaining what my family lost—but you come first with me and always will."

Spencer brushed his lips with a fingertip. "Then ye'll not be terribly disappointed if we dinna have enough money to buy back yer family's farm and refurbish it with fine stock?"

"Yes, I'll be disappointed. But I'll get over it and find something else to do. All that matters I have in my arms, right here, right now. And my manhood is aching to prove what I'm saying."

"I'd almost forgotten about yer poor abused

manhood!" She kissed the tip of his nose. "Almost, but not quite. Oh, Jordan, I'm in danger of burstin' with happiness!"

He dipped his head, and his mouth fastened on hers. They shared a deep, possessive kiss. Jordan's hands began to rove her body, tenderly at first, then with growing urgency. They shed their clothing and came together with small cries of joy. Spencer could feel Jordan holding back, trying to prolong the rapture of their lovemaking and make certain she was ready for him. But she was more than ready; her body begged for his possession. Changing positions, she climbed on top of him and guided him into her, sliding down his turgid length with a whimper of pleasure.

His hands cupped her breasts; his thumbs teased her nipples. She placed her palms flat on his chest, found the small nubs hidden in the crisp, curly hair, and lightly stroked them. Jordan thrust upward, embedding himself deep within her. "Ah, love . . ." he growled. "You are so warm and tight, so giving!"

"And ye are so hard and strong." A tide of need and want swept Spencer. She undulated her hips, glorying in the friction the movement created.

Without breaking their union, he turned her onto her back. "I want to go slowly . . ." he rasped in her ear. "But you're making that impossible."

"It's impossible for me, too! I want ye so much. I canna wait, Jordan . . . please, please take me."

The entire universe gathered and compressed itself into the throbbing cradle of Spencer's hips. Sweet, burning need engulfed her. She lifted herself to receive the ultimate pleasure—and he gave it to her, thrusting long, hard, and deep. Her body convulsed and shuddered. Her heart thundered in unison with his.

"Now you are truly mine," he whispered. "Mine, mine, mine . . ."

"And ye are mine, Jordan. Me own true love . . ."

Chapter Twenty-eight

They slept late the next morning. When Spencer opened her eyes, she saw that Jordan was already awake. Without moving, she studied his handsome profile. He was lying on his back, staring at the ceiling. She lifted her head in alarm. When he saw she was awake, he turned to her and grinned as if nothing was wrong. But it was too late. She had already witnessed the dark frown puckering his eyebrows and the downward tilt of his mouth.

"How's my beautiful wife this morning?" he cheerfully inquired, but the cheer seemed forced.

"Worried . . ." she answered truthfully. "Jordan, what is it? Last night, ye seemed so happy. This mornin', ye look as if ye lost yer best friend. Ye havna, ye know. I'm here beside ye, and I've no intentions of goin' anywhere without ye."

With an overly hearty laugh, he reached for her. "You're imagining things, sweet wife. I'm as happy as a man can be. I'm married to you, aren't I? What more could I want?"

"Oh, Jordan . . . ye aren't still broodin' about Arana, are ye?"

"If I am, I shouldn't be—not when I've got you beside me."

He kissed her long and passionately. The distraction proved irresistible. They made love again, then napped in blissful contentment, wrapped in each other's arms. It was past noon when Spencer awoke for the second time. She sat up. Jordan was still asleep, this time with a smile on his face. She would have to work very hard to keep it there, she realized. Whether he would admit it or not, Jordan was deeply bothered by the possibility that Arana might never have to pay for his crimes. She wished she knew what to suggest, but the situation seemed as hopeless as ever. They were lucky to have escaped Paraïso alive. Now they had to think about Abelardo, and Jordan's sisters, and building a new life for themselves. Revenge—no, justice—would have to wait until a time when they were far less vulnerable.

Hunger finally drove her out of bed. Suddenly starving, she groped for her nightgown and wrap and slipped them on without awakening Jordan. After tugging up the sheet to cover his nakedness, she went to the door, opened it, and tiptoed to the stairwell.

"Abelardo? Chico?" she called softly.

Almost immediately, Abelardo appeared at the bottom of the stairs, his small round face worried. "You and Senhor Rei are sick?" he inquired.

"No, Abelardo, we just slept late. You weren't worried about us, we're you?"

He vigorously nodded. "You did not stay at the hotel. And you did not get up with the sun. So Abelardo think you sick."

Spencer stifled a smile. "We're fine, dear. Please tell Chico to make fresh coffee and bring it up. I'm going to wake Senhor Rei, and I'm sure he'd appreciate some, too."

Abelardo nodded, his black eyes shining. "I tell him. I help. Chico teach me many things."

The boy darted toward the kitchen, and Spencer allowed her pent-up amusement to blossom. Abelardo was wearing the proper pants and trousers she had bought for him, though he had made it clear he would much rather be running about half-naked. He had not, however, put on his stiff new shoes; even at the church during the wedding, he had taken them off and held them clutched under one arm. They probably hurt his feet, but in time he would become accustomed to the restrictions of civilization.

Returning to Jordan's bedroom—their room, now—Spencer awakened her new husband with a kiss. He responded by trying to pull her down on top of him in the bed. Fending off his caresses, she warned him that Chico would soon be bringing coffee.

"We should have stayed at the hotel after all," Jordan groused. "Here I feel like I have to get up and dress to please my house servant."

Eyeing his tousled blond hair and the muscular, bronzed chest above the white sheet, Spencer was tempted to agree. "It's not Chico you must worry about; it's Abelardo. He was afraid we were sick."

"I *am* sick. I'm prostrate with love." Jordan flopped back on the pillows in a parody of illness. "Come back to bed and make me feel better."

Spencer tossed his trousers at him. "Ye must get up, Jordan. Ye canna spend yer whole life in bed."

"Why not?" Jordan grasped her hand and

flipped her onto the rumpled sheets beside him. "Spending our lives in bed together is a wonderful idea!"

"Jordan, let me up!"

They began to tussle, and Jordan was getting the better of her when a knock sounded at the door. "Damn my aunt Milly's corset!" he exclaimed. "Can't a man have a minute alone with his new bride?"

"Dinna be swearin' no more, lad," Spencer scolded in a mock-angry brogue. "Ye can have more time after we eat. Yer bride is faint wi' hunger."

She scrambled off the bed and opened the door to admit a beaming Chico and Abelardo, bearing trays. They set them on the table near the bed. "Break-fast . . ." Chico announced triumphantly.

Jordan sniffed the air appreciatively. "At least it smells good."

Chico took Abelardo's wrist and began to drag him out of the room. When the boy hung back, Spencer waved her hand. "Let him stay, Chico. A son can come see his parents anytime."

Jordan frowned at her. "Not *any*time . . . but he can stay for now."

"I serve," Abelardo said. "Chico show me how."

"Sĩm," Chico affirmed. "I show him . . ."

"Then you can go about your duties, Chico," Spencer said. "We'll send him downstairs with the trays as soon as we're finished."

Chico nodded, then left the room. With bright-eyed pride, Abelardo poured out two cups of coffee. When he started to sprinkle salt into one of them instead of spooning sugar, Jordan stopped him. "No, no, Son! That would be better on the eggs than in the coffee."

Abelardo dipped a finger into the sugar and tasted it, then sprinkled salt into his palm and licked it up. A smile of understanding lit his round face. "Sugar better!" he announced.

"The sooner we get him home to the United States and into school, the better," Jordan muttered. "There's so much he has to learn."

"He'll soon catch on. A little at a time is the best way to teach him." Spencer reached for her coffee. As she picked it up, she noticed a long envelope lying beneath the cup. The handwriting on it was familiar; eagerly, she replaced the coffee cup on the tray and grabbed the letter. Bless Chico! He had remembered her instructions to bring any mail from Peru directly to her, rather than tossing it into the overstuffed mail basket.

"Reading my mail already?" Jordan inquired.

"This is for both of us. It's from Walter Hardenburg."

Jordan scowled. "How do his letters always manage to reach us at inopportune moments?"

"This isn't an inopportune moment. It's the perfect time to get a letter from him. I wonder what progress he's made in finding witnesses to testify against Arana." Excitedly, she broke the seal on the letter, tore it open, and scanned the contents of the first page. "Oh, Jordan, listen to this!"

"I expect I have no choice in the matter," Jordan dryly quipped.

Undeterred by her husband's lack of enthusiasm, Spencer began summarizing the contents of the letter. Now that she and Jordan were married, there was no longer a reason for him to be jealous of Walter. Besides, this might be just the news for which she'd been hoping—a solution to the problem of Arana.

"Walter says he's had a devil of a time in Iquitos trying to locate anyone who will talk about Arana, much less say anything damaging. He's encountered lies and deceit at every turn. But he is beginning to amass a body of evidence against him. He begs us for our continued support. It may take years, but he's sure he'll eventually be able to force an investigation, if not here in Brazil than in London, where Arana's financial investors move in the highest circles of government and business."

"I'd rather see what we can do on our own, if we can do anything," Jordan said darkly. He was glowering as he always did when either Arana or Walter Hardenburg's names were mentioned. "In view of the profits involved, Arana's American investors probably won't listen to a word I have to say. However, I intend to approach them as soon as we get home."

"But Jordan, it makes no sense to act independently! Walter wants us to hold off doing anything until he's got enough damning evidence from credible sources that it will be impossible for Arana to bury the truth any longer. We're still his prime witnesses, Walter says. But wait until he hears about Abelardo! Think of what the testimony of a real Indian could do!"

"I won't have my son paraded before the insensitive press and put on display as some sort of freak from the jungle!" Jordan's raised voice made Abelardo jump backward in alarm. On the tray, the coffee cups rattled. "Don't think he wouldn't be regarded as such, Spencer. I forbid you to tell Walter Hardenburg anything about Abelardo."

"But Jordan . . ."

"But nothing . . . Don't look at me like that, Spencer. This time, your 'looks' won't work. I know what I'm talking about. Are you never going to have faith in me or my judgment?"

Spencer thought back to all that had happened. She did have faith in Jordan. He had never once let her down. Oh, he had blustered and grumbled and insisted on doing things his way—and his way had often turned out to be the right way, after all—but the one thing that stood out most in her mind was that no matter how much they argued and fought, no matter how much they disagreed, she could always depend upon him to come through in the end. He was always there for her, reluctantly perhaps, but there just the same. And he always would be.

Walter Hardenburg had said it might take years before Arana's downfall was assured. By then, Jordan would surely change his mind and decide to cooperate. For now, it was better not to argue. Abelardo's participation might or might not be necessary. In any case, it was something to be decided in the future. Calmly, she refolded the letter and put it back in the envelope.

"You're right, of course," she said. "I mean, about Abelardo. As for the rest, why don't we wait and see what Walter manages to put together? I'd still like for us to be a part of it. I know you don't particularly like Walter, but he's very brave, idealistic, and dedicated. He deserves our support, Jordan. If we don't support him, who will?"

Jordan glared at her for several long moments; then a tiny smile began to play about his mouth. "I guess I do have a weakness for brave, idealistic, dedicated people. After all, I married one. We'll wait and see what the fellow comes up with, and if we can, we'll back him to the hilt."

"Thank ye, Jordan," Spencer whispered. She caressed his face with her eyes, loving him even more, if that was possible. "Now, let's have our coffee before it gets cold."

Several weeks later, they boarded a ship headed downriver for Belém, retracing the journey that had brought Spencer to Manaus so many long months before. From Belém, they set sail for Boston. The voyage brought brimming delight to Abelardo and Jordan, and great misery to Spencer. By then, she was in her first months of pregnancy, and though her joy abounded, she felt physically ill. For the first time in her life, she experienced seasickness, which alternated with morning sickness and a desire to sleep all the time. Only Jordan and Abelardo's solicitous care enabled her to endure the long, arduous journey.

By the time they arrived in the United States, Spencer felt better. She met and befriended Jordan's sisters, then traveled to Kentucky where Jordan succeeded in buying back Castle Acres and stocking it with horses few in number but fine in quality.

On a stormy, rainswept night, she gave birth to a red-haired, green-eyed baby girl. They named her

Marta. Abelardo and Marta grew and flourished, frolicking in the blue-green meadows of Kentucky alongside spindly-legged colts destined for greatness on racing tracks all around the country.

Except for the hovering black cloud of Arana, and the way their memories of El Encanto affected both of them—causing Jordan to sink into occasional periods of dark brooding—Spencer's life was full and joyous. In time, she resumed practicing medicine on a modest basis but with warm acceptance from the residents of the nearby town of Lexington. The townspeople respected the Kings and were therefore unafraid to trust in Spencer's medical abilities. The years passed, and Spencer's only dissatisfaction lay in the knowledge that Don Julio César Arana continued to harvest rubber on the Putumayo and to grow richer and more unassailable every year.

Then one day another letter from Walter Hardenburg arrived. Spencer had advised him of their address the moment she first knew that Castle Acres would be their home, but in the press of living, they had exchanged letters infrequently. Standing in the front hallway, where summer sunshine was spilling through the long, stained-glass windows beside the front door, Spencer opened it with trembling hands. She began reading and was suddenly back in the jungle, encased in a dark green gloom where danger hid behind every fern. As she read, her heart hammered, and perspiration popped out on her brow.

> "It has been many years, but I hope you have not forgotten the sufferings of the Indi-

ans on the Putumayo. Can you both come to London? I am finally ready. Don Julio César Arana cannot escape now. I have worked too hard and planned too carefully. But I need your help. You must come and tell the members of Parliament and the shareholders of the Peruvian Amazon Company (PAC) what you personally witnessed on the Putumayo and at La Reserva. In the main, these are British noblemen who have opened their homes, hearts, and bank accounts to Arana, and given him access to the highest levels of British society. His family lives here now, in great luxury. It has been difficult, but I have persuaded the House of Commons to investigate Arana's business dealings. Thus far, their investigations have not been as revealing as I had hoped, but I remain confident that the upcoming hearings will see the truth finally come to light . . ."

So the time has come, Spencer thought, lowering the letter. She smoothed it out between her fingers as visions of the atrocities she had witnessed at El Encanto danced before her eyes. Once again, she saw the gaunt, starving Indians, the bloodstained whipping post, the row of cages, the bleached bones in the burial pit.

"Mama? Is something wrong?" Five-year-old Marta was tugging at her skirt. "Mama, you look all sad and white—like a ghost."

"There are no such things as ghosts, Marta," Spencer automatically corrected. She looked down at the little girl with the fiery red curls and huge green eyes but scarcely saw her. "Where's your brother? I want to see your brother at once." Her need to assure herself that Abelardo was safe and sound was overwhelming.

"He went down to the barn with Papa to help exercise the horses . . . Mama, where are you going?"

"Stay here, Marta. I'll be right back." Spencer yanked open the door, flew out into the front yard, and began running down the hill toward the stables. "Jordan? *Jordan!* Oh, me darling, I *need* ye!"

Six weeks later, they arrived in London—Spencer, Jordan, Abelardo, and Marta, clutching her favorite stuffed toy, a bay pony with a black mane and tail. The first thing Jordan did upon their arrival was buy a copy of each of London's newspapers. They brimmed with news of the hearings being held in the House of Commons by a select committee of Parliament appointed to investigate Walter Hardenburg's charges against the Peruvian Amazon Company.

"What do the papers say?" Spencer asked Jordan on the carriage ride to the hotel where they were staying.

As the carriage lurched through streets crammed with motor cars, other carriages, dray wagons, and pedestrians hurrying to and fro, Jordan tried to make sense of the conflicting articles. "Apparently, your Walter Hardenburg convinced *Truth,* London's leading weekly periodical, to run a series of articles revealing the scandals on the Putumayo. That's what initiated the hearings. Then it came out that Hardenburg was a blackmailer who previously approached a high official of PAC and demanded seven thousand pounds to refrain from publishing a book damaging to the company's image. When the official refused, Hardenburg then went to the editor of *Amazonas* in Manaus and demanded similar sums for handing over the same information."

"I dinna believe a word of it!" Spencer exclaimed. "Arana's trumped up the whole thing to paint Walter as a liar and opportunist . . . and he isna *my* Walter, either."

Jordan raised a scornful eyebrow. "They're saying that *your* Walter, having failed to extract money from either PAC or *Amazonas,* then forged a ten-pound bill of exchange, converting it to almost nine hundred pounds, after which he escaped scot-free to London."

"Lies . . . all lies, which I'm sure Walter will explain as soon as he knows we've arrived, and we can arrange t' meet with him."

Jordan impatiently rattled the newspapers he had been devouring. "I don't like it, my love. I hope we haven't been deceived all these years and put our trust in a charlatan. If so, Arana will emerge from this stronger than ever. The entire focus of the investigation seems to have shifted from Arana to Walter. The *Times* is now defending Arana. It describes him as being a sensitive, cultured gentleman under attack by an upstart American out for his own personal gain. Arana has been living in London for some time, his children attend prestigious schools here, and he socializes with the elite and powerful, none of whom want to believe the worst of him. By contrast, Hardenburg does appear to be a crass, money-grubbing opportunist. Righteous as his cause is, Walter may be an opportunist, Spencer, whether you like to think so or not."

"He's not and ye know it!" Spencer said heatedly. "When we're called upon t' testify, we'll set all of them straight. We'll be tellin' the truth, and they'll have t' listen."

"Just remember that I don't want Abelardo dragged into it, unless it's absolutely necessary," Jordan warned.

"But I want to testify, Father," Abelardo spoke up from the opposite seat.

Spencer gazed at him with great pride. He was a striking young man, now—still bright-eyed, curious, and intelligent. He was also thoroughly Americanized, with flawless English and remarkable grades in school, where he excelled at everything from mathematics to sports. His bearing was princely. With his dark hair, flashing black eyes, and careful manners, he could easily compete with the sons of British noblemen. His Indian heritage revealed itself only in his broad features and his affinity for animals, from horses to dogs to birds, all of whom instinctively trusted him.

"If your mother or I testify, that should be enough," Jordan said sternly. "Arana doesn't know about you, and I would just as soon keep it that way."

Spencer understood her husband's reluctance to expose Abelardo to danger; there was danger in what they had come here to do. The newspapers held proof of it. What was happening to Walter Hardenburg amounted to character assassination. She would not be surprised to learn that Walter's life was in danger, too.

"There's the hotel!" she cried, pointing out the window.

"Oh, Mama!" Marta squealed. "Are we finally here?"

"Yes, sweetheart . . . we're here." Spencer glanced at Jordan, who returned the look with a silent, brooding one. He had put no stumbling blocks in the way of their coming to London, but she knew he was doubting the wisdom of it. Not only was he still wary of Walter, but if Arana employed the same tactics to discredit them as he had used to discredit Walter, it could destroy the family business. Many of Jordan's buyers were Englishmen who regularly came to America for the purpose of securing fine-blooded animals to strengthen their racing stock. While in England, Jordan planned to contact them. Unfortunately, they would never consider doing business with Castle Acres if the King name became controversial or, worse yet, besmirched.

As the carriage drew to a stop in front of the hotel, Spencer took Jordan's hand and squeezed it. He gave her a wry grin and squeezed back. *Saint Brigid, after all this time, dinna let us fail now,* Spencer prayed. With her family in tow, she alighted from the carriage and passed into the hotel.

Chapter Twenty-nine

"This is my wife, Mary." Walter Hardenburg beamed as he made the introduction. "I can't remember if I told you I'd gotten married, but don't let my forgetfulness be an indication of my true feelings for this darling girl. I don't know what I'd do without her. She's stood beside me through all of this, and more than once prevented me from sinking into despair."

Spencer took the young woman's hand and drew her forward so she and Jordan could get a good look at her. "Ye canna know how delighted I am t' meet ye, Mary! What a lovely young woman! Ye're exactly the sort of wife I meself would have picked for Walter! Isn't she perfect, Jordan?"

Jordan's lips puckered in amusement at Spencer's effusiveness. "Perfect, indeed. It's high time you got married, Walter, and it certainly appears you made an excellent choice."

Though Mary Hardenburg couldn't know the underlying reasons for the Kings' delight in her and Walter's marriage, she blushed becomingly. A slender brunette with melting blue eyes, she was quite the most wholesome-looking person Spencer had ever met. "Walter may have failed to mention me, but he's told me all about you, Mr. and Mrs. King. I'm honored to make your acquaintance. It was very good of you to have come all this way to verify my husband's claims."

"Observations, Mary," Walter corrected. "I've been careful to make no outrageous claims which could be construed as libel. All I've done is tell what I've seen with my own eyes and what others have also seen."

"Let's sit down." Jordan gestured to a cluster of overstuffed chairs drawn up near the windows of the small parlor in their hotel suite. "I want to hear everything that's happened."

Spencer rang for tea, then joined Jordan and the Hardenburgs. For this important meeting, the children had been sent to an inner bedroom with instructions not to interrupt for any but the most serious reasons. As she sat down and arranged her striped taffeta skirt around her ankles, Spencer smiled at Mary who smiled back, then turned an adoring, rapt gaze on her brown-eyed, balding husband. Walter Hardenburg had lost none of his youthful zeal and earnestness, though he now exuded a steadfast maturity Spencer found most appealing. How anyone could look at this man and see a forger and blackmailer seemed well nigh impossible—yet, according to the newspapers, it was happening.

"I'm most encouraged by the direction of the hearings . . ." Walter began. "Sir Roger Casement's revelations are having a great impact."

"Sir Roger Casement?" Jordan questioned. "Who is he?"

"Forgive me," Walter apologized. "You've only

just arrived and so cannot know all that's occurred recently. With all the demands on my time, I fear I've been seriously remiss in keeping you informed. Did you receive my last letter? I did mention Sir Roger in it."

"We only received the one urging us to come for the hearings," Spencer informed him.

"Then I shall strive to enlighten you as best I can. The Peruvian Amazon Company, or PAC, as it's called, has for many years had a board of directors composed entirely of Englishmen, the only exceptions being Arana himself and his brother-in-law, Abel Alarco. When the directors first became aware of my allegations, they selected Sir Roger to journey to the Putumayo and report back to them on conditions there. Of course, by then, the worst abuses had been eliminated. But Sir Roger is not a man to accept only what he is shown; he set out to interview the Barbadian overseers Arana had imported to control the Indians. After being granted sanctuary for themselves and their families here in England, the Barbadians confirmed that they had been forced to gun down Indians, torture them, and employ methods of great cruelty in order to keep them at the task of collecting rubber."

"Didn't Arana discredit the Barbadians? In his bigotry against anyone with a darker skin, I'm sure he tried to paint them as being only a cut above savages." Jordan crossed one elegantly trousered leg over the other and leaned back in his chair. The years had done nothing to diminish his handsomeness, Spencer thought fondly, pleased by her husband's attentiveness. Her fingers suddenly itched to push back the errant lock of golden hair that dipped low on his forehead. If Jordan only knew how attractive he was, he would never have been jealous of Walter.

"Many Englishmen look at the Barbadians that way," Walter conceded. "But Sir Roger also amassed figures to buttress my contention that the Indians have been slaughtered like animals. With the help of the British Foreign Office, he determined that over a five year period, the Indian population declined from fifty thousand to no more than eight thousand. He discovered some of the same 'battlefields of bones' that you discovered. Though no one can blame these things entirely upon Arana, there can be no doubt the Peruvian knew about the destruction and condoned it."

"But what of the accusations against you?" Spencer interrupted. "We were outraged to read of them. Has anything occurred to restore your credibility?"

"Not yet," Walter admitted, frowning glumly. "Those who claim I went to them demanding money are all liars, beholden to Arana in some way. Some have since disappeared entirely, and the rest are still in Manaus, which makes it difficult to refute their sworn statements. Arana claims those statements made him doubt I had anything of truth or value to offer; hence, he was justified in ignoring my accusations."

"What about the forged bank note he accused you of circulating? Can that be disproved?" Jordan questioned.

"No, because I did present it," Walter bitterly stated. "On behalf of a friend I erroneously trusted while in Manaus. His name was Julio Muriedas. Finding himself short of funds, Muriedas begged me to loan him twenty pounds, which I did. When I went to collect the debt, he claimed to be ill and gave me a bank note to present to the Bank of Manaus on his behalf. Never suspecting it had been doctored to change the amount of money he had coming, I presented it, received the money, and took it back to him, whereupon he paid me my twenty pounds. The fellow then made a miraculous recovery and disappeared. Even then I did not suspect he was Arana's henchman, hired for the express purpose of entrapping me in wrongdoing. I never thought a thing about it until Arana produced documents attesting to the forgery. According to the Bank of Manaus, I am the guilty party, not this mysterious Muriedas."

"Can't Muriedas be found and offered immunity from prosecution if he will cooperate and reveal who hired him to lure you into the trap?"

Walter shook his head. "Believe me, I've tried to locate him, but to no avail. He's disappeared. The only witness to his existence is a clerk from the hotel where we were staying at the time, sharing expenses, for we were both short of funds. The clerk must also be in Arana's pay, for he told a representative of the committee that he found it exceedingly strange that two gentlemen were sharing a room together, and one of them, the Spaniard, had feminine mannerisms."

"Can you believe it?" Mary Hardenburg burst out indignantly. "Such shameful innuendos! My Walter is the most manly of men, yet Don Arana has managed to cast aspersions on his very manhood! Why, it's . . . it's positively disgusting!" She sputtered in indignation, her blue eyes flashing.

Jordan grinned. "Well, at least your presence here must serve to dispel any notions that Walter is a 'peculiar' gentleman."

Mary sat up straighter in her chair and said proudly: "We have two small sons who could dispute those notions even better than I. But Walter won't let me bring them to the hearings. He says they are no place for our precious, innocent babes."

"I can understand his reluctance to have his family exposed to public ridicule and censure. I feel the same way about my family," Jordan said.

Walter's brows lifted in concern. "Does that mean you will not permit your wife and son to testify? When Spencer wrote me about Abelardo, I was ecstatic. The boy is just the witness we need to tell of Indian life along the Putumayo, and how it was affected by the world's demand for rubber in general, and by Arana's greed, in particular. Your son, more than anyone, can disprove the theory that the Indians are mere animals meant to be exploited as beasts of burden by superior white men. Arana has actually claimed himself to be their hero—a kindly, godfather who rescued them from the dark clutches of cannibalism and idol worship. He claims he was only 'civilizing' them for their own good."

Spencer waited with bated breath to see what Jordan's answer would be. She knew he still had strong reservations about allowing Abelardo to testify.

"If it can be avoided, I wish to avoid it," Jordan

finally said. "I don't care what the press says about me, if they do say unfavorable things, but I care very much what they may say about my wife and son."

"Perhaps, we can avoid it. Do you know what I hope and believe?" Walter asked, leaning forward. "Arana is dangerously close to breaking. Thus far he has conducted himself with admirable restraint and won sympathy even from his detractors. But I think he's very near the edge. He cannot maintain the pretense of civility and innocence forever; the hearings are wearing him down. All the speculation is unnerving him. He has built his entire life on a pack of lies, and I doubt he can endure the cold glare of suspicion much longer."

"Don't forget he's a Peruvian," Spencer pointed out. "If the committee does find him guilty of everything of which you've accused him, they cannot punish him—other than to banish him from London in disgrace and to dissolve PAC."

"For a man like Don Julio César Arana, reputation and good name are everything. Losing them would be punishment enough," Walter said. "The bottom is falling out of the Amazon rubber market, anyway. More and more buyers are looking to the East to make their purchases. Each year, the yields in India are increasing. Arana's days are already numbered. I'm sure he knows that. What he doesn't want is to become a pariah before it's over. All he really has is his reputation and the respect of his friends and family. In the end, that's all any man has."

"No," Jordan protested. "I disagree. All a man really has is his self-respect. Arana must have lost that years ago."

"Maybe your testimony will be the one that drives him over the edge," Walter speculated, looking at Jordan.

"I hope so," Jordan said. "We'll find out tomorrow, won't we?"

A knock at the door signaled the arrival of the tea tray Spencer had ordered. As she went to answer it, she shivered with combined excitement and anxiety. Would Arana find some way to discredit Jordan, as he had Walter? Or would Jordan succeed in toppling the monster, once and for all?

The next day, Spencer watched the fifteen members of the Parliamentary committee file into room number 11 and take their seats on the dais of the lofty, green-and-brown chamber on the first floor of the House of Commons overlooking the Thames River. It was a chilly autumn day, but the chamber was so overcrowded she felt stifled by the heat. Spectators lined the walls. Every leather chair was taken. It amazed her that this tribunal had so captured the public's fancy; it had no real legal authority other than to assess the guilt of the British board of directors, yet the atmosphere was one of a courtroom, where a man was standing trial for his life.

And in a way, that was exactly what was happening. If the tribunal decided that Hardenburg's allegations were true, then Arana was finished. No one would ever do business with the Peruvian again. He would be destroyed. On the other hand, if the tribunal labeled the charges as lies, then Walter

Hardenburg and her own husband would suffer dire consequences.

Spencer moistened her lips and smiled at Jordan, already seated at the witness table across the crowded chambers from her. The look he gave her in return warmed her heart. It was a look that said, "I love you. Be brave. No matter what happens here today, I'll always love you." Once again, Spencer thought of the risks her brave husband was taking. Today's proceedings would brand either him or Don Julio César Arana as a liar and a charlatan.

Jordan had dressed carefully. He wore a somber brown suit that emphasized his rugged, muscular build and lean blond looks. It was not, however, as impressive as the turn-out of most of the committee members. Black-robed, white-wigged barristers dotted the room, conferring with clients whose rich clothing bespoke an air of wealth and privilege. Spencer suspected that the barristers were coaching the committee members on how to ask the most probing, truth-revealing questions.

Looking about, she spotted the important men Mary had taken pains to tell her about; there was Raymond Asquith, the attractive, sardonic thirty-four-year-old son of the prime minister. There was the earnest, frock-coated William Joynson-Hicks, also known as Lord Brentwood. The youngest son of the Marquis of Bath, Lord Alexander Thynne, sat at a nearby table, flanked by other noblemen. But the most impressive figure of all, to Spencer's way of thinking, was the sixty-four-year-old Irishman John Gordan Swift MacNeill. Known as "Swifty" to his adoring public, he was said to be a wit and firebrand, a lover of courtroom histrionics who possessed a tongue like a lash where injustice was concerned.

Spencer expected a great deal from this fellow Irishman who had risen to the pinnacles of power through his intellect and charisma; if anyone could destroy the pompous, secretive Arana, it was he. Her eyes searched for the Peruvian but did not find him. A sudden commotion in the anteroom signaled the arrival of someone important. Craning her neck, Spencer saw Arana enter the chambers and walk to his place at the shiny, mahogany table.

He had not changed much over the last several years, except he had gained in bulk and appeared even more formidable. His expression was unreadable, and he looked neither to the left nor to the right, but took his place in silent dignity. Spencer reluctantly admitted he was an impressive figure in his impeccably cut black clothing. His heavy-lidded eyes surveyed everything and everyone with cool disdain. Upon his arrival, the hearing was called to order and the first witness summoned to the witness box.

Spencer wished Mary was there to explain things, but due to the sudden illness of the woman who usually watched their children, Walter's wife had elected to stay home and had invited the King children to join her at the modest apartment Walter had rented in London. Walter himself was seated at the same table as Jordan, so Spencer had to make her own judgments as to what she was seeing. The first witness was Henry Lex Gielgud, former secretary and manager of the Peruvian Amazon Company, who had evidently been interviewed before.

In answer to questions put to him by Swifty MacNeill, he continually and annoyingly referred to past explanations. Spencer quickly began to think him a dunce. His only response to pointed inquiries regarding his knowledge of happenings on the Putumayo was that he himself knew nothing, and had accepted Arana's explanation for every irregularity brought to his attention.

Swifty MacNeill disgustedly dismissed him, then called out Jordan's name. As Jordan rose, dwarfing the men nearest him with his height and bold, American presence, Spencer had to clasp her hands together to keep them from trembling. Jordan did not look at all nervous. He sat down with the easy grace of a man used to spending many hours in the out-of-doors on horseback.

"Sir, please tell us your name and residence," Swifty MacNeill requested.

After Jordan had done so, the silver-haired elder statesman directed him to "recount his story." Jordan began by describing his first meeting with Miguel Loayza, when the overseer had tried and failed to purchase Paraĩso. In chronological order, Jordan related every event involving Loayza and Arana. Following the format he and Spencer had discussed the previous evening after Walter and Mary had gone home, Jordan told what had happened and what he had directly witnessed or experienced. At no time did he accuse Arana of anything; rather he allowed his listeners to draw their own conclusions.

During his recital of events, there wasn't a sound in the chambers, except for several gasps of outrage as Jordan revealed what he and Spencer had seen at El Encanto and La Reserva. When he finished, the chamber remained hushed for several moments while everyone digested the incredible tale. Then it exploded into a babble of shouted questions and the frantic raising of hands.

Swifty MacNeill banged a gavel to restore order. "Ask your questions one at a time, gentlemen. Please give Mr. King ample opportunity to answer."

The questions flew like arrows or poison darts. "Sir, is it true that you and Don Julio Arana were competitors—vying for control of the entire Putumayo region?"

"Is it true you threatened Arana's life in Manaus, then tried to kill him by poisoning his food with an Indian dart tipped with curare?"

"Mr. King! Do you desire to destroy Don Arana's good name because he has proof that your late father obtained Paraïso in a devious manner, by cheating at cards?"

"Mr. King, aren't you exaggerating the atrocities you claim to have witnessed because you despise Don Arana for being more successful than you?"

The questions were shocking and outrageous, leaving no doubt in Spencer's mind that Arana had made elaborate preparations to refute Jordan's testimony. It was as if Jordan himself were the accused, instead of Arana. She twisted her hands in anguish while Swifty MacNeill banged the gavel.

"Gentlemen! I said one question at a time! Silence . . . silence in these chambers!"

Gradually, order was restored, and Jordan given the opportunity of responding. He did an excellent job, patiently explaining everything he could, but Spencer could see from the cynical faces around her that doubts and hesitations still existed. These rich, titled Londoners, born to wealth and privilege, wanted to believe the worst of her self-made American husband. Arana was, after all, one of them—a man who had eaten at their tables and drunk their fine wine and brandy. If he had indeed done all Jordan had said he'd done, then they were guilty of being hoodwinked, at the very least.

"Mr. King, have you anything else to add to your testimony?" Swifty MacNeill asked.

"Yes," Jordan said, standing and glancing scornfully around him. "I came here today in good faith that I would be telling my story to unprejudiced men—men who desire to hear the truth and see justice done. Obviously, before I opened my mouth, you had all swallowed the lies carefully spoon-fed to you by the man who has the most to lose if I'm telling the truth . . ." Jordan turned and looked pointedly at Arana. "Gentlemen, isn't it time you ask yourselves if you have not been fed lies all along? Don't let your pride stand in the way of admitting that you have been wrong about the smooth-talking villain in whom you placed your confidence, invited into your homes, and entrusted with your money. Wrong about the manner in which you hid from your own selves the knowledge of what was happening on the Putumayo. Did none of you ever bother to ask how all that rubber was collected? And at what price?"

Jordan paused to let his words sink in, then quietly continued. "I, too, wanted to be rich and for many years was able to ignore the ugliness of the system whereby most of the world's rubber is harvested. I thought I could retain my self-respect by doing it differently on my own plantation. I tried to remain ignorant about what was going on, so I could take my profits without a qualm of conscience. But one day I met someone who refused to allow me to bury my head in the sand any longer, someone who forced me to open my eyes, to look and really *see* the evil I was helping to perpetrate . . . Now, I thank God every day for my good fortune in meeting that person. Because of her, I can face the mirror without flinching every morning. I can call myself a man and be the father to my children that I wish to be. God willing, my children will never have cause to be ashamed of me, as I sometimes was of my own father . . ." Jordan's voice broke with emotion. His eyes met Spencer's across the room.

Her cheeks flushed a hot crimson, but she returned his gaze proudly. Never had she been so proud of Jordan or of the beliefs and values they shared. They had done what they could. Let Arana do his worst. In the end, he would only destroy himself, while they would survive. They had each other, and it was enough. More than enough. It was everything.

"Gentlemen," Jordan said. "I have told my story, so I will take my leave. Deny it, if you can. But as God is my witness, Walter Hardenburg and I have told the truth."

Moving swiftly, Jordan came around the table and walked toward Spencer. He stretched out his hand to her. Conscious of all eyes on them but not caring what anyone thought, Spencer took it. Together, they walked out of the crowded chambers, accompanied first by silence, then by a wild, thunderous applause that shook the very walls and rafters. Thinking it the sweetest music she had ever heard, Spencer smiled into Jordan's jungle-green eyes.

"We've won," she whispered. "Oh, Jordan, we've won!"

Epilogue

"You should have seen it, Mary!" Walter exclaimed. "After Jordan got done, Arana didn't stand a chance. Jordan's testimony was the straw that broke the camel's back. The Peruvian lost all confidence and hemmed and hawed and contradicted himself like a guilty schoolboy hauled up by his ear before the headmaster."

"I wish I had seen it." Mary sighed wistfully. "Wouldn't you know that the one day I miss the hearings would be the day Arana's smooth facade finally cracked?"

"I'm rather sorry we missed it, too," Spencer said with a scolding look at Jordan. "I wanted to stay and hear Arana's testimony, but I could hardly refuse to escort my husband out of the chambers when he so gallantly took my hand and dragged me away."

"I didn't drag you," Jordan protested. "What I should have done was knock that bastard on his ass before I left. Excuse me, Mary, but it's how I felt—how I still feel."

They were sitting in Walter and Mary's nearly threadbare apartment, rehashing the day's events while the children laughed and played noisily in the background. Abelardo was giving pony rides around the parlor to Marta and the Hardenburgs' two small sons while the adults occupied the only chairs available—the ones around the long dining-room table.

"What will happen now, Walter?" Spencer asked.

"The committee will vote and issue its findings—a mere formality, I should think. Arana will be pronounced guilty of the atrocities perpetrated by his agents and employees on the Putumayo. He cannot be brought to trial in London, of course, and Peru will never prosecute him, but Arana's career is now ruined . . ."

"And his British codirectors? What will happen to them?" Spencer pursued.

"That's harder to say. While certainly guilty of negligence, they weren't directly involved in the atrocities and so cannot be held accountable. However, PAC can and will be dissolved. For all practical purposes, the company no longer exists."

"Thank God," Spencer murmured. "I only wish it had happened sooner—in time to save more Indian lives."

Mary reached over and patted her hand. "You mustn't brood over it, Spencer. You've saved one Indian's life, at any rate." She nodded toward Abelardo whose snorts and whinnies were a perfect imitation of a real pony's.

"I can't wait to get him safely home," Spencer admitted. "I'm glad we didn't take him to the hearings. The press thronged us after we left the House of Commons and only returned to the hearings when Arana's name was called as the final witness. When we go back to our hotel, they'll be waiting for us. I don't know what we'll say to them; Jordan already said everything there is to say."

"Why don't all of you stay here tonight?" Mary suggested. "We have enough room. We may not possess much in the way of furnishings, but we do have beds . . . Oh, Walter! Do convince them to stay." Mary turned to her husband. Her pleading eyes were impossible to resist.

Walter shrugged helplessly. "What do you say, Jordan? Will you spend the night? In the morning we can study the morning newspapers together over coffee and hot croissants."

Jordan glanced at Spencer for her approval. Happily, she nodded. "How can I refuse your hospitality?" he inquired. "Especially now that I know you aren't interested in my wife."

"Your wife?" Walter looked questioningly from Jordan to Spencer. "I was never interested in your wife. At least not in a personal sense."

"I knew that, Walter, but Jordan didn't," Spencer explained. "For years he's been jealous of you—so jealous, in fact, that I sometimes feared he wouldn't testify against Arana when the time came."

"My, my . . ." Walter said, shaking his head. "I can't imagine anyone being jealous of me."

"Maybe that's because you underrate yourself, dearest," Mary scolded. "I'm not surprised Jordan was jealous. From the moment I first saw you, I set my cap for you; it's a wonder Spencer didn't do the same."

"By the time I met Walter, I was already in love with Jordan," Spencer informed them. "Isn't it amazing how it all turned out? I expect the fates knew what they were doing when they brought us all together."

"Fates, hogwash!" Jordan exclaimed. "The fates had nothing to do with it, at least not for you and me, Spencer. That we met and fell in love was pure, blind chance—augmented by a serious lack of competition. I was the only man around, and you were the only woman. In any other setting, we'd not have taken a second look at each other. Even when we did take that second look, we each had our reservations; you wanted an idealist like Walter, and I wanted someone far less prim and proper."

"It must be true that opposites attract," Spencer mused.

"But Walter and I aren't opposites. If anything, we're very much alike . . ." Mary disputed.

Walter grinned. "This is an argument that could last all night."

"It better not last all night," Jordan protested. "Your company is most agreeable, Walter, but I have an overwhelming need to be alone with my wife. I don't care if we have to sleep on the floor."

"Jordan!" Spencer gasped, red-faced.

"Well, I do," Jordan asserted. "I'm not ashamed to admit it. That's what's wrong with the world today. People hide their real desires from themselves and from each other and do such a good job of it that soon even they don't know who they are anymore."

"Do you think that's what happened to Arana?" Mary questioned. "Do you suppose even his wife doesn't really know him?"

Jordan spread his hands on the tabletop and

looked down at them dispassionately. "We'll never know, will we? But I wouldn't be surprised to learn that's the case. My experiences with Arana taught me one thing; I'm determined to be perfectly honest with everyone—and that means that when I want to be alone with my wife, I say so! Damn my—"

"Aunt Milly's corset!" Spencer finished for him.

Walter and Mary stared at them, and Spencer smiled sheepishly and covered Jordan's hand with her own. "You'll have to excuse us. It's a private joke, one of those silly things that make sense only to a man and woman who have lived together a long time."

She caught Jordan's eye and discovered he was giving her an intensely hungry look, one that conveyed his growing ardor and desire to be alone with her. When he spoke, she had no doubt of his intentions, and neither could the Hardenburgs. "If you can direct us to the nearest flat surface, I'd be most obliged," he said. "Really, we'd be perfectly happy sleeping on the floor. Don't worry that we won't be comfortable. In Brazil, we slept in a number of unusual locations . . ."

"Ye should be ashamed of yerself, Jordan!" Spencer admonished. "Ye're makin' it worse and worse! Whatever will the Hardenburgs think of us?"

"That we're madly in love . . ." Jordan smiled a teasing, unrepentant smile, then turned to Mary Hardenburg. "Just don't assign us a hammock, Mary. I detest hammocks. Had enough of 'em in Brazil. They're utterly impossible."

"We don't own a hammock," Mary assured him.

Her blue eyes were wide, as if she disbelieved what she'd been hearing.

"Mary, love," Walter said. "Could you stand to have my help making up the beds for tonight? I think the Kings would like to be alone together, this very minute."

"Of course, Walter. How . . . how accommodating you are!"

Walter winked at them as he went out the door behind Mary, then gently closed it to give them complete privacy.

"How wicked ye are!" Spencer rapped Jordan on the knuckles. "I'm positively mortified."

"I'm not. I'm positively amorous . . ." He pushed back his chair and reached for her.

"Jordan, not here! Not now!"

"Yes, here. Yes, now," Jordan growled, taking her into his arms.

"But the children!"

"Are playing horsy . . . ."

"And the Hardenburgs!"

"Won't bother us for at least an hour. You never know what trouble two people can get into, making up beds together."

His kisses soon dissolved her hesitancy. As his hands began to skim her body, tugging at her clothing, Spencer sighed her acquiescence. Then she was reminded of something she had always wanted to ask him.

"Jordan?"

"Yes, love."

"Did ye really have an Aunt Milly and did she really have a corset?"

"I can't remember. At a time like this, does it

matter?"

He cupped the fullness of her bare breast in one hand, and she had to concede it didn't matter in the slightest. Raining kisses on her cheeks, lips, and hair, Jordan pressed her backwards against the dining room table. *This is insane,* she thought. *He's going to make love to me on top of the table!*

Surprisingly, the table top did not feel as hard as she might have expected. But then with Jordan, nothing was hard; everything was easy, especially loving him, which she planned to do each and every day and night for the rest of her life.

"I love ye, Jordano Rei," she whispered. "I love ye wildly, totally, shamelessly . . ."

"I love you more," he whispered back.

Then he set about proving it with the passion of his strong, virile body, arousing and possessing every inch of her, so that nothing existed but the blazing inferno of their need for each other . . . a fire that would never go out.

Afterword From the Author

Spencer O'Rourke and Jordan King, the hero and heroine of my story, are fictitious, but Walter Hardenburg and Don Julio César Arana are not. They actually existed. (More information about these two men can be found in *The River That God Forgot,* by Richard Collier.) The rubber-boom period in the Amazon did not last long, only a few decades, but while it did, Arana and many others destroyed entire tribes of Indians and made incredible fortunes.

Twenty years ago, my husband and I flew up the Amazon River to Manaus, where the luxurious Opera House still stands. While in Manaus, we toured an Indian museum and marveled at blow guns, darts, basketry, and other artifacts, remnants of those lost civilizations. From the missionaries, we heard stories of the continuing exploitation and destruction of the jungle people.

According to news reports today, the Amazon region remains a place of great mystery and controversy. It is so vast as to be largely unknown and is one of the few places on earth that continues to defy man's efforts to plunder its hidden wealth. I hope my story entertained and enlightened you. As the Brazilians say, *ãte logo,* which means good-bye until the next time . . .